The
RED HAND ADVENTURES

Rebels of the Kasbah
BOOK I

Wrath of the Caid
BOOK II

Legends of the Rif
BOOK III

Thieves of the Black Sea
BOOK IV

PRAISE
for the
RED HAND ADVENTURES

"O'Neill has an eye for detail, atmosphere, and action...this is a
rousing period piece."
—*Publishers Weekly*

"Whether intended for a YA or adult audience, this is a book the entire
family can enjoy reading...The book reads like a Boy's Own adventure
and is filled with action involving bandits, pirates and rebels, reminding
the reader of such grand entertainments as Rudyard Kipling's *Kim*,
Michael Chabon's *Gentlemen of the Road* and John Milius'
The Wind and the Lion...Four Stars."
—Kenneth Salikof for *IndieReader*

"Debut author O'Neill incorporates a great deal of cultural and
historical context in his story...and will make the readers feel as
though they have traveled back in time and fallen into that world.
An exciting, exotic tale...The cliffhanger ending all but demands that
readers jump to the next installment of the series."
—*Kirkus Reviews*

"Block out the next few hours, because you won't want to put
this book down!"
—Kevin Max, Founder and Editor, *1859 Oregon's Magazine*

MORE PRAISE
for the
RED HAND ADVENTURES

Selected for School and Library Battle of the Books Contests
around the country
(Rebels of the Kasbah)

Selected for the National Battle of the Books Contest
(Rebels of the Kasbah)

Selected as a *Publisher's Weekly* indie select book
(Rebels of the Kasbah)

Silver Medal Winner for the Mom's Choice Award
(Rebels of the Kasbah)

Bronze Medal Winner for Best Book Series—Fiction
in the Moonbeam Children's Book Awards
(Red Hand Adventures)

Gold Medal Winner of the Independent
Book Publisher's Living Now Award
(Wrath of the Caid)

2015 Preferred Choice for Kids Chapter Books
Creative Child Awards
(Rebels of the Kasbah)

2015 Seal of Excellence for Kids Chapter Books
Creative Child Awards
(Wrath of the Caid)

— WORD ON THE STREET —

For Rebels of the Kasbah

KCamp (Denver, CO USA): Great to have for *Battle of the Books*.

Eva Jones (Age: 11 Grade: 5): *Rebels of the Kasbah* is an amazing novel. It is spun together with foreign elements, gore, trickery, and leadership. One excellent aspect is the personality you get from each character. The description he gives is impeccable—it feels like you're standing right there in the scene. I don't know how Joe O'Neill did it, but he did!

Xander ForeverBookish (Top Middle Reader Book Review Blog rated it 5 of 5 stars): AMAZING! You NEED to read this!

Books on the Edge (Middle Reader Review): It reminds one of the classics like *Treasure Island, Oliver Twist,* and *Aladdin* while written in a language suitable for young readers of today. Yup it's one of those books that you hope your son or daughter would read and find heroes among its pages....and who couldn't use a well written hero or two?

Dr. Jean Lowery, CEO *Battle of the Books*: "When I sat down to begin reading *Rebels of the Kasbah*, I couldn't turn the pages fast enough until I reached the last page and said—NOOOOO, I need to know what happens next! "

Franny: I could feel the sand stinging my face, this story is so descriptive, and so creatively told by the author. *Rebels* was heartwarming, exciting and inspiring. I can hardly wait for the sequel!

Heather P (M.Ed.-Reading & Language Arts-Former Classroom Teacher-Book Lover!): Hands down a great book for middle school readers, all the way to adults!

This Kid Reviews Books (Top Middle Reader Review Blog): O'Neill writes a captivating story that kept me on the edge of my seat! I couldn't put down! The characters are believable and...have a unique personality.

— WORD ON THE STREET —

For Wrath of the Caid

Margaret rated it 4 of 5 stars on Good Reads: The kids at Remann Hall Book Club truly love this series. They no sooner finish one book, than they want the next one. I love the maps, the sense of adventure in far-away places, and the longing the stories create for the reader to know more.

Marie rated it 5 of 5 stars on Good Reads: I was so excited to finally read this book! It picked up right where *Rebels of the Kasbah* left off and just amazed me again. I liked the fast-paced action of this story and how it takes you all over the world and back again! There were some good humorous parts that made me laugh, some scary scenarios that made my heart race, and an ending that once again makes me NEED the next book! I highly recommend *Wrath of the Caid*.

I Be Readin: Can we get up and cheer for this one? This novel reminds me of the famous series written by J. K. Rowling. No...there are no wizards or broomsticks, but the battle of good versus evil continues in O'Neill's writing and you can't help but get caught up in this story, and would totally adapt to big screen.

For Legends of the Rif

Kumara rated it 4 of 5 stars on Good Reads: "It is exciting from start to finish reminding me a lot of the *Boys Own* adventure story's I read when I was a lot younger. ...it's impossible not to cheer on the good guys as the bad guys get their comeuppance in these scenes. Each time this happened it left a smile on my face as we have been through a lot with these characters over three books."

C. Anderson (Middle School Teacher, Portland OR): As a teacher, I recognize how this series is a major draw for reluctant readers...my favorite element of this installment is the increasing sense of morality discussed in the book through narration, character dialogue and character action. Thank you Joe O'Neill!

Eli rated it 4 of 5 starts on Good Reads: "Extremely enjoyable. I think it holds great lessons and teachings about the past and issues even today that would be valuable for kids to learn, and I loved all of the themes inside it. I'm really looking forward to the next book."

Erik of This Kid Reviews Books rated it 5 of 5 stars on Good Reads: "Wow. Just 'Wow.' This was amazing. Mr. O'Neill really knows how to draw you in. It makes you feel like you are there in the Middle East. I've always enjoyed this series because of the characters and setting...the third book is my favorite so far."

Black Ship

PUBLISHING

Adventure Novels with a Shot of Wry

EX LIBRIS

The
RED HAND ADVENTURES

BOOK IV

Thieves of the Black Sea

JOE O'NEILL

This novel features some events that are historically accurate. However, all characters are fictional and any similarity between characters within the book and actual characters is purely coincidental.

A portion of proceeds from the sale of all *Red Hand Adventures* books will be donated to help the many impoverished and enslaved children in the world.

Thieves of the Black Sea

COPYRIGHT © 2016 BY JOE O'NEILL
Art Direction by Kristin Myrdahl
Graphic Design by Anna Fonnier
Composition by Margaret Copeland/terragrafix.com
Cover illustrated by Lamont Russ
Maps designed by Josh Espinosa
Interior Illustrations by Lamont Russ
Edited by Sara Addicott
Copyedited by Bedelia Walton
www.redhandadventures.com

Black Ship

PUBLISHING

ISBN 978-0-9905469-9-3

SPECIAL THANKS

*Last year I had the privilege to visit the Remann Hall Book Club in
Tacoma, Washington. This is a program for incarcerated youth to
encourage them to read. In spite of initial skepticism by some, the
program has been a resounding success with over five hundred participants!
As I sat in a bland, soulless room, I was moved to tears when the young men
and women were brought into the room in small groups of four, five, or six and
watched closely by a prison guard. Wearing innocuous orange jumpsuits,
they sat on the floor and waited for me to speak.*

*What I saw were not hardened felons, but young people that should be
worrying about prom, learning to drive, making a sports team, or studying
for a test. Instead, some of them would be sent to an adult penitentiary for life,
their young lives over before they ever had a chance to begin. I was amazed by
their intelligent questions and, most of all, by their sense of humor in spite of
being locked up and leading amazingly tragic and difficult lives.*

*This book is dedicated to the youths of Remann Hall and the founders of the
book club—Margaret and Craig Ross—who are not state or
federal employees, just concerned citizens who wanted to
help some kids who sorely needed a little bit of encouragement.*

— Joe O'Neill

*"I and the public know
What all schoolchildren learn,
Those to whom evil is done
Do evil in return."*

— W.H. Auden

TABLE OF CONTENTS

CHAPTER   PAGE

1	Dreams of an Osprey	3
2	The Call of the Hunter	15
3	A Friend Indeed	19
4	Two Lost Rabbits	27
5	Mandolins in the Moonlight	37
6	A Ripple in the Desert	43
7	The Trail Is Not Dead	47
8	The Tutelage of Foster Crowe	53
9	Gravediggers	63
10	The Beinhoff-Muller Gang!	81
11	Lhak-Pa	95
12	The Hunter or the Hunted?	99
13	Cat Burglars	107
14	To The Black Forest	117
15	The Den of Abdullah Ozek	123
16	Catacombs of the Red Hand	135
17	A Fly in the Wine	141
18	Crow's Delight	151
19	Tour de Constantinople	167
20	Lessons of a Different Color	179
21	Bruised, but not Broken	183
22	Galatasaray!	187
23	Reinhold and the Black Forest	197
24	To Sleep with the Fishes	219
25	A Bucking and Kicking Iron Horse	229
26	The End is just the Beginning	233
27	Shattered and Numb	245
28	Revenge Served with a Stiletto	263
29	The Clock Strikes Midnight	271
30	Stepping into the Breach	283

CONSTANTINOPLE
1914

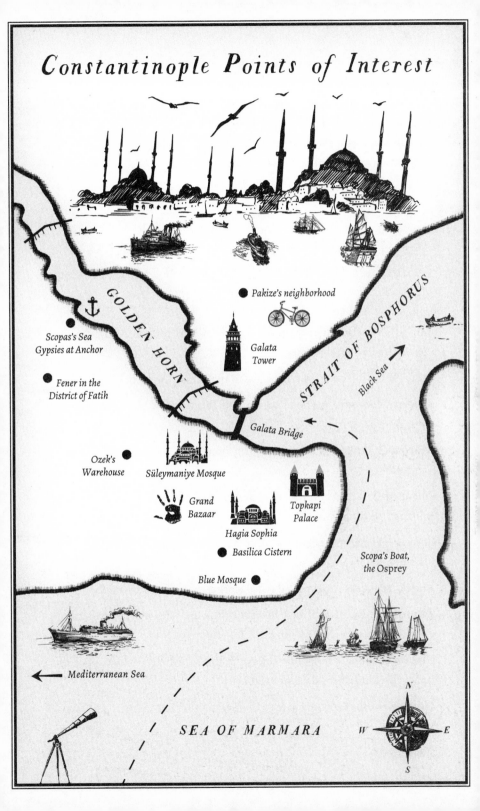

Please note: We strongly suggest first reading *Rebels of the Kasbah*, *Wrath of the Caid*, and *Legends of the Rif* before reading *Thieves of the Black Sea* because the Red Hand Adventures books are meant to be read in chronological order. Each book has several plot points, character introductions, and events that can be fully understood and enjoyed only by having read the entire series in order.

CHARACTERS RETURNING FROM
REBELS OF THE KASBAH, WRATH OF THE CAID, and *LEGENDS OF THE RIF*

Tariq (tah-reek): An orphan; kidnapped and sold to Caid Ali Tamzali to race in deadly camel races

Fez: A friend of Tariq's; fellow slave to the tyrant Caid Ali Tamzali

Aseem (ah-seem): A friend to Fez and Tariq; fellow slave to Caid Ali Tamzali

Margaret Owen: An English girl; kidnapped and sold to Caid Ali Tamzali

Aji (ah-jee): Tariq's best friend on the streets of Tangier; killed by a street thug named Mohammad

Sanaa (sah-nah): A beautiful Moroccan assassin; part of the resistance, instrumental in prison escape

Malik (ma-leek): A respected tribal leader; part of the resistance

Zijuan (zee-wan): A gifted Chinese woman and sage martial artist; rescued Tariq from streets of Tangier

Charles Owen: A decorated colonel in the British army; kidnapped by pirate crew, father to Margaret and David

Louise Owen: A devoted wife to Charles; mother to Margaret and David

Caid Ali Tamzali: An evil warlord; feared ruler of the Rif Mountains, killed in an epic battle

Note: For definition in this series, a Caid (k+aid) is a warlord in Morocco who answers only to the Sultan, the sovereign ruler of Morocco. He controls his own territory, but pays taxes and owes all allegiance to the Sultan. However, a more common definition of a Caid is a Muslim or Berber chieftain, who may be a tribal chief, judge, or senior officer.

The Black Mamba: The most ruthless assassin in Morocco; a loyal servant to Caid Ali Tamzali, killed by the honorable assassin Sanaa

Melbourne Jack: An Aboriginal adventurer trained by Foster Crowe in Australia; searching for the diary of Alexander the Great, assisting the boys in a battle to take down the Caid, died tragically in a hot air balloon crash

Foster Crowe: A master of the Red Hand. He runs a circus that travels across the world which is actually a training ground for agents of the Red Hand. Pursuing Wu Chiang; determined to protect the Red Hand teachings.

Amanda: A teenage girl; took care of young Melbourne Jack in the circus

Timin: A former betting parlor boss, imprisoned and left homeless; friend of street boys

Sister Anne: Head of St. Catherine's School in the south of France

The French Students: Sophie, Etienne and Inez; roommates of Margaret's at St. Catherine's

Wu Chiang: A suspicious character plotting a world war

Azmiya (az-mee-uh): A girl rescued from an evil uncle by Tariq and friends

CHARACTERS INTRODUCED IN
THIEVES OF THE BLACK SEA

Captain Scopas: The Captain of a band of sea gypsies. He is seeking Abdullah Ozek.

Lhak-Pa: A mysterious sage that young Foster Crowe meets in the Himalayan Mountains.

Major Lars Hostetler: The officer in charge of the German internment camp.

Leopold: A former advisor to the Kaiser. Inez and Margaret meet him in the German internment camp.

Mia: The leader of a resistance group in Germany.

Pakize: A thief who assists Fez, Tariq, and Aseem in Constantinople.

Abdullah Ozek: An evil gangster in Constantinople and the rival of Captain Scopas.

Reinhold: A German boy who helps Inez and Margaret.

PREVIOUSLY IN THE RED HAND ADVENTURES

Morocco. 1912. In Book I, *Rebels of the Kasbah*, Tariq, Fez, and Aseem are three young boys kidnapped and sold into the Kasbah of Caid of Ali Tamzali to race in deadly camel races. Along with Margaret, an English girl who was also kidnapped and sold into the harem of Caid Ali Tamzali, they plan a daring escape with the help of an undercover assassin named Sanaa, who was dispatched to help Tariq by his guardian—the venerable sage Zijuan.

Following their successful escape, the kids join a resistance tribe in the Rif Mountains led by a man named Malik. After gaining valuable information on the kasbah's vulnerabilities, Malik and his warriors stage a daring raid on Caid Ali Tamzali and his kasbah.

Meanwhile, Margaret's father, Charles, is kidnapped by a pirate named Captain Basil and joins forces with him when he learns a corrupt British Lieutenant named Dreyfuss is attacking helpless African fishing boats and villages.

In Book II, *Wrath of the Caid*, the Caid unleashes a man named The Black Mamba to find and kill, Tariq, Aseem, and Fez, and destroy the resistance tribe. Margaret is sent to live in England, as it's no longer safe for her in Morocco. In England, she gets in a bit of trouble and is quickly sent to Saint Catherine's boarding school outside of Marseilles, France where she befriends some French school girls.

Lieutenant Dreyfuss sends a spy by the name of Sharif Al Montaro to capture Captain Basil and Charles Owen.

Tariq, separated from his friends, meets a friendly Aborigine named Melbourne Jack who begins to explain the secrets of the Red Hand and the exploits of his mentor—Foster Crowe.

In Book III, *Legends of the Rif*, Tariq, Fez, and Aseem are adrift in the Mediterranean Sea and clinging to life after their hot air balloon crash landed. Melbourne Jack, their friend and mentor, tragically died in the accident.

PREVIOUSLY...(CONTINUED)

Sanaa, Zijuan, and Malik successfully defeated Caid Ali Tamzali and his evil henchman, The Black Mamba, to free the countryside of Morocco from his iron grip. Inez was suddenly missing after identifying German spies near her school in the French countryside.

Finally, Foster Crowe follows the mysterious Wu Chiang to Europe from the jungles of Ceylon after discovering Wu Chiang's dark vision to plot a war the likes of which the world has never seen.

Thieves of the Black Sea

CHAPTER
— *I* —

DREAMS OF AN OSPREY

1914—HOLD OF THE VAGABOND SHIP—THE OSPREY

Tariq awoke to the sounds of clinking glass and the smell of salt water. Shards of green, red, and blue glass moved rhythmically over him—a mobile gently swaying back and forth, blown by the wind from an open porthole just over his bed. The room creaked. It seemed to breathe, inhaling and exhaling, to the ebb and flow of the sea. Soft cotton sheets covered his bare skin. Slowly stretching his body and then his toes, Tariq tried to register his new surroundings.

Around his bare neck was the medallion of a black panther worn by his best friend, Aji, and on a table next to him sat the diary of Alexander the Great, nestled in its protective bag. Lying next to the diary was a sheathed knife that Tariq always kept strapped to his right calf.

For a few moments, Tariq was disoriented. He couldn't shake the images of being stranded on the balloon basket for days without food or water after Melbourne Jack died.

Then it came to him, the urgency of his mentor's parting words: "You must return Alexander the Great's diary to my circus in India. You must find Foster Crowe."

Flashing images filled his head—of falling into the sea, watching the surface fall away, and then a boy and shark. A boy and a shark?

Where was he? He had to find some answers.

He suddenly remembered Fez and Aseem and felt panic creep in. He had to find their whereabouts and if they had survived.

As Tariq began to lift himself out of bed, he saw the doorknob slowly turn and then the door opened. It was an old woman. She smiled broadly and started talking in a foreign dialect. She sat on the side of Tariq's cot, gently kissing him on each cheek and making the figure of the cross with her right index finger on his forehead. She brought her wrinkled hands down to his cheeks. As she held Tariq's face in her hands, she looked into his eyes. Tariq saw pure joy in her expression.

He tried to get out of bed, but she motioned for him to stay.

Retreating to the hallway, the woman returned with a large glass and a beautiful ceramic pitcher painted with intricate designs in vibrant colors.

She handed Tariq a glass of water, and when he had emptied it, she poured again and again, until Tariq had consumed four entire glassfuls and the pitcher was empty.

Tariq's entire body felt like one big bruise. His head was wobbly and felt full of cobwebs. He thought of nothing else but Fez and Aseem, and he had an urgent desire to discover if they were still alive or if they had perished in the sea along with Melbourne Jack. His chest felt tight as panic returned, worrying about his friends and their safety.

His pants were hanging beside him on a wooden peg, only now they had been cleaned and smelled of soap and lemon. He put them on, dressing under the sheet. When he stood up from the bed, he instantly fell to one knee. His equilibrium was thrown off from being at sea for so long, and his lightheadedness from dehydration only added to his lack of coordination.

The old woman came to him and urged him to lie back down. He shook his head and forced himself to stand up, and then stumbled to a wall, holding onto it for balance. He pointed out the door, hoping the old woman understood that he meant to find his friends.

Understanding Tariq's gesture, she held him by the arm and guided him as they wobbled and staggered out of the bedroom like two drunken sailors.

Down a narrow and cramped hallway, they continued until they came to some stairs. The hallway smelled damp, and the weathered and warped floorboards creaked beneath his feet. It was difficult to balance as the boat rocked to and fro with every wave. The old woman motioned for him to climb up the stairs, which he did slowly, then he smiled and thanked her with a kind look and a small bow. He was still woozy and weak, but was able to slowly make his way up the stairs with the help of a handrail.

At the top of the stairs, Tariq reached for the hatch, pushed it open and emerged to find himself on the deck of a large sailboat. Sunlight blinded him, and he stood still for a few seconds to allow his eyes to adjust.

"Tariq!" Aseem yelled and ran to him and hugged him.

Tariq smiled haggardly, still tired and dizzy, but managed to hug him back. Aseem's strength seemed to have completely returned to him and even the sun sores on his face were largely healed.

"You're looking good, my friend. A bit skinnier, but aren't we all?" Aseem said with a laugh.

"It is so good to see you, Aseem," Tariq said, and he meant it. The last time he'd seen Aseem, he had been clinging to life—near death from dehydration. To see him healthy and alive brought Tariq a deep kind of relief.

The two boys stared at one another for a few moments, each grateful for the life of the other, not knowing exactly what to say. Finally, Tariq spoke.

"Fez? Is he okay?"

"Look!" Aseem said and pointed upward to the main mast of the boat.

On the mast, forty feet in the air, Fez dangled, pulling in a slack line. A sailor beneath him was giving him instructions, laughing as Fez pulled until, finally, it was snug.

"Tariq!" Fez yelled down from his perch on the mast.

Quickly he and the sailor made their way down until Fez was able to jump onto the deck of the boat.

Once he landed, he sprinted to Tariq and hugged him.

"Wow Fez, you were up really high!" Tariq said with a smile.

"We thought you would sleep forever!" Fez replied.

"I feel like I could have. I'm still confused as to exactly what happened," Tariq said and began studying his surroundings more carefully.

The boat was long, over eighty feet, with three masts. Laundry hung from every available railing and line. The floorboards were warped and scratched from salt. Green paint flaked and peeled from the cabin walls and roof. Many of the lines were aged and looked to be on the verge of shredding. Black mold spread in the corners of the floorboards where moisture had collected. Crewmembers, their shirtless torsos bronzed and rugged, shouted and waved to Tariq and he waved back. An old man with gray stubble on his cheeks, his body skinny and tan, came over and smiled and shook Tariq's hand. He was missing his two front teeth, and there was a huge scar down his neck.

Raggedy sails attached to each mast held steady in an eight-knot wind.

"Where are we?" Tariq asked.

"We were rescued by Captain Scopas and his clan. They call themselves sea gypsies and travel around the Mediterranean. They are the nicest people, and we owe them our lives!" Fez replied.

"How long have I been asleep?"

"Five days! Aseem and I woke up two days ago and have been exploring the boat."

Tariq looked over the side and saw a dorsal fin next to the boat. The fin skipped up and under the water and reminded Tariq of a dog running next to a wagon. Sailboats of all different sizes and shapes surrounded theirs, all sailing close together. Most were in equally poor condition as their boat.

"Was I dreaming, or was I rescued by a boy and a shark?"

Aseem and Fez looked at each other and started laughing.

"You weren't dreaming. There is a boy named Panos and he rides a shark! Apparently, he rescued the shark when it was just a baby, and he and the shark became best friends. The shark's name is Lako, and he's kind of a scout for the fleet—that's how they found us! Lako came upon us, and when he was circling the basket, he was trying to help us! Amazing isn't it?" Fez explained. He was obviously very excited.

"So, he wasn't trying to eat us?" Tariq asked.

"No, he knew we were in trouble but didn't know what to do. He stayed with us until the fleet was close enough and he could return with Panos to help us."

"I thought I was dead. I thought I saw Aji," Tariq explained, still half believing that the boy he saw was real and not a dreamlike image of his old friend, Aji.

His mind was still confused.

The old woman then appeared with a tray of fresh fruit and more pitchers of water. She opened a large tin of aloe vera, which she applied to their faces and lesions. Immediately their skin felt cooler.

The boys eagerly shoved pieces of orange and watermelon in their mouths and gulped glass after glass of fresh water.

"So, you must be Tariq," came a bold voice from behind them.

They turned as a big man appeared in front of them—the same man who had been on the mast with Fez. He was large, but not fat—all bone and muscle. His face carried the look of a boxer, while the gleam in his eye gave a hint of a rogue and a gypsy. His posture and voice suggested that he was a man of some authority on the boat. A soft black beard covered his square jaw. His right ear was deformed and resembled a gnarly mushroom.

"You speak Arabic?" Tariq asked.

"Yes, of course I speak Arabic. I also speak Greek, English, Turkish, Spanish, French, and a smattering of Russian. It sounds like you've all had quite an adventure! Another ten minutes and I don't think we could have saved you."

Tariq approached the man and extended his hand. The man smiled and shook it with massive hands. Tariq thought the man might break his fingers, his grip was so tight.

"Thank you for saving me and my friends. May I ask your name?"

The man laughed.

"Ah, I always appreciate a boy with good manners. I am Captain Scopas and this is my boat—the *Osprey*! As your friends may have explained to you, this is my clan and we live on the sea, traveling by boat from port to port. That is my mother, Helen, who took care of you. You met my boy Panos and his shark, Lako. Quite a story, eh?"

"I've never heard of a boy swimming with a shark before," Tariq answered, who was mesmerized by the man's deformed ear.

"In the Greek Islands, where I am from, it's not so uncommon. Many of the village boys would swim with sharks. Ah, the world is a wonderful place, is it not?"

Captain Scopas laughed and hugged Tariq. Tariq felt like a mouse being squeezed by a python.

He let go and noticed Tariq staring at his ear.

"You're wondering about my ear, eh? I was wrestling with a Russian and this happened—he popped my entire ear and blood went everywhere. This Russian was so afraid of blood he fainted on the spot and I won the match. Ha! That will show those damn Russians, who think they wrestle better than anyone."

Tariq was embarrassed for staring.

"I'm sorry, it's just…," he tried to explain

"No need to explain. Tonight, we will prepare a feast in your honor. I must attend to my duties, but, please, enjoy yourselves. We dock at Constantinople in four days' time if this wind holds up."

"Constantinople?" Tariq asked, suddenly remembering his dream where Melbourne Jack told him to find a panther in Constantinople.

"Ah, you're wondering why a proud Greek such as myself would set foot in Constantinople with the dreaded Turks? Well, I have some unpleasant business to attend to, my friend, that's all I can tell you."

Captain Scopas suddenly turned very serious and then disappeared below deck.

"What did he mean by 'the dreaded Turks'?" Aseem asked.

Fez and Tariq shrugged their shoulders.

Tariq couldn't help but feel as if he were in a dream. He recalled the voice of Melbourne Jack in his head, telling him to find a panther in Constantinople—and now a sea captain was telling him that's exactly where they were headed.

He took another drink of water and ate some more orange slices.

Inez couldn't move or talk. Her hands had been tied behind her back and her feet were bound together in front of her. A dirty cloth had been stuffed into her mouth.

Her head felt like a sack of cement.

Two burly and dour German men stood in front of her smoking cigarettes, studying a map, and occasionally giving her an angry glare.

Inez's long red hair was caked with blood and dirt. Just fifteen years old, she'd recently gone through a growth spurt, and her gangly legs and arms ached as the rope dug into her skin. Her brown eyes, wide with terror, studied the men as they glanced at her. She breathed heavily, almost hyperventilating. For the first time in her life, she felt helpless.

Once, she had gone rabbit hunting with her father and they had laid a steel trap with turnips and carrots. Half a day went by, and when they returned, they found a hare in the trap, the steel teeth gripping its left leg. The terrified hare had tried to scramble and break free from the trap's teeth, but the steel pressed deep into its skin and wouldn't release. The animal screamed in fright as they edged closer to it.

Inez remembered what it felt like to grab the hare by the scruff of its neck, and how it looked at her with such fear. As if it knew it was headed for certain death.

Inez felt like that hare—trapped and horrified, and completely at the mercy of her captors.

The last thing she remembered, before waking up with her hands and feet bound, was spying on these same men from up on a hilltop. Then everything had gone black. One of the men must have snuck up behind her and knocked her unconscious.

The men clearly weren't happy, as they kept arguing in German, scratching their heads, and pointing at Inez, until finally they put the map away. Two of the men picked her up—one at her armpits and the other at her feet—and threw her into the bed of a truck that was covered with a cloth canopy made from heavy cotton and held up by steel girders.

She landed hard on the steel grate and it stung her back sharply. The truck reeked of oil and gasoline and the bed was a mess of rust and mud.

Looking up, Inez saw one of the men stare intently at her with such evil that she shuddered. He screamed something at her in German and waved his hands, motioning for her to move to the back of the bed. Complying, she scooted until her back felt the hard, cold steel.

Satisfied, he flicked his cigarette at her.

The truck's engine roared to life and soon rumbled along the dirt road. A similar truck tailgated so closely behind, Inez could see the growth of the driver's beard.

The two trucks drove away from the farmhouse and away from her school and the safety of her home and friends.

Inez had never felt so alone.

Rain slapped down on the tent roof like the pitter-patter of thousands of pairs of little feet.

The night was especially dark, as the sky was filled with thick, gray clouds. Strands of water fell from the sky to the dirt below, forming huge mud puddles on the battlefield, which was now a temporary encampment. The blood of thousands of fallen warriors created red streams that seeped into the earth.

Zijuan slept fitfully in her tent when the dreams came to her.

A boy swimming with a shark.

A faraway city.

An old book of some importance.

A black panther.

A sea captain with a beard.

Then the images changed, and she saw Melbourne Jack sitting above them, almost floating, smiling in an angelic haze.

She tossed in her sleep as more images filled her mind.

A city, gray with smoke, appeared, its buildings bombed and smashed, as if a tornado had ripped them apart. Soldiers fought and butchered one another. In the background, some kind of shadow watched over it all. Images of Fez, Aseem, and Tariq came into view. A red handprint dissolved like sand through an hourglass.

The sound of hundreds of thousands of people crying out shattered everything.

The images were so prolific and horrifying that she awoke with a start and sat up in her bed, completely confused by her surroundings. Her pulse raced and she felt her heart beating as if she'd just run a marathon. Beads of sweat dripped down the side of her face and her hair stuck to her neck.

Unable to shake the nightmare, Zijuan walked over to a basin and splashed cold water on her face.

She lit a lantern and laid a small rug down on a dry part of the dirt floor so that she was able to sit down cross-legged. She then removed a scroll and fifty sticks of equal length from a small chest. Breathing deeply, she began to throw the sticks across her tent. After making a series of throws, she interpreted the sticks' positioning.

She was performing a variation of *I Ching*—an ancient form of fortune telling.

With each throw, she felt herself grow tense, each outcome more ominous than the previous one.

"Tariq…," she muttered with her last throw.

She stared at the sticks in disbelief. Never had the readings been so foreboding, and never had she felt such fear. She was about to pick up the sticks when a voice came from outside her tent.

"Zijuan, are you awake? May we enter?" Sanaa asked.

"Yes, please come in," she answered.

Malik and Sanaa entered the tent.

"Sit down," Zijuan instructed.

Malik and Sanaa sat down on the rug. Outside, the rain started to pour down harder and Zijuan could hear thunder in the distance. The smell of smoke and charred flesh lingered in the tent. The smell had been thick in the afternoon, when they'd cremated hundreds of dead soldiers before the flesh could rot. The welcome rain had begun to wash the smell away.

Together in that small tent sat the three deadliest, and most respected, assassins in all of Morocco, and perhaps all of Arabia and Africa.

"We're having nightmares."

"Both of you?"

"Yes," they replied at the exact same time.

"Tell me about them."

"We see Tariq, Fez, and Aseem, but they are in a foreign city with some kind of captain. A large black cat. Then we see strange men, one Caucasian and the other Asian, and then a war of some kind and a red handprint. We can't make sense of it," Malik explained.

"How long have you been having these nightmares?"

"Since the boys disappeared into the clouds. The day of our victory over the Caid."

Zijuan sighed.

"What is wrong?" Malik asked as they sat across from Zijuan.

"I have been having the exact same nightmares. I didn't understand them until I performed an *I Ching* reading just before you came to my tent. I believe that Tariq and the boys are alive, but are far away. I believe they are, for the moment at least, in safe hands. They must engage on a quest of some kind and we must not interfere. This quest will be very dangerous and some—or all—of them may perish."

"What are you talking about? I don't understand. What quest?" Malik asked.

"I do not know," said Zijuan.

"Can we help them?"

"No, it was clear to me that they must complete this quest on their own accord."

"How is it possible we've all been having the exact same dreams?" Sanaa asked.

"Everything is connected, Sanaa. Our thoughts and our actions, both in the physical world and the spiritual one. Think of everything like a spider web, all woven together. Most people forget, or refuse, to believe

12

in such an interconnected world. But I believe that the world is headed for a dark place, and what is happening now is breaking through our consciousness and enabling us to know the whereabouts of the boys."

"And we can do nothing? Just sit back and hope they survive?" Sanaa asked.

"But they are so young," Malik said worryingly.

Zijuan nodded.

"I will meditate for them each and every day to try to tip the scales in their favor. As I have answers, so will the both of you."

Sanaa listened attentively. By nature, she was subdued and stoic, but the disappearance of the boys had been weighing on her.

"All I care about is that they are alive," she whispered.

Zijuan stared at the husband and wife across from her. They were the two people she trusted more than anyone else in the world.

"I don't know why we were all given the exact same dreams, but it's not a coincidence. The Red Hand is reaching out to us—for what reason, I am not sure."

Malik nodded his head as he listened.

"You've always had a gift for the metaphysical, Zijuan. We will listen to your premonitions. If we are told that we must not interfere, then so shall it be. Please know that Sanaa and I will do anything for those boys."

"I know. And please, if you have any new dreams, please describe them to me immediately."

Sanaa stared straight ahead. Her face was lean and angular, and her black hair was tied in a ponytail that hung to the small of her back. A dagger was omnipresent at her side, even at night, in the safety of Zijuan's tent.

"I can't help but think of Tariq when I first saw him being tortured and held prisoner in the Caid's kasbah. Never once did he complain or cry or whine," she said.

Malik took her hand.

"Or when I started training him with the other boys in the mountains, how eager they were to learn, and how brave."

"Perhaps it is not an accident they were chosen for this quest? Perhaps all of their learning and perseverance has been to prepare them for the test and trials ahead?" Zijuan replied.

"Like training?" Sanaa asked.

"Exactly like training," Zijuan agreed.

"That makes me feel a bit better," Malik answered before sighing deeply and continuing.

"We will retire to our tent. Thank you, Zijuan."

Sanaa and Malik stood up, bowed gently to Zijuan, and then exited the tent, back into the driving rain.

Zijuan stared at the scroll she had laid out in front of her. A weight seemed to hang from her shoulders as they slumped when she stared at the scroll.

She hadn't told Malik and Sanaa everything. There was an evil force at work in the world. Zijuan had never felt such a malevolent and brutal presence in her thoughts. This evil presence had somehow been awakened and was plunging the world into a darker and more sinister time than any in history. She couldn't shake the sick feeling in her bones. She'd never felt anything like this—such evil and such terror. The gruesome images and voices of all those suffering people lodged in her mind.

Even more troublesome was her realization that Tariq, Fez, and Aseem could be on a collision course with this darkness.

CHAPTER
— 2 —

THE CALL OF THE HUNTER

1914—AMSTERDAM

The harbor of Amsterdam lay under a blanket of gray and smothering fog. Smoke belched from the many chimneys of the factories that lined the waterfront. Longshoremen and sailors moved slowly, still waking up, as they began unloading ships and preparing freighters for journeys to distant shores.

A pelican flew overhead. Foster Crowe stood on a creaky dock and watched the harbor come to life. Soon he began walking toward the train station at a brisk pace. After a week-long journey aboard a freighter from Ceylon, his legs were a bit wobbly, but his face was a picture of determination. Carrying only a small leather backpack, he needed to move fast. At fifty-two years old, he had some gray hair around his temples, but was otherwise in peak physical condition. Always dressing as a gentleman, his tan suit coat remained starched and clean, and his brown leather loafers were polished. As he walked, he could feel the tip of a dagger he'd hidden up his left coat sleeve.

Foster Crowe was on a hunting expedition.

He was hunting a man by the name of Wu Chiang.

A month prior, Foster had discovered a temple deep in the heart of the Ceylon jungle. He broke into the temple and stole a journal from Wu Chiang. The journal told of a secret society that had existed for centuries. This society was responsible for countless acts causing death and destruction dating back to the bubonic plague in Europe, and possibly even before that. Using the principles of the Red Hand Scrolls for evil, the society developed inventions and devices built explicitly to maim, murder, and cause mayhem.

Even more sinister, the diary revealed that Wu Chiang and his agents had been plotting some kind of world war for decades.

A war that would be the most destructive in the history of mankind.

Unfortunately, Wu Chiang had escaped on a freighter headed for Bremen, Germany. Unable to follow him to Bremen, Foster had secured passage on a freighter headed for Amsterdam in the hopes of catching up to him once he arrived in Europe.

However, Foster wasn't even sure what Wu Chiang looked like. His only description of the man had been provided to him by a dockworker in Colombo, who described Wu Chiang as a portly Asian man with thick glasses—most likely of Chinese descent—dressed in plain clothes.

Once he arrived in port in Amsterdam, Foster ran on the hard cement through the city, hurrying to the train station. He needed to get to Bremen, and the four-day journey by train was the fastest route possible.

He had to find Wu Chiang and stop him.

The Asian man sat cross-legged with an upturned, dirty brown derby hat in front of him. He'd stuffed his pudgy body into ragged and tattered clothes. Thick glasses sat on his nose.

This was the man known as Wu Chiang.

Pedestrians stepped around him, and a few dropped coins in his derby.

From where he sat, Wu Chiang could see the Serbian embassy across the street. Two guards casually stood at the gated entrance, smoking a cigarette and sharing a joke.

Suddenly, an enormous explosion rang out from the embassy! It was so powerful that it shook the ground and even shattered the glass from a lamppost. Smoke billowed from the windows. The guards, shocked into action by the blast, opened the gate and ran to the building. People on the street ran to the site to see what had happened.

After a few moments of silence, Wu Chiang began to hear the screaming and the moaning of the injured and the maimed. The smell of sulfur filled the air. Acrid smoke began to sting the eyes of stunned onlookers who had gathered around the embassy walls to see what had happened.

Then, without warning, a second explosion tore through the area, this time just inside the embassy gate.

Wu Chiang was blown back into the brick wall behind him by the force of the blast.

Instantly, the street became a gruesome scene of butchery, death, and destruction.

Dead bodies were everywhere. A decapitated leg, bloody at the thigh, landed in the street across from where Wu Chiang was sitting. A man staggered backward, his entire body engulfed in flames, screaming until the flames overtook him and his charred body fell to the ground. Dust and chalk blew upward and settled on anything and everything within a several-block radius. A large crater, six feet in diameter, appeared where the gate had been; now only fragments of steel blown to bits remained. Bricks and dust scattered around everyone on the street.

More screaming. Not just the screaming of the wounded and dying, but the agonized cries of people who arrived at the scene, soon realizing that their loved ones were dead or wounded.

Wu Chiang watched the carnage in front of him.

And he smiled.

CHAPTER
— *3* —

A FRIEND INDEED

Inez had been in the truck for hours and hours. Her stomach growled and she huddled her arms around her legs, pulling them against her chest to keep somewhat warm. With nobody to talk with, and nothing to read, she was resigned to staring at the back of her truck and the windshield of the truck behind them. Everything about the bed of the truck was noisy and uncomfortable. The hard steel bruised her butt and tailbone. Occasionally, she nodded off and her head drooped to one side, only to be woken up with a jolt when the truck tires hit a big bump.

Her ankles and wrists were tied, making escape an impossibility. Her mouth was gagged so she couldn't call for help.

For the moment, she was resigned to being a prisoner.

At last, the truck stopped and a German man opened up the tailgate, grabbed her roughly, and proceeded to untie her and drag her by the arm to a bathroom in the rear of a filling station. Once she was finished with the facilities, he removed her gag, handed her a sandwich and a bottle of milk. After she'd finished her meal, he put her gag back on, tied her up and returned her to the back of the truck.

He did all of this without saying a word.

Once back in the truck, Inez felt much better. The truck rumbled along for hours and then, once again, they stopped at a filling station, she was allowed to relieve herself, given another sandwich and milk, and directed to the back of the truck.

A full day passed and once again it turned to night.

At one point, Inez thought she heard what sounded like Italian when the truck stopped to ask directions.

Again, the truck stopped, she used the facilities, was given yet another sandwich, and then got back in the truck. The man never said a word.

He closed the tailgate and, instead of starting the truck, she heard him saying something to the other driver and the men disappeared.

That's when someone leapt over the tailgate into the bed of the truck! The figure was like a shadow, and it moved so quickly that Inez thought she may have imagined it.

"Inez, don't make a sound," the voice said.

"Margaret!" Inez said in a muffled voice from behind her gag.

"Ssshhhhh," Margaret whispered.

Inez could clearly see her friend Margaret Owen's blond hair in the pale moonlight.

Margaret moved behind Inez and frantically began sawing at the ropes that tightly bound her hands.

"I have to cut these before those men return," Margaret whispered.

Inez felt her arms being pulled and pushed as Margaret hurriedly tried to cut the rope with nothing but a rusty piece of steel. Inez began to feel the ropes loosen and then, finally, her hands were free.

They heard the men's voices returning. Margaret immediately ducked behind one of the crates. Inez kept her hands behind her back when one of the drivers peeked in to check on her.

Inez tried to look pathetic.

Satisfied, he threw out his cigarette and went to the cab of the other truck. The two engines roared to life and the trucks began rumbling down the road once again.

"Keep your arms behind you in case he can see into the bed of the truck. We'll have to wait for a chance when he's not so close, and then we'll jump out," Margaret explained.

Crawling on her belly, Margaret began cutting loose the ropes from Inez's ankles. She sawed at the rope in quick, scissor-like motions. Inez could hear her labored and quick breathing. She hoped Margaret wasn't panicking.

Margaret stayed on her belly next to Inez for ten minutes. The second truck followed so closely that Inez could smell the engine oil just behind them.

The first truck went over a hill and then began to pass around a bend. The second truck's engine faded into the background and its headlights dimmed from view as it struggled to keep up.

"We're going too fast! The roads are slippery from a rain," Margaret whispered aloud.

The truck continued to gain speed, whipped around a corner, splashed through a mud puddle, tossing both Inez and Margaret to the right side of the truck's bed.

"What a fool!" Margaret whispered again.

The truck edged around another corner and both girls began to feel the tail end swerve. Then, the left side of the truck tipped up, both wheels off the ground, until the truck was completely out of control, moving on only one of its two right wheels.

The truck toppled over and down a dirt embankment. Margaret and Inez bumped and tossed around the back of the truck. Everything seemed to move in slow motion as the truck rolled down the hill.

At one point, the rolling slowed to a temporary stop, and Margaret saw an opportunity. Grabbing Inez by the armpits, she launched both of them toward the back of the truck, out of the bed and into the mud as the truck began to roll again, this time with much more momentum. The truck stopped only when it crashed into a tree.

Then there was stillness. The smell of gasoline permeated the air. The truck was smashed to bits. The windshield was crushed and broken glass was everywhere. The front grill was bent. The back was a mess of shards of steel and ripped pieces of cloth.

Inez could see the torso of one of the German soldiers slumped out of the passenger window. Blood poured from his head as his arms drooped to the side. She reached up to feel something sticky on her scalp, and her left elbow throbbed. Margaret looked a bit dizzy and was holding her ankle and grimacing. Inez couldn't believe it when Margaret sprung to her feet and started barking orders.

"Let's go!" Margaret ordered, and the two schoolgirls, bloodied and covered in mud, limped away from the carnage and into the beginning of a forest. They heard the second truck stop and then the voices of men behind.

"Hurry up Inez, we don't have much time," Margaret urged as they ran into the forest and away from their German captors.

The day wore on and the boys went about helping the crew with various chores and learning more about the *Osprey*. After a couple of hours, Tariq felt light-headed and tired. He carefully returned to his room, closed the door, and felt an odd sense of dread begin to overtake him.

The awful image of Melbourne Jack dying in his arms flooded his mind. Watching the life drain from Jack's face, and then having to make the horrible decision to let his friend's body slip into the sea.

Slumped on the bed, Tariq placed his face in his hands. He felt as if the strength was leaving his body.

Then, inexplicably, different images began filling his head. Images of places he had never been and memories he didn't have.

A field covered in mud and barbed wire. Two trenches, only a hundred yards apart, and then two armies running at one another. Thousands of men, some in strange masks, charging at one another across the field through a light fog, rifle shot after rifle shot ringing out, and a collision of bayonets and the sick sucking sound of a young soldier's breath leaving his body, his belly pierced by a bayonet. Blood spurted from the boy's mouth and dribbled down his chin. Tariq watched the scene unfold in his mind—so clear and so real—until the young soldier collapsed onto the muddy battlefield. A young boy with blond hair, barely older than himself.

He was so close that Tariq could have touched him.

The awful images continued until he forced himself to sit up and relax in the stillness and safety of his cabin.

What were these images?

Looking at the side table next to the bed, he noticed his brown and green bag, which was made from crocodile skin and resembled a small knapsack.

Opening it up, he pulled out a diary, its pages made from some kind of thin leather. Sketched on the pages were words in an ancient dialect, alongside many diagrams and calculations.

This was the diary of Alexander the Great.

Tariq had guarded it with his life on the ocean and now scolded himself for leaving it unattended in his cabin. From now on, it would never leave his sight.

He rubbed his hands along its cover.

Find the panther to begin your journey. Return the diary, Tariq!

The voice belonged to Melbourne Jack. Tariq heard it so clearly that he almost jumped. During his delirium, he thought he had just dreamt about Melbourne Jack, but now he understood that Jack's continued presence in his life wasn't just a dream. And now, Jack seemed to be in the room with him, giving him instructions.

Breathing heavily and still dazed, Tariq held the diary in his hands. It felt sacred, like it was becoming a part of him.

"Are you here, Jack?" he whispered.

Begin your journey, Tariq! Find the panther in Constantinople!

There was the voice again inside his head. It was unmistakably that of Melbourne Jack.

Tariq suddenly felt himself tire. A sense of peace came over him, and he leaned back on the bed, holding the diary tightly to his chest, until he fell into a deep and restful sleep.

Tariq awoke with a start, still clutching the diary. Miraculously, he felt refreshed—the dizziness and weariness had left him. His body was no longer sore. He wasn't sure how long he had slept, but his energy had returned.

After placing the diary in the bag, Tariq put his head and arm through the strap and wore it around his neck and shoulder. The crocodile skin felt cool against his chest. Melbourne Jack had ingeniously designed the bag so it would be completely waterproof and impervious to almost any puncture. There was an interior lining made of ox leather, treated so it would be fire resistant and then folded over once more to prevent any kind of water from seeping in. The outer layer, made of thick crocodile skin, was so strong it could almost stop a bullet. It was secured by a leather strap, braided to add strength and then woven into the lining of the bag.

Putting on a cotton shirt to cover up the bag, Tariq made his way back up on deck. It was almost dusk; the sun would descend in the horizon in another half an hour.

Fez and Aseem were playing with Panos and throwing scraps of fish to Lako over the side of the boat. The boys laughed as the shark eagerly ate the chunks of tuna and mackerel.

Standing next to them, Tariq smiled. Panos handed him a piece of fish and Tariq tossed it to the hungry shark.

"Are you okay? We checked on you a couple of hours ago but you were sound asleep," Aseem asked Tariq, obviously concerned.

"Yes, I am fine, thank you," Tariq replied, appreciative of his friends' concern.

"Tonight, Captain Scopas told me he would begin teaching us about celestial navigation. That's how sailors navigate by the stars. They've been doing it for thousands of years," Fez explained.

"How far is it from Morocco to Constantinople?" Tariq asked.

"Just over one thousand six hundred nautical miles. We're traveling about eight knots an hour and a knot equals one nautical mile. So, we're travelling approximately one hundred and ninety nautical miles per day!" Fez explained.

"Why do they call it a knot? Why not just say mile?" Tariq asked.

Fez shrugged his shoulders and said, "I'm not sure—maybe because a nautical mile is longer than a regular mile?"

"That's silly," Aseem said.

"Everything is different on a boat. It's not even called a rope; it's called a line. Left is port and right is starboard. The front is the bow and the rear is the stern."

"Why do they call everything different?" Tariq asked.

"I guess when you're stuck at sea for weeks at a time, you get pretty bored," Fez replied.

After explaining about how a keel keeps the boat upright beneath the water, Fez and Aseem sheepishly looked at one another.

"Tariq, we wanted to do something to honor Melbourne Jack, but we didn't want you to think it was dumb," Aseem explained.

"What?"

"We were talking—that when Aji died, Zijuan told you to light a lantern to honor him. I was thinking we could make lanterns to place on the ocean in memory of Jack?"

Tariq nodded his head and put his hand on Aseem's shoulders.

"I would like that very much," he replied and smiled.

Aseem went over to a wooden pail and took out some small pieces of driftwood and tiny pieces of candle cut from a much larger candle given to them by Scopas. Fez helped place the pieces of wood and candles on the deck between Aseem and Tariq.

As the boys constructed the small floating lanterns, Tariq shared with his friends the last conversation he had with Melbourne Jack.

"Jack told me he didn't want to be mourned. He wanted us to be bold in our lives and be true to ourselves and each other," Tariq said quietly. "He made me promise to return the diary to his circus, to Foster Crowe. He didn't know where the circus is now, but that if I go to India I can learn its location."

Fez and Aseem nodded and solemnly focused on the project of making lanterns from the pieces of driftwood, each with a tiny candle in the middle. They were careful to provide plenty of leverage on either side so the wood wouldn't collapse. Once finished, they lit the candles and then placed them in the wake of the *Osprey*. Slowly, the floating lanterns all drifted away, flickering in the dusk.

Each boy closed his eyes in silent prayer for Melbourne Jack, and then each bowed in deference to his memory.

CHAPTER
— 4 —

TWO LOST RABBITS

Margaret and Inez stumbled through the forest. Margaret's right ankle throbbed, while Inez felt a sharp pain on her temple and blood trickled down her face.

Through the thicket of trees, in the darkness, it was impossible to see any kind of trail. The girls ran blindly—falling, picking themselves up, falling again, and continuing to move in any direction they could, so long as it was away from the crash site they had fled. Their knees, elbows, and palms were covered in dirt and scraped with blood. The only sound that could be heard, in the otherwise stillness of the forest, was the crackling of branches under their feet and their labored breath.

They ran until their legs screamed with pain and their lungs shouted to stop. Finally, when they arrived at the edge of a small stream, Margaret allowed them to rest.

Both girls doubled over, gulping air into their pleading lungs. Sweat poured down their necks and soaked their shirts. They were bloodied and bruised, a feeling of shock resonating throughout their bodies.

After a moment, Margaret leaned down to the water's edge and began scooping handfuls of water into her mouth. Her ankle throbbed, and she wanted nothing more than to take off her boot and let it soak in the cool water. Inez followed suit until both girls felt their breath return to normal and their bodies cool a bit. They rinsed the blood and sweat from their faces.

"Let's go," Margaret urged and soon they were running through the forest again, staying as close to the stream as they could.

Inez ran, and Margaret limped, for another twenty minutes, until Margaret finally stopped and leaned against a tree.

"Inez, I have to stop. My ankle is killing me. Besides, I don't hear them following us anymore."

Inez was bent over in exhaustion as well, and her face was drenched with sweat.

"Yes, let's stop for a minute."

After catching her breath, Inez looked at Margaret. Margaret was dirty and sweaty and grimacing with pain, but Inez had never been happier to see anyone in her life.

"Margaret, how did you find me? What happened? I thought I was all alone—those men were so scary," Inez said and went and hugged her friend tightly. Margaret, unaccustomed to any kind of display of affection from Inez, was taken aback for a moment. She held her friend close, and could feel Inez shake in her arms as she cried into Margaret's chest.

"You would have done the same for me," she whispered in Inez's ear.

Finally, Inez released her grip on Margaret, her eyes watery from tears.

"How did you find me?" Inez asked again with a sniffle.

"When you went missing from school, I knew there was only one place you would have gone, and that was to spy on the Germans. I found your notebook and binoculars on the hillside by the farmhouse. I saw them put you in the truck, so I ran down and hopped in the second truck. It was luck, really," Margaret said, remembering her British humility to never embellish.

"You're a hero! That is the bravest thing I've ever heard of!" Inez exclaimed.

Margaret had to smile at the enthusiasm in her friend's face. She never thought of herself as brave, or as any kind of hero, but seeing the joy in Inez's eyes, she now realized how alone she'd been.

"It was nothing. Now, we've got to figure out where we are," Margaret replied, wanting to shift the attention from herself.

Margaret tried to peer through the darkness, but it was hopeless. Without some kind of light, they would simply be walking blind.

"I think we need to rest a bit until dawn and then begin walking. We mustn't go to the main road because they might be patrolling it, so, we'll stick to the forest."

"I have no idea where we are," Inez said.

"We traveled for a long while. I think we're in Germany."

"Germany! Why would they want to bring me to Germany? If they were going to kill me, why not just kill me in France?"

"That's just it. I don't think they wanted to kill you, but I also don't know what they wanted with you."

Inez stood and thought for a moment.

"It's getting cold, Margaret," Inez said.

"Let's make a quick shelter. Grab as many long branches as you can and I'll collect leaves. The drier the branches, the better," Margaret ordered.

The girls gathered all the leaves and branches they could find, and then Margaret went about preparing a kind of teepee fort made of branches with leaves for flooring and spread on the outside for insulation.

Inez watched her in amazement.

"That is so neat. Who taught you how to make a fort?"

"My father. I'm making it small so it will keep us warm. It will be cramped, but that's the point."

In no time, the fort was built and both girls crawled inside. It was small, so they had to curl up together. Still, it was warm.

Inez felt Margaret next to her. She finally posed a question that had been bothering her.

"Margaret, all the time you were in that truck, how did you go to the bathroom?" she asked.

Margaret shook her head in frustration.

"Really, that's what you're asking me right now? After I risked my life to save you, and we're stuck nowhere, and we have no food or water?"

"Um, yeah, I guess," Inez squeamishly answered.

"There was a bucket, okay?" Margaret tersely answered.

"Any paper?" Inez questioned.

"Oh my goodness, be quiet!" Margaret admonished and Inez knew better than to ask any further questions.

Both girls curled together. The shock in their bodies subsided and gave way to exhaustion. Soon, they drifted into a fitful sleep.

"Inez, wake up!" Margaret said.

Inez slowly opened her eyes. Margaret was kneeling and looking into the shelter from outside. It was now daylight, but just barely, and the chirping of many varieties of birds could be heard all around them.

Inez was notoriously crabby in the morning, and at school, the girls avoided waking her at all costs. Once awake, she was the most courageous of all of them, but early in the morning, she had the sensibilities of a two-year-old baby.

Stretching her arms, she brought her torso up and yawned.

"I'm stiff and sore and hungry," she complained.

"So am I. Let's get a move on."

"Do we have to? I want to sleep for a few more minutes," Inez pouted and turned over.

"Inez, we don't have time for that, we have to move!"

Inez sat up, folded her arms, and stared crossly at Margaret.

"Fine!"

Trying to ignore her, Margaret walked over to the stream, put a bit of water in a large leaf, and then produced a pin from her hair. She rubbed the pin a few times on her clothes to charge the pin. She then broke off a blade of grass and floated a small, wide piece in the leaf and carefully placed the hairpin on the floating grass. Slowly it spun around until it stopped.

"This is a trick my dad taught me. Float a small piece of metal in a leaf with water and it should point to magnetic north. With sunrise on one side, we can determine which end of the hairpin is north. We know we want to head south, so—that way," she said, pointing.

Inez stared at the hairpin in the water.

"Are you sure that thing works?" she asked, wrinkling her nose.

"Of course it works, now let's get a move on."

Inez stood up and soon the two girls were tramping through the forest. Margaret winced in pain from her ankle, but it wasn't so bad she couldn't walk. They had found a long stick for Margaret to use as a cane, which helped. Twigs snapped under their feet and mud caked to their shoes. They walked for two hours until the morning was bright and the sun was in full view.

"If we are in Germany, it means they may have taken us through Italy and through Switzerland. No, that doesn't make any sense, because I don't remember going through a mountain pass. They would have taken us north through France and then headed directly east. I would imagine it would be southern Germany and the Alps would be just below us. I think those are the mountains we've been staring at."

Inez gazed at the mountain range in front of them.

"The Alps?"

"I've visited them several times on skiing vacations. They're very beautiful," Margaret explained.

"So how do we get out of here?"

"I'm not sure. But we need to stay away from the main roads and towns. No doubt the Germans will be looking for us."

"How will we eat?"

"Inez, I don't know. We'll figure something out, just keep walking."

The girls continued on, at one point finding another stream, where they washed their hands and faces and cooled themselves off. Walking up a hill, Margaret thought she heard something on the other side. As they drew closer to the crest of the hill, the noise became louder. It sounded like a hammer hitting a nail.

"Get down Inez, let's see what's over that hill."

The two girls crouched down, stayed hidden behind trees, and then continued their walk to the top. The forest was dense so it was easy to hide.

Over the hill, the girls came upon a scene that both amazed and surprised them.

Approximately a quarter-mile down, they could see a makeshift camp. It looked to be about two hundred yards square. Barbed wire surrounded the outskirts of the camp, and a guard tower was at each corner. To the right were a series of large canvas tents, about twenty in all. The camp was a buzz of activity, but it was difficult to see who occupied it from such a distance.

"What is this?" Inez asked.

"I don't know, maybe some kind of army camp? I think those are all soldiers," Margaret answered.

Suddenly, as they were peering down at the camp, both girls were grabbed from behind. Strong hands dug into their triceps and pinched their skin. Then they heard shouting in German.

They were staring at a couple of German soldiers dressed in black uniforms.

"*Was is das?*"

"*Was is die?*"

Inez and Margaret felt the gruff hands on them. The two young soldiers continued to question them in German. After a few moments, four more soldiers joined them.

"I don't speak German," Margaret in both English and French.

"*Was?*" one of them answered, an older and squalid man who was obviously the one in authority.

He motioned for the others and soon Inez and Margaret were being led down the hill to the camp. As they approached, the barbed wire around the fence now looked ominous. Margaret spotted people dressed in rags who looked at them as they were marched down the hill by the group of soldiers. Coming closer, Margaret could see that some of the people were in chains and were being forced to work, overseen by German soldiers. Many people emerged from their tents to stare at the girls. They looked malnourished and Margaret could clearly see the despair on their faces.

"Margaret, this isn't a camp…it's a prison!" Inez whispered.

Foster Crowe arrived in Bremen on an early morning train. The ride had been comfortable, and he had managed to get some much-needed sleep after the rigorous sea journey. The aroma of a bakery filled the air as Foster stepped out of the train station. He followed the delicious smell to a door in an alleyway. It was a small bakery with just one table. Although it was early, the baker had already been up for four hours and was just now taking pans of pastries from his wood-fired oven. Foster negotiated for a Berliner, a type of doughnut without the hole, filled with fresh raspberry filling. The baker poured Foster a cup of strong coffee as they spoke to one another in German.

Looking out onto the Bremen city streets, he was reminded of his childhood in Belgium.

In the early morning, Bremen was chilly and gray and a fog held steady on the cobblestone streets. Foster was in some kind of city square. A large fountain with the statue of a robed man, most likely a saint, with tiny angels surrounding him anchored the center of the square. Spouting water shot up from the basin of the fountain. On one end of the square was a Gothic cathedral with long and narrow stained-glass windows and a stone griffin—a mythical lion and eagle hybrid—on the roof, acting as a guardian of the supposed gold and riches hidden inside the cathedral. Statues of saints were sculpted into the facade just above the massive wooden door that acted as an entrance.

Foster surmised it might have taken twenty or thirty years to build the cathedral, even with hundreds of masons working tirelessly on the tiniest of details.

The entire square was surrounded by Gothic-looking apartment buildings with gray bricks, long windows, and pointed arches at the top. The apartments were crammed together.

In front of the cathedral, steel tracks made way for a lazy red streetcar moving slowly through the rising fog.

Gathering his thoughts, Foster went and sat at the fountain and took out a black leather notebook he carried with him for jotting down notes and ideas. He'd been thinking about nothing else but Wu Chiang on the journey over. He took a minute to look over his previous notes.

He had tried to put himself in Wu Chiang's shoes. What would he do? Where would he stay?

He knew next to nothing about the man—only a vague outline of his appearance and not much more. He didn't know his travel habits. He had no inkling if he had any friends.

Foster decided the first thing he would do is visit the harbor to see if the ship from Ceylon was still docked. If it was, perhaps he would get lucky and a dockhand might remember Wu Chiang. If that didn't work, Foster could check the passport office next.

It was a start.

The baker came out with a cup of coffee and sat next to him.

"Such a peaceful plaza, and such a shame about the Serbian embassy," he said, taking a slurp of his coffee.

"Serbian embassy?" Foster asked.

"You didn't hear? It was bombed two days ago. Two bombs actually. Over fifty people dead, and now the Serbs are blaming the German police. Such madness in the world. This is such a peaceful city; why would anyone want to kill innocent people?"

"This happened two days ago?"

"Yes, here, let me get you a paper. You can read for yourself."

The baker went back inside his bakery and returned with a paper. He handed it to Foster.

The headline was in large bold font: **No clues into bombing of Serbian embassy. Serbs still blame German police.**

The article included a photograph of the scene after the bombing. It showed a blown-up building with bricks scattered everywhere, and a woman in a white dress who was crying in the street.

Foster read about the bombing, and about the mobs in Serbia who blamed the Germans, even beating a German tourist who found himself in the wrong place at the wrong time.

It all made perfect sense.

Wu Chiang was behind this bombing. That's why he was in Bremen. He was creating tensions between Serbia and Germany. Tensions that might eventually lead to a war.

Foster hoisted his backpack over his shoulder, asked the baker for the general vicinity of the Serbian embassy, and made his way across town.

Two hours later, Foster stood at the Serbian embassy bomb site.

The outside of the embassy looked like a giant monster had chewed it up and spat it out. Spikes of steel that were once the embassy gates stuck up from the ground like broken toothpicks. The front of the building was completely blasted away—like a wrecking ball had shattered the front wall and only a few lonely bricks remained. Dust had settled everywhere.

There was a constant crowd of mourners, and people had taken to placing bunches of flowers along the outer embassy wall. The bouquets numbered in the hundreds and stretched down the wall for over a block. In one section, someone had erected a makeshift shrine on a column and pasted a piece of paper with a note to someone lost in the blast and a candle underneath. Others followed suit until the shrine was covered in leaflets and letters with dozens of candles on the ground.

An old woman dressed in black sat next to the wall where she had slept through the night. Her body and face were covered in dust. She held her hand against the brick wall in the faint hope that her dead husband would come for her.

Over one hundred soldiers dressed in gray uniforms surrounded the embassy. They were positioned outside the embassy gate and all around the interior grounds. Absolutely no one was allowed in or out of the building without specific clearance—clearance that Foster Crowe most assuredly did not have.

He had hoped to get inside the embassy grounds to the blast site for a clue of some kind, but he now saw that would be an impossibility.

Foster stared at the old woman and the hundreds of people gathered around the embassy. A small group circled together in prayer, while others merely stood and observed the destruction.

A man called out with fresh pastries and hot apple cider. Foster purchased a strudel and cider and then approached the old woman by the wall.

"I'm sorry," he said to her.

She looked up at him. Her eyes wanting and full of pain. Her face and gray hair covered in dust.

"Who would do this?" she asked him.

Foster shook his head.

"Only someone who cares nothing for the world."

"A person such as this should not be allowed to exist," she answered.

He wanted to say something, anything, to comfort her. But the pain and grief in her eyes told him that was impossible.

"I brought you some breakfast. Do you need anything else?" he asked, and placed the cider and strudel next to her.

"You are very kind. No, I just need to be here. To be here with him."

"I understand," Foster answered, put his hand on her shoulder, and then returned to the crowd outside the former gate.

He thought deeply about Wu Chiang. He understood, now, that he planned to create tensions among countries. He probably already had agents in place around Europe. It was as if he'd been building a bonfire and now he was lighting a match.

There was something else that was bothering him.

The newspaper article had stated that tensions were high in Serbia and mobs were already forming to attack German tourists.

It was peculiar how fast these German newspapers had the story, Foster mused.

Too much of a coincidence—was it possible that Wu Chiang had someone within the German newspaper writing planted stories about events in Serbia?

If Wu Chiang's work in Bremen was now done, Foster knew he would be on the move toward his next target.

Foster slung his backpack over his shoulder and ran back to the train station.

CHAPTER
— 5 —

MANDOLINS IN THE MOONLIGHT

That night, the boys were treated to a magnificent feast by Captain Scopas and his clan. A long and fat sea bass was being grilled on a spit over an open fire pit on deck. The fish, still whole with its eyes and tail, was being turned and doused with a mixture of olive oil and herbs until its skin began dripping and the luscious white flesh was solid and meaty. Some sardines were fried in a huge black pan and given as appetizers.

"Aji and I used to beg for sardine scraps in the harbor. These are much better than the raw ones we used to suck on," Tariq said.

"Raw sardines? That sounds disgusting!" Aseem said and the boys laughed.

Captain Scopas played a mandolin and sang song after song in his native Greek. Eventually, the entire clan gathered in a circle and sang with him, stomping their feet and clapping their hands in a frenzy of song and movement. The boys' faces lit up with excitement watching the dancers in the firelight on the old boat.

The eyes of each sea gypsy glowed in the darkness, illuminated by the fire. Unlike city dwellers, these people didn't know how to hide their emotions. Every song was sung with full voice, as if the words resonated from some deep place within their hearts. The dancing increased in intensity and raw energy with each song. The laughter was honest and true, as if unfettered joy were pouring out from their souls.

Each clan member came and hugged the boys and even kissed them on the cheeks. Everyone immediately accepted the boys into their clan without trepidation or judgment. The boys were now to be treated as members, and even looked up to with a certain amount of respect for surviving such an ordeal.

Tariq watched the festive scene in front of him and felt mesmerized by the people and their dancing and singing. These people were so full of life that it was hard to feel the grief that had been consuming his thoughts. Looking up at the stars, Tariq was struck by the immeasurable beauty of life. Only days ago he had been inches from death, and now he was singing and dancing on a gypsy ship.

He knew, at that moment, that Melbourne Jack would have loved this ship and these joyful people. He couldn't help but smile.

Eventually, Scopas gave up the mandolin to another man and brought Panos over to join the boys.

"You must tell me. How did you train your shark?" Fez asked.

Scopas translated and Panos excitedly provided an answer, again translated by Scopas.

"It's a nurse shark, and not so dangerous. Lako was attacked by another shark and seriously injured, so, Panos created a shallow pool and fed him until he was healthy enough to swim fast. After that, Lako would always find Panos in the sea and allow him to ride on his fin. When the clan left for another port, Lako followed us and has been with us since."

The boys laughed and slapped Panos across the back. Panos beamed with pride at being the center of attention with these older boys.

"So boys, how did you happen to be stuck in the middle of the Mediterranean?" Scopas asked.

The boys looked at one another, not sure if they should go into detail about their former lives. They nodded as an affirmation that Captain Scopas could be trusted.

"We were part of a resistance in Morocco, where we fought an evil caid. Our friend, Melbourne Jack, built the hot-air balloon. We crashed into the sea after we were attacked by a French airplane," Tariq explained.

Scopas lit his pipe and took a long drag.

"A resistance?" he asked.

"Oh yes, we were spies against Caid Ali Tamzali. We watched his troops. Aseem and I infiltrated the military, posing as soldiers. We stole vital secrets. Tariq even managed to hijack a shipment of arms from a boat," Fez explained.

"Tell me more, if you feel comfortable," Scopas asked.

"Well, we were trained in the Rif Mountains by a man named Malik. He taught us to fight, to hunt, to track animals, and how to be warriors. In the cities, our friend Timin taught us how to be spies—by blending into the environment and using a set of codes to communicate," Fez answered.

"Very interesting…what happened to this Melbourne Jack?" Scopas asked gently.

"He died at sea," Tariq answered mournfully.

Scopas could see that Jack's death still affected Tariq more than the other boys.

"And did you defeat this caid?" Scopas asked.

"We don't know. The battle was still raging when our balloon went out of control in the clouds," Aseem answered.

"I am sorry for your loss. I have lost many friends in battles through the years. Although lost, they are never forgotten. Here, let me say a toast to your friend Melbourne Jack."

Scopas stood up and motioned for silence. Eventually, all eyes of the clan were on him and the boys. Then, in Greek, Scopas gave the following eulogy:

"My friends, these brave lads lost a friend as they were fighting an evil caid. His name was Melbourne Jack and he died in the sea. As you can see, the boys have been through a horrible ordeal. Please raise your glasses for their good friend Melbourne Jack. May he find peace in heaven and smile down on these boys throughout their lives."

Everyone in the clan raised their glasses and looked at the boys. Tariq, Fez, and Aseem stood up and raised their glasses as well, although they had no idea what was being said.

"To Jack!" Scopas said, drank a whole glass full of ouzo, and then threw the ceramic glass down on the boat's deck, shattering it to pieces.

"To Jack!" everyone screamed, drained their glasses, and then threw them down, breaking them as the captain had.

Scopas urged the boys to down the contents of their own glasses and then break them. The boys looked at one another, gulped down their water, and then threw down their glasses hard and watched as they shattered.

The deck was quickly covered in shards of broken ceramic, and just as quickly, the clan resumed singing and laughing.

"Ah, that is the Greek way. We say a toast to our fallen friend and then break the glass as a way to say goodbye…to finish it. You understand?"

"Yes," the boys answered.

"Good. The song they sing is a song for the dead. You see, it is not a sad song, but a song to celebrate life! That is our way," Scopas instructed and then sat back down and urged the boys to do the same.

"Boys, I have some serious business in Constantinople. I need some assistance, and you just might be the right boys to help me."

"What kind of business?" Tariq asked.

"I'll explain everything when we dock. Now, enjoy the song and do not be sad!"

Captain Scopas smiled and tousled the hair on each boy's head, and then they went about listening to the beautiful singing of the clan.

Later that night, Scopas made his way to his quarters where he was joined by his wife, Calliope. She was a little younger than he was, with long, dark hair that went down past her shoulders. She was already dressed for bed in a white nightgown and was quietly brushing her hair.

Scopas sat at the edge of his bed and washed his bare feet in a basin of cold water.

"There's something about these boys," he said to her.

"What do you mean?"

"There's something about these boys that is different. I can't place my finger on it. They are very wise for their age…and very courageous. I get this feeling they are meant for bigger things."

Calliope smiled and continued brushing her hair.

Scopas was deep in thought.

"I do not know why it is. I have dreams of them each night and they are constantly in my thoughts. It is very strange. I may ask them to spy for me in Constantinople."

Calliope briefly paused brushing her hair and then continued.

"They remind me of you when you were younger," she said. "So full of life…if you feel they can help you in Constantinople, then ask them."

Scopas thought a moment before answering.

"You think I am taking advantage of them?" he asked.

"Of course not."

"Then I shall ask for their help."

Scopas began to ready himself for bed when his wife finished brushing her hair and went to a small dresser, opened up the top drawer, and took out an object covered in burgundy cloth. She gave the object to Scopas.

"What is this?" he asked.

"You'll see."

He unwrapped the object. In his hands was a white chess piece. It was carved from marble in the shape of a king.

"It was your brother's. He gave me his favorite chess set just before he died. He said it was to encourage you to play, however, I think it was as if he had a premonition of his own death," she said somberly.

Scopas felt the piece in his hand. It was smooth and perfectly carved. His brother had spent over a year carving the board and each individual piece. This king was a representation of the British King William the Conqueror. His brother had been studying medieval history, and his favorite king was William.

"Elektra plotted her revenge, and so must you, but never forget why you seek your revenge," she explained to him.

Scopas felt the piece in his palm. His brother had been a huge advocate of chess since they were both young children. While Scopas was out having adventures and enduring no end of mischief, his brother would be home studying chess strategies or have his nose stuck in some book. The piece brought back so many memories of him trying to teach the finer points of the game to Scopas, but ultimately he didn't have the aptitude, or the patience, to ever be much competition to his brother.

"Thank you," he whispered and kissed her before going to bed.

Scopas placed the piece in his coat pocket as a token to remember his departed brother.

CHAPTER
— *6* —

A RIPPLE IN THE DESERT

The rain had stopped and the sun slowly ascended above the horizon. Sanaa sipped on a hot cup of tea with a blanket over her shoulders to keep her warm. Stoking a fire with a stick, her breath disappeared into the crisp morning air.

Looking across the battlefield, she stared at the spot where she had slain the Black Mamba just days earlier. Her body was still sore and bruised from the battle, and her mind was fatigued. There was a cut on her upper lip that had still not healed. When she spoke, her skin pulled at the edge of the wound, a reminder of the fight to the death she had just endured which had taken every ounce of her strength. To mark the spot where the Mamba had been killed, the Tuareg had boiled his head in a hot cauldron of water and placed the bare skull on a cross for all to see. The tribespeople placed colorful necklaces made of bead, bone, and feather around the skull. It was a grisly token, but a deserved one. The Mamba had terrorized the country for too long, and it gave the tribespeople pride that his skull now sat atop an old, battered piece of wood.

This monument also paid homage to Sanaa, as she was now a celebrity within every tribe in the region.

Around her, people began to emerge from their tents to prepare for the day. Soon, more fires would be built.

Malik had made the decision to stay for a week to allow his warriors to rest and make preparations for their next assault. He was considering marching on Tangier to battle the French, but was still undecided. His indecision was, in some ways, a wise move, as it gave the people a chance to relish their victory and time to heal.

As Sanaa sipped her tea, she noticed one of their falcons circling in a manner that suggested visitors were approaching. At intervals throughout the day, their falcons flew circles around the perimeter of the encampment, acting as scouts and alerting the tribe to any potential threats.

She studied the falcon's movements, which relayed to her that the approaching group was small.

Returning to her tent, she reached inside to grab her sword. Malik stood by, shaving, as she slung the sword across her chest.

"We have guests," she said and left the tent without leaving him time to reply.

Malik toweled himself off, dressed, grabbed his *bō* stick, and then joined Sanaa outside.

Soon, Sanaa spotted a small contingent of about ten people on horseback on the adjoining hillside. The sun was behind them, and they were backlit so their torsos were dark like shadows. One of the horsemen raised a flag and began to trot slowly down to the encampment.

"What is happening?" Malik asked, unable to see for himself because the Black Mamba had blinded him.

"A small group, one of them is coming to us with a raised flag."

Others spotted the visitors and soon a contingent of soldiers had surrounded Malik and Sanaa. The assembled soldiers had come from tribes around the Rif Mountains and surrounding countryside. Some had ventured from as far as the Sahara desert—and even the Atlas and Jbel Saghro mountain ranges.

Sanaa looked at Malik.

"I'll be the one to greet them," she told him.

She went to fetch her camel, which sat tranquilly in a herd of other camels. She urged it to its feet, threw herself on its back, and then sprinted out to meet the lone rider.

Zijuan joined Malik.

"Did you ask her to ride out alone?" Zijuan asked.

"You think I could give her an order?" Malik replied and they both smiled.

As Sanaa rode out, she could see that the man was a fellow Moroccan, dressed in her native country's garb. He was undoubtedly a warrior of some kind—he wore a white turban and robe and had dark skin and a black beard. His flag was white as well.

As she edged closer, she slowed her camel to a walk and carefully approached the rider, who was walking his own horse.

They finally came face to face.

"My name is Adel Kharja. I am an emissary and advisor to the Sultan," he explained.

"What do you want?" she asked sternly.

"I have come with some French generals. They want to discuss an accord."

"An accord?"

"They want to negotiate the peace."

"And you trust these French dogs?" she asked.

"I think you will want to hear what they have to say," the man answered. Although dressed as a warrior, he had the tongue of a diplomat.

"I hear the Sultan's troops ran like cowards from the imperial palace and the Sultan is in hiding like a rat. Why should we trust you? Or follow him?"

The man studied Sanaa. He had heard of her reputation, and that of Malik.

"Because we all want peace for our country, and you have the advantage. We are coming to you to negotiate a peace," Kharja explained.

She studied him for a few moments.

"If it was up to me, I would cut you to shreds and then ride up and kill these French generals. Thankfully, my husband is the reasonable one and chosen to lead our army. Tell your French masters to ride and we will meet with them. You have my word none of you will be harmed."

"There's just one more thing," Kharja added.

"What is it?"

Kharja whispered something to Sanaa. After a few moments, she nodded and rode back to the encampment.

"What was that about?" Malik asked.

"The French, and a diplomat from the Sultan. They want to negotiate a peace."

"That is good news. I was worried about attacking a city. We've taken heavy losses and I'm not sure we could stand up to the French artillery. We will need to be careful though…it could be a trap."

"There is one more thing," she said.

"What is it?"

"They want to name you as the next caid," she said, and a slight smile came across her face.

CHAPTER
— 7 —

THE TRAIL IS NOT DEAD

Wu Chiang sat in third class on a train headed for Paris, France. While biting into a baguette layered with hard-boiled eggs, salami, and lettuce, a bit of egg dropped on the lapel of his shirt. He wiped the yellow glob from his front, looked forward, and breathed deeply.

The passenger car was full of people, crammed together like cattle. People huddled together on the hard floor, as there were no empty seats in third class. Two windows on either side of the car were open and provided the only ventilation. Outside, the French countryside buzzed by and the rhythmic beating of railroad tracks was omnipresent. Most of the people were silent, just trying to get through an arduous journey.

Wu Chiang had spent the duration of the trip crammed into a corner with an obese man who reeked of body odor and sweated profusely pressed up against him. The man's torso kept pushing against Wu Chiang, jamming him against the hard steel of the railway car and leaving sweat smudged stains on his entire left side.

He travelled in third class because nobody inquired about third class passengers, whereas a first class passenger might attract conversation and attention.

His thoughts turned to an ambassador's dinner in three nights at the Hotel du Cecil. He knew from his spies that the Austrian ambassador to France would be in attendance. It was common knowledge that Austria and Germany were the closest of allies and neither country was on friendly terms with France.

He'd alerted one of his agents that there would be a mission and for her to ready herself.

A vendor came into the car selling cups of tea from a steel tray placed around his neck. The obese man purchased a cup, and as he turned to ask the vendor for some sugar, while the man's back was to him, Wu Chiang casually placed four drops of liquid into his cup from a vial he'd hidden in his suit pocket.

The man continued to eat his sandwich and sip his tea. He licked the crumbs from his chin with his long, pink tongue and continued to look straight ahead.

After a few moments, the man's face flushed and he began choking and gasping for breath. He grabbed his chest and fell forward. The other passengers, panicked, surrounded the choking man. His face turned a disturbing shade of purple as he gasped for air. Stewards rushed in. Someone loosened his shirt, but he suddenly went into convulsions, his body spasming so violently it shook the entire cabin.

Then the man stopped breathing and moving altogether.

A doctor was found on the train who arrived in time to pronounce the man dead. Everyone around was astonished, staring at the obese body, his left cheek on the floor and his lifeless eyes frozen open.

A few children cried and some of the older women said prayers and crossed themselves.

It took six stewards to remove the man's body and place it in a baggage car.

Through all the commotion, Wu Chiang casually stood up and watched without emotion as the man died in front of him.

He calmly sat back down, stretched out, and finished his sandwich.

Going over his plan in his mind, he nodded into a deep sleep.

Foster stood at the Bremen train station, trying to decipher the train schedule. There weren't a tremendous number of trains departing each day, perhaps a dozen, and most were spread throughout the day. Wu Chiang probably would have departed in the early afternoon, a few hours after the embassy bombing.

Only two trains left the station in the afternoon on the day of the bombing: a train to Paris, France and a train to Florence, Italy. Foster asked around among the many railway station workers, but none of them could remember seeing an Asian man on the platforms or in the waiting area.

Foster took out a coin from his pocket.

Well, he thought, *we'll just have to do this the old-fashioned way.*

Flipping the coin high in the air, it rotated half a dozen times before coming to rest in his palm.

The side of the coin with the bearded head of Prince Luitpold stared back at him.

I guess it will have to be Italy.

He put his hands together and said a quick prayer that this was the right decision.

"What are you looking for, mister?"

The voice was that of a boy. Foster looked down and saw a street boy looking up at him. He was about fourteen and wore a brown flat cap with a dirty tan wool coat, brown trousers with a hole in one knee, and leather loafers that were at least three sizes too big for his feet.

"Eh, nothing, just trying to make a decision," Foster replied.

"A decision about what?" the boy asked.

"A decision about a person," Foster answered somewhat agitated.

"A person? I know just about everything that happens in this train station. What person are you looking for?"

"He would have been a passenger and only here for a few moments. You wouldn't know him."

The boy took a step forward.

"A mark if I can tell you about your passenger," the boy replied.

"I can't imagine you could assist me."

"Try me."

Foster was exasperated with the conversation.

"Fine, he would have been an Asian man carrying a large trunk leaving perhaps two days ago."

"I know exactly who you're talking about," the boy answered in earnest seriousness.

"How could you possibly know?"

The boy lifted his sleeve. On his right forearm was a burn about the size of a cigarette burn.

"Because the man you're looking for gave me this."

Foster stared at the burn. It was deep and red and already oozing with pus.

"How on earth…?"

"He was having a bit of trouble with his trunk and I offered to help him—for a price of course! At first, he ignored me. When I tried to take the trunk handle from him, he took my arm and dug his cigarette into my skin."

Foster immediately felt sorry for the boy.

"Do you remember what train he was getting on?"

"The train to Paris."

Foster stared at the boy and flipped him not one, but two silver coins. The boy's face immediately lit up.

"Thanks, mister!" he said and ran down the railway station.

Foster purchased a ticket on the train heading to Paris, which was scheduled to leave in twenty minutes. He placed his leather bag in the compartment above his bed, and looked out the window as the train began to rumble and move away from the station. Onlookers cried and waved to their departing loved ones, all smartly dressed for a trip to the station, and Foster felt a slight longing for the circus and his friends. He noticed a mother with her young children waving—a boy about ten and a little girl about six. The little girl was sobbing. Foster guessed that their father was on the train. Foster smiled at the crying girl, who was dressed in a pink velvet bonnet and a black wool coat.

He settled into his compartment for the journey. Leaning back into a pillow, he closed his eyes and calmed himself. After a few moments, visions began to fill his mind.

Images that were neither memories nor dreams.

Two armies colliding, thousands of dead soldiers fallen in the mud and cold. Three young boys of some kind of ethnicity. A black panther. A sea captain. An ancient city. A Red Hand disintegrating and falling into the sand.

The Red Hand was reaching out to him, and he became immediately certain that time was of the essence.

If he didn't stop Wu Chiang soon, the world would be plunged into chaos.

CHAPTER
— 8 —

THE TUTELAGE OF FOSTER CROWE

1872—THE HIMALAYAS

Young Foster Crowe was just ten years old when his father called him to his study one afternoon. While lighting his pipe, which was filled with stringy brown tobacco, Foster's father gave his son some surprising news—he was to accompany his father on a hunting expedition to Nepal.

Foster would spend a semester away from his boarding school in Belgium, which he had attended since the age of six. This was the first time that Foster's father had invited him anywhere other than the occasional deer hunt in the woods surrounding their small castle—an estate that had been in their family for over twelve generations.

His father, being a military man, was a very strict disciplinarian, and most of Foster's summers were spent ironing his own clothes, polishing shoes, cleaning horse stables, and continuing his studies. Each morning, at precisely seven o'clock, his father gave him—and his room—a full inspection, and any grievances were given a black mark. Five black marks, and he would have to bend over his father's knee and have his backside whipped with a riding crop.

Foster was an only child, and his mother had died giving birth to him. His father, uninterested in rearing a child by himself, had Foster sent away to a school in Belgium. His actual name was Viscount Frederick von Crowe. His nanny since birth, an Algerian woman, couldn't pronounce the name "Frederick," so she called him "Foster."

The name stuck.

Six weeks later, Foster found himself on the deck of a clipper ship sailing through the Suez Canal. His father had insisted he work to earn his board, so most of the time Foster could be found scrubbing the decks, coiling the lines, washing dishes or laundry, and on occasion, helping the crew hoist and tighten the many sails.

The Suez Canal, completed just three years prior, shaved months off the journey as they would be spared sailing down the coast of Africa and cutting through the Cape of Good Hope.

Foster was amazed at the sights and sounds of Calcutta and by the nautical journey they had taken to get there, which took only six weeks, followed by a caravan to Kathmandu, which took three weeks. Nepal was notoriously closed to any foreigners, but Foster's father had bribed the right officials. After Kathmandu, it had been a four-day journey to the town of Pokhara.

In Pokhara, his father hired two sherpas; they purchased the appropriate provisions, and their hunting party disappeared into the Annapurna range of the Himalayan Mountains. His father justified his time away from school by saying a little "worldly" experience would do him good.

Foster always wanted to be close to his father, yet his father remained distant and aloof. A tall man with jet-black hair and a narrow moustache, his father almost never smiled and rarely showed emotion. He was a decorated Belgian soldier who had fought in the *Force Publique* in the Congo and helped subdue Congolese insurrections. He smoked his pipe incessantly and spent every waking moment watching everything around him, his eyes darting about like a lizard eyeing a fly. Nothing escaped his father's gaze, and every mistake Foster made was instantly recognized, ridiculed, and corrected. His father seemed to relish, a little too much, finding fault in all of Foster's endeavors and personal traits.

His father loved hunting for sport more than anything else in the world. Their castle in Belgium was adorned with hundreds of stuffed heads from animals killed by his father over the years. Tigers, wolves, lions, cheetahs, apes, deer, antelope, and even the full body of a black bear stood at attention in the cold stone interior. Each animal head was displayed with its mouth open, in an attempt to emulate its terrifying nature.

On this expedition, his father was hunting a rare tiger only found in the high altitude of the Himalayas. The tigers were said to live only above

10,000 feet and were able to navigate the steep and treacherous terrain of the stark landscape. Even in the snowy landscape, these tigers were little more than ghosts, as there was scant evidence of their existence.

Foster wanted nothing more than to please his father by killing a tiger. He practiced shooting each day—his father had given him a brand new Springfield 1871 rifle, a new model from the United States. It was the first gift his father had ever given him, outside of one present each year on Christmas day.

Day after day, Foster practiced shooting until his shoulder was so sore from the rifle's recoil that he could barely move it in any direction. Every night, he studiously cleaned the rifle both inside and out. After dousing it with linseed oil, Foster carefully oiled the chamber and ran a cotton cloth over and over the steel barrel. He polished the handle with a homemade beeswax formula. When he'd finished, it was so shiny that Foster could see his reflection in the wood.

When they set out on the trek, his father informed the sherpas they were planning on going to Machapuchare—a smaller mountain in the Annapurna range.

The sherpas looked at each other and then shook their heads. In broken English, they explained that the mountain was revered and considered to be sacred to the Hindu god Shiva and not to be climbed.

Foster's father took out some gold sovereigns, enough money to feed these men's families for a year, and then told them, in no uncertain terms, that they *were* going to climb Machapuchare.

The sherpas looked at one another and had a brief discussion in Nepalese. In agreement, they took the coins and then hoisted the bags on their shoulders to begin the arduous trek.

"Do you think we should go if this mountain is sacred, Father?" young Foster had asked.

His father shook his head at him.

"Do we look like simple peasants who believe in superstitions?" he replied and then set off behind the sherpas.

It took two weeks to reach Machapuchare, and the hunting had been almost completely fruitless. The only thing his father managed to shoot was a wild yak—which the sherpas made into stew and then prepared the hide, which later would be dried and made into jackets and pants.

Reaching the base of the mountain at last, Foster noted the stillness in the air. He felt like he was trespassing on sacred ground. He couldn't shake the feeling that he was being watched. A few times he even looked over his shoulder to see if someone was watching him from behind, but each time he saw only the mountain staring back at him. At night, in the confines of his small tent, Foster swore he could hear voices in the wind.

As they continued up the mountain, the air became thinner as they climbed higher and higher, and it became more difficult to hike. Foster needed to stop for a break every five or ten minutes. His surroundings became nothing but rock, snow, and ice.

Setting up camp well below the summit, his father declared they would camp for two days to rest and hunt.

The next morning, Foster and his father headed out to hunt early, before daybreak. The air was cold and Foster stomped his feet as they walked. He was still sleepy, but he knew better than to complain to his father. The sun had just come up on the horizon, and Foster struggled to keep up with his father's long stride.

They had walked for two hours in silence when, after coming around a bend, they saw a huge albino tiger standing right in their path!

The tiger was massive, perhaps three or four hundred pounds, and looked to be of the Bengal variety. Albino tigers were the rarest of all tigers, and only a select few had ever been seen in the wild. The big cat's fur was completely white, save for the black stripes down its body and head. Its coat was wet around the back, and droplets of water dripped from its rib cage. The cat was gently licking the melted snow off a rock and did not notice Foster or his father nearby.

Quickly and silently, Foster's father brought the rifle stock to his shoulder, steadied his gaze down the front sight at the end of the barrel, and aimed the chamber right at the cat's midsection. After taking a quick breath, he relaxed and allowed his right index finger to pull back on the steel trigger. Foster mimicked his father, bringing his own rifle to his shoulder and looking through the sight at the tiger. He understood that he was to wait for his father to fire first.

Instead of firing, his father's rifle jammed!

The tiger, hearing the click, looked up and growled and looked right at Foster.

"You've got the shot, Foster, take him down!" his father shouted.

Foster pressed the butt of the rifle against his shoulder, allowed his right index finger to caress the trigger, closed his right eye, and brought the tiger within his sight.

The tiger growled, but it did not attack. Perhaps a hundred feet away, it stared at Foster and growled again. Looking into the tiger's eyes, Foster felt a strange, otherworldly connection to it. For a moment, Foster could swear he could hear the tiger's thoughts.

"Take the shot!" his father ordered.

But Foster did not shoot. He thought of all those animal heads in their trophy room in their cold castle. He looked at the tiger and something from deep within his soul told him not to shoot—he just couldn't see a reason to. All this time, all he wanted to do was please his father, but in that moment, he didn't care about his father's approval at all. He knew, intrinsically, what he was doing was wrong.

Lowering his rifle, he looked up at his father.

"No," he whispered.

His father hit him in the face with the back of his hand, knocking Foster down, then grabbed the rifle, brought it up and pointed it at… nothing.

The tiger was gone.

His father glared down at Foster, his rifle in his hand, in disbelief that his son had passed up such an easy shot.

"An albino tiger! You passed up an albino tiger! A once in a lifetime animal. You ever pass up a shot like that again, I'll shoot you myself."

He threw down the rifle at Foster, who was now bleeding profusely from his lip.

The next day, the sherpas packed up the camp to move to higher ground. Foster's father hadn't spoken him to him all night, and Foster traveled in the rear of the caravan—away from the sherpas and his father. It was as if he had been banished by his father. Walking far in the rear, the snow crackling beneath his feet, and his breath dissipating in the mountain air, Foster felt so very alone. He should have felt safe being with his father, but instead, he felt as if he were unwanted. That his father wasn't just disappointed in him—more that he was no longer wanted on the hunt at all.

They trekked through the snow all morning and then came to a narrow crossing that required the group to walk in a single-file line. Foster stayed in the rear, still fearful of his father, who gruffly barked out orders at the sherpas.

After a few moments, Foster's father proceeded across the narrow path, followed closely by the two helpers. The crossing was only about eighteen inches in width and required each climber to press his back against the cliff behind and sidestep down the path.

As his father and the sherpas moved farther away from him, Foster felt a tinge of fear as he looked down the sheer face of the cliff. It was at least a thousand-foot drop to the ground below.

Foster felt a gust of wind and his entire body froze in paralysis. His palms instantly became clammy and wet. He realized that one false move would send him plunging to his death. He tried hard to control his shallow, nervous breathing.

His father called out to him as he was about halfway across the pathway.

"Foster, hurry up, we don't have all day!"

Taking a deep breath, and steadying his gaze to focus on nothing but the trail, young Foster was about to take his first step when, suddenly, his father let out a horrible scream followed by the terrified screams of the two sherpas.

Just one moment before, Foster had been staring at his father and the two men, and the next moment they had dropped from sight.

The path had given way under the weight of the three men!

His father continued to scream as he was plunged down the mountain. Foster watched in horror as his father and the two sherpas fell faster and faster until they landed with a 'thud' on the snow-packed ground a thousand feet below. As Foster watched, everything seemed to move in slow motion. It felt like an eternity before his father hit the ground.

Aghast, Foster stared down at his father's unmoving body, splayed out in an unnatural position on the cold plateau of the Himalayan tundra.

"Father!" Foster yelled, but his father's body didn't move an inch.

"Father!" he yelled again, his voice bouncing off the cliff and echoing in the valley below.

His father's body never moved.

He was dead, as were the two sherpas.

After standing there for ten minutes, still in disbelief about what had just happened, Foster finally managed to move his legs and looked around. He couldn't possibly move forward as there was now a fifteen-foot gap in the narrow path. His only solution was to return to the place they had camped the night before.

Slowly, Foster moved away, taking one last look at the lifeless figure of his father. Another gust of wind blew through his hair, and Foster noticed the complete silence around him. Nothing moved. Everything was still as though frozen in time.

For three hours he walked until he found the spot where they'd been the night before but now it was just an empty, snowy patch of land. Foster sat down and pulled out a hunk of chocolate, took a bite, and then returned it to his pocket. He really wasn't hungry.

It was still daylight, so he decided to keep moving to keep his body warm. He didn't think of his father. He didn't cry. He just wandered in solitude along the mountain trail, until he came upon a strand of Buddhist flags stretched between two rocks. The flags were somehow peaceful, colored like a rainbow. They flickered in the wind like the flames of a candle.

He was completely lost, but at least now he'd seen a sign of life.

All of his gear had been lost. He no longer had a tent, a sleeping bag, a stove, or even a lantern. Fortunately, he was dressed warmly enough, but the only supplies he carried on his person were a hunting knife, a compass, and some chocolate.

Foster stood there, watching the flags snapping in the wind, when he was suddenly awed by the sight of the Himalayan mountain range in front of him, like gods emerging from a mist. He had never bothered to notice their beauty before, as his father would have admonished him for such novelty.

He spent the rest of the day constructing a snow fort, as his father had taught him, then dragged himself inside to settle in for the night.

Lying in the snow, his back against a rock, Foster hugged his knees and brought them up to his chest. The snow was a bit cold underneath him, but his wool pants did an excellent job of keeping him warm. Pulling his hood even further down his face to block the cold, he slowly felt himself fall into sleep as the sun descended and the day turned to night. It was a fitful sleep, and he awoke a dozen times during the night to the sound of the wind swirling around him in the starkness of the night and the snapping of the Tibetan flags. After hours of tossing and turning, he finally managed to drift into a deep sleep.

He awakened with a start to someone smashing through his snow fort with a stick and then poking him in the shoulder.

Looking up, he saw a man dressed in a brown jacket made entirely of yak fur. A brown hood partially covered his face. The man stomped into the fort, wearing massive brown leather boots lined with yellow fur and caked with mud, and waving a long stick made from a mangled piece of wood with a huge knot in the middle.

The man looked like some kind of snow yeti.

He poked Foster again.

Foster immediately stood up and realized he was just an inch or two shorter than the man in fur. The man reached into his pocket, causing Foster to take a couple of nervous steps back, but instead of a weapon, the man brought out a large hunk of yak cheese, called *chhurpi* and offered it to Foster. Foster took the cheese and practically inhaled it, he was so hungry.

The man pulled back his hood and Foster could see that he was an older Nepalese man, maybe sixty. His head was bald, but his eyes were the most sparkling shade of green.

"Hello Foster. My name Lhak-Pa. Must follow me."

Foster stared at the man, who smiled at him.

"How did you know my name?"

"All in good time. Come, need to get off this mountain. Not good to disturb Machapuchare. Do not speak for three days—must mourn father."

"But, who are you? How did you find me?" Foster asked.

"No questions now. Must get early start. Storm is coming. Follow close behind me."

With that, the man turned and started heading down the mountain path. He walked farther and farther away until Foster decided to jog and catch up to him. He didn't know anything about the man, or how the man had found him. At the moment, he was just thankful he wasn't alone anymore.

CHAPTER
— 9 —

GRAVEDIGGERS

Margaret and Inez sat across from the German officer. His desk was small and orderly. He had a trim physique, a tight black moustache, and the look of a military man. His eyes seemed to shift as he studied the girls.

"How did the truck crash?" he asked in French.

Margaret and Inez looked at one another.

"We don't know. We were in the back…in the bed," Margaret sheepishly answered.

He studied them both, still in their school uniforms.

"I was told there would only be one girl. Was I misinformed?"

"No, my friend Margaret tried to save me by hopping in the back of the second truck."

He sighed, nodded his head, and leaned back in his chair.

"A very brave act, but also a foolish one."

He stood up and walked over to look at a map on the wall. He seemed tired, or maybe preoccupied.

"Well, I'm stuck with you until I receive further orders. My name is Major Hostetler and this is my detention area."

"Sir, what is this about? Why did you take Inez?"

The man stared at her.

"Because your friend doesn't know how to mind her own business. Now, I have more important things to think about than two French schoolgirls. Guard!"

"But I'm innocent, Sir. I didn't see anything…I was just having a bit of fun!" Inez cried.

"Unfortunately, the world is coming to a place where 'fun' will be in short supply," he answered sternly and then turned his back on them, ending the conversation.

A guard came in and escorted Inez and Margaret out of the room, grabbing them both hard by the arm.

The girls were led to a bath area and forced to stand against a brick wall. A pail of freezing water was thrown first on Inez and then on Margaret. Dripping wet, they were given thirty seconds to scrub themselves with a single bar of soap.

A German woman, burly and thick-boned, watched them wash, and then took another bucket of cold water and doused each of them to rinse off the soap.

Afterwards they were given a ratty towel and told to dry off.

Finally, they were issued drab, gray prison uniforms and a pair of old shoes that were held together by the barest of threads. The same female guard ushered them out of the bathhouse and shut the heavy wooden door behind them.

They were now standing in the prison yard.

Their shoes sunk into soft mud as they entered the yard. To their left were the rows of tents they had seen from up on the hillside. A small garden had been planted and was starting to show the tiny beginnings of greenery. Some guards watched lazily from the prison towers on each corner of the yard. Inmates meandered past the tents, and a few more were playing a game of fußball, also known as soccer.

The girls held hands and slowly began walking toward the tents.

"I'm glad you're with me, Margaret," Inez whispered.

Margaret squeezed her hand.

"We'll get out of this," she replied.

"How do you know?"

"Because I've escaped from one prison and I can escape from this one," Margaret answered. She suddenly felt not only calm, but confident. The imagery of escaping from the Caid's kasbah, having to kill a man, and fleeing with Sanaa flooded her mind.

An older woman immediately spied the girls and walked toward them.

"*Hallo*," she said.

"Hello," Margaret replied.

"*Deutsche?*"

"English and *Français.*"

"Oh."

The woman smiled. She was perhaps fifty, skinny with long hair littered with gray streaks. Dark bags sagged under her eyes.

"So what brought you to such a place?" she asked in French.

"I was spying on some Germans in a farmhouse when they captured me. My friend Margaret here tried to rescue me," Inez answered.

"All the way from France? The Kaiser must be getting more and more paranoid."

"The Kaiser?" Margaret asked.

"Oh yes, that's why we're all here...for supposed crimes against the Kaiser. Everyone here has been accused of spying, or plotting his downfall."

"So this is a prison?"

"Yes, it's definitely a prison. But the crimes are more political in nature."

"My name is Inez and this is Margaret, what's yours?"

"I am Clara. I've been in this camp for over a year, I think. It's difficult to keep track sometimes."

"Why were you brought here?" Margaret asked.

"I ran a small newspaper in Frankfurt that questioned the Kaiser and his government. One day, his troops knocked down my door, burned my papers and destroyed my printing press, and threw me in a truck. I've been here ever since."

"My goodness! What kind of stories did you write?"

"Oh, stories that depicted the Kaiser for what he is...a paranoid and small little man who is going to start a war that will likely be the ruin of Germany."

A man who looked to be in his fifties walked up to Clara and the girls. He was small and slight with a bald head and glasses.

"Girls, this is Leopold. Leopold, this is Margaret and Inez. They were spying on some Germans, captured, and brought here."

"All the way from France?" he asked in French.

"Yes, at our school just outside of Marseilles," Margaret replied.

"Well, you've had quite a journey."

Leopold had a kind nature and a soft voice. His eyes were a light hue of blue, and he seemed socially awkward. He nervously shifted on his feet and had trouble making eye contact.

"Leopold is undoubtedly the most important prisoner here. He was an advisor to the Kaiser on all things military," Clara explained.

"What are you doing here?" Margaret asked.

"Oh, once I saw that the Kaiser was preparing for war, I began to question some of his motives and decisions."

"So you were a general?" Inez asked excitedly.

"Hmmm...no, I was more of an inventor. I helped in the design of guns, ships, and even a new invention I modeled after Leonardo da Vinci's design from the fifteenth century. I called it a 'tank'—an armored vehicle impervious to bullets or bombs. I even designed a submarine suited for war."

"Like in *Twenty Thousand Leagues Under the Sea*? Captain Nemo's ship?" Margaret asked.

"Well, yes, that's a very good analogy. Only my submarine was designed specifically for war and could attack a city from a mile out at sea."

"Wow," Inez answered.

Just then, a burly guard with a beard walked up to Inez and Margaret. He was smoking a cigarette. He addressed them gruffly in German.

"So, you're the girls who wrecked the truck. You know, two of my friends were injured in that accident, all for bringing some little snot-nosed French girls," he said and threw the cigarette down and walked away.

"What did he say?" Margaret asked.

"He blames you for the truck accident. His two friends were hurt transporting you."

"But it wasn't our fault! We were stuck in the stinking back and tied up!" Inez exclaimed.

"I know, but he doesn't see it that way. That is Klaus...he's probably the most brutal guard in the prison. I'm afraid this isn't very good," Clara explained worriedly.

"What should we do?" Inez asked.

"Do anything he asks, and don't make trouble."

Just then, the guard named Klaus returned with two shovels and practically threw one each at Inez and Margaret and then said something in German.

"What did he say?" Margaret asked.

"He said to follow him. Girls, I fear for your safety. I mean it—just do what he says," Clara said, with genuine panic in her voice.

The girls followed Klaus to the farthest corner of the prison. The guards on the watchtowers laughed as Inez and Margaret nervously looked at one another.

"What are we doing Margaret?"

"I don't know, just do what he says."

Klaus stopped, pointed, and ordered the girls to dig. The ground was hard, and it took tremendous effort to get even half a shovel full of dirt. Within minutes, blisters had formed on their palms from the wooden handle digging into their skin.

"I think…I think we may be digging our own graves," Margaret said.

"Why do you say that?"

"Because Klaus took out a pistol, that's why."

Inez looked over her shoulder and, sure enough, Klaus was leaning against a fence post, polishing a black pistol with a white handkerchief, the barrel pointed out prominently beneath the white cloth.

"What should we do?" Inez whispered.

"Just keep digging."

Margaret and Inez both focused on digging a hole, ignoring the pain from their raw and bleeding hands. Inez wanted to stop on several occasions, but Margaret urged her on. Some of the guards watched and laughed at them, and a few even came over and told them to dig deeper. After two hours, the shovel handles were covered in blood and their hands were a mess of popped and bloodied blisters. Sweat drenched their necks and chests and the muscles in their shoulders and forearms screamed from exhaustion. Each had managed to dig a good-sized hole, as the ground was soft underneath the tough outer layer. The girls peered up from inside the holes they'd dug, which now reached their armpits. Klaus casually walked to the edge of the small pits. The girls cowered and didn't look him in the eyes—they stood silently holding their shovels, terrified of what might happen next.

"Are you ready?" Klaus asked in broken French and smiled sadistically. His pistol hung casually in his right hand, and he studied the girls as a circling hawk might watch an injured mouse in a field.

Fez, Aseem, and Tariq stood at the bow of the *Osprey* in the early morning as the armada came upon the ancient city of Constantinople.

The sun snuck up from the horizon as they passed through the Sea of Marmara. To their left, on a giant cliff, was a massive palace surrounded by a stone wall. To the right, up ahead, was a giant lighthouse.

"We are approaching the entrance to the Golden Horn. She is protected by Topkapı Palace there on the cliff. That is Galata Tower to the right. She guides ships into the Horn," Captain Scopas said as he joined them.

The boys studied the scene in awe as hundreds of tiny fishing boats edged out into the sea for the morning's catch. The fishermen, dressed in wool sweaters with black caps on their heads, smiled and waved, and the boys waved back.

"Topkapı Palace has protected Constantinople from invaders for eight hundred years. The only time she failed, the Ottoman Turks took the city from the Byzantine Christians in 1453," Scopas explained.

"So Constantinople is Muslim?" Fez asked.

"Yes, mostly, but the Christians were never driven out completely. You'll see," Scopas explained.

"The Byzantines, those were Greeks, right? Your people? That's why you don't like the Turks?" Fez asked.

Scopas laughed.

"Fez, you are too smart for your own good."

Rounding Seraglio Point, the boys took in a scene that, literally, took their breath away.

The ancient city of Constantinople presented herself in full glory to the three boys. Her buildings were cast in a golden hue as the morning layer of fog lifted off the sea. Blue herons, nesting in Gülhane Park, flew by the thousands overhead. On the hillside of the city, seven humongous and beautiful mosques, each with long and narrow towers called minarets, glowed in the morning sunshine. Wooden houses filled the many hillsides.

"That big one on the hill is Hagia Sophia mosque. It was first a church until the Ottomans converted it to a mosque after taking the city. Behind Hagia is the Blue Mosque, the most splendid mosque in all the world. Decorated in blue tile, it was built to dwarf Hagia Sophia."

"What's that big one in front of us?" Aseem asked.

"The mosque of Süleyman the Magnificent."

The call to prayer, or ezân, suddenly sounded out from the city as the müezzins each scaled their respective mosque's minaret and sang out for Muslims to begin one of their five daily prayers—facing toward Mecca to honor Allah.

"These are your people, eh?" Scopas asked.

Tariq listened closely. In Tangier, the familiar call was omnipresent in his life.

The sound reminded him of home.

Scopas could see the fascination and curiosity etched into the face of each boy.

"Look boys, to the right is Asia and to the left is Europe. Constantinople is the only city in the world with feet on two continents. Yes, for centuries she controlled the trade between Europe and Asia. It was said that whoever ruled Constantinople ruled the world."

"That's why they built all the walls and Topkapı Palace? To protect the city?" Aseem asked.

"Yes, invaders have tried to capture this city more times than can be counted. These waters have run with blood since the time of the Romans. She is a city that is to be respected and honored," Scopas said with dead seriousness in his voice.

The other boats in the gypsy clan moved parallel to the *Osprey*. The boys gave the adjacent crews a smile and a wave, which were quickly returned. A fleet of pelicans flew in a vee formation and glided with the wind current just a few feet above the water.

Tariq, for a moment, forgot about his troubles and was simply glad to be alive and able to witness the scene unfolding in front of him.

"I've never been to a city outside of Morocco," Fez admitted.

"Neither have I," Tariq replied.

"Boys, prepare to dock. We'll make shore in about thirty minutes. Then, I have some serious business to discuss with you," Captain Scopas explained to them.

Soon, all three boys were helping the crew take down the sails, preparing lines for docking, and throwing fenders over the side. Scopas navigated the *Osprey* to a loading dock, secured the boat, and all three boys jumped off onto the wooden dock. Instantly, all of them wobbled until their knees buckled and they fell down. Their minds and legs hadn't adjusted to being on dry land after so long at sea. After several tries, and a bit of laughing, each of them found their balance and hurried after Scopas, nervous and excited at the prospect of exploring the city.

"We are in the neighborhood of Fener. It is a Greek neighborhood, and I can travel safely in its confines. But, I must be careful. As a Greek, if I travel into the wrong neighborhood, I could easily have my throat slit." Scopas said as the four of them walked off the dock and into the city.

The sky was blue and gold and the morning dew dripped from the leaves of many trees that dotted the sidewalks. Cobblestone streets, so narrow that a donkey and cart could barely fit side by side, were enclosed by wooden houses stacked on top of one another—each colored brightly in turquoise blue, amethyst purple, canary yellow, and cabernet red. Laundry of hand-sewn cotton shirts, woolen pants, long underwear, and Ottoman vests were strung on lines fastened between the houses. Gnarled ancient vines, cascading down the walls, were overflowing with clusters of ripe grapes for wine. Vendors, pushing small wagons, called out their wares as they meandered from street to street. Everything from *lokma*, a delicious doughnut-like pastry, to roasted chestnuts—the aroma was enchanting to anyone within a stone's throw. A squadron of sparrows darted in and out of the many trees like squeaking neighbors meddling in one another's affairs. Old men played backgammon, screaming obscenities and slamming their chips on the black mahogany boards, while the younger men stood in small groups, discussing the day's work ahead of them, warmed by apple tea served in small glass cups. Merchants in gray and black suits, their heads adorned with hats, congregated together talking commerce and making deals. Women stuck their heads out of windows, chatting with one another in Greek, scolding their children to dress for school, and acting as overseers of their beloved neighborhood.

The neighborhood of Fener, in the district of Fatih, was entirely Greek and had existed for five hundred years since Sultan Mehmed II overtook Constantinople, declared Islam as the primary religion, and burned almost every Christian church in the city. It was, at times, the only neighborhood in all of Constantinople where a Christian could live safely.

Making his way through a back alley, Scopas entered a small and dark café with only a Byzantine symbol above the door. He made the sign of the cross with his fingers before entering the café, then ushered the boys in and closed the door quickly behind them.

The doors, ceiling, and walls of the café were made entirely from mahogany, giving the place a dark and foreboding feeling. The tables and chairs were wooden as well, and only a small window allowed in any light. Lamps at each table provided the café's only illumination.

"What kind of place is this?" Aseem asked.

"A place where Greeks talk of things forbidden by law. The owner is a friend of mine," Scopas whispered and suddenly the boys felt a twinge of danger.

A short and stout man, perhaps sixty, came out and hugged Scopas tightly. They spoke Greek to one another for a minute. The man studied the boys, then Scopas said something, and the man rubbed his chin while deep in thought. He then nodded, said something else in Greek, and disappeared back to the kitchen.

"That is George—the owner. He'll bring us some breakfast so we can talk some business," Scopas said, sat back down, and leaned back.

"Ah, revolutions have been plotted in this café for three hundred years. It has survived major earthquakes, war, famine, even infernos that burned down the entire neighborhood of Fener," he explained, relaxing and enjoying the small space.

In the meantime, George returned with a copper pot and four small cups and spoons. He spooned a large amount of sugar into each cup and then poured steaming hot coffee to the brim. He then delivered a huge platter of food—a morning feast of yogurt, bread, jam, fresh berries, butter, eggs, and a salty cheese called *beyaz peynir*.

"Did you boys know that drinking coffee started in the Ottoman Empire? The Turks take their coffee very, very seriously. Even their word for breakfast is *"kahvaltı,"* which translates to "before coffee." The coffee is amazing, but very strong," Scopas explained as he stirred his coffee.

The boys looked inquisitively at the dark mixture.

"Okay, boys—when you drink the coffee, you must drink it in one shot and not sip it. Are you ready?" Scopas asked.

Tariq, Fez, and Aseem each gingerly took the small coffee cup by its tiny handle, brought it to their lips, and waited for Scopas's signal.

"Go!"

The boys tipped back the cup and downed the entire contents in one gulp.

Immediately, all the boys started gagging and making faces.

"That's the worst thing I've ever tasted!" Tariq yelped while making a face as if he'd just sucked on a raw lemon.

Aseem was too busy coughing and grimacing to say anything.

Scopas and George laughed at the three boys as they continued to cough and lick their lips. Scopas happily drank his cup and eagerly refilled it.

"Ah well, it's an acquired taste. Please, fill your plates and eat some breakfast."

The boys hurriedly drank water and took bites of bread and cheese to rid their mouth of the foul coffee taste.

"Captain Scopas, can we send a telegram after breakfast? It would mean so much to us to let everyone know we are safe. I can hardly focus on anything else until I know that we've given word that we are alive and well," Fez asked.

"Yes, of course, let me pay for our breakfast and we'll go find an office. But first, we have some business to discuss."

"What business?" Tariq asked.

Captain Scopas took another sip of coffee before he continued to speak, very deliberately.

"There is a man, a Turk by the name of Abdullah Ozek. He is what you might call a gangster. He killed my brother in a knife fight in Corfu. I came to Constantinople to find him and avenge my brother's death."

He said the words very quietly and with the utmost of seriousness. The boys all watched him, eagerly anticipating what he might say next.

"Your experience as spies may come in handy. I've been thinking that perhaps there is a way I could use your services."

"What is it you need us to do?" Tariq asked.

"I want you to try to find Abdullah Ozek. I know for sure that he is in the city. I have information that he owns a warehouse, but that is all I know. I would do it myself, or ask one of my people, but a Greek hanging around Constantinople is a suspicious target. He is a very powerful man and the leader of the Turkish underground. You'll have to be extremely careful."

The boys looked at one another and then huddled together, whispered in one another's ears, and finally came to an agreement.

"No problem at all, Captain. Just tell us where and when to get started," Aseem replied.

Scopas laughed out loud and threw some coins on the table to pay for breakfast.

"I like you boys. You're courageous and you say what you mean. But this could be dangerous, and always remember one thing…"

Captain Scopas leaned in and the boys leaned in together. It was obvious he was going to whisper something very important.

"If you find yourself in a vicious knife fight with a dreaded Turk… spare no quarter, because no quarter will be given."

After they had finished breakfast and discussed the plan in detail, Scopas escorted the boys to the Grand Post Office. A magnificent building, constructed mostly of marble and erected just five years' prior as a symbol of modernity for all of Constantinople. Inside, over thirty postal operators collected mail, sent mail, and delivered telegrams. The boys were amazed at the building's construction and its beautiful white marble. Scopas approached a desk clerk and said something in Turkish. The boys watched as the clerk replied, shaking her head.

"Boys, I have bad news. All the cables are out between here and Morocco. They don't know how long it will take to repair them. Maybe two weeks or longer."

The faces of all three boys instantly sagged in disappointment.

"So there's no way to get a message to Zijuan that we are safe?" Tariq asked.

"Unfortunately, no. But perhaps we can try again later," Scopas said and tried to console them.

Dejected, the boys stood there, hoping perhaps for another solution, when Scopas noticed many of the men in the post office were looking at him and the boys.

"Come boys, it's not safe for me in here. We must leave immediately."

Looking up, Tariq noticed the stares and sneers of the people—mostly men—in the post office. Some whispered to one another while they looked at Scopas.

Exiting the post office, Scopas hurried outside.

"Boys, I must leave this area and return to Fener. A Greek walking unescorted through Constantinople is an invitation for trouble. I have written down the address and general vicinity of Abdullah Ozek's warehouse. Please be careful and report back to me the minute you've found anything," Scopas said and gave a piece of paper to Fez, along with some Turkish coins.

He stopped for a moment and addressed the three boys.

"My friends, if you ever feel like this appointment is too much, please don't hesitate to abandon it and return to me. I do not want anything to happen to you," he confessed with the utmost of sincerity.

"Captain Scopas, you rescued us from certain death. We owe you our lives, so this is the least we could do to repay our debt," Tariq answered and the other boys nodded their heads in agreement.

"Thank you, boys. Your courage is an inspiration. Please do be careful, though," he answered and a hint of emotion could be heard in his voice.

With that, Scopas flipped up the collar on his jacket and walked with a brisk pace down the street and back to the Christian neighborhood of Fener, leaving the boys standing by themselves in the crowded town square, surrounded by Turks, in a city completely foreign to them.

"What should we do?" Aseem asked.

"I don't know, but I'm disappointed we were unable to send a telegram," Fez answered.

"Come on, let's get going," Tariq instructed and they walked out of the town square and into one of the many roadways of Constantinople.

For hours they walked in a maze of tiny alleys and streets. Losing all sense of direction, they soon found themselves following a crowd into a huge building. It was a marketplace of some kind, with stalls of merchants selling their wares lining both walls.

As they continued down the narrow corridor, the boys' mouths fell open in awe; they were transfixed by the sheer magnitude of goods being sold. Hundreds and hundreds of stalls seemed to go on for miles. Spice markets; tea and coffee merchants; rug hawkers by the dozen; a man blowing glass into the shape of a vase; a man selling fezzes; suit tailors; shoemakers; a blacksmith forging knives and swords; a café where men drank tea and played backgammon; a stall full of musical instruments; and another with tiny bamboo cages holding finches. Anything could be found here: wedding dresses, furniture, copper pots, fish, and cheese. They passed a man selling vats of goat milk and a larger stall where a man sheared a sheep and his wife spun the wool into a blanket on the spot.

Tariq felt something guiding him through the mazes of stalls and merchants. As if he were dreaming, but still very present in the physical world.

All around, men yelled at the boys, urging them to visit their stalls. Suddenly, a middle-aged man with hollowed cheeks and a light-gray beard appeared in front of them. He was thin, wore a red turban, and a gold tooth showed prominently when he talked.

"You Arab, eh?" the man asked in Arabic.

"Moroccan," Tariq answered.

"I am from Egypt; my name is Ammon. Come to my stall and have some tea. Come, boys."

Tariq looked around and noticed the stall was full of maps. His mind suddenly flashed back to Melbourne Jack telling him to go to India and find the circus. He was immediately shaken from his dream-like state.

"You sell maps?" he asked.

"Of course. Come, boys. I need a reminder of home."

"Should we?" Aseem asked.

"Tea sounds good, and maybe he has a map to show a route to India?" Fez responded.

The boys slowly followed Ammon to his stall.

Open to the corridor, with an old blue globe affixed to a pergola just below the ceiling, the stall had a stack of Turkish rugs on the floor, and covering the walls were dozens of maps enclosed in aged brown frames. Hundreds of other maps were rolled and stored in copper containers around the room. Four lanterns, each encased in glass, provided the stall's only light. The boys proceeded to inspect the maps on the walls. Some looked to be dated all the way back to the sixteenth century, and one even featured what looked like sea monsters off the coast of Africa. Many were yellowed and stained, while others looked to be new. There were maps of every area of the world—from the highlands of Scotland to the valleys of China.

A small table with six wooden chairs was in the back of the stall. Ammon said a few words and then a boy of about eight appeared and then disappeared just as quickly. At Ammon's insistence, the boys took a seat at the table. The lanterns provided some hazy light, but the corner was dark and secluded.

Ammon sat down across from them. The light from the lanterns cast thick shadows down his face, making him look ominous. His gold tooth gleamed in the dim light, but the bags under his eyes appeared darker.

"So my boys, what brings you to the Grand Bazaar?" Ammon asked slowly.

"That's what this is?" Fez asked.

"Of course, this is the Grand Bazaar, the most famous market in all of Turkey. You did not know this?"

"No, we're kind of lost."

"Ah, it is easy to get lost in Constantinople. Here, you can find anything in the world. Is there something specifically you're looking for?"

Instinctively, the boys understood to not mention their errand.

"No, just looking around," Fez replied apprehensively.

"Ah, there must be something you need, everyone needs something."

The boys stared at him, not knowing what to say.

"How much money do you have?" Ammon asked.

"Nothing," Tariq answered sternly.

"Ah, a shrewd negotiator. Okay then, let's play a game. It is something I only do for a few select customers. Pick a map, any map from a bin, and I'll give it to you for just one lira."

"We don't need any maps," Tariq answered.

"For just one lira? Come now, my boy. A map can tell a lot about a person. It can tell where you've been, and sometimes even where you're going. My maps are from all over the world. Some are very young and others are very old. It is said that you don't choose a map...the map chooses you."

"We still don't have any money," Tariq answered sternly.

Ammon smiled as the servant returned with glasses of mint tea.

The servant boy was dressed in a white shirt and pants. He smiled nervously at the boys as he served their tea. After taking a sip of the tea, Aseem smiled at the boy, who skipped off, content that his tea was satisfactory.

"Come on, have a little fun with me. Just look around. Pick a map. The only rule is you can't look at it. Then, I will tell you about the map and your future. If you don't like it, don't buy it. What could you lose?" Ammon asked while slurping a bit of his tea.

The boys looked at one another, and after a few moments of hesitation, all stood up from their seats. They cautiously began to look through the many maps in the bins. They searched through the rolled up maps, casually talking with one another, until Tariq stopped them, and insisted they take a closer look at one that appeared to be older with some dust on its edges.

"How about a newer one?" Aseem asked.

"No, this is the one," Tariq said.

They returned to Ammon's table, and Tariq placed the map down authoritatively.

"This one!" he said.

Ammon smiled, put down his tea, unfurled the map, and placed paperweights on each corner to hold it in place on the table.

His expression instantly changed. He went from being gracious and amiable to scared and even terrified. His fingers shook as he examined the dusty map.

"Why did you choose this map?" he asked cautiously and slowly.

"I don't know. I just chose it. Or, I don't know, it kind of chose me, like you said."

The boys looked at the map. It was a very old one, with crinkled edges and brown wrinkles along the seams. It was in an unfamiliar language, with many symbols and numbers.

"Where is it?" Fez asked, naturally inquisitive about the contents.

The map intrigued Tariq. He leaned over it and studied it, transfixed by its design, language, and symbols—as if the map were speaking out to him. Then Tariq saw something. Near the Black Sea was a red hand print right on top of Constantinople.

"We'll take it," he announced and slapped a lira hard down on the table.

Ammon looked up at him. His eyes seemed to register something.

A warning.

"Are you sure?" he asked.

"Yes," Tariq answered.

Ammon quickly rolled up the map and secured it with a string. From behind a shelf, he produced a dusty leather map case with a shoulder strap. After placing the map in the case and snapping it closed, he handed it to Tariq.

"Keep your money, I don't want it!" Ammon exclaimed with dire seriousness in his voice.

"What's this map? You said you would tell us our future," Aseem answered.

"I cannot tell you your future. I am sorry. Take this map and leave my place at once," Ammon ordered, ushering them out of his stall and back into the corridor of the Grand Bazaar.

Just as they reached the corridor outside, Ammon bent over to say something to them. His breath smelled of licorice, and his skin smelled of lemon. He trembled as he put his hand on Tariq's shoulder. "Be careful, son. A gypsy witch gave that map to me many years ago. It has sat in a bin collecting dust until now. She said whoever chose it would be thrust into a war that could end all of mankind. A war so great that even the supernatural would be forced to get involved. Do not let anyone else have it, and listen to what it says to you. That is all I can say. Goodbye, my young friends."

Ammon turned his back on the three boys and disappeared into his stall. Slowly, the boys walked away, the map slung over Tariq's shoulder.

"Why did you choose that map, Tariq?" Aseem asked.

"I don't know. It's like Ammon said would happen—it kind of chose me. And, once it was opened, I saw three things. A red hand print, a route to India, and in the corner, I saw the mapmaker's name 'Abhijaat.' That's the exact name Melbourne Jack gave me."

"Really? I didn't see that!" Fez answered excitedly.

"That's got to mean something!" Aseem agreed.

"This is going to be a great adventure! I'll bet that map will get us to the circus. That has to be it!" Fez responded, growing more animated by the moment.

Tariq nodded, trying to act as optimistic and excited as his friends, but he felt dread in his heart. The shock on Ammon's face had frightened him. He hadn't told anyone, but when he touched the map, the image of Melbourne Jack had appeared in his mind.

That's why he had chosen it...

As if Jack were reaching out to *him*.

CHAPTER
— 10 —

THE BEINHOFF-MULLER GANG!

The wooden crate was filled with feces and urine. A fetid brown ooze bubbled near the surface. Dozens of flies buzzed around the crate's nauseating odor.

Inez dry heaved as she tried to grab a handle. Margaret was on her knees throwing up.

Klaus and the guards on the watch towers all laughed as they watched the girls struggle.

Finally, Margaret stood up.

"This is not how you treat ladies or prisoners!" she yelled at Klaus.

"Yes, good, you bring to hole and then cover up," he instructed and started laughing so hard that tears rolled from his eyes.

Inez glared at him.

"Let's just do it, Inez. We'll show them," Margaret instructed and even managed to stomp her right foot.

Gingerly, she grabbed a handle on the side of the crate and began dragging the crate through the dirt. It had metal wheels on the bottom, which made it easier to move, but still took a tremendous effort. A fly buzzed against her cheek and she tried to hold her breath. She didn't want to go too fast for fear of spilling the contents.

A week's worth of waste from two outhouses was enough to make a Viking gag.

After ten feet she stopped and threw up again.

Inez, just getting started on her own crate, suddenly began shrieking and hopping up and down.

"I got poop on my arm! I got poop on my arm!" she yelled and instantly rubbed her right arm in the dirt.

Klaus was now doubled over in laugher, as were the guards on the towers. Tears streamed down his face and his cheeks were flushed.

Inez, indignant at the laughter, composed herself, held her breath and dragged the crate twenty feet before running off and dry heaving again.

The girls followed a similar pattern of dragging the crates while holding their breath and then running ten feet away and dry heaving. Major Hostetler even came out to see what the commotion was about. He saw the guards and the scene in front of him and started shaking his head and chuckling before returning to his office.

Finally, the girls dragged the crates to their holes, lined them up, and then spilled the contents into the hole. The sound of the brown goo dripping onto the dirt, and the stench it unleashed, caused both girls to open their mouths and gag even more in disgust.

After emptying the crates, they were ordered to grab their shovels and fill the holes with dirt, which they did gladly, as each shovelful slowly helped to dissipate the smell, until the hole was covered.

Afterward, they rinsed the disgusting, smelly crates by throwing pails of water into them. Once they were somewhat clean, they returned them to the pits underneath the outhouses.

Klaus, his eyes still watering, returned the girls to Clara and made his way off.

"A bit of fun on your part?" Clara remarked, shaking her head.

Margaret and Inez, sweaty and dirty, sat outside one of the tents.

"I guess we're in prison now," Margaret remarked.

"Prison stinks!" Inez answered.

For a week the girls tried to make themselves comfortable in their new surroundings. They were allowed a "shower" every other day, which consisted of buckets of cold water being thrown on them. Only two meals a day were served: breakfast, consisting of oatmeal, and dinner, usually some cabbage and potatoes. There wasn't a lot to do other than work in the garden and play fußball. They weren't even allowed any kind of books or reading materials. They did their best to learn a few German phrases, but it seemed a very difficult language with long and strange-sounding words.

Inez fought homesickness more than Margaret, and every night cried herself to sleep. Accustomed to being the tough one, this was the first time she'd known true danger, and she hated being confined to a prison. Her natural spirit was that of an explorer, and being confined to a court-yard was almost as bad as being locked in a cage.

One day, just before dusk, Major Hostetler called the girls and Leopold into his office. Hostetler sat rigid in his chair, staring at the three of them. Leopold stared at the floor while Margaret and Inez waited for Hostetler to speak. A moth circling a lamp was the only noise in the room.

"You three are being transferred," he finally explained.

"Transferred to where, may I ask?" Leopold answered.

"Another camp. I have my orders. The truck is waiting."

"No explanation?" Leopold asked.

"No, just that I have my orders, and you're going," Hostetler coldly answered.

A guard came in and shackled their wrists in front of them, and soon all three were sitting in the bed of a truck as it rumbled out of the camp and along a dirt road. Inez mournfully waved to Clara, who was at the fence and waving back.

The guard sat in the back of the truck with them. He was young, barely twenty, and looked sleepy.

"Where do you think they're taking us?" Margaret whispered in French.

"I haven't a clue. I've never been moved before," Leopold answered.

"Why just the three of us, I wonder?" Inez questioned.

"I don't know. We're hardly alike."

"What do you mean?" Margaret asked.

"Well, I'm an inventor and military strategist and I had direct access to the Kaiser. It's understandable why they would want me in secure confines. But you're just a couple of girls who stumbled upon a farm-house. I should hardly think there's reason at all to keep you locked up."

Margaret looked disdainfully out the back of the truck. Her shackles were loose and didn't hurt her wrists nearly as much as she thought they would. The truck was uncomfortable, but it was at least different from their normal prison routine, which had gotten ridiculously disgusting and terribly dull.

For fifteen minutes, the truck rumbled along until it suddenly stopped so hard and fast that Leopold and the girls tumbled across the truck's bed.

They could hear shouting coming from the front of the cab! The shouting was loud and very animated.

"What's happening, Margaret?" Inez asked fearfully.

"I don't know. It sounds like the truck is being hijacked!"

The young guard, also tossed around by the sudden stop, had begun to bring his gun down from around his shoulder when a figure appeared at the back of the truck and hit him square in the jaw with the butt of his rifle. Instantly, the guard slumped forward—unconscious.

"No!" Margaret yelled instinctively, feeling empathy for the young guard who now lay in a heap on the bed of the truck with blood pouring from his head.

There was more shouting up front and then a loud burst of gunfire. Someone was leaping on the roof of the cab while shouting continued around the truck.

Margaret could see the figure from the back of the truck as he came into view—the man who had knocked out the young guard. Solidly built, the man wore a brown leather coat and brown gloves A black burlap sack covered his head, hiding his identity, with slits cut for his eyes and mouth so he could see and breathe. His machine gun was polished, and he pointed its black muzzle into the bed of the truck.

Margaret thought he looked like a scarecrow.

He peered in at them, appearing to be somewhat confused, and then yelled something in German.

Three other men soon appeared in back, all of them with the same black burlap bags over their heads to hide their identities.

They all carried machine guns.

More shouting in German, and then one of the figures jumped up, leaned into the cab, and began yelling at them. They moved so fast, and their voices were high pitched, almost panicked.

Next, a woman's voice sounded out and began yelling at Leopold and the girls.

Leopold said something back and held up the shackles on his wrists. Margaret and Inez lay in the bed of the truck, petrified, as the masked gunmen—and woman—continued to yell and frantically run around the truck.

The man closest to them searched through the pockets of the unconscious guard, found some keys, and began unshackling the girls and Leopold. He worked quickly and nodded to them after releasing their hands.

"They said they are liberators and are here to free us! Hurry, girls, follow me!" Leopold told them.

The woman's voice sounded out and Leopold said something in return, and soon they were ushering the girls out of the truck and leading them at a full run into the woods. Margaret wanted to ask a million questions—who were these people? And why had they attacked the truck? Instead, she kept quiet and ran.

After about half an hour, the group stopped at a clearing. Everyone was breathing heavily and a few of the "scarecrows" leaned over, sucking in air and trying to catch their breath. Inez and Margaret were still too shocked at what had just happened to say anything at all.

The scarecrow closest to them removed its hood to reveal the face of a woman.

She was perhaps sixty years old, but it was hard to tell exactly. Her face was like granite, with hard edges for cheekbones and an angular chin. A silver ponytail ran down the length of her neck. She was the only one not dressed in a leather jacket. Instead, hers was made of deerskin and looked to be sewn by hand and stitched together with thick thread. A leather strap with a long bear's tooth hung down from her neck. Her steely, ice-blue eyes shone in the light of the woods.

Inez thought she looked like a mountain woman.

The woman said something to Leopold, and after he responded, she began speaking French to the girls.

"Who are you?" she asked.

"We're nobody," Margaret replied.

"Why were you in the truck? It was just supposed to be Leopold."

"I have no idea why we were in the truck," said Margaret.

"Are there any others like you? From France?" the woman asked hurriedly.

"No, just us. My friend Inez here was spying on a farmhouse just outside our school, near Marseilles, when she was kidnapped and thrown into a truck. I followed to help her escape, but we were captured and sent to that prison, where we met Leopold."

The woman first studied Margaret and then Inez. It looked to the girls as if she didn't have an ounce of fat on her body. She looked at them with a penetrating gaze before turning her attention to Leopold. Margaret and Inez watched her every move.

After asking Leopold a question in German, the woman commiserated with her comrades, each of whom had taken off their scarecrow hoods. All of them were men—one was about forty, thick with a beard, and the other two were younger, perhaps in their mid-twenties.

The girls had no doubt that she was the leader.

They held an animated discussion for five minutes and then she spoke to them.

"Your school, would they help us?" she asked.

"Help with what?"

"Would they harbor Leopold? Would they keep him safe?"

Margaret thought for a moment before answering.

"Yes, I think so. Sister Anne, who runs the school, once harbored my father and a wanted pirate from a vicious British lieutenant. She's very political."

"Your father?"

"Yes, he's a colonel in the British Air Corps."

"Hmmm…that might be good," she answered and then began talking with her comrades once again. Finally, she moved closer to the girls and Leopold and leaned in.

"You really have no idea who he is, do you?" she asked.

Inez and Margaret shook their heads.

"He might be the only man in Germany who knows how to defeat the Kaiser. We've been watching that camp for two months, planning his escape, and we finally got him out. We now have an important opportunity."

"Who are you?" Inez asked.

"My name is Mia, but you do not need to know my friends' names. We are enemies of the Kaiser and his government. We call ourselves the Beinhoff-Muller gang!"

"That's a mouthful," Inez remarked, only to be hushed by Margaret.

"We have decided that I will escort you and Leopold back to your school," Mia added.

"What?" Margaret asked.

"It is the safest thing for him. If we can get him into France, we might be able to prevent the Kaiser from starting a war."

"How?" Margaret asked.

"If the Kaiser knows that Leopold is in the enemy's hands, he may be hesitant to attack, because Leopold will be able to advise the French on how to defeat him."

Margaret looked at Leopold.

"Do you want to do this, Leopold? You're the one who's important to the Kaiser," Margaret said.

Leopold didn't hesitate before answering.

"I will do anything to defeat the Kaiser. This is a good plan. If I am proven to be with France, then the Kaiser will think twice about attacking any countries in Europe."

"Okay, it is settled, then. I will escort you and these girls back to their school in France. We don't have a moment to waste. Once they've found out we've taken you, there will be soldiers after us," Mia said.

Inez and Margaret looked excitedly at one another.

"You'll take us home?" Inez asked.

"Yes, this is the best plan. Like I said, we don't have a moment to spare. Follow me!"

Without hesitation, Mia began running through the woods, followed closely by Margaret, Inez, and Leopold. Inez and Margaret were smiling from ear to ear. Suddenly freed, their hopes were renewed and their enthusiasm returned.

"I told you we would escape," Margaret joked to Inez.

For hours, the boys wandered aimlessly through Constantinople.

They hoped they were heading in the direction of the warehouse, but, truthfully, their thoughts were on the mysterious map and its contents. Walking through an alley and onto a larger street, Fez looked up and saw the street sign they'd been looking for.

"Inonu Sok!" he exclaimed.

The boys stopped and looked at the street name. It was the exact same as the one on the piece of paper that Scopas had given them, which said *"Inonu Sok Nolu 2."* They searched the buildings until they saw the number 2 above two huge doors. The building seemed to take up the entire block.

"This sure looks like a warehouse," Aseem exclaimed.

"What do we do now?" Fez asked.

"Just wait around, I guess. Just pretend like we're street boys," Aseem answered.

Tariq spotted a mosque on a hill that looked down on them from about four blocks above. He knew it was the mosque of Süleyman the Magnificent. The opaque-white mosque truly was breathtaking, with huge colored domes and four tall minarets. It dwarfed every other building in any direction.

"You guys take the first watch, I've got something to do," he said, before walking away without further explanation.

Fez and Aseem eyed one another and then sat down on a nearby stone wall to watch the doorway of the warehouse across the street.

As he walked through the neighborhood, Tariq felt the weight of the world on his shoulders. This map, the diary of Alexander the Great—it all seemed too much for him. He'd never even been out of Morocco, and now he was supposed to travel to India?

Leaning against a wall, he watched as some boys played soccer in the street. They seemed so free and happy, without a care in the world. Would their world come to an end soon?

Suddenly, like a bolt of lightning, the image of Melbourne Jack began filling his head. Visions of thousands of dead soldiers and bombed-out buildings flashed through his mind until finally he saw an image of the Red Hand. The eyes of the soldiers—frozen open in death and staring up at him—were haunting. The dead soldiers' skin was a ghastly gray. They weren't people any longer; they were just empty, lifeless shells.

These images terrified him. He just wanted to be home, back with Malik, Sanaa, and Zijuan and in the safety of his clan. He so deeply hoped they had won the battle and now everyone was safe. He felt an urgent desire to reach out to them.

But he was a thousand miles away.

Shaking his head, he began walking again. Up on the adjacent hill were the domes and minarets of the mosque. He wasn't sure why, but he knew he wanted to visit it. He needed to go somewhere, anywhere, that might provide some answers and calm the brewing panic inside him.

Making his way through meandering streets, he finally came to the courtyard of the Süleymaniye Mosque.

Tariq strolled through a large stone doorway into the mosque's courtyard. The mosque was surrounded by walls and beautiful gardens with flowering trees and shrubs lined the perimeter. Families mingled together in the courtyard, and groups of single men congregated and spoke politely to one another. Some washed their hands, feet, and faces, as was customary before entering a mosque. As it wasn't prayer time, most people just mingled and visited with one another. Children behaved themselves as was required in the mosque confines. Nobody swore. Nobody spat or threw trash.

It was a sacred place.

In all his time in Morocco, Tariq had never entered a mosque. Growing up a poor street orphan, he never saw the need. Mostly he was ignored by society, so why bother with religion? Families went to mosques, and he had none. It actually hurt his heart to be so near to loving families, so he avoided any situations that might make him feel vulnerable.

Yet, at that moment, he felt so homesick and so afraid, that he longed for something to remind him of home.

The call came for prayer time. It was the exact call he used to hear back home: the voices of men calling Muslims to prayer—almost songlike.

Gingerly, he took off his shoes and washed his feet, then his hands, and then his face. As he placed his shoes in a waiting area, he felt anxious about going inside. What if someone told him to leave? What if he was found out as a foreigner or a non-believer? What if he was scolded for being a street boy?

Pushing away his nervousness, he bravely entered the mosque and was instantly struck by its majestic beauty and peaceful environment.

The floor was covered in a soft and clean red carpet. Huge chandeliers were supported by hundreds of long pieces of wire that stretched all the way to the ceiling. Thousands of lit candles filled the chandeliers and illuminated the room.

Looking up, Tariq guessed that the massive domes were well over a hundred feet high. White, orange, and yellow tiles covered almost every square inch of every wall. Intricately designed stained-glass windows lined the walls, casting colorful beams of light through the huge room. Tariq knew that visual depictions of people were strictly forbidden in Islam, and so he appreciated all the Arabic prayers, beautifully written in black ink, adorning almost every wall. He imagined that the utmost of care had been given to every stroke and line.

Dozens of men kneeled on the carpet, some reading from the Koran, and others softly praying. They prayed in a separate area away from the women, as was the custom. It was dead quiet, save for the soft whispers of prayer.

Tariq didn't know what to do. He didn't know any prayers. He didn't know the Koran. He just felt a need to be someplace safe.

Then a kindly old man, dressed in traditional clothing, approached Tariq and gently took him by the elbow, guiding him to kneel in front of an altar.

The man kneeled along with him.

He motioned for Tariq to close his eyes and then, in Arabic, whispered in Tariq's ear.

"I watched you come in, my boy. You seem lost and lonely. All are welcome here. Clear your mind. This is a place of peace."

Tariq closed his eyes and tried to clear his mind, but all he could see in his mind's eye was the image of Melbourne Jack dying. His own feeling of drowning and being close to death. The images of dead soldiers sickened him. Again, a wave of homesickness overcame him, and he thought he might retch right there in the mosque.

"Such grief for so young a boy. Give your tears to Allah and then go back out into the world. Life is precious, never waste a moment of it."

Tariq sat there, kneeling, and allowed his grief to pour from him until, after a moment, he did feel a kind of peace. New, more positive feelings washed over him. He suddenly felt sure that Melbourne Jack was safe and that his spirit was there in the mosque alongside him. A sense of relief came over him, a feeling that the world was exactly as the way it should be, and that every moment had a meaning, including death.

His breathing slowed and became less labored. He felt himself relax.

Opening his eyes, he was welcomed by the smile of the old man next to him.

"There, my friend. Leave your burden and go back out into the world."

Tariq stretched his toes and fingers and smiled at the man.

The old man kissed Tariq on both cheeks, as was customary, and then bowed to him slightly as Tariq went back outside. As Tariq slipped his shoes back onto his feet, he felt a world apart from when he entered the mosque—unburdened and free.

He felt confident. He felt alive in a way he wasn't sure he'd ever felt before.

With renewed energy, Tariq returned to find Fez and Aseem perched on the stone wall across from the warehouse. He sat down next to them.

"Anything happen while I was gone?" Tariq asked.

"No, where did you go?" Aseem asked.

"Just…to stretch my legs a bit," Tariq replied.

The boys stayed on lookout for an hour, pretending to be normal street boys, when Tariq heard a sound he wasn't immediately able to identify.

"What is that?" Tariq asked and took off to see what the commotion was about.

As he turned onto the next block, he saw a man cracking a whip into a small cage. Inside the cage was a huge, black panther that had to curl itself into a ball just to fit inside. The panther growled and hissed as the man continued to whip it. Its ears lay back on its head, its eyes flashed with fear and rage, and the big cat's fur was lined with blood where the whip had dug in.

The cage was on a wheeled wagon being pulled by two men. The boys followed as the wagon moved slowly up the city block until it came to rest in front of the same warehouse they had been watching. Just then, the panther let out a loud yowl. Tariq, though far enough away that he hadn't yet been noticed by the men, made eye contact with the wailing panther. Its black eyes revealed its suffering, as if it knew a dreadful fate was ahead. Tariq, seeing the fear in the panther's eyes, felt a sudden knot in his stomach.

"We're supposed to help that panther," he whispered.

"What?" Aseem asked.

"They're going to do something awful to it, I just know it. I can't explain it, but I know we're supposed to help it. I've been having dreams where Jack tells me to find the panther in Constantinople."

"Dreams?" Fez asked.

"Melbourne Jack told me the history of the Red Hand. How a tiger appeared from the jungle and led a girl named Lakshi to the Red Hand Scrolls. How cats, especially big cats, are sacred. Since then I've been having dreams where he tells me to find a panther in Constantinople, and here we are in Constantinople with one right in front of us."

"Do you think the panther is *owned* by this Abdullah Ozek?" Fez asked.

The other two boys shrugged and looked at one another. They nodded their heads and Aseem put his arm around Tariq's shoulder.

"If we're supposed to help that panther, then we're going to help that panther. What's the plan?" Aseem asked with a smile.

Tariq nodded and watched as the caged panther disappeared into the building. It made him sick to see a wild cat being whipped and beaten. But there was also something else. Ever since Jack had died, Tariq had felt something change within himself that he had a hard time putting into words. He felt more focused and highly attuned to the world around him, as if he had been injected with renewed energy and intuition.

Something had changed in him. He wasn't sure what it was. He didn't understand his feelings.

A year ago, he might not have even noticed the panther. If he had, he probably would have shrugged his shoulders and moved on. Now, he knew he had to do something. He couldn't sit there and watch as the cat was tortured.

He watched the massive warehouse doors close behind the panther's cage and he was absolutely sure of one thing.

Whoever was hurting that animal was going to pay.

CHAPTER
— II —

LHAK-PA

1872—THE HIMALAYAS

Young Foster Crowe hiked with Lhak-Pa for three days to the foothills of the Himalayas. The journey had so far been almost seventy miles, and Foster's legs were sore and tired from the arduous pace. They were covering over twenty miles a day. Lhak-Pa, however, looked as if he could keep hiking for another hundred miles.

It was getting colder—autumn was peeking around the corner. Foster bundled himself up warmly each night in a blanket made of yak fur and spent each morning stomping his feet to get warm and watching the clouds from his breath disappear into the brisk morning air.

On the third night, they sat around a campfire as Lhak-Pa heated some water for black tea.

"Wondering how Lhak-Pa found you?"

"Yes."

Lhak-Pa sighed as if he was solving a riddle.

"Will not explain at this time. Will, however, offer condolences for loss of father."

Foster said nothing to this.

"Why did I have to remain silent for three days? Is that some kind of Nepalese ritual?"

Lhak-Pa laughed.

"Oh no. Prefer hike in silence. Knew Foster would have questions. Did not feel like answering them."

"So I've been silent for three days for no reason?" Foster asked, clearly agitated.

"Not no reason. Witnessed beauty of nature. Did not pollute with nonsense."

Foster said nothing as he was given a hot cup of tea. Lhak-Pa spooned a dollop of yak butter into Foster's tea. It was still bitter, but warming.

"I haven't cried for my father," he said.

Lhak-Pa went about preparing their dinner and arranging a series of pots and pans.

"Then do not cry," came the only answer.

The next day they marched out of the foothills and came to a dirt road, which they followed the rest of the afternoon.

"Where are we going?" Foster asked.

"Kathmandu."

"That's a long way away."

"Not for a Nepalese."

They walked for another week, camping when necessary and enjoying the hospitality of teahouses when possible.

On the last day of the trek, Lhak-Pa started asking Foster questions.

"What home do you have to return to?"

Foster thought about this before answering.

"I don't know. My mother died when I was very young, and I don't have any brothers or sisters, or any relatives for that matter. I suppose I could go back to my school...," Foster said, his voice trailing off.

"Are you happy in your country?"

"No, not really," Foster whispered.

"Are you happy here?"

"Yes, very much. At first, the camping was hard, but once I was accustomed to it, I quite enjoy living this way. The people are so friendly and..."

"And what?" Lhak-Pa asked.

"Now I don't have my father constantly bullying me. I know that's not a nice thing to say, but that's how I feel."

"So, no family and not happy at home?"

"I guess not."

"How about stay here?"

"What? Stay in Nepal?"

"For training."

"Training? What kind of training?'

Lhak-Pa continued to walk and it looked to Foster like he was enjoying the conversation.

"Tiger tell Lhak-Pa...Foster need help. How knew exactly where to find Foster."

Foster was confused by this answer.

"What tiger?"

Lhak-Pa stopped and stared at young Foster.

"Tiger saved by not shooting. Stood up to father. Took bravery."

"Oh," was all Foster managed to reply.

They walked for a couple of hours, and the whole time Foster was deep in thought about the offer in front of him. He wondered how Lhak-Pa had talked with a tiger. It was true, he really didn't have a family back home. His boarding school was okay, but he wasn't missing it very much.

"You didn't answer my question. What kind of training?" Foster asked.

"Training to be warrior, of course."

"A warrior?"

"Warriors must be brave. Must be smart. Above all must have good heart. Foster pass test."

"Test?"

Just as Foster spoke, he looked up and saw the ancient city of Kathmandu right in front of him. He'd been thinking so hard he hadn't noticed they had walked right to the edge of the city.

Foster followed Lhak-Pa down a mountain path and into Kathmandu. He was struck by the sights and sounds of a city that was considered by many to be one of the most beautiful on earth. Yaks pulled wooden carts filled with vegetables and wood. Tibetan prayer flags hung from almost every rooftop. The city was a maze of temples, buildings, and houses—all thousands of years old. Houses were literally built on top of one another. The roads were narrow and rough, either made from dirt or cobblestone, and they twisted and wound around the city with no visible reason or pattern. Foster saw no advertisements of any kind; in fact, there were almost no signs at all. Finding one's way meant asking perfect strangers for directions, and they always obliged. Kathmandu was nestled in a valley and surrounded by the Himalayan mountain range, which provided an expansive view from almost every angle in the city. The buildings were a traditional pagoda architectural style, with multiple roofs that grew smaller as the building grew higher. Walking into Kathmandu was like entering a sacred burial ground. In that valley, it seemed as if the spirits of the dead watched over the city and used it as their personal resting place.

A mist was descending over the city, and Foster felt as if he were entering a dream.

CHAPTER
— *12* —

THE HUNTER OR THE HUNTED?

Wu Chiang checked into a dingy and decrepit hotel just a few blocks from the prestigious Hotel du Cecil. The ambassador's dinner was the next night and he had many preparations to make. Security would be tight at the dinner, and he needed to make just the right accommodations. He knew he might only get one chance.

Opening his trunk, Wu Chiang brought out a number of small vials full of liquid and began mixing a few different components into a beaker. After a few moments, the mixture, which had begun as a pale, cloudy yellow color, became completely clear and odorless. Satisfied, he produced an empty pencil sized glass vial and filled it with some of the mixture from the beaker. He sealed it with a cork, upending it once to be sure it did not leak.

He noticed there were rat droppings on the floorboard next to the east wall. Pulling out some Camembert cheese, he tore off a chunk and then put a few drops of the liquid directly on the cheese. Placing it on the floorboard, he sat on his bed and watched and waited. Soon enough, a mouse emerged from a small hole in the wall, and made its way to the stinky morsel.

Scurrying quickly, the mouse went to the cheese, took a few bites, and then put the entire piece in its mouth and began scampering back to its hole. Halfway there, the mouse suddenly fell on its side, gasping for breath as its body seized and shook, and, in a matter of seconds, fell dead on the spot.

Satisfied, Wu Chiang put the dead rodent and the chunk of poisoned cheese in a bag and tossed it in a rubbish bin in the hallway.

He then placed the vial in a brown envelope before taking a quick nap. After about an hour, he was awakened by a knock at his door. He rose from his bed and opened the door about six inches and held the envelope just inside the opening, where it was snatched from his hand and he immediately closed the door.

The plan was now set into motion.

Outside the hotel, a beautiful young woman placed the envelope in her coat pocket and hurried down the street. She was a waitress at the Hotel du Cecil and was on her lunch break. A light rain began to fall as she crossed the street, dampening her hair and wool coat.

She had long auburn hair, and her face was narrow and symmetrically perfect. Pale blue eyes complimented her skin and hair. She knew every man in the hotel was already in love with her, and she teased and manipulated them to do her many chores.

Her name was Jacqueline.

In truth, she was a terrorist and a servant of Wu Chiang. She was from a very wealthy family in Bordeaux. Great sums of money had passed from generation to generation in her family. Like many intelligent and idealistic young women, she rebelled against her family, rejecting their stodgy lifestyle. Wu Chiang had recruited her when she was just fifteen. By the time she was twenty, he had moved her to Germany to manipulate a subject. When that mission was completed, she was relocated to Paris and employed at the Hotel du Cecil.

A telegram had come to her just a week prior with instructions on her next mission. She was to knock on the door to room 310 at a hotel across town, receive a brown envelope, which she would then hide in her room. She was not to open it. From there, she would wait for further instructions. Under no circumstances was she to open her door.

Wu Chiang packed up his room and checked out. He took his things and moved to another dilapidated hotel about six blocks away to make his whereabouts more difficult to track.

He jotted down instructions for Jacqueline in code on a piece of paper, which he placed in his suit pocket. He would leave the instructions in the bottom of a bird feeder just across from the Hotel du Cecil, which Jacqueline knew to check each morning. These careful plans and elaborate steps were taken so that in the event anyone discovered Jacqueline and the vial of poison, they wouldn't know who was the subject of the attack or when it was to take place. This strategy was called "compartmentalization," and Wu Chiang was a master at compartmentalizing.

Back at the Hotel du Cecil, Jacqueline went about her business and began preparing the dining room with the finest silverware and porcelain dishes. The ambassador's dinner was the following evening, and representatives from Serbia, Germany, and Austria would be in attendance. Tensions were already high between the countries as Austria increasingly sided with Germany in political matters. The dinner was seen as an opportunity to forge a more cordial relationship between Serbia and Germany.

Jacqueline knew that all the diplomats would be on edge. Anxiety was already escalating throughout Europe, as both Germany and Austria were making threats of war. The dinner was seen as an opportunity to ease hostilities among the nations.

After she completed setting the ballroom, Jacqueline prepared the main dinner room and went about her normal dinner service. After her shift ended, she took a long hot bath and wrote a lengthy letter to her father, which she signed with a prick of blood from her thumb. She placed the letter in an envelope, sealed it, and put the appropriate number of stamps on the front. She made sure it would be delivered to the concierge the following morning.

That night, she slept fitfully in her bed.

She wondered if it would be the last night she spent on the earth.

Foster Crowe emerged from the train station with nothing but a backpack and a vague notion of Wu Chiang's plans. A light drizzle descended from the gray Paris skies. Foster pulled up his collar and tugged down his fedora so that it almost covered his ears. He could see his breath in the damp, cold air. The aroma of fresh-baked Parisian bread filled his senses, reminding him he was in the culinary center of the world.

He spotted a street boy hanging around outside of the train station. The boy had an innocent look about him, but based on his clothes, it looked to Foster like his life hadn't been easy so far. The boy's black pants had holes in both knees and he wore an unraveling brown sweater and a dirty cap that covered his stringy hair. He looked like he hadn't slept in a bed or taken a bath in some time.

Foster always made it a point to spot urchins. Most were boys, as orphan girls were normally placed in homes to become maids. He found that, if dealt with correctly, younger boys could be trusted; they often wanted nothing more than to feel important about something in their lives.

Foster approached the boy. The boy started to walk away, probably thinking Foster was a policeman. Foster picked up his pace until he caught up to him.

"How would you like to earn fifty francs? Ten now and the rest later," Foster said to him.

The boy stopped and measured up Foster.

"What do you mean?"

"I'm looking for someone. If you happen to see him, simply follow him and take note of where he goes. That is all."

"Who is this person?" the boy asked suspiciously.

"Just someone I'm trying to locate," Foster replied and pulled up a ten-franc note.

"That's a lot of money, what if I just take off with it?"

"Then you miss out on a much bigger payday. Besides, what else do you have to do? The man I'm looking for is a very bad man. Under no circumstances should you attempt to speak to him."

The boy suddenly perked up and grabbed the ten-franc note from Foster's hand.

"I'll do it! A bad man? What has he done?"

"It's what he's *trying* to do that I'm worried about. I need you to watch for a Chinese man, overweight, wearing thick glasses, most likely wearing a suit and sweating a lot. He'll be in a hurry and won't want to talk to anyone. Can you do that for me?"

The boy crumpled the ten-franc note in his pocket.

"Mister, for forty francs, I would wait here for a month!"

Foster smiled at the answer.

"No, it shouldn't be more than a couple of days. I'm counting on you," he said and looked the boy square in the eyes. He had a sixth sense about people, and he had a feeling this was a good boy who had just fallen on difficult times.

"I will be here, you can count on me," the boy said and his voice softened. Secretly, he was already thinking of the dinner—and perhaps even a pair of new gloves—he was going to buy with the francs.

"My name is Foster, what is yours?"

"My name is Laurent," the boy replied with a bit of pride.

"Nice to meet you, Laurent."

"And you as well, Foster. I will keep my eye out, do not worry."

A murder of crows squawked from a barren oak tree as Foster exited the train station. Rain drizzled from the gray sky as he made his way along the cobblestone streets and through the dark alleys.

Foster was excited, and his fingers tingled with anticipation like an old west gunfighter preparing for a duel. He was closing in on his prey, he could feel it. His senses were more alive. His heartbeat quickened. He reached down and found the butt of his revolver in his suit jacket, caressing the wooden handle with his fingertips.

He'd decided to make his way to the German embassy. If Wu Chiang was in Paris, it most likely had something to do with politics or diplomats. The embassy seemed the most logical place to start.

The only problem was finding it. The taxi drivers were all on strike, and for the third time this year, no less.

He didn't have a map of the city, so he was going to have to find the embassy by asking directions, making wrong turns, and meandering through the miles and miles of Paris alleys and streets.

Foster found himself passing under the Arc de Triomphe and entered the Place de l'Étoile. Couples strolled arm-in-arm and young parents walked patiently with their children. Everyone was dressed elegantly—men in their topcoats and hats and children in warm wool coats. The Arc was the intersection of twelve avenues, and perhaps the most famous landmark in all of Paris. Foster purchased a crêpe and a coffee and took a moment to savor the scene around him before heading back under the Arc de Triomphe.

The Arc took thirty years to build and honored those who fought and died in the Napoleonic Wars and the French Revolution. It was originally commissioned by Napoleon himself and finally completed during the reign of King Louis-Philippe. Foster knew that in the attic of the Arc were shields from every major French victory during the Napoleonic wars. He walked under the Arc and read the names of the many French generals that were inscribed on the pillars.

Such history all around him. He wished he had a week, or even a month, to spend in Paris just to study the architecture and soak up the history of a city that had stood since 300 BC.

Finishing his crêpe and coffee, he asked directions once again and, finally, was given definitive instructions on how to reach the German embassy.

He made his way down Avenue des Champs-Élysées, turned left on Avenue Victor-Emmanuel III and within minutes was standing in front of the embassy, an old brick building completely surrounded by an eight-foot cement wall. At the gate was a German guard. Foster went to him and asked to go inside.

"Passport, please," the guard stated and Foster produced his passport and handed it to the man.

The guard was older, maybe fifty, and his large belly hung over his belt. His cheeks were flushed and he had a tiny moustache over his lip.

"This is a Belgian passport?" the guard asked.

"Yes, I'm a Belgian citizen, but I need to talk with someone in the embassy," Foster answered.

"Sorry, sir. No visitors are allowed inside the embassy who are not German citizens."

"That's strange, I've never had a problem before. Why all the security?" Foster asked. He took out a pack of cigarettes, lit one, and then offered one to the guard.

The guard seemed to relax and relish the company. He stepped forward, took a cigarette, and kindly accepted a light from Foster.

"Since the bombing in Bremen, security is tight. With the diplomats' dinner tonight, everyone is especially on edge. I think it's all a bunch of nonsense," the guard answered.

"Diplomats' dinner?" Foster asked.

"At the Hotel du Cecil. There's even a rumor the king is going to make an appearance."

"Hmmm…so there's no chance of getting in today?" Foster asked.

"No, try back in a couple of days once everyone relaxes a little."

Foster thanked the guard and walked away. That had to be it! A diplomats' dinner would be the perfect place for Wu Chiang to create an international incident.

His instincts told him he was following the right scent.

He hurried back to the Place de l'Étoile. Cursing the striking taxi drivers under his breath, he managed to find someone who knew of the Hotel du Cecil, and was told it was located across town.

His mood was turning black. All this running around was annoying him. He needed to find Wu Chiang.

The day was turning to night and the slop from the muddy streets had soaked his pant legs. While cutting through an alley, Foster noticed two men lurking in the shadows—one to his right and another to his left.

Instantly his senses heightened. Out of the corner of his eye, he could see that both men were watching him, and their manner suggested ill intentions.

As he continued walking through the alley, two more men stepped directly in front of him. One was small, with a face like a rat; the other was muscly and big-boned.

"Your wallet or your life, monsieur," the rat-like one said.

"I don't have time for this," Foster answered directly and continued to walk straight toward them.

The two thugs in front appeared put off, probably expecting Foster to stop, cower, and hand over his wallet rather than walk right toward them.

"Stop," the smaller one stammered.

The bigger one smiled and stepped toward Foster, obviously thinking his size and strength gave him a significant advantage.

He was wrong.

The man reached out to grab Foster, only to grab handfuls of empty air. Foster avoided his grasp and brought his right foot behind the man's legs, grabbed him across the chest, and threw him down to the cold ground, spinning him as he tossed him down so the man landed hard on his back.

Foster then grabbed the smaller man's left arm and snapped it at the wrist. The man with the rat face screamed in agony. Once the two men in back of him heard the screaming, they stopped in their footsteps. Foster knew he'd no longer have any trouble with them and walked straight ahead as if nothing had happened. He had no mercy for thieves or men that attacked in groups.

Every hunting instinct in him was coming out. He felt his anger swell up inside him like a red mist. His fingers twitched in anticipation. His eyes were wide and he felt a wildness within himself begin to grow.

He was going to the Hotel du Cecil. He was going to find and kill Wu Chiang.

CHAPTER
— 13 —

CAT BURGLARS

Mia, the girls, and Leopold walked for hours through the dense woods until it was dark and the moon was visible overhead. Mia seemed to know every rock and tree and easily guided them along a path that seemed otherwise invisible to the human eye. Margaret and Inez were hungry, but they didn't complain or whine. Their clothes weren't warm and their shoes were falling apart, but they knew anything was better than being in the prison camp.

As they slowed on the path, they could hear shouting in the distance. It came from far away, but somehow it was distinct.

Then they heard dogs barking.

"Hurry! We must hurry! They are on to us!" Mia exclaimed and suddenly they were running through the forest, twigs snapping beneath their feet, branches scraping their faces and arms.

They ran for fifteen minutes until they came upon a wood cabin with moss growing on the roof. The planks of wood that made up the walls were weathered and looked old from the outside. Mia opened the door, which squeaked, and hurried them inside.

The inside of the cabin was dark and covered with animal rugs. There was a bearskin rug on one wall and deer and rabbit skins on others. A single shelf on the east wall held dishes and pots that looked to have been cast out of stone. Wooden chests lined another wall. Spears were propped up in one corner and in another, coats and clothes of all kinds hung on pegs. It was amazingly well stocked for such a small cabin.

Mia immediately began throwing clothes at the girls and Leopold while packing knapsacks with provisions. The girls dressed themselves in pants and jackets made from the skins of various animals. They even found some hiking boots under the piles of clothes. Margaret asked for something to stuff in the toes, as her boots were too big.

Mia gave each of them a huge stick of elk jerky and urged them to eat it quickly, and the girls gladly obliged. Afterward, she handed out the knapsacks made of heavy cotton.

Finally, Mia handed them long spears that she said could double as hiking sticks.

Just outside the cabin, they all stood and listened to Mia's stern instructions.

"It is imperative that we bring Leopold to France. He must not fall into the hands of the Kaiser, do you understand me?" she said and the girls nodded and shuddered at the seriousness of her voice.

"Follow me and do exactly as I say. There is no time to waste!"

At once they were running through the woods. But this time, they were warmly dressed with provisions to keep them going.

The shouting and dogs had grown louder since they'd stopped at the cabin.

They ran through the darkness—the only light provided by the moonlight peeking through the tall pines. Leopold struggled to keep up as he was older and not as spry as the others. Still, he never complained and maintained a good pace.

The barking of the dogs grew even louder.

"They're getting closer!" Inez gasped and the group ran faster.

In the moonlight, Margaret and Inez could see a river and a wooden raft tied up on the embankment.

"Get on!" Mia yelled.

They all hopped on the raft and then Mia loosened the lines tethering it to the embankment and used her walking stick to shove off. While floating down the river under the cover of darkness, they could hear the dogs bark and whine through the night.

Mia stood on the rear of the raft, pushing with the long stick, and guiding the raft around the many boulders in the river. They continued for about a mile, going at a modest speed. Soon, the raft picked up momentum and sped faster with the current, and a strange sound could be heard in the darkness.

The sound of rushing water.

"Hold on!" Mia yelled.

Leopold and the girls hung on tightly to the wooden planks of the raft. As the sound grew louder, they saw why Mia had yelled.

There were rapids directly ahead of them for about a hundred yards.

Not little rapids, but big rapids that ducked and dove under huge boulders and jumped up into the sky.

"Oh my Gahh..." Inez screamed as they went directly into the string of whitewater.

They hit the first set of rapids perfectly and were plunged about eight feet down, nose first, into a swirling whirlpool. Mia bent her knees and pushed off the rocks with all of her strength until the raft was released from the grip of the whirlpool, righted itself, and continued onto the next set of rapids.

They were not so fortunate this time.

The raft hit a large boulder and spun around in the opposite direction. Mia leaped over the three of them to the other end of the raft just as they were thrown down a chute and into yet another whirlpool. The raft was sent in a series of dizzying circles.

Mia braced her stance and tried to steady the raft as it continued in circles, each time going a little deeper under water. She fought the current with all her strength, but this time, the whirlpool wouldn't release them. If they couldn't get out, eventually the water would suck them all under.

She waited until there was a point when there was a bit of a lull, then thrust her stick into a boulder, and pushed with all of her weight.

It didn't work.

The raft continued to go down into the water.

Margaret and Inez screamed as they felt the icy water. Their eyes were wide with fright.

The raft came around again and Mia knew she only had one chance.

As the boulder came to view, she reared the stick back, stuck it straight into the rock, and strained as hard as she could, leaning her weight into the rock.

There was a sucking sound and the raft released from the whirlpool just enough to jump out of the tumbling water, but still not enough to be completely free.

Were they being sucked back in?

Tariq, Aseem, and Fez waited until dark outside the brick building which looked to be several centuries old. White paint flaked and chipped off some of the woodwork around the windows and doors. Rust was caked onto the door hinges and even on the ancient-looking lock.

Once darkness fell, Tariq whispered, "Okay then, let's move."

The boys crossed the street and Fez pulled a tiny nail from his pocket, about the length of a match, and began picking the lock.

It came open in just under five seconds.

"That was easy," he whispered.

Carefully opening the door, the boys slipped in quietly and closed the door behind them.

They couldn't see anything in the dark, but they instantly smelled something quite foul. They also heard noises. Not human noises, but animal noises.

And not just one animal, but dozens.

They saw a hallway in front of them, about fifteen feet long that led to another door.

Walking single file down the hallway, they made their way to the second door, opened it, made sure no one was watching them, and then walked into a gigantic warehouse.

The enormous open room was filled with caged animals of every kind: lions, tigers, monkeys, zebras, hyenas, and even a couple of giraffes.

There must have been hundreds of them.

"Oh my goodness!" Fez exclaimed.

"I don't see any guards, but they must have a few—where do you think they are?" Aseem asked.

Tariq looked around and pointed to the faint glow of candlelight coming from the far end of the warehouse. It was on the east side and it looked as if there might be an adjacent room down there.

"You two go look for the guards and check out that light over there. I'm going to look for the panther."

"Okay," Fez and Aseem agreed.

Tariq looked at the animals and saw that all of them were in terribly small cages. There was scarcely any food or water and no bedding, so they were forced to sleep on the hard steel bars. Some of the animals were housed three or four in one cage.

To him, the animals looked sad. Even the lions, who Tariq thought might normally watch his every move, didn't pay him any attention. A zebra whined to Tariq in such a way that Tariq swore it had to be asking him for help.

A couple of monkeys huddled together in their small cage looked at Tariq with mournful faces as he passed by.

After walking up and down two more rows, Tariq finally came to the panther.

The big cat was lying down in his cage and barely looked up when Tariq approached. Tariq supposed he had been abused so much, and starved for so long, that he had almost given up all hope. Once in a while he would whimper like a homesick child, but mostly he just lay there. Tariq could clearly see that the cage was too small for him and he had been forced to curl up in a ball. It was doubtful he could even stand up in the cage.

"I know just how you feel," Tariq whispered to him.

The panther simply blinked and looked ahead.

Tariq watched the cat and his heart felt so low. He hated seeing anything in a cage, but, for some reason, seeing this magnificent animal caged really tore at his soul. He reached out and gingerly petted and scratched the panther on the back. The big cat looked up and made eye contact with Tariq and let out a slight purr-like sound, as if any kind of contact of kindness was so needed and appreciated.

He continued to stroke and whisper to the panther when, suddenly, he felt the cold touch of a knife blade at his throat. The blade just barely touched his skin. Whoever held it understood exactly what they were doing.

Tariq froze. He held his breath. He stood there paralyzed, waiting for whatever came next.

He'd been discovered.

A whisper came in a language he didn't understand.

The blade pushed against Tariq's chin, moving his head up until he was suddenly face to face with a young woman.

"I don't speak Turkish," Tariq tried to explain.

The woman looked at him with surprise.

"You're Arabic?" she asked in Arabic.

"Moroccan."

"Why are you here?"

"I've come to rescue this panther."

The woman looked at the cat, still curled up.

"What do you want with that cat?"

"Never mind, what do you want?"

The woman wasn't a guard—she was different! She seemed intrigued by Tariq.

"I am Pakize, the best thief in all of Constantinople."

"You're a thief?"

"Not just any thief, my friend—the *best* thief!" she answered and seemed to study Tariq. "You want to steal this panther to sell him?"

"No, to save him."

"Save him?" she answered.

"Yes," Tariq whispered back.

"You're no ordinary thief…you're something else," she seemed to say to herself.

"You're right, I'm not a thief. I just want to save this panther. He's going to be killed, isn't he?" Tariq answered.

Tariq stared at Pakize. She had spiky short, black hair and a thin, almost elfish face. Her complexion was lighter than he'd seen on most

Turks. She wore all black, and dressed like a boy, and a brown leather bag hung over her shoulder. Black slippers were on her small feet. She looked to be about twenty years of age.

Light footsteps could be heard around the corner as Fez and Aseem walked up to see Pakize and Tariq standing face to face.

"Shhhhh, do you want to wake all of Constantinople?" Pakize whispered.

"Sorry, uh, Tariq, who is this?" Fez asked, noticing the knife still at Tariq's throat.

"I don't know. She says her name is Pakize, she's a thief."

"The *best* thief," she interrupted.

"Fine, the best thief in all of Constantinople," Tariq corrected himself.

"What's she doing here?" Aseem asked.

"Stealing, what else do you think I am doing here? Your friend was so noisy I thought he might wake the guards," she interrupted again.

"What are you stealing? There's nothing here but caged animals," Fez asked.

"There are always things to steal if you know where to look," Pakize answered with a smile and she finally put away her blade. She was still alert, but decided that these boys were no threat to her.

"There are only two guards and they are in that room playing cards. I think they might be drunk as well," Fez finally answered.

"Good, we're going to steal this panther right now!" Tariq answered.

All three individuals looked at Tariq with a complete look of shock.

"We're going to steal that panther?" Aseem asked.

"Yes." Tariq answered boldly.

"That panther belongs to Abdullah Ozek," Pakize replied.

The three boys looked at her with a blank expression.

"Ozek is the most notorious gangster in all of Constantinople. You do not know this?" she asked.

"Well, we knew he was some kind of gangster, but, we're kind of new here," Fez explained.

"Nobody steals from Abdullah Ozek if they value their life."

"You're stealing from him," Tariq answered.

"Yes, but I am an exceptional thief, and I only steal small things that will not be missed."

"Like what?"

Pakize reached into her bag and pulled out a couple of bracelets and a small roll of cloth.

"Some gold bracelets and some silk. He has more treasures than a king."

Tariq looked around at all the animals in the warehouse.

"Well, he has all these animals. I don't think he'll miss one panther."

"How are we going to steal this cat, Tariq?" Fez asked.

"We're simply going to roll him out of here."

Aseem had been studying the situation and Tariq. He noticed something in Tariq's voice, a determination, or even, a kind of desperation.

"You're doing this because of Melbourne Jack, aren't you?" he asked.

Tariq stared at Aseem and then nodded his head.

"Jack would not want this cat to suffer, and in my dreams he told me to find the panther," he replied softly.

Aseem smiled and put his arm around his friend.

"I don't want the cat to suffer either. Come, let's get moving and get this cat out of here. Tariq, let's you and I pull, and Fez, why don't you push from behind."

The boys got into position as Pakize stood with an exasperated look. She was about to leave them but, for an inexplicable reason, she stopped.

"Wait," she scolded, disappeared down a hallway, and reappeared with a small bottle. She began spraying all the wheels and hinges.

"Grease for the hinges, you don't want them to squeak," she whispered.

The boys smiled in appreciation.

"Okay then, let's go!" Tariq whispered.

The boys began to try to move the wagon. It was heavy and required all of their weight and strength. Its metal wheels didn't provide the best traction, so Pakize decided to help Fez push.

They carefully and successfully got the wagon out of the warehouse, closed the door behind them, and began rolling the cage down the dark street. A fog had descended on Constantinople and the cage disappeared into a gray haze.

Pakize placed a blue shawl over her spiky black hair. It wasn't a hijab, a traditional Muslim headwear, but a simple shawl, intended only to cover her head, as required by Ottoman law.

Slowly they rolled the cage through the city streets. The buildings of Constantinople were outlined by the moon and shrouded in secrecy by the fog.

Tariq checked on the panther in the cage. It was awake and alert, yet it didn't make a sound.

CHAPTER
— *14* —

TO THE BLACK FOREST

The German internment camp was alive with activity. Prisoners were rounded up for roll call and extra guards were posted as sentries. It was cold and the prisoners stamped their feet to keep warm. Lanterns were lit in every corner to illuminate the surroundings.

The guards who had been attacked in the truck and had let their prisoners escape were forced to work double shifts and take over latrine duties as punishment for their ineptitude. One of them had a broken jaw, and lay incapacitated in the infirmary.

Major Lars Hostetler was in the prison yard to inspect the prisoners, who stood in straight lines shivering and coughing.

Once they had learned of the escape, a small contingent of eight guards had taken three of their hounds to track the lost prisoners. In the distance, Hostetler could hear the group returning.

Klaus stood next to Hostetler.

"What do the prisoners say?" Hostetler asked.

"They all say they were sleeping and knew nothing of the planned escape."

Hostetler continued to inspect the prisoners. There really wasn't much to inspect or even to do. The truck had been ambushed. Who had done it was a mystery, but why they had done it was perfectly clear.

They wanted Leopold.

The group of returning guards led the dogs into the prison yard and went straight over to Major Hostetler.

"I'm sorry, Major, but they escaped in the river and we were unable to give chase," one of them reported.

"The river?"

"Yes, they had a raft waiting for them."

The major thought carefully about the escape. He was a patient man and quite methodical. Above all, he was highly intelligent. He'd been a physician before being drafted into the army and stationed at the internment camp. Now in his mid-forties, he liked being in the country, and he tried to run an orderly prison. Most of the prisoners were German citizens and were awarded a certain amount of lenience in terms of propriety and comfort. They weren't at war, after all.

Major Hostetler moved slowly and deliberately; he usually walked with his hands grasped behind his back. In spite of his scholarly face, he had a very athletic build. He had the posture of a military man, but the cunning of a weasel.

"Sergeant, prepare a party to go after the prisoners. I will be leading the expedition. I want eight soldiers and three hounds. Do we have a boat?" he asked.

"A boat, Major?"

"Yes, a boat to follow the raft down the river."

"Well, not officially, sir. There are a couple of fishing boats just up the river, but those are private boats, sir."

"Commandeer them in the name of the German army. I want to track this group as quickly as possible," Hostetler replied.

Mia loosened her grip on the stick for a moment before pushing hard against the boulder again, trying to release the raft. It wasn't working. The raft continued to be sucked under the icy cold water, and the girls were screaming with fright. There were only seconds to spare before the whirlpool sucked the raft under and its passengers along with it. Margaret felt the frigid waters splash against her bare skin. Inez stared wide-eyed, feeling the power of the rapids all around her, transfixed by the sounds of the rushing water.

Mia's muscles ached and stretched as she dug in her heels and pushed with all of her body weight. She felt a slight tug and then in an instant, the raft freed itself from the whirlpool and shot itself out of the swirling rapids.

After bouncing through one last set of tiny rapids, the raft slowed and landed in the calm waters of the shallows.

Nobody said anything for a few minutes as the shock of the journey subsided.

"Can we do that again?" Inez asked with a smile.

Margaret shook her head and then giggled.

"Who *are* you people?" Leopold asked, and even Mia had to smile at his question.

They continued down the river for another five miles and then Mia pulled the raft to the riverbank in an area with calm, shallow water.

"We hike from here," she instructed.

"Where are we going?" Inez asked.

Mia pointed at the mountain range in front of them.

"Through the Black Forest. I will deliver you to France and get Leopold safely out of the country."

Mia hurried to get the raft completely up on the river's edge, and then had the other three help her pull it all the way behind some trees and then covered it with a series of branches. From the river, it was now almost completely invisible. Next, she took a branch and wiped away all traces of their footprints leading into the forest.

In a few minutes, the group was marching through the dark and into the trees.

After perhaps half a mile, Mia stopped and took a glass canister from her knapsack. She sprinkled some kind of liquid all over the trail. An owl screeched in the distance and the pleasant aroma of pine needles filled the night air.

"We rest for five minutes. I've no doubt they will find our trail, so I'm hoping this stuff will throw off the dogs."

"What's it made of?" Inez asked.

"A mixture of chili powder and the scent of an elk. If they're tracking us, it will confuse the dogs. At least, that's my hope," Mia answered resolutely.

"Yuck, it smells really bad," Inez replied.

"It's supposed to. It will render the dogs' noses useless for a couple of hours until their normal sense of smell returns."

Margaret and Leopold took off their knapsacks and sat on a log. Already, their shoulders ached from the weight. Leopold had said very little during the entire journey. He always seemed preoccupied, as if his thoughts were in a faraway place. His demeanor was that of a man who had spent his entire life in a windowless laboratory.

"Leopold, why are you so important to the Kaiser? I mean, if he has all your inventions, why does he want you so bad?" Margaret asked.

Leopold was quiet for a while before answering, as if he were contemplating some complex mathematical problem.

"The enemies of Germany, especially Russia, use codes to communicate. I developed a machine that could break almost any code. Only, when I learned of the Kaiser's plans, I hid the machine away. With it, the Kaiser would have a huge advantage over other countries."

"And he didn't find it?" Margaret asked.

"Oh, he tried. Believe me, he tried," Leopold responded and lifted up his right pant leg. Huge scars wrapped all the way around his leg.

"I was tortured for a month, maybe more, by his interrogators. These scars came from when they wrapped barbed wire around my leg and pulled it tight. They tried to break me, but they failed. I wouldn't give up the machine."

"Why didn't you just destroy it?" Inez asked, suddenly interested in the conversation and studying Leopold's deformed leg.

"Excellent question, Inez. I sometimes think I should have destroyed it. I suppose, as an inventor, I was proud of that machine. It took me years of hard work to create it, and I didn't want it to go to waste."

"So now it's hidden away where nobody can find it. I think that's good, Leopold. You should keep it that way," Inez replied.

Mia looked back at Inez with a blank expression, but she seemed to have a bit of curiosity in her eyes about the little red-headed girl.

"So if we get you to France, you will actually be able to prevent a war?" Margaret asked.

"Well, I suppose that's one way of looking at it. But, yes, the machine could prevent the outbreak of war. Or, if the Kaiser finds my invention, it could even start one."

"This is so exciting! A code-breaking machine! A jailbreak! I thought getting kidnapped and sent to prison was the worst, but it's actually just about the most exciting thing that's ever happened to me!" Inez exclaimed.

Margaret shook her head.

"Well now, I guess someone is back to her normal self."

"I thought Leopold was just some boring old man. It turns out, he's the most wanted man in all of Germany!"

Leopold looked incredulously at Inez.

Mia came up to them. She seemed a bit more anxious than usual.

"Come, we must hurry. There's not a moment to waste."

With that, they all put on their knapsacks and began tromping through the dense foliage of the Black Forest.

CHAPTER
— 15 —

THE DEN OF ABDULLAH OZEK

"You brought me a panther? What was Abdullah Ozek going to do with this cat?" Captain Scopas asked.

The boys looked at one another. They actually had no idea what Abdullah Ozek was doing with all the animals.

"And who is this?" he asked while looking Pakize up and down.

"You didn't tell me you worked with a dirty Greek!" Pakize admonished the boys.

"You brought me a dreaded Turk along with this cat?" Captain Scopas bellowed.

"What do you mean 'dreaded Turk'? I would rather eat with a mangy dog than a dirty Greek," Pakize yelled at him and Captain Scopas stepped forward with a clenched fist.

Fez quickly stepped between them.

"Um, I know the Turks and Greeks don't like each other, but, right now, we kind of need to hide this cat," Fez said.

Pakize and Scopas stood only three feet apart. They glared at one another for ten seconds until, finally, Scopas looked away.

"Boys, I need you to explain yourselves. You have put me in great danger bringing this Turk to me. What is this all about?

Pakize stepped forward.

"The panther will be sold to animal traders in China and then sold at auction at a later date."

Scopas studied Pakize. She was fierce, and confident, and that impressed the captain.

"How do you know this?" he asked.

"I just know. All of Ozek's animals get shipped to China to be sold for slaughter. The Chinese think that eating the flesh of a wild cat, or the fin of a shark, will make them strong and virile. His heart and liver will bring the highest price, and his pelt will be sold to the highest bidder as a trophy."

The boys all stared at Pakize, disbelieving what they were hearing.

"They *eat* them?" Fez asked mournfully.

"Yes, the Chinese believe that by eating them, they will gain the animal's strength."

Fez stared at Pakize with his mouth open.

"That is literally the dumbest thing I've ever heard in my entire life," he answered.

Scopas even had to smile a bit at this.

"You say they eat shark fins as well?" he asked.

"Yes. Shark fin soup is a delicacy. The fin fetches a small fortune, so the fishermen just cut off the fin and throw the shark, still alive, back in the water. The shark dies a very slow and miserable death. It will drown as it struggles to swim, unless the other sharks attack it first."

Scopas's shoulders slumped. His passion and fire could just as easily turn to compassion and softness. He thought of Panos and his pet shark, Lako.

"I couldn't bear something like that happening to Lako," he whispered.

Scopas went to look at the panther and had to admire the cat's regal nature. He studied its granite-like muscles and velvety black fur. The panther's piercing yellow eyes looked relaxed and Scopas watched as he licked his whiskers with his pink tongue. Then, as if he knew Scopas was pondering his fate, the panther rolled on his back and kicked his legs like he was playing. He lay on his back, his belly exposed, still and docile.

Scopas knew that it was a sign of trust for a wild animal to show its belly, the most vulnerable part of its body. And the panther was making an unusual sound, almost purring.

Yet, the purring wasn't like that of a house cat. It was the wildest, most exhilarating noise that Scopas had ever heard. He felt euphoric from being this close to a big cat.

"Where does Abdullah Ozek get these animals?" he asked.

"Poachers trap them from all over Africa and ship them to Constantinople. Then Abdullah Ozek ships them to China. He controls the entire black market animal trade on behalf of the Sultan," Pakize paused before continuing. "I am a proud Turk, and he is a disgrace to the Turkish people. He is my sworn enemy."

"Why?" Scopas questioned her, suddenly suspicious of why a Turk would hate another Turk.

"He poisons my people and imprisons them in poverty. He steals from the poorest of the poor and gives nothing back. That's why I steal from him every chance I get."

"You steal from him?"

"Yes, but everything I steal goes to my people," she answered, now considerably more relaxed with Scopas. In fact, she liked him. She could tell he had a good heart.

Captain Scopas lit his pipe, took a long drag, exhaled, and continued to study the cat.

"We'll bring him on my ship and put him in the hold. Perhaps, somehow, we can get him into a bigger cage so he'll be more comfortable," he finally said.

The boys jumped with excitement and all three hugged Captain Scopas, who smiled at the generosity of the boys' affections.

"One more thing," he said.

"What?" Pakize asked.

"We're going to take down this animal trade of Abdullah Ozek. We're going to burn it to the ground."

His voice was cold and forbidding.

"Then, I'm going to find Abdullah Ozek. He has a debt to answer for murdering my brother."

The Turkish gangster named Abdullah Ozek was fifty years old. His hair was close-shaven, as was his face and chin. A large black moustache matched his bushy eyebrows. His jaw was square and his thick neck disappeared into his shoulders and huge bulging muscles led down to his strong-looking forearms.

Ozek tightened his arms around the neck of his opponent. They were both drenched with sweat and were a tangled mess of arms and legs. The stink of body odor, olive oil, and fish surrounded them. Both men grunted as exhaustion set in from almost thirty minutes of nonstop wrestling.

Ozek's eyes were dark and menacing and he rarely smiled.

The men were "oil wrestling," the national pastime of Turkey and a sport thought to be over a thousand years old. Both men, wearing only *kisbets*—pants similar to lederhosen, made from water buffalo hide—doused themselves in oil and then engaged in a type of freestyle wrestling. The oil made their bodies very slippery, and it was extremely difficult to grab ahold of one's opponent. Usually brute force won out.

Ozek bent his opponent's shoulders back to a point where he knew pain had to be shooting up the man's spine and down his arms.

The man writhed in agony.

Ozek didn't care.

He continued to squeeze and bend the man's shoulders back until Ozek heard a "snap" and the crackling of muscle tendons.

When Ozek finally let go, his opponent screamed and writhed in pain, grabbing his right shoulder. Where the man's rotator cuff had been was now shredded muscle tissue and raw nerve endings.

Ozek, completely drenched in sweat, walked off to find a drink of water. All around were his henchmen, perhaps thirty in all, smoking and hollering and congratulating him on his victory.

Normally, oil-wrestling matches ended with the opponent on his back, but uninjured. Ozek, however, didn't want to just beat his opponents.

He wanted to disable them.

Ignoring the traditional modesty and respect given in the sport, he took a huge swig of water and spit at his opponent on the ground, who continued to twist and moan in his suffering.

"Give him some coins and get him out of here," Ozek instructed one of his many assistants. The injured man, a local champion from a neighboring district, was carried off by three assistants and given a small bag of coins for his troubles.

Ozek loved oil wrestling more than anything else. He'd been doing it since he was seven and was considered to be perhaps the best wrestler in all of Constantinople. Nobody could remember him ever losing a match. Partly, that was due to his skill and partly to the fact that no opponent dared beat him. They understood that humiliating Ozek in that way would mean a stiletto to their kidneys, or perhaps across their throat, by one of his many assassins.

He rubbed himself down with a large cotton towel and continued to take gulps of cold water from a glass jug.

"Bugra, I will go to the *hamam* now and then lunch," he said to his assistant, who was only twenty-five and quite meek. His only desire in life was to serve Ozek.

Bugra stood next to his master, his eyes at the ground, shifting on his feet.

"What is it?" Ozek asked, annoyed that Bugra was standing so close to him.

"Master, we have a problem."

Ozek stopped wiping his sweaty and oiled body and looked up at Bugra. He didn't like to hear about problems, he only wanted to hear about solutions.

"What problem?"

"The panther has been lost."

Ozek stared at Bugra and wondered if he was joking.

"What are you talking about?"

"The black panther. It is missing."

Ozek continued to stare Bugra down.

"What do you mean 'it is missing'?"

"It's not in the warehouse. We can't find it anywhere."

Ozek took a drink of water and actually managed a little bit of a smile.

"If it's missing, then it's been stolen. Do you know anyone dumb enough to steal from me?"

Bugra shook his head.

"Bring me the guards who were stationed at the warehouse last night. We need to send a message."

"Yes, master."

Bugra retreated and left the courtyard. Ozek continued to rub himself down with the towel as he drank water and considered these developments.

The panther was rare, much more rare than the usual assortment of animals that passed through his warehouse. Still, he was so feared in Constantinople that he couldn't imagine anyone stealing directly from him.

The next day, two bodies hung from a beam outside of the warehouse, approximately six feet off the ground. Their hands had been tied behind their backs and their legs tied together.

They were the bodies of the guards from the warehouse.

Crows circled and then landed on the shoulders of the dead men and began pecking at the eyeballs of the corpses—a delicacy for these black birds. The largest crow sucked an eyeball, stringy veins still attached, from one of the eye sockets and gulped it down.

A sign, made from old wood, hung from one of the guard's necks. In large black letters, it read simply:

THIEVES OF ABDULLAH OZEK

The inhabitants of the neighborhood looked on in curiosity and fear at the men hanging from the beam. Mothers shielded their children's eyes and quickly walked away while men cowered at the sight.

Abdullah Ozek's message had been received and understood.

That night Abdullah Ozek sat in an oversized brown leather chair and drank *rakı*, also known as "lion's milk," the national liquor of Turkey. He had been troubled since he learned that the panther had disappeared. Something just didn't seem right about it. Why would anyone want to steal a panther? It made no sense to him.

Ozek drank himself to sleep on most nights. He had no family and every fiber of his life went into building his criminal empire. He had hundreds of henchmen working for him and it took every ounce of his energy to manage them all. Yet, in spite of his numerous employees, he trusted absolutely no one. Just last week he had to kill one of his lieutenants because the man had been plotting a robbery behind his back.

In his den, he was surrounded by treasures too numerous to count. The floors were covered with dozens and dozens of the most expensive rugs from around the world. On his shelves were countless gold artifacts and jewelry. Necklaces dripping with emeralds and rubies, stacked high on top of one another, overflowed from an ivory box carved from an elephant's tusk.

A stuffed adult lion stood in one corner, frozen in time to look fierce, its shiny black mane waxed and fluffed. The heads of dozens of animals personally killed by Ozek adorned his walls, including a zebra, a bear, a wolverine, a giraffe, cats of many varieties, a wolf, a giant ape, and even the massive head of an elephant.

He kept his den almost completely dark. The windows were shuttered so nobody could see in or out, and one solitary lantern provided the room's only light.

He preferred the dark.

He tipped the glass of rakı, his eighth, to his lips and then set it down on the mahogany side table next to him.

He began to drift off when, inexplicably, he heard a voice in his head. The voice was clear and distinctive.

The voice of a man he'd known for almost thirty years.

The voice of his master and teacher. The man who had helped him develop and form his underground and criminal empire. The man who had opened up contacts all over the world and opened up his black market trade of exotic animals, opium, weapons, and even people.

The man who had taken Abdullah Ozek, a small-time street thug, and turned him into the most notorious gangster in all of Turkey.

The only man Abdullah Ozek had ever trusted.

Watch for three boys.

His master's voice said it four or five times. It was unmistakable.

Watch for three boys.

Abdullah Ozek felt a chill run down his spine as he heard the words. He was not a man accustomed to feeling fear, but suddenly he felt his palms become clammy.

His master had been dead for five years.

This was a warning from the grave.

Watch for three boys.

And then the voice went silent.

The thief named Pakize sat across from an elder from her neighborhood. The elder was over seventy years old, with a gray moustache and a face that looked as if it had seen more than its fair share of life. He wore a gray jacket and pants with a white shirt, as he had every day for the last thirty years. Brown leather shoes, which he shined each and every morning, sat comfortably on his feet.

They met in a blacksmith shop that belonged to his son. While his son pounded away in front, repairing a cast iron table, the old man sat in a back room with Pakize, completely hidden from the street and any customers in the shop. The small room smelled of smoke and oil and was cold from the morning chill.

The man was a mentor of sorts to Pakize, and she shared with him the encounter with the boys and the panther, as well as with Captain Scopas.

"Tell me of this Greek," he asked.

"He is a captain of some kind, mostly of gypsy boats. He seems to have a vendetta against Abdullah Ozek," Pakize replied.

The old man nodded and studied Pakize. He had tutored her since she was only ten years old and considered her a daughter.

"There are changes happening in our country, Pakize. The Ottoman Empire is going to end. The Sultan is barely hanging onto control, and what little control he still has is due to his association with thugs such as Abdullah Ozek. He has silenced any kind of discontent in Constantinople, yet people meet in secret to discuss their disgust at his rule. He has already lost control of the countryside," he said.

"I see the same thing," she replied.

"For years you have been a thorn in Abdullah Ozek's side…stealing objects here and there and giving them to the less fortunate. But the time for revolution may be near. It may be the time to strike at Abdullah

Ozek, and this Greek might be just the man to do it," he said, rubbing his callused hands and stomping his feet to keep warm.

"I thought you distrusted Greeks?" Pakize asked.

"Oh, the only difference between Greeks and Turks is our religion and the divide created by rulers. I have known many an excellent Greek. Our true enemy lies within. Turkey is a proud country with centuries and centuries of history. All of the Ottoman Empire and Arabia has been ruled from this very city. I want for Turkey to retain her proud heritage, while evil men like Abdullah Ozek try to keep her antiquated and corrupt," he explained.

Pakize straightened up and rubbed her hands together, the frost numbing her fingertips.

"It is strange, but I do trust this captain...and these boys. I can't explain it. They were so determined to save that cat, I had to help them," she said.

The old man laughed.

"You have always had a good heart, Pakize. That is why you give what you steal to the poor and the needy. I'm sure you saw something in these boys, and this captain, that made you trust them," he replied.

"So, what are you going to do?" Pakize asked.

"There are men, young men, who meet in secret and discuss a future for Turkey without the rule of the Sultan. I will arrange a meeting between one of these men and this Greek captain. Perhaps he can set the wave of revolution in motion."

"It is a bold plan," Pakize replied.

"The times are afoot for bold plans...and for bold men...and women!" He answered with a smile.

The boys had named the panther "Cafu."

Cafu now sat in a much larger cage. Actually, it wasn't a cage at all. Scopas had a compartment in the cargo hold with bars halfway down the middle that was usually used to hold livestock. With no livestock on board, it made a perfect home for the panther. There were even two portholes to allow sea air to freshen it up and they had found a blanket for the panther to lie on. The panther seemed to appreciate his new home and looked content lying on the floor. He panted softly.

Tariq, Fez, and Aseem stood over a rickety wooden table in the hold of the *Osprey*. The boys had spread the map out on the tabletop, and by candlelight, they studied it fastidiously.

Fez stood over the map, his eyes mesmerized by the contents.

"How is this possible?" he whispered.

At the center of the map was the Ottoman Empire, and just up to the left was a red handprint. At the edge of the Black Sea was a route shown by a dotted line that went through Russia, above the Caspian Sea and the Aral Sea, near Persia, through Afghanistan, and finally into India.

"It's the exact route we should take to return the diary to India," Aseem replied, equally as awed as Fez.

Tariq studied the map. It was ancient, with crinkled corners and frayed edges. There were longitude and latitude lines and a several compass roses. At the bottom right corner was a small box with writing in it.

The boat rocked with the rhythm of the waves and the wood creaked as it expanded and contracted. A gush of wind came in the room sending the hairs on each boy's neck on edge, but didn't extinguish the candle.

"We were supposed to find this map," Tariq said.

Fez shook his head.

"We didn't find this map Tariq...this map found *us*."

Tariq couldn't explain his feelings as he peered down at the map. It was as if they weren't alone—that this map was proof that somebody, somewhere, was watching out for them. He felt invigorated and excited when he looked at it. It awakened something deep within him, and he began to feel that Melbourne Jack's death had not been in vain.

He felt like a true adventurer.

Fez continued to study the map and the outlined route.

"This is not an easy route. It will mean crossing through mountains and deserts over many thousands of miles. It won't be easy."

Tariq went over to a blanket he'd placed on the floor and sat back on a pillow. All the boys had spread blankets on the floor so they could be close to Cafu. Subconsciously his fingers toyed with Aji's black panther medallion hanging from his neck.

"We need to pay a return visit to the map seller. We need to ask him where he received this map and exactly who gave it to him," he said.

The next morning the boys returned to the Grand Bazaar. The area was bustling with activity and it took a half hour of wandering before they arrived at the spot where they'd first met the map seller.

Only his booth was gone.

The space was empty, as if nobody had ever been there.

They walked to the middle of the stall. The floor was completely bare.

The boys tried to ask around to find out what happened to the map seller, but nobody could understand their Arabic. Most merchants simply brushed them aside thinking they were street boys and not real customers.

"Are you sure this is the spot?" Aseem asked.

"I know this is it. I remember that café and that rug merchant over there. This is exactly where we got the map," Tariq answered.

Fez stood at the center of the stall. There was nothing. No clues. Not a trace left behind.

"C'mon, let's go. Some of the merchants are looking at us strangely. Besides, we said we would meet Pakize."

"What do you think happened to the map seller?" Aseem asked.

Tariq shook his head.

"I do not know, but I think it had something to do with the map he gave to us."

Fez, feeling a lump forming in his throat, gave the other two boys a serious look.

"If he left in such a hurry, maybe it was because he felt his life was in danger…"

"Which means that our lives might be in danger," Aseem finished his friend's sentence.

Suddenly all three boys began looking over their shoulders, their eyes scanning the area.

"Are we being watched?" Tariq asked.

"Let's get out of here...I have a very bad feeling," Fez answered and soon they were all practically running down the corridor and out of the Grand Bazaar.

In their haste to leave, what they didn't notice was a man in dirty, ragged clothes hiding behind a column across from the now-empty stall. His face was gaunt and skinny and resembled that of starving dog. His eyes darted about and he had studied the boys when they'd stood in the middle of the booth.

He'd made a mental note of their appearance before losing them in the crowd.

CHAPTER
— *16* —

CATACOMBS OF THE RED HAND

1872—KATHMANDU

Young Foster Crowe and Lhak-Pa walked through the streets of Kathmandu until they came to a tiny house at the far corner of a neighborhood block. The neighborhood looked poor, as could be seen by the houses in various states of decay and the number of people sitting on their stoops, seemingly without purpose.

"Lhak-Pa house. Foster need sleep and bath. Training in morning," Lhak-Pa explained.

"But I haven't agreed to any training!" Foster answered.

"Try one month. You do not like, return home. Deal?"

Foster thought about it for a moment. He had no family to return to and really nothing that was calling to him in Belgium other than a cold boarding school. If he didn't like Kathmandu, he could always leave.

"Deal," he replied.

The house was small, with only two bedrooms, a living room, and a tiny kitchen. Lhak-Pa prepared a dinner of wild rice, goat curry, and greens. It was surprisingly delicious and Foster ate three helpings.

Foster then took a warm bath and slept for fourteen hours.

The next day, some simple clothes were laid out for him. Foster felt a bit funny without his normal European clothes. Still, they were comfortable and he was happy to fit in with the local populace.

Foster wasn't sure what to expect as they left Lhak-Pa's tiny house and ventured into the streets of Kathmandu. After walking for twenty minutes, they came to a temple with a green door. Lhak-Pa opened the door to the temple, which was musty and sparsely furnished. The two walked to the back and down a flight of steps to a cellar. Lhak-Pa pushed aside some straw from the floor, uncovering a hatchway with a wooden handle. He pulled it open, and Foster could see that an opening proceeded straight downward.

"What's down there?" Foster asked.

"First lesson."

The two carefully climbed down a ladder into the darkness of the underground. It seemed to go on forever, until finally, they hit solid footing.

Lighting a lantern and handing it to Foster, and then lighting one for himself, Lhak-Pa began to lead Foster down a corridor. It was pitch-dark except for the illumination of the lanterns. The only sound that could be heard was the slow dripping from multiple leaks, as water droplets splashed onto the floor. Surprisingly, it didn't smell bad; in fact, it smelled fresh.

Foster pointed his lantern at one of the walls and was shocked to see that it was covered in hieroglyphics—paintings from an ancient time and civilization.

Walking for five minutes and taking a series of turns, they came to a wall that was covered in red handprints and nothing else.

"What are those?" Foster asked.

"Messages from dead," Lhak-Pa answered.

"Messages from the dead? This is all very creepy."

Lhak-Pa laughed.

"Just wait."

They walked a bit more, until Foster came across a most gruesome scene. As far as his eyes could see—along a wall measuring a hundred feet or more—there were nothing but human bones and skulls. The bones were crammed so tightly together they actually formed a wall that acted as part of the tunnel's foundation. All the bones looked to be very old, and were dark and dusty. Some were cracked and others splintered, and others were crumbling to dust.

"What are these bones?" Foster asked.

"Bones of dead."

"I know that, but why?"

Lhak-Pa stopped and shrugged his shoulders.

"They die. Something has to happen to bones."

Foster continued to try to digest all of these new sights and new information as they continued on a bit farther. Lhak-Pa led him into a room that was completely covered in writing. Even the floor and ceiling were covered in writing and symbols. The writing was all in white.

"Today start learning secret language."

"Won't I need a pencil and paper?" Foster asked.

"No, commit to memory. Start in corner and work our way over."

They studied in the room for two hours. The language was unlike any Foster had ever studied or seen. The letters were little more than strange symbols and elegant lines. When sounding out the letters, Lhak-Pa instructed him never to talk loudly, and to always whisper when speaking this language. When Lhak-Pa spoke the language, he spoke so softly it could barely be heard, and so rapidly it sounded like a strong wind brushing up against a tree with dead leaves on its branches.

Finally, satisfied with the first lesson, Lhak-Pa guided them back above ground, where they walked for another half an hour to a large building.

"What is this place?" Foster asked.

"Library."

"We're going to do training at a library?"

"Of course. Many free books—what better place?"

The three-story library had books stacked in every available space. Foster could not find any rhyme or reason to the order of the books; they were simply stacked in piles until they were so high that not another book could be added, at which time a new pile was started. The result was a maze of books that needed to be carefully navigated in order to walk about the library.

Lhak-Pa sat Foster down at a large wood table, disappeared into the maze of books, and returned with a big stack of ten books. He put them down in front of Foster, turned around, departed, and returned ten minutes later with another stack.

After fifteen minutes, Foster was surrounded by stacks and stacks of books that looked to be both ancient and new. There were books on Chinese acupuncture, oceanography, celestial navigation, metallurgy, astronomy, astrology, physics, mathematics, anthropology, geology, medical science, mechanical engineering, ten different languages—and that was just the beginning.

"Do I have to read all these books?" Foster asked, quite intimidated by the stacks in front of him.

"No, have to learn from all these books. Understand difference?" Lhak-Pa asked.

"Yes, I suppose so."

"Good, get started."

"Um, I thought we would study at a temple hidden in the mountains or something?" Foster asked sheepishly.

Lhak-Pa looked incredulously at him.

"Why do that? Sounds boring. Here, study books."

For five hours they studied, starting with a book on anthropology and then moved on to the study of ancient Greece. After that, Lhak-Pa gave Foster an introduction to algebra and concluded with the basics of every bone in the human body.

Foster's head hurt from studying so much, but that was not the end of the day's lessons. Lhak-Pa showed him to a small park just outside his house. The park was pleasant, with a bench and some simple fruit trees and birds that jumped from tree to tree. After going through a series of breathing exercises, Lhak-Pa showed Foster the correct formation for a fighting stance—feet more than shoulder-width apart, legs bent slightly, shoulders straight, elbows tucked into the body, and arms at forty-five degree angles.

They sparred for two hours until Foster's arms and legs were a mess of welts and bruises from being kicked and punched by Lhak-Pa.

Lhak-Pa then showed Foster to a shelter that provided room and board to homeless and broken men. They went about helping prepare food, served it to the men, and then saw to it that the elderly men in the shelter were taken to bed. Foster even sang them a lullaby he knew from his childhood. The old men smiled with appreciation for the young white boy who had taken the time to feed them and sing them a song.

Their lessons continued like this for a month. Intense study all day, martial arts training, and helping the needy and unfortunate at night.

It was extremely different from the rigid and authoritarian studies at his boarding school. Lhak-Pa didn't want him simply memorizing facts, he wanted him to learn and understand their meaning and importance. Foster found that Lhak-Pa rarely had to goad him into learning; he wanted to study for the sake of learning. Once in a while, Foster's thoughts drifted to his father, but never for long. He'd never really known his father, and what little he had known of him, he hadn't liked much.

One night, Foster dreamt of a woman. She was young and beautiful and smiled adoringly at Foster. She seemed so familiar, until Foster suddenly awoke.

It had been his mother in the dream.

He had never dreamt of her before, but he knew her face from a photograph his father kept next to his nightstand. The photograph was in gray and white. It showed his father sitting and his mother standing to his right. They both had stern expressions, and were dressed in their finest clothes, as only the wealthy had portrait photographs taken.

But in his dream, his mother was smiling. He continued to dream of her each night. In some dreams, she sat next to him. In others, she would lead him through a forest to a lake. Yet, she never spoke. She simply looked at him the way only a mother can look at her son.

Foster began to feel that she was with him during the day. All his life he had felt alone, even in his crowded boarding school. For the first time, he felt calm and loved. He could never quite explain it, but he knew in his heart his mother was watching over him.

After a month, Lhak-Pa sat Foster down at his kitchen table and asked him if he wanted to continue.

Foster already knew the answer.

"Yes, please."

Lhak-Pa smiled and they went out to start the day.

Foster found that he was learning so much, at such a rapid pace, he could hardly contain himself with happiness. Knowledge seemed to flow so easily through him, and his mind expanded more each day with his studies of new worlds and inventions and exciting discoveries. He didn't miss his boarding school, and he didn't miss Belgium. The world presented to him by Lhak-Pa was so interesting and the lessons so invigorating that he hardly ever gave his old life a second thought.

And always he felt his mother with him.

In time, Lhak-Pa incorporated vigorous mountain and rock climbing to the regimen.

Their martial arts training became more and more intense, and the use of weapons was introduced.

One day, down in the underground crypt, Lhak-Pa took Foster down a passage through a strange chamber until they reached a locked steel door. He opened the door and lit a series of candles until the room was completely illuminated.

It was a laboratory.

Shelves and shelves of beakers and test tubes and glass canisters were stacked neatly on one wall. Another wall was a mass of hundreds of small drawers, each one marked with a unique symbol. In the drawers were all makes of powders and ingredients, such as sulfur, potassium, amethyst, quartz, topaz, mustard seed, dried cocoa leaves, valerian root, and hundreds of others. One entire wall was blank and had been smoothed over to be used as a place to write down formulas. There were now dozens written on this wall in chalk. A large wooden rectangular table sat directly in the middle of the room, with two stools at one side, providing a large and uninterrupted working area.

"What is this place?" Foster asked.

"This where young Foster become apothecary."

Lhak-Pa pulled out a glass canister, produced some powders from a drawer full of ground herbs, and placed everything down on the table.

"New task—make potion, help sleep."

CHAPTER
— 17 —

A FLY IN THE WINE

Foster walked with haste through Paris to the Hotel du Cecil—a three-story colonial hotel, painted white, built in the classic French style. Many visiting diplomats had begun to arrive at the hotel. They were dressed to the nines in tails and top hats and most appeared to be friendly with one another. Foster spotted a couple security guards in the crowd.

The diplomats' dinner was in full swing.

Foster milled about the outside of the hotel until the security guards were preoccupied, then entered the lobby and pretended to be a guest. He spotted an open door to the dining room and a waiter dressed in a white apron and tie. There was a guard posted outside the dining room, but Foster patiently waited for an opportune moment, and then slipped past the guard as the man kneeled down to tie his laces. He followed his nose to the kitchen.

Normally, most kitchens had an employee changing room. After opening two doors, Foster managed to find it and went inside. Clothes hung from hooks as workers changed into their restaurant uniforms. Seeing a stack of white aprons, Foster put one on and fastened a black tie under his collar. Grabbing a large circular tray, he exited the room and prayed his ruse would work.

Along the way, he'd made note of the exit doors and mentally created three possible exit strategies should things go awry.

After making his way to the kitchen and pumping through two swinging doors, Foster was presented with a scene of absolute chaos. A huge team of chefs and cooks stood over their stoves managing dozens of copper pans and skillets at one time. Fire jumped in the air from sauté pans as a variety of sauces, fish, and meats were prepared on the burners. Sous cooks scurried around the chefs and chopped herbs and vegetables at hummingbird-like speed. Once dishes were complete, waiters grabbed the plates and delivered them to the dining rooms.

Foster spied a bottle of red wine, hurriedly placed it on his tray, and made his way through the doors of the dining room.

The large, rectangular dining room featured a piano player at one end who played a little-known ballad from an obscure French composer. The diplomats appeared to be enjoying their drinks and gossiping with one another, and most of them smoked either a cigarette or cigar. Foster began offering wine to the guests. These encounters were important, because he was listening for their accents. He could also tell by looking who the foreign diplomats were: the ones who didn't speak French often had a translator standing alongside them, usually a young man.

The problem was that Foster wasn't totally sure who, or what, he was looking for. He didn't even know if he was in the right place. All Foster had were his instincts to go on. And today, he had a hunch that he was definitely in the right place, hopefully at the right time. If Wu Chiang had already bombed a Serbian embassy, then logic would follow that he might try to target a German or even an Austrian official.

Overhearing someone speaking French, he turned around to notice a slender, well-heeled gentleman.

"Pardon me, monsieur, do you know where I might find the German ambassador? I have the wine he requested," Foster said.

Quite politely, the man nodded toward a large man with a red walrus moustache, who chortled as he chomped on a cigar and joked with his companion. Foster thanked the man and continued in that direction.

"*Vin, monsieur?*" Foster asked.

The German diplomat nodded his head and Foster poured him a glass of wine and walked away. Now that he had his target, his only solution was to sit back and watch to see if anything developed. He had to make sure he continued to look busy, pouring wine and milling about the dining room, hoping that none of the staff would question a man they had never seen before.

Scanning the faces around the room, Foster was hoping to notice someone, or something, that seemed out of place. None of the diplomats appeared nervous or preoccupied. Yes, there was a general feeling of tension, in a political sense (most likely from the bombing in Bremen), and emotions had been running a bit hot of late. But tonight, none of them seemed especially agitated.

What would Wu Chiang do?

Foster knew, from experience, that Wu Chiang had a tendency for either bombings or poison. This suggested a man who liked to keep his distance from his targets. A bomb might make sense, but why kill all the diplomats? Countries might band together against a common enemy if they all lost members of their diplomatic corps.

Because of that, Foster was increasingly sure it would be an assassination—and it would be made to look like the Serbians were responsible. He was also sure it would happen in setting like this one, because a spectacle had to be made to make the statement he was after.

That might suggest a poisoning.

Which might mean kitchen staff.

Foster made a point to observe every member of the staff, with special attention to anyone handling drinks (the most obvious way to slip in a bit of poison). For fifteen minutes he went about his business, pouring wine, and watching the hotel employees. Nobody bothered him or even asked him for credentials.

Talk about lackadaisical security, he thought to himself.

Continuing to make his rounds, at last he noticed something unusual. A young server, a beautiful woman, seemed to have slipped something into the pocket of one of the diplomats. Her movements were so subtle that most people might not have noticed it.

Moving quickly, he made his way to the diplomat.

"*Vin, monsieur?*" he asked.

"No thank you," came the reply.

"You're from Russia?" Foster asked. He couldn't quite make out the accent.

"No, the Kingdom of Serbia."

Foster felt the color drain from his face as his worst fear was being realized. Without a moment's hesitation, he pretended to trip—falling into the Serbian diplomat and reaching into the man's pocket, hoping to find what the waitress had planted. He deftly grabbed the object and hid it in the palm of his hand.

"Apologies, monsieur," he said to the Serbian diplomat while walking away.

He returned to the kitchen and found a secluded corner behind some dry goods. There, he inspected the object he'd taken from the diplomat's pocket.

A small glass container was filled with some kind of liquid.

Foster didn't have to taste the liquid. He didn't even have to smell it. He knew what it was—an odorless, tasteless poison that was probably the same that had killed his faithful servant Melgrave.

The plan now seemed obvious: poison the German diplomat and blame the crime on the innocent Serbian representative.

Foster returned the vial of poison to his pocket and made his way back to the dining room. He scanned the room, looking for the beautiful server who had slipped the vial into the Serbian ambassador's pocket.

He spotted her standing next to the German diplomat, flirtatiously smiling, and offering him a glass of wine to replace the one that Foster had served him a few minutes before. The German, obviously affected by the woman's charms, put down his glass, grabbed the one on her tray, and had begun moving it toward his mouth.

If the German swallowed that glass of wine, it could be the start of a world war.

Foster had only seconds to act.

The German diplomat brought the glass of wine to his lips. Foster was still twenty feet away across the room. He began to sprint toward the diplomat, but he knew he could not get to him in time. Then, serendipitously, the diplomat lowered his wineglass and looked at the ground. Some of the ashes from his cigar had fallen to the carpet.

"Damn, could someone bring me an ashtray?' he asked, to no one in particular.

That slight hesitation provided Foster just enough time to reach him. Without skipping a beat, he grabbed the glass of wine from the man's hand and carefully lifted it away.

"I'm sorry, sir, a fly seems to have found its way into your wineglass. Let me find you another," Foster said and turned and walked away.

The German diplomat, a bit stunned, merely wrinkled his nose and took another puff on his cigar.

Foster had just prevented an assassination and eventual international catastrophe, but it was doubtful anyone would ever know about it, except for Jacqueline, who witnessed the scene from the far corner of the room.

It was clear to her that she'd been found out.

Stricken with panic, she realized she was no longer anonymous. As she stumbled through the kitchen, everything was a blur. Reaching the rear exit door, she looked behind her and saw exactly what she feared the most.

Foster was chasing her, and he was gaining ground fast.

Sprinting out of the hotel, Jacqueline dashed through a courtyard and onto a street. The street was heavy with automobiles and horse-drawn carriages. Darting through the parked carriages, she had no idea where she was going. She couldn't move fast in her uniform, and she knew Foster would be on her in seconds. She was desperate. She reached into her pocket and pulled out a small vial—the original one she'd been given by Wu Chiang—and emptied the entire contents into her mouth, swallowing hard.

She had saved enough for just such an emergency. It was the last decision she'd ever make.

In seconds she had collapsed on the wet pavement. Staring up at the overcast French sky, the world seemed to dull around her. Noises softened and the streetlights became hazy.

She thought of her mother and father.

Within moments, Foster appeared above her.

"Dear God, you've poisoned yourself, dumb girl," he scolded her and tried to revive her.

It was no use; the poison was working too fast.

"Tell my parents I'm sorry," she whispered.

"No, no, tell me where Wu Chiang is! Help me!" Foster admonished.

The girl's eyes shifted to the right and Foster watched as the life drained out of them. Her body went limp, and in moments, Foster was holding a corpse.

Hanging his head, Foster sighed. *This wasn't supposed to happen,* he thought.

As he considered his next move, he saw something out of the corner of his eye. It was quick, but deliberate. Looking over, Foster saw a figure—an unmistakable figure—staring right at him. It was the direction the girl's eyes were facing. In her last gesture, it was as if she were trying to show Foster where to find Wu Chiang. Perhaps it was her way of asking for forgiveness.

The shadowy figure was across the street nearly a block away. Foster strained his eyes, hoping to get a glimpse of the man's face. Just then, the man took a step backward. The glow of the streetlamp illuminated an unmistakably Asian face.

It had to be Wu Chiang!

Without missing a beat, Foster began sprinting across the street after him. Wu Chiang, obviously surprised that he'd been found out, began running away and down the block in the opposite direction.

After almost getting hit by a carriage, Foster ran on the sidewalk, sidestepping pedestrians, and turned right down the block where he'd spied Wu Chiang.

Up ahead, he saw Wu Chiang turn left. Foster had already made up a lot of ground on the slower man. Continuing to sprint around cars, carriages, street vendors, musicians, and the many patrons going for an evening stroll, Foster's legs pumped like pistons and his arms chugged at his sides like the gears on an oilrig.

Foster saw Wu Chiang duck into a restaurant, obviously trying to throw Foster off his trail. But Foster followed, bursting through the front door, knocking down the maître d', and causing the entire dining room to stop and stare at him. He dashed through the dining room into the kitchen, where the chefs were busy at work. That's when it happened!

Foster looked up to see a projectile coming his way. At the last moment, he ducked, and immediately afterward an explosion rocked the kitchen. The explosion sent him flying through the kitchen, crashing into a shelf of pots and pans and sending it, and him, to the floor. Landing hard, his ears rang and his left elbow felt numb. Blood gushed from his right hand. Shaking his head, he picked himself up and noticed the sharp smell of sulfur in the air. Smoke now filled the kitchen and the cooks were either on the floor or coughing and trying to help the ones who had been knocked down.

As Foster regained his bearings, he glimpsed a door closing in the rear of the kitchen.

Foster tried to run toward the door, but felt a sharp pain in his left knee. It wasn't completely debilitating, just bruised enough to slow him down a bit. His ears still ringing, he ran after the figure, ignoring the pain in his elbow, knee, and hand.

Foster ducked through the back door and spotted Wu Chiang in the distance, perhaps half a block away. He had him in his sights now—Wu Chiang wouldn't be able to duck him this time. Normally, he would have been on him without a problem, but the injury to his knee slowed him down. He could stay close enough to keep Wu Chiang in his sights, but couldn't make up much ground.

Wu Chiang tried anything and everything to lose Foster. He ran in and out of shops. He twisted around pedestrians. He ran through traffic and down alleys.

After two minutes, it seemed he was also starting to fatigue.

Foster saw that he was now gaining on him and now only trailed by about forty feet. Being this close urged on his confidence. Ignoring the pain in his knee, he sprinted faster.

Gradually gaining ground with every minute, soon he was only twenty feet behind and then ten. Foster could see the fear in Wu Chiang's eyes as he continually looked behind him as Foster edged closer. For the first time, he got a very good look at the face of his enemy. The man was sweating profusely, and his thick, black hair stuck to his forehead.

His face was chubby and Foster could see how labored his breathing had become. He looked scared.

Foster was only a couple of feet behind him now. They were running on a hard cobblestone street and there was nowhere for Wu Chiang to hide. As he grew nearer, Foster threw himself forward and tackled Wu Chiang. He hit him hard in a classic rugby tackle, bringing his left arm down over Wu Chiang's left shoulder and pulling him down to the ground.

Foster landed on top of his adversary. They both hit the cobblestone very hard and Foster instantly felt pain surging up his left ankle and into his knee. His ankle had landed awkwardly and twisted severely.

Hanging onto Wu Chiang's jacket with a vise grip, he was determined not to let go of his prey despite being in considerable pain. Wu Chiang was scrambling and squirming, like a walrus trying to fit through a water hose. He jerked and twisted his body until, finally, his arms slipped out of his jacket. Bursting forward, Foster was left holding nothing but a sweaty jacket as Wu Chiang escaped from his grasp and sprinted ahead. He gave one last look back to Foster. His glasses had come off and blood was gushing down his face to his chin.

Foster immediately tried to get up and give chase but his ankle screamed out in protest. His leg gave way and he stumbled to the ground, landing hard on both his hands.

He watched in agony as Wu Chiang sprinted down the street and out of view.

Slowly and gingerly rising to his feet, Foster noticed a pair of glasses with the right lens smashed to bits lying next to Wu Chiang's empty jacket. Picking up the glasses and coat, he began hobbling down the street.

Foster's training with the Red Hand had taught him to always control his emotions, but this time he couldn't help himself. As he watched the area where Wu Chiang had just disappeared, Foster felt anger rise up in his veins and in his heart. His fingers clenched and he ignored the searing pain in his ankle. He should have captured Wu Chiang easily, yet something seemed to be working against him. A dark force of some kind had entered into the equation and had sabotaged his efforts. He'd first felt it when he started to run after Wu Chiang. He'd never experienced anything like it...as if he were fighting, and reacting, in a fog. A step slower than usual.

He didn't understand this force, but he was determined not to allow it to slow him down in the future. He was going to find Wu Chiang and stop him. He hated to lose, and Wu Chiang had been nothing but lucky to escape.

Next time he wouldn't be so lucky.

CHAPTER
— *18* —

CROW'S DELIGHT

Tariq, Fez, Aseem and Pakize gawked wide-eyed at the bodies hanging outside the warehouse. The ropes swung lightly and creaked softly as they swayed back and forth. Crows had devoured the eyes and even some of the skin from the men's faces.

One man's face was a pale gray, and his lips were caked with flakes of skin and dried blood. He almost looked as if he were delivering a warning directly to the boys. The deep sockets where his eyes had been stared straight at them.

"This is what happens when you steal from Abdullah Ozek," Pakize whispered.

Tariq looked at the lifeless bodies. For some reason, this display of cruelty didn't scare him. He'd known brutality all of his life and what was one more street killing? He was thinking more about the map than anything else.

Tariq noticed that Aseem and Fez were taken aback by the gruesome scene.

"This is nothing, you should see the inside of the kasbah of Caid Ali Tamzali," he said with a slight smile.

Aseem and Fez nodded to him.

"Pakize, we'll show this Abdullah Ozek how we handle things," Tariq added.

Pakize was silent for a while.

"I am endangering my life, and even the lives of my people, by associating with you and Scopas. A Turk befriending a Greek is unheard of in Constantinople. Yet, something tells me you might be instrumental in defeating Abdullah Ozek. But before we proceed, I must have your word that you will embark on this appointment with seriousness and resolve. There is no retreating once we go down this road, because

Abdullah Ozek will never stop hunting us if he learns of our identities. Do you understand?"

The boys, impressed by Pakize's serious tone, nodded in agreement.

"No, I must have your word. I must have a blood oath."

Pakize took out a knife and slit her palm. Blood began to drip from her palm as she handed the knife to Aseem, who slit his own palm, and then to Fez and Tariq, who both followed suit.

Then, Pakize shook each of their hands, smearing their blood with her own, and looked them in the eyes.

"Do you pledge to show courage and honor? Will you deliver on your promises?" she asked.

"Yes, I will," each boy answered.

"Good, let's go to my neighborhood and I'll show you why I fight. We'll be safe there to make our plans."

Pakize led the boys over the wooden Galata Bridge and into her neighborhood. It was an extremely poor neighborhood, with inhabitants crammed into stacks of wooden apartment buildings. Shop owners sold fish, vegetables, cheese, eggs, and many Turkish pastries from their small shops. Children kicked a ball around in the street with their bare feet. Mothers sat on stoops gossiping and embroidering. Men played backgammon and drank tea while shouting and pounding their fists on the wooden board. Clothes hung from the windows of the apartment buildings, creating a collage that resembled a bright, exploding firework.

Overhead, the Galata Tower looked down on the neighborhood like a hawk studying the ground. For centuries it had acted as both a lookout tower for enemy ships and lighthouse for friendly ones.

The streets, not yet cobblestoned, were wet and muddy and dirt caked their shoes and the bottom of their pants. Horses, camels, and carriages plodded through the mud with ease.

"This is my neighborhood, boys. I was born in that house right over there, and over there I had my first fight when I was just six. If you need a new pair of shoes, that is Bulent, he makes the best shoes in all of Constantinople. You see smoke from that chimney? That is Emre, the coffee maker. All day he stokes a fire to roast his coffee beans. Yes, there is no place in the world I would rather be," Pakize exclaimed as she puffed out her chest with pride.

People shouted and waved to Pakize and she shouted and waved back. They looked with curiosity at the boys, welcoming them with happy smiles because they walked with Pakize.

"That shop over there has the best ceramics. That family has been making ceramics for almost five hundred years! That old lady there is kind of crazy, she goes around the neighborhood feeding all the cats. No cat ever has to worry about starving here."

Feral cats, protected by the writings of Muhammad, lazily basked on a fence or stoop, each one cared for and fed by the many inhabitants.

"Where are all the dogs?" Fez asked.

"That is quite a story in our history. A few years ago our governor ordered every stray dog to be rounded up and shipped to an island called Hayırsızada. The island is very barren, without much shelter or water, and many of the dogs died. Soon after, a great earthquake ripped apart Constantinople and, in particular, the governor's neighborhood. People said it was God's revenge on him for abandoning the dogs. Now, they are welcomed back, but we take better care of them."

Pakize continued to walk, pointing to favorite spots and attractions.

"Here, you have to try this. It is my favorite dish," she explained. They had stopped in front of a wooden cart where a man was roasting some kind of delicious-smelling meat on a spit over a wood fire.

Pakize said something in Turkish, the man laughed, and then he set about making their lunch. He took four bread rolls, cut them each in half, and cut off generous portions of the meat, which he piled high on the rolls. Wrapping each sandwich in brown paper, he handed them to the boys.

"Here, try it," Pakize ordered.

The boys took a mouthful and their eyes lit up.

"This is really delicious," Fez said.

"Very good," Tariq agreed.

All four sat in front of the cart, devouring their sandwiches, and when they were finished, they licked the juices from their fingers, savoring every last taste.

"What *was* that?" Fez asked.

"It is called *kokoreç*. Sheep guts wrapped in sheep intestine and then roasted to perfection," Pakize explained.

"Sheep guts!" Aseem exclaimed.

"Sheep intestine!" Tariq yelped.

Just then, the cook handed each boy a long stick with an eyeball at the very end. The eyeball had been roasted and was burnt around the edges.

"Ah, now for the best part," Pakize said and then ate the eyeball from her stick, chewed on it, then gulped it down.

The boys stared at Pakize and then at one another. Not one of them wanted to be the first to chicken out.

Fez, sensing the draw, finally put his mouth over the stick, and then bit off the eyeball and chewed it.

"Hmm, it's not bad actually. Kind of chewy," he said as Tariq and Aseem watched him.

Not to be outdone by anyone, especially little Fez, Aseem and Tariq shrugged their shoulders, then each ate their own eyeball.

Nodding his head, Aseem licked his lips as he finished chewing.

"Very nice, kind of salty," he explained.

The cook laughed at the boys and then came and gave them each a big bear hug. He was built like a bull, with thick arms and shoulders and a gleaming bald head.

"He likes you. His name is Arda. He's been making *kokoreç* for as long as I can remember at this very street corner," Pakize explained, then paid Arda and thanked him.

"Come, there's something I want to show you," Pakize said.

The boys followed her up a steep set of rickety wooden stairs with ivy on either side. At the top of the stairs was an archway covered in purple and orange flowers, and long and bushy grape vines. Passing under the archway, they came across a beautiful park overlooking the city of Constantinople and the glistening water of the Golden Horn. In the park, old men played chess and bocce, laughing and arguing with each move and throw. Children played as their mothers sat nearby discussing the happenings in the neighborhood. A huge garden, with every kind of vegetable and herb, had been planted, and a few men and women happily pruned vines and poured water from a steel bucket with a wooden spout. An enormous willow tree anchored the center of the small park, providing shade and shelter. A man played a modern tune on the mandolin and couples danced nearby.

"This is our neighborhood park. Believe it or not, a giraffe used to live here. All the inhabitants took care of the giraffe, and it lived to a very old age. My people have gathered here for centuries. Those old men playing chess and bocce are the neighborhood elders. They meet and hold judgment on all things pertaining to the neighborhood. That garden helps feed all the people. It is my favorite place to relax and take in the view of Constantinople," Pakize explained.

The boys and Pakize took in the view, enjoying the skyline of Constantinople and observing the many boats going in and out of port.

"This park is very important to my people. It is where we meet, and play, and come to relax because we live in such cramped houses. But now, let me take you to my home," Pakize said as they meandered out of the park.

They walked up four blocks until they came to an old and decrepit apartment building—four stories high with chipped green paint splotched with white.

Pakize was swarmed by a group of young children playing on the front steps of the building. They hugged her as she and the boys entered the lobby, which had termite-infested planks for floorboards and peeling paint on every wall. Wax dripped from holders on the walls from candles that provided the only light in an otherwise dark stairway.

They walked up two flights of stairs and came to a hallway. Pakize opened the third wooden door on the right and led them into a room that was at once petite yet still very inviting. The small room was painted blue from ceiling to floor, and the trim on the doors and windows was bright red. Four kids read books on the wooden floor. Sitting in a chair was a young girl trying to play a *bouzouki*—a Turkish guitar. She patiently strummed and did her best to keep her fingers pressed down, but she was obviously a beginner, as the notes were off and the guitar wailed with a "twang" for each missed note.

The children all stopped their activities and ran to Pakize and the boys, smiling at them in complete amazement. The oldest was perhaps nine years old and the younger ones hugged Pakize around her waist and legs.

She spoke to them in Turkish, and they giggled and continued to smile and stare at all the boys.

"This is Arif and this is Eser," she said and pointed to the two boys, who both smiled and nodded their heads.

"And here we have Damla, Ece, and the youngest is Selim." The young girls giggled and waved their hands at the boys. The boys smiled and waved back.

Pakize kissed them all on the cheeks, said a few more words in Turkish, and then the children ran back to continue their studies.

Just to the left of the main room was a very small kitchen with one cramped counter and four wooden boxes stacked on top of one another. Each box was filled with jars and metal tins filled with spices and herbs. On the counter was a small stove with a solitary burner. To generate the heat, pieces of coal were placed in a small compartment directly beneath the burner. Some kind of yellow mixture simmered in a copper pot on the cooktop.

An old woman patiently stirred the contents of the copper pot with a wooden spoon and then went about slicing vegetables piled high next to the stove.

"Nana, I have some new friends. This is Fez, and Tariq, and Aseem," Pakize announced in Arabic. Then, she said something that sounded similar in Turkish.

The old woman stopped cutting and took very small steps toward the boys. Pakize took her hands. The woman looked off into space.

She smiled, said something in Turkish, and then continued her cooking.

156

"My grandmother is blind, but she's the best cook I have ever known. Turkish people hardly ever eat in restaurants because the best meals are always at home. In fact, people think if you eat out that you must not have a home," Pakize explained.

"Come, we'll eat later. I want to show you around."

"Pakize, I've been wanting to ask you. Why do you steal?" Fez asked as they exited the apartment building.

"All these people I've shown you, half of everything they make goes into the pockets of Abdullah Ozek. If they don't pay him, then his thugs beat them up. If they still don't pay him, then they find themselves at the end of a rope as a warning to everyone else."

"So why hasn't anyone eliminated him?" Tariq asked.

"Because he is too strong and I am just one girl. I steal from him to give back a little of the money he extorts from my people. I've never had anyone around me who I thought could stand up to Ozek," she explained and then looked at each one of them.

"Until now. Until I met Scopas. He is a man who can defeat Ozek, and you three boys showed more courage than I have ever seen in stealing that panther. You see, you are my hope."

Tariq took in the scene around him and studied Pakize. He felt safe in the neighborhood. It had a familiar feel, like being wrapped in a warm blanket. Everyone was friendly and said "hello," which was a bit foreign to him. In Tangier, people kept to themselves. He saw how much this neighborhood meant to Pakize. How her eyes lit up when she talked of its people and history. He couldn't help but feel warmed by her enthusiasm.

They continued to walk through the neighborhood until they came to an alleyway. Pakize knocked four times on a solitary wood door and waited until it slowly opened.

"Come in," a voice whispered.

At once, Pakize and the boys were whisked into a darkened room as the door closed behind them.

The room was empty with the exception of a large desk. Behind the desk sat a man with a derby hat, who smoked a cigarette and eyed the boys warily.

He said something in Turkish, annoyed, and Pakize said something back, equally as annoyed.

"He doesn't like that I brought you here," she whispered.

"Where are we?" Tariq asked.

"This is the man who buys all my stolen goods."

Pakize produced the trinkets from her bag and handed them to the man. He studied them fastidiously, and then said something in Turkish.

Clearly perturbed, Pakize began scolding him in Turkish and yelled something in return.

The man relented, nodding his head and reaching, into a desk drawer for some coins, which he placed in a small leather pouch and handed it to Pakize.

Without delay, they left the man's office and returned to the crowded streets.

"What did you argue about?" Fez asked.

"He tried to cheat me on the price, but I reminded him the money was for his people. It is always like that."

They walked down a flight of stairs and came to another apartment building. An old man came to greet Pakize and they kissed one another on the cheek. Pakize took a gold coin from the pouch and gave it to him. He smiled, kissed her forehead, and then said a prayer to the sky.

As they walked away, she explained.

"That is Berrak. He takes care of a center for the elderly."

Next, they crossed four streets and stood in front of a large brick wall. Pakize gave a loud whistle and soon the gate was opened. A man with round spectacles emerged and talked quietly with Pakize. She gave him a gold coin as well. He bowed slightly and then disappeared behind the wall, closing the gate behind him.

"That is for the leper colony."

They continued like that for three more stops, until they finally reached an old apartment building with chipped white paint. Water

158

dripped from the cracked and broken roof tiles, which were patched together with rusty nails. A group of men were gathered outside, most of them missing limbs. A few wore a patch over one eye.

"This is the home for veterans of Turkish wars," she explained.

A man approached Pakize. Missing both legs, he used crutches to move about and she greeted him with a smile. He was dressed in full military regalia, including five medals that hung from his left breast pocket. Pakize whispered to him, kissed him on both cheeks, and gave him a coin.

They walked away from the building and Pakize shook her head.

"These brave men fight and die and become crippled for their country, yet nobody helps them. It is so sad."

Fez looked back at the soldiers.

"Pakize, normally I do not agree with thievery. But, seeing what you do with the money, I think you are doing a very good thing."

Tariq and Aseem agreed.

"Yes, you protect your neighborhood and that is a great deed. I am proud to be your friend," Aseem explained.

Pakize smiled at the praise.

Then, she stopped smiling, and looked straight ahead as the boys immediately saw why she had developed such a stern look.

A group of five men had surrounded one of the shopkeepers. The man was diminutive and slight, but stood defiantly in front of his display of vegetables as the men antagonized and mocked him.

A woman and two small boys, presumably the man's family, stood off to the side. The woman had her arms around the boys and looked terrified by the five ruffians.

Tariq immediately understood what was happening. The men were bullies and were shaking down the merchant for money. He had seen the same scene countless times in Tangier.

"Those are Abdullah Ozek's men, aren't they?" he asked Pakize.

"Yes, but we shouldn't make trouble. They do this all the time."

Tariq watched as the men laughed and mocked the merchant. The man tried to be brave, but they were five strong men and he was one feeble one. Tariq studied the humiliation on his face and heard the desperation in his voice. He didn't understand what he was saying, but he didn't have to. The man's voice conveyed a mixture of fear and a cry for sympathy.

As he watched, Tariq became more and more angry. He thought of the moment that Melbourne Jack died in his arms, and suddenly he was absolutely furious. He didn't know why he was so angry, but he just wanted…to hurt these men.

Fez studied him and whispered to Aseem.

"Tariq's going to do something, make sure we have his back."

Aseem looked at Tariq and then back at Fez and nodded his head in agreement.

"Pakize, you better stay back," Aseem whispered to her.

"If there's going to be trouble, then you include me," Pakize answered.

Tariq continued to stare at the men as they ridiculed the shopkeeper and then, without thinking, he burst forward.

Fez and Aseem followed him.

Seeing a rock about three times the size of his fist on the ground, Tariq grabbed it, ran straight ahead toward the closest man, and, with a full wind-up, smashed the rock down on the his head.

The sharp edge of the rock went straight into the man's cheekbone and he let out a loud yelp and stumbled to the ground. The other men froze with surprise.

Nobody had ever attacked them before.

Without a pause, Tariq continued to run straight at a second man, brought his left leg up and pounded his foot on the man's right thigh, pushed him, and smacked the rock down on his skull. The thug stumbled to his knees and held his head in his hands—already a huge knot was forming.

Tariq landed, spun around, and was tackled by the leader of the gang. He was a brute of a man, strong, and his breath smelled of garlic and fish. He managed to get both arms around Tariq and squeeze him. Although the thug outweighed Tariq by at least one hundred pounds, every ounce of Tariq's body was poised for a fight. He was like a hungry alley cat, all muscle and fury. Tariq struggled and brought his right arm up to the thug's throat, gripped his jugular, and pinched his fingers together around his windpipe. Gasping for breath, the man released his grip and Tariq was able to roll on his back and get away.

Now on his knees and holding his throat, the huge man looked up as Tariq rammed an elbow straight into his nose.

Breaking it.

The man staggered to his feet and Tariq kicked him in the groin, dropping the man back to his knees.

Looking up, Tariq saw that both Aseem and Fez were in considerable trouble. The two other men had them both in headlocks while Pakize was wrestling with a third.

Grabbing the same rock, Tariq hit the first man in the back of the head. It was enough to get him to release his grip on Aseem so that Aseem could roll away.

Running to the other thug, Tariq dug the rock into the small of his back. The man shouted in pain and Fez scrambled out of his grasp.

The three boys, now back together, suddenly realized the men had regrouped from the surprise attack. With a look of murder in their eyes and their faces flushed with rage, three of Abdullah Ozek's gangsters started running directly for Tariq, Fez, and Aseem.

Inez sat chewing a piece of hard, salty elk jerky.

Mia stood above her, watching the woods, and keeping an eye on the group sitting on the ground. She had not wanted to stop, but Leopold's slow pace finally forced her to give them a ten-minute break.

Leopold looked tired. He was dirty and probably wasn't accustomed to this amount of rigorous exercise.

"Leopold, do you think there will be a war?" Margaret asked.

Leopold wiped his glasses once again and took a drink of water.

"I do not know. The Kaiser is a very insecure man and insecure men always start wars. He has been building an arsenal for years and, eventually, he'll want to use it."

Mia perked up at this conversation.

"If we have a war, it will be worse than any in history," she replied.

"Why do you say that?" Margaret asked.

"Technology," Leopold answered for her.

"Technology?" Inez asked.

"The modern weapons we have now are designed to kill humans at a rate that was previously inconceivable. Because of the steamship and the railroad, we can now move soldiers around in the hundreds of thousands. Because of the telegraph, we can now communicate more quickly and easily. It all makes the world a smaller place," Leopold answered.

"Wasn't the Gatling gun supposed to end wars because it was so devastating?" Margaret asked.

"Yes, that's what the gun's inventor, George Gatling, said when he invented it. The gun was so powerful that he thought no nation would ever want to engage in a war again because the human cost would be so high."

"Of course, he was wrong," Mia replied and Leopold nodded.

"What will you do if you get to France?" Inez asked.

"I am hoping that if the Kaiser knows that I am in France, he will think twice about engaging in a war. My presence there will deal him a serious blow."

"What other kinds of things did you invent besides this decoder?" Margaret asked.

Leopold waited a few moments before answering, as if he were trying to figure out if he should divulge all his secrets.

"I studied and tested all the new weaponry and even invented a few new weapons—those were my main functions."

"Like what?" Inez asked.

"Gases that can kill with just one breath. A new kind of tank that is impervious to regular bullets or even artillery shells. Planes outfitted with machine guns so they can attack from the air."

"My God, you're a monster!" Mia exclaimed and the sound of her voice was a mixture of surprise and contempt.

Leopold stared at the ground. It was easy to see the remorse on his face and the great regret he carried with him.

"Why did you do it, Leopold? You seem like such a good person," she asked.

Leopold dragged his finger through the dirt and sighed a deep breath before answering.

"I had a family once. A lovely wife and small daughter. They both died of pneumonia about ten years ago. For the longest time, I wasn't interested in life. But then a woman came into my life. She was younger, and beautiful, and I don't know, my life started changing."

"What do you mean?" Inez asked.

"She was the one who got me a job with the Kaiser's staff. I don't know how she did it, but she did. She was the one who—I suppose 'manipulated' is the word—manipulated me to pour all of my efforts into these inventions. She assured me they would be good for Germany and would be used only to prevent war but that was a lie. Everything I did was just helping the Kaiser prepare for war."

"So, it sounds like you did it for a girl?" Inez asked.

"Yes, I suppose I did," he answered mournfully.

"Where is she now?" Margaret asked.

"I do not know. Once I discovered the extent to which the Kaiser would use my inventions for war preparations, I began to raise questions and voice my disapproval. About the same time that happened, she suddenly left one day and I never saw her again. A week later I was sent to that internment camp."

"Do you know of other military plans? The size of the Kaiser's army, his navy, that sort of thing?" Mia asked.

"Of course. I was in on all the strategic military meetings. The Kaiser has created a massive army and navy. He has a real inferiority complex and feels that Germany should have a bigger navy than Britain."

"But Britain has the largest navy the world has ever seen." Margaret interrupted.

"I know, but the Kaiser feels the British and French don't take Germany seriously."

"Leopold, there is something you're not telling us," she said.

Leopold looked at the ground.

"This woman, I think she manipulated me the entire time. Once, I saw her writing a note in code and questioned her about it. She said it was just a silly game and burned the note. Sometimes she would be gone for days at a time and not tell me where she had gone. But when I was really stuck on a problem, amazingly, it seemed she could always come up with a solution. I simply thought she was brilliant, but I think someone was pulling her strings. It turned out I was the puppet."

"She was a spy?" Inez asked excitedly.

"Yes, she was a spy. But for whom? I do not know."

Inez felt sorry for him. He had just wanted to love and be loved, but he had been used by that woman.

"Don't worry Leopold, I know what it's like. Boys never pay attention to me and I'm always the girl who is alone at a dance. I'm sure you just thought you were in love—you didn't know."

Leopold smiled at Inez; it felt good that someone had showed him a bit of sympathy.

"I just can't believe I was so naïve. Me, a grown man," he said softly.

"You just wanted someone to love you, Leopold. It could have happened to any of us," Margaret said.

Mia began to pack up, and in a few moments the gear was ready. All this talk of emotions made her feel uncomfortable.

"Come, we must move," Mia ordered and soon they were moving at a brisk pace through the German countryside.

Inez now looked sympathetic to Leopold and walked closely behind him. It seemed she could tell that he was having trouble keeping the pace, and she wanted to make sure he wasn't too exhausted.

"I'm sorry you lost your wife and daughter, Leopold," she told him.

He looked behind at Inez and smiled a bit.

"They were everything to me. My daughter was the light of my life and such a fun little girl."

"Will you tell me about them? I lost my father and he meant everything to me. I know what it's like, and it's good to remember," she explained.

"How did he die?" he asked.

"In a mine," she replied softly.

"I'm sorry, Inez; it's true that mines are dangerous places."

"I know. My mother always tells me to be thankful for the time I had with him, but I miss him all the same."

They continued to walk and then Leopold turned and looked at Inez.

"Inez, you're a very pretty girl. Don't worry about boys, because boys can be very foolish. You will find someone who loves you for who you are, I want you to remember that," he explained. This made Inez smile.

"Thanks. Sometimes I do wish they stared at me like they stare at Margaret or our friend Sophie. Boys are *always* staring at Sophie. I just wish that they liked me for something other than sports."

"You're an athlete?" he asked.

"The best in our school. In fact, I'm better than most of the boys," she replied, not with pride, but with a kind of embarrassment in her voice.

"That's wonderful, Inez! I like to see girls excelling in sports."

"Boys don't seem to like it," she answered softly.

"To hell with those boys. If they cannot handle being bested by a girl, then forget about them and just try harder. Keep being yourself, Inez—don't try to be someone you're not. That was my mistake. I thought, *why would a beautiful, young girl be attracted to me?* I should have known something was wrong, but I wanted to believe it could be true. In reality, I'm an old man and not very interesting."

There was a now a hop in Inez's step at these words of encouragement.

"Don't worry Leopold, you can make everything right when we get to France, you'll see!" she said.

Just then, Mia told them to stop and to be quiet. In the distance, they could hear the barking of dogs and men's voices.

"They are on our scent. Come, we must move fast!" she ordered and soon all four were sprinting through the woods. As she ran, Mia threw down more of her powder to throw off the dog's scent. The barking was getting closer.

The farther they ran into the dense forest, the darker it became. Tall pine trees cut out the sun. Weaving between the limbs, the group resembled ghosts as they disappeared into the forest.

At a full sprint when they finally reached the edge of the forest, as they ran into a small clearing, each of them stumbled and fell—into a lake full of mud!

"Aaaaggghhhh!" Inez yelled as she felt her body sinking into the goo.

"Oh my goodness, I'm stuck! I'm stuck!" Margaret cried as her legs became immobilized in the smelly muck.

The mud was thick as stew and stank like an outhouse. It was so dense, they could barely move their legs or feet.

Then they started sinking into the mud. First, the mud covered their knees, and then it crept up to their waists, and then began to slowly devour their torsos. Everyone tried to move, but the more they moved their bodies, the more they sank into the mud.

"What's happening ?" Margaret screamed.

"Don't wiggle, it will only make it worse!" Mia answered.

Mia surveyed their surroundings. The mud pool was thirty feet wide. She spotted the trail about four or five feet away. She managed to keep her hands out of the muck. Mia heard screaming to her right and saw Inez trying to keep her head above the mud and watched as she sank into the dank pool. Reaching over, she grabbed beneath the surface, felt for Inez's shirt collar, and lifted her up, which took all of her strength. She pulled and pulled and finally Inez's head popped out and she let out a scream. Her face was covered in slimy muck, and her eyes were wide with terror.

Mia hoped their feet would soon touch bottom, but the mud was too deep. She was sure it would consume them all.

Inez tried to hold her head above the surface, but she kept slipping until all she could do was tilt her face to the sky so that only her face and lips were above the mud.

She began to scream.

TOUR DE CONSTANTINOPLE

"We better run!" Tariq said, to the agreement of Fez and Aseem. The boys tore down the street followed by Abdullah Ozek's three henchmen, two of whom were bleeding profusely from the face. The men were enraged and screaming every kind of profanity at the boys.

Down the street the boys ran, to the encouragement and cheering of the many onlookers who watched in astonishment as three young boys dared stand up to the gangsters of Abdullah Ozek. A small alley led off to the right and a man on the street pointed for the boys to run down it, and they happily obliged.

The alleyway was very narrow, with only room for two people side by side. The boys continued running and were dashing down a steep set of stairs. On both sides were apartment buildings and doors, and the stairs wound around in a circular fashion until they ended at a road.

Directly in front of them was a bicycle shop with a dozen or more bicycles standing out front. Wasting no time, Tariq grabbed a bicycle and, as he climbed on to ride, he yelled.

"Get on!"

"But I've never ridden one of these!" Aseem replied.

"Aseem, get on the back. Fez, jump up on the handlebars."

Fez and Aseem climbed on and it took Tariq a minute to get going with all the weight on the bike. The shopkeeper screamed and started to give chase. Tariq urged his legs on and at last the bike picked up momentum.

He could see a downward slope perhaps twenty yards ahead. If they could make it there without being caught, they might be able to make their escape.

All around, people stopped to gawk and yell as the bicycle with three boys hanging on for dear life sped past them with the shopkeeper and thugs in pursuit. Most yelled words of encouragement and clapped their hands in appreciation of the excitement.

Tariq stood up, hands on the handlebars, legs churning with force.

Fez, his backside on the handlebars, placed the tips of his toes on the knobs of the front wheel. Aseem held onto the seat and somehow managed to place both feet on the frame holding the rear wheel.

Aseem looked back as the thugs gained speed—they were now only about thirty feet behind them.

"Hurry up! They are almost on us!"

Tariq pedaled even harder until mercifully the ground began to slope downward. The bike began a gradual descent before picking up speed as the downhill slope increased.

The skinniest of the thugs ran faster than the others and soon was only a hair's breadth behind Aseem. He reached out, about to grab Aseem by the hair when Aseem bent forward and the man's fingers missed Aseem's neck, grabbing only a handful of air. The thug lost his balance and toppled hard to the ground.

Aseem looked back and laughed.

The bicycle continued to gain speed on the downward slope, putting more and more distance between the boys and the men in pursuit. The road was uneven—dirt in some places, rock in others, and gravel in still other spots. The bike jiggled and shook as it went over some gravel and Tariq almost lost control as the wheels tried to spin out.

They approached a slight curve, and Tariq yelled at Aseem and Fez.

"Lean your weight a little to the left!"

They did as instructed, and the bike tore through the town. Up ahead, they were heading right toward a man crossing the street with a string of fish attached to a pole on his shoulder.

"Look out!" Fez screamed repeatedly.

At first, the man ignored Fez's cries but once he realized the bike had much too much speed to stop, he tumbled out of the way, just as the bike came within inches of hitting him. Dead fish splattered under the bike's tires and the man jumped up and began shaking his fist and yelling a string of profanities at the boys.

"Sorry!" Aseem yelled at him and shrugged his shoulders.

"Tariq, where did you learn how to ride?" Fez yelled from the front.

"I was a delivery boy for Zijuan at the orphanage."

"You'd think you would have been a better camel jockey!" Fez answered.

"I know!"

The street flattened out and Tariq continued to pedal ferociously. The men, who had lost some distance, were still running at a full sprint and were now gaining ground.

"Hurry up!" Aseem yelled.

Tariq took a glance backward, saw the men were closing on them, and made a quick decision. There was a sharp right turn up ahead and he wanted to make it. Taking an outside line, he yelled to Fez and Aseem to lean with him to the left. Moving the pedals parallel to the ground so they wouldn't touch, the bike pulled to the right and Tariq had to make a slight adjustment to keep it from falling to the ground.

Going wide, they headed straight for a building where a crowd of women had gathered in front. The women watched as the bicycle rounded the corner and many began screaming.

"Aaaaahhhh! Watch out!" yelled Tariq as the out-of-control bike hurtled toward the group of women. The women were all dressed in bright colors and wore colorful head scarves. Their arms were full of baskets of fruits, vegetables, and meats.

Tariq urged the bicycle tightly inward to the corner, allowing gravity to take them. The bike tilted more and more on its side until it was nearly parallel to the ground.

Yet, somehow it didn't topple.

Instead, the bike missed the mob of women by just inches as it roared past and onto the next street. The thugs behind them, however, misjudged their speed and the angle of the turn and two ran straight into the women—sending the two thugs and half a dozen women to the ground. The remaining women, yelling and screaming, began berating the two men and hitting them with bread loaves, whole fishes, and large eggplants.

They came to another downhill slope, with a descent so steep that the bike had reached maximum acceleration down the street. The boys all leaned forward and, for a moment, allowed themselves to enjoy the exhilarating sensation of speeding downhill and the rush of adrenaline that accompanied the chase.

The descent finally ended and they were traveling at a pretty good clip, still gaining distance from the henchmen. Onlookers waved at the boys and got out of their way.

"I think we lost them!" Aseem yelled.

"I think you're right!" Fez yelled back. They all relaxed a bit until suddenly they heard more yelling coming from behind them. To their astonishment, when they looked back, they saw Ozek's men staring back at them. On their own bicycles!

The thugs looked comical on bicycles which were way too small for their large bodies. They screamed and shouted into the crowd and pedestrians dove out of the way.

Tariq pedaled harder and harder, but on the flat streets, all the weight he was carrying on the bike was slowing them down. When going downhill, however, all the extra weight worked in their favor, as they were able to pick up speed faster than the men on their own bikes

"That way!" Fez yelled and Tariq turned the bike sharply into a small alleyway.

"Aaaahhhhh!" all three boys yelled.

The alleyway was actually the entrance to a very, very long set of winding stairs.

Instantly the boys were bumping and bouncing downward on the stairs. They leaned back on the bike (as leaning forward would have sent them flying over the handlebars) and it took all of Tariq's strength to keep the bike straight.

Down the stairs they flew, bumping so hard their vision was blurred and their heads felt like marbles bouncing up and down on a wood floor. Everything became a blurred mess of colors and shapes as they sped downwards.

The stairs ended at a pathway headed downhill.

At the bottom of the hill, the end of the path led to a narrow plank, only twelve inches wide, that took them toward a building under construction. Little more than a skeletal creation of a series of wooden planks and scaffolds, the six-story structure had a rickety wooden walkway that connected the building to the edge of the cliff.

"Tariq! Stop!" Fez yelled.

"I can't!" came the reply.

The bicycle was going much too fast for him to try to stop it.

Tariq wanted to scream and close his eyes and jump off. But, he knew if he did, they would fall to their deaths. Instead, he gripped the handlebars tightly and focused all his energy on the narrow plank ahead. It was about twenty feet long, and if he could keep the bike steady, they would make it over the gap.

Lifting the pedals parallel to the ground, he aimed the bike dead center at the plank and didn't slow down at all. He knew from experience that speed meant safety on a bicycle. With speed came balance—and they needed all the balance they could get right now.

As the plank came into view, Tariq kept the handlebars steady and focused on keeping the front tire aimed straight down the middle of the plank. Tariq worried they were going way too fast. But suddenly, they were halfway across the plank and felt as if they were suspended in the air. On either side was a sheer drop of six stories. Construction workers stopped to gawk at the crazy boys on the bicycle going over their makeshift bridge.

Before they knew it, the bicycle had somehow made it across the plank and onto the roof of the building. Tariq applied the brakes and they skidded to a stop.

All three boys were breathing heavily with smiles on their faces.

"That was a close one!" Fez said.

"Nice driving, Tariq!" Aseem said and patted his friend on the back.

Tariq was about to reply when he saw the three gangsters still following them! They hadn't been so bold as to attempt to ride across the plank on their bicycles like the boys had. They had, however, abandoned their bikes and were now slowly walking across the plank with outstretched arms like tightrope walkers.

"Uh oh," came his reply.

The other boys looked and saw the gangsters coming for them.

Behind them, the gangsters gingerly walked across the plank.

"Trying to catch these boys is like trying to catch a chicken covered in grease," one of them lamented.

"My gut aches…I need to cut down on the baklava," another replied.

"Shut up, you two!" the leader shouted, tired of their complaining.

Up ahead, the boys were on the roof, thinking they had no way to escape, when Fez saw a way out.

"Tariq, look!"

Fez pointed to a ramp the workers had constructed for carting things up and down the building. The ramp was wooden and made of the same planks as the bridge.

"Let's do it!" Aseem shouted. Tariq steadied the bike, they all hopped on, and Tariq pointed it downward toward the ramp.

Soon they were gaining speed and rushing down the wooden planks.

"Left!" Fez yelled.

All three boys leaned their body weight to the left and Tariq turned the handlebars as the bike left the first ramp, landed on the fifth floor, went left, and was soon zooming down yet another ramp.

"Yaaaaaa!" Fez screamed as workers stopped what they were doing and pointed at the bicycle as it made its way down each floor.

Aseem looked behind and briefly saw the three men running after them.

"They're still coming. Go faster!"

The bike hit the second ramp with more speed and Tariq struggled to maintain control.

Behind them, the three gangsters were flushed with fury.

"Keep following them. Once they hit ground, they're ours for sure. When I get my hands on these kids, they'll be sorry they were ever born!" the leader growled as he took baby steps down the ramp and was already starting to tire.

Up ahead, the boys continued to speed down at a dizzying pace from the fifth floor to the fourth floor. Tariq could feel the bicycle wobble in his arms. They were going too fast, he was starting to lose his balance.

As he took the turn to go down to the third floor, he knew they were in trouble.

The bike sped down the ramp at such a high speed that there was no possible way they could make the next turn. Try as he might, Tariq was unable to hold the handlebars steady and instead of turning down the next plank, the bicycle continued to go straight.

Straight into a mess of boards standing upright against a wall.

With a mighty crash, the boys—and the bike—went flying in all directions. The bicycle smashed into the wall, instantly crushing the front rim and flattening the tire. Tariq landed on his back with a thud and felt a throbbing in his right elbow. It had been scraped badly in the fall and blood dripped down his arm.

He heard the men on the floor above them, their footsteps making very loud sounds.

"Get up!" Tariq yelled and went to hoist Fez up, who looked dazed. He lifted a plank off of Aseem and helped him up, too.

All three boys stared at the ramp, saw three pairs of feet approaching, and simultaneously exclaimed, "Oh no!"

They were sure they would be caught.

Then Aseem spied a cart, three stories below them. It was a garbage cart, used to haul out garbage from the various districts, filled with old and rotten food and waste.

Without speaking, all three boys knew what Aseem was thinking.

"Aim for the middle!" Tariq yelled.

"This is crazy!" Fez screamed.

They stood on the edge of the building, waited for the cart to come into the perfect location, and launched themselves off the side of the building. Floating through the air, they each moved their legs as if they were trying to walk through the air and flapped their arms like birds. The cart came closer and closer to them with increasing speed, but now it looked like they had mistimed their jump and would miss the cart.

All three boys screamed as they realized they were falling straight down onto a cobblestone road that would surely break their legs, and possibly kill them.

The world blurred by as they dropped faster and faster until the hard road was only seconds away.

"Hold on!" a voice shouted.

From the corner of her eye, Inez saw a boy of about fifteen standing on the edge of the swamp. He had blond hair and blue eyes and looked kind. He was dressed in the finest hiking attire and wore a pair of quality leather hiking boots.

The boy tossed a rope to Inez, who used all of her strength to lift her hands from the muck and grab the rope.

"Hold onto me!" she yelled.

Margaret and Leopold clung to her as the boy quickly wrapped the rope around a tree for leverage and began pulling them out.

Gradually, they rose above the surface of the muck. Mia grabbed onto Leopold's legs like a caboose at the end of a train.

The boy strained with all his muscle. The rope burned into his skin and his legs screamed in agony. Once he had pulled Inez out, he moved forward and began to carefully lift the rest of the group out of the mud.

Exhausted, they slowly crawled away from the swamp to solid ground. Everyone was covered in muck and grime and smelled awful. Although they had only been in the thick mud for less than three minutes, it had taken everything they had to keep their heads above the surface.

In the distance, the barking of the dogs grew louder and louder.

The boy, hearing the dogs, urged on the group of four.

"*Deutsche?*" he asked.

"*Français?*" Margaret replied.

"Come, we must hurry!" he yelled in perfect French and helped everyone to their feet.

They followed the boy into the forest as fast as they could. The trees were still thick and the boy wasn't following any particular trail—he knew the forest intimately.

They ran and ran, desperately trying to distance themselves from their pursuers.

Major Hostetler maintained a fast pace with his soldiers. His three Dobermans were quick on the scent and he was sure they would have their captives before nightfall. The dogs were getting more and more excited as the scent grew stronger and stronger and dashed ahead of the group about thirty or forty yards.

Suddenly, Hostetler heard a loud yelp and then sounds of his dogs crying. He and his soldiers ran ahead, stopping just short of the swamp full of muck.

All three dogs had fallen in and were now whining and crying.

Without thinking, Major Hostetler jumped into the mud and grabbed two of the dogs by the collar to keep them above the surface. The other dog disappeared beneath the muck, and Hostetler had to let him go.

"Throw me a rope!" he yelled.

One of the soldiers threw a rope over to him. He tied a knot around the collar of the two dogs and then ordered his soldiers to pull.

After pulling the dogs out with the rope, the soldiers reached down and hoisted the major out by his armpits. Hostetler was soon standing on solid ground, covered in the slime from his chest down to his leather boots. His socks were soggy, and his toes squished inside his boots, which were now filled with water and mud.

Bending over, he paused to catch his breath.

"Get the dogs back on the scent. We can't spare any time," he ordered.

The soldiers tried to send the dogs ahead but the dogs seemed confused. They whined and circled and then looked up at the soldiers.

"The mud must have done something to their noses—they have lost the scent," one of the soldiers said.

"You're right, the mud has covered the scent. The dogs will be useless," Hostetler agreed.

Hostetler stared into the forest, exasperated at their run of bad luck. It would be dark in half an hour. He and his soldiers would need to set up camp now. He'd just have to take a chance that they would be able to find the trail in the morning.

Captain Scopas sat in his living quarters, deep in thought, drinking a strong cup of coffee, and smoking a pipe. The room was almost completely dark, except for the glow of his lit tobacco.

His wife, Calliope, entered the room and immediately pulled back the curtains from the two portholes to allow in some light. Then, she lit two lanterns and sat across from Captain Scopas.

"What is wrong? Why are you here in the dark?" she asked.

Scopas took a long pull on his pipe and then a sip of dark coffee before answering.

"I am thinking of these boys...and my clan. Am I running a fool's errand? Endangering my clan out of blind revenge?" he answered flatly.

Calliope held her husband's hands in her own and allowed his callused palms to warm her soft and delicate hands.

"Do you know what holds our clan together?" Calliope asked.

Scopas shrugged his shoulders.

"It's knowing that if anything happened to any one of us, the rest would instantly take up arms. It goes beyond family, our clan. We are everything to one another. If you allowed your brother's death to go unavenged, it would create a divide in our clan that might never heal itself," she explained.

"The others don't question me?"

"Of course not, my darling. In fact, they are proud of you. They feel protected, and they are fighting for a cause. They are fighting for one another. If anything, this errand has made the clan stronger. It has given them a purpose."

Scopas smiled and took another drag on his pipe.

"These boys, Tariq, Fez, and Aseem…they remind me of myself when I was young. Fearless and longing for adventure. They are such good boys, and their bond is unlike any I've seen from boys so young. I just hope I'm not placing them in too much danger."

"This troubles you?"

Sighing deeply, Scopas thought before answering.

"It does. Because these boys are not ordinary. Imagine being stranded for days in the ocean, with death at your door, and finding a way to will yourself to survive. They fought in a war in Morocco. They have seen more pain and adversity in their short lives than most men twice their age. I believe in them, but I feel responsible for them at the same time."

She smiled at him.

"A very sensible answer," she replied and kissed him on the forehead.

Scopas stared deeply into his coffee as Calliope continued.

"This Abdullah Ozek is not a soldier. He is a vicious, murdering thug who cut down your younger brother and has murdered dozens of people. He is a very evil man, Scopas. A very evil man. If you do kill him, God will not judge you for such an action," she explained.

He nodded in agreement.

"And these boys, you must look after them. They are so young. Make sure you are there for them."

Nodding, Scopas got up from his seat and kissed his wife.

"Thank you," he whispered to her.

Breathing deeply, he went to the porthole and stared out at the water and the boats passing by. How he loved the sea. Allowing the salt air to fill his nostrils, he tried to clear his mind and forget his troubles. Slowly, he remembered the day that he rescued Aseem, Fez, and Tariq. He thought of how weak and dehydrated they had been and how close to death. He had been so worried for them, and had checked on them constantly until it was clear they were out of danger.

He couldn't help but think that none of this was an accident. Somehow he was meant to find these boys, and somehow he played a role in their play.

CHAPTER
— 20 —

LESSONS OF A DIFFERENT COLOR

1882—KATHMANDU

Young Foster Crowe was now twenty years old and still living with Lhak-Pa in Kathmandu. Today he was dressed as a beggar, with a tin cup in hand, asking pedestrians for alms. Some dropped a coin in the cup, but most continued on their way without a glance in his direction.

For a week he begged, even going from house to house asking for food. Some households were friendly and readily gave him a plate of warm food and offered blessings, while others slammed the door in his face.

"Why are you having me do this?" Foster asked Lhak-Pa.

"Must learn empathy for others. A true human being sees life from many eyes—not just eyes of rich man. Lhak-Pa have saying, 'Measure person by how treat poor and unfortunate, not how treat rich and powerful.' Will Foster shut door in face of beggar? Or offer meal and kind word?"

Foster nodded in understanding.

The lessons continued in this fashion—less studying in the library and more exposure to life. Foster worked many jobs and talked with hundreds of people. He traveled through Nepal and even down to India over to Bangladesh. His world was expanding with each passing day.

He continued to explore the catacombs underneath much of the city of Kathmandu. In them were secrets from thousands of years ago and remnants of languages that had long been forgotten. The catacombs became like a second home to him, and he could now find his way through them without the use of a lantern. He no longer found them creepy, quite the opposite—they were fascinating.

The dead whispered their secrets to him, and he gladly listened.

One day, Lhak-Pa came to find him and said he had an assignment like no other.

"What is the assignment?" Foster asked.

"Must kill a man."

"What?"

Foster stared at Lhak-Pa and he could see he was serious.

"Are you kidding me, Lhak-Pa? You've taught me so much about compassion and empathy, and now you want me to kill a man?"

Lhak-Pa nodded solemnly.

"Very evil man. Brought much destruction and pain to the land. Worse, is spreading an edict of fear and hatred."

"You want me to be an assassin?"

"When time right, yes."

"Who is this man?"

"A general who has enslaved many Tibetans and slaughtered hundreds."

"And you know this for a fact?"

"Yes."

Foster breathed deeply. He was at odds with what was being asked of him.

"Will I have many of these assignments?" he asked.

"Only when last resort."

"And how was judgment laid down for this man? Was there a trial and jury?"

Lhak-Pa shook his head.

"If man not stopped, will slaughter hundreds of thousands of people."

"And how do you know this?"

"Because power corrupts this man's mind. Because Lhak-Pa looks into future."

Foster didn't know how to respond.

"Are you some kind of fortune teller?"

"Yes."

Foster stood up and paced around the room.

"I won't do it—just like I wouldn't kill that tiger."

"Different."

"How is it different?"

"Tiger, as all animals, innocent. Simply survive in life. This man evil. This man lives for subordination, bondage, and death of others. This man like cancer that must be cut out of body."

Foster stared at Lhak-Pa.

"Do I have a choice?"

"No."

Foster left the house very agitated. He went to their park and meditated by doing a series of breathing exercises as he tried to focus his mind. Recently, images had been coming to his mind when he meditated, and he wondered if they would come to him today. He breathed deeply and relaxed his body. Suddenly, he saw visions of Tibetan people being killed by the hundreds and many more being chained and forced to work sixteen hours a day. He saw the face of this general, and even managed to see into his soul, which was a dark and twisted place. As his mind saw these images, his heart felt the pain of the Tibetan people and heard their call for help.

He accepted the assignment.

CHAPTER
— *21* —

BRUISED, BUT NOT BROKEN

Resting on his small hotel bed, Foster elevated his injured ankle on a couple of pillows to release the blood flow. He'd wrapped it in a bandage to help stop the swelling. If he put any amount of weight on it, his ankle throbbed and ached. His left hand and elbow were also sore and his head hurt.

He still hadn't forgiven himself for allowing Wu Chiang to escape. Failure was not something he was accustomed to, and it stung. Replaying the night over and over in his mind, he was sure there must have been something he could have done differently.

Foster took a sip of his tea, closed his eyes and thought of Wu Chiang. What he knew, and what he might do next. The only thing he was really sure of was that Wu Chiang was traveling by train. He didn't know where he was going, or when, or anything else.

All his hope fell on the shoulders of a random street boy who may have run off with his ten-franc note.

After struggling to get his bag packed, he hobbled down the hotel stairs, paid his bill, was able to hail a taxi, and instructed the driver to take him to the train station. Along the way, he purchased a walking cane to help him get around on his injured ankle.

It took forty-five minutes for the taxi to finally arrive at the train station. Between traffic, and some dubious wrong turns, Foster was sure that if he'd had the normal use of his ankle, he could have walked to the station faster.

He scanned the area, but didn't find Laurent hanging around outside where he'd first met him. There was no sign of him anywhere. After fifteen minutes, he still hadn't shown up, so Foster shuffled inside the station. It was full of people, and the smell of fresh bread and strong coffee filled the air. Walking up and down the platforms, Foster couldn't find any sign of Laurent. He studied the train schedules, but it was fruitless trying to guess where Wu Chiang might be headed. Dejected, he had just purchased a double espresso when, from behind him, he heard his name shouted.

"Foster, there you are. I've been trying to find you everywhere!"

Foster turned around and there was Laurent, who was breathing heavy with his hands at his hips.

"Laurent, I thought you'd disappeared with my money. I'm so grateful to see you," Foster answered.

"I found him. I found the man you're looking for!" Laurent said with a great deal of satisfaction.

"Really? Well done! Where?" Foster asked excitedly.

"He is on the train to Sarajevo. It left thirty minutes ago."

Foster immediately looked up to see when the next train to Sarajevo was departing. He scanned the departing schedule and finally found it.

Three days!

"The next train for Sarajevo doesn't leave for three days, I'll never catch him," Foster mumbled under his breath.

"I have that covered. I have a friend who is a steward on that train. When the train reaches Sarajevo, I told him to follow the man and report to you. Same deal, you give him fifty francs. Is that okay?"

Foster laughed and hugged Laurent tightly.

"My boy, that is utter genius!" Foster exclaimed and produced a fifty-franc note and gladly handed it to him.

"But the deal was for forty francs?"

"You've earned the rest. Now, who is this friend of yours?"

"His name is Gerard. I told him to leave you a note at the concierge desk in the Sarajevo train station under the name 'Foster.'"

"That is outstanding work, Laurent. Thank you so much. Now, I just have to figure out how to get to Sarajevo," Foster said.

"How about a motorcycle? I have a friend with a motorcycle for sale. It would get you there."

"A motorcycle? I've never ridden one."

"Ah, it is no problem. Very easy to learn and he'll give you a great price."

"Where is this friend of yours?"

"You wait here and I'll go get him. Don't move," Laurent replied. Within a second, he ran off through the crowd and disappeared from sight.

Foster studied the departure schedule and tried to do some manual calculations in his head. It was a two-day train ride from Paris to Sarajevo. It would be almost impossible to catch the train before it arrived, as it traveled a route that didn't follow any main roads. He would need to traverse over country roads. He imagined some of the roads would be dirt and pretty rough. Still, with a bit of luck on his side, he could make it in about two days if he took minimal breaks.

He was awakened from his daydreaming by Laurent, who was with a gruff-looking man in grease-covered overalls.

"This is Franck. He's a mechanic with a great bike for sale. An Indian 61 Twin—top class with a great engine!" Laurent explained.

"Where is it?" Foster asked.

Laurent and Franck led Foster outside, where the motorcycle was parked directly in front of the train station. It was a beautiful bike— silver with a leather seat and two leather bags on either side.

"Five hundred francs for it. It's almost new," Franck explained.

Foster winced at the price, but he knew it was his best hope. The circus didn't bring in much money, but he had a fortune stashed away from inheriting his father's estate. He never really needed the money, but it certainly came in handy in times of emergency.

Franck and Foster shook hands and agreed to the deal. Franck took the money and did a double take between Foster and Laurent.

"You weren't kidding he needed a bike," Franck laughed.

"Okay, now show me how to use this thing," Foster asked.

Franck started the bike and it roared to life. The engine was a bit noisy, but it purred like a finely tuned machine. Franck revved it a couple of times and then had Foster get on the seat.

After about ten minutes and a few quick tips from Franck, Foster had learned all the basics of shifting and using the clutch and brakes. He rode in circles in front of the station, and soon seemed to have the hang of it. He secured his belongings in the side cargo bags and tied his empty travel bag on the back.

"For five hundred francs, I'll throw in some riding goggles and gloves. It will be quite cold. Do you know where you're going?" Franck asked.

"Not at all," Foster answered.

"Okay, then I'll draw you a map on how to get out of Paris and then onto the main road to Sarajevo. You'll need to ask directions along the way."

"That's no problem," Foster replied. Franck proceeded to draw a map using Laurent's back for a writing surface. After five minutes, he handed the map to Foster, gave him some verbal instructions, and then patted him on the back.

"Thank you, Franck. I'll be off, then." Foster said, pulling his riding goggles over his eyes. He smiled and saluted to Laurent who saluted back. He kicked the bike into first gear, and it jolted forward and then sputtered along before Foster gave it enough gas to get it going. He was on his way.

"I hope he doesn't kill himself on that thing!" Franck remarked, watching as Foster jolted and jerked along the road.

"I think he'll be okay. Now, where's my commission? That's fifty francs for setting up the deal!" Laurent said and held up an empty palm.

Franck placed a fifty-franc note into the boy's hand and slapped him on his back. Laurent now had one hundred francs in his pocket, more money than he'd had in his entire life.

"So, what are you going to do with that fortune?" Franck asked him.

"I'm going to get a warm coat, some wool pants, and a nice pair of leather boots," came the reply.

Franck smiled with appreciation.

"A sensible investment."

CHAPTER
— 22 —

GALATASARAY!

Falling faster and faster, the boys were sure they were going to hit the ground when the garbage cart suddenly accelerated. It was now directly below them. Tariq stretched out his legs as he, and the other boys, landed directly in the middle of the oncoming cart. Amazingly, the landing was soft and none of them were in any pain from the impact.

However, the stench was absolutely terrible. Fez wrinkled his nose, and Aseem almost gagged. Tariq started dry heaving. The smell was a toxic mixture of moldy and rotten food and termite-infested sawdust. Spoiled meat was a constant problem anyway, but this particular garbage cart had the remnants of a decaying cow. Flies buzzed around the carcass and maggots covered the rotting meat—so many, in fact, that it gave the illusion that the entire bottom of the cart was moving.

Fez looked down, saw the maggots crawling everywhere and let out a primal scream. The other boys looked down, saw the same thing, and started screaming and scrambling to find a way out of the cart. They pulled themselves up to the side, and jumped out, screaming all the way. They frantically brushed off the maggots that had managed to attach themselves to their clothing.

They ran past the navigator of the garbage cart, an old man with only a few teeth remaining. Two mules pulled the cart. The old man had a piece of straw in his mouth and had long since grown accustomed to the nauseating smell. He smiled at the boys as they ran past him, as if it were a usual occurrence for children to run screaming from the foul contents of his wagon.

Continuing to run down the street, the boys noticed a mob assembled up ahead. Thousands of men, each clad in red and gold shirts, were yelling chants in Turkish and obviously very excited about something.

Joining the mob, the boys did their best to zip through the throng of men to lose their pursuers. However, the thugs, fueled by adrenaline, were closing in on them fast and were now only about ten feet away.

"Faster!" Tariq yelled, as he could see the anger on the thugs' faces as they closed in on them.

Aseem and Fez looked back in panic.

Suddenly, Pakize appeared next to them and began shouting at the men dressed in red and gold and then pointing at the thugs. The mob stopped and focused all of their attention on the three gangsters.

Without further provocation, the mob attacked the three thugs, hitting them and throwing them to the ground. Abdullah Ozek's henchmen, taken by surprise, tried to defend themselves, but they were outnumbered by the dozens of men, who hit and kicked and spit on them. Barely finding their feet, the thugs retreated, bruised and beaten. The mob continued to shout at them and chased the gangsters until they had vanished from view.

The boys walked with the mob along with Pakize.

"Pakize, how did you find us? And what did you say to those people?" Fez asked.

"I chased after Ozek's men as they ran after you," she answered casually.

"Who are these men dressed in gold and red?" Tariq asked.

"They are supporters of Galatasaray futbol club. There is a huge match today against Fenerbahçe. They are marching to the grounds. I told them those gangsters were Fenerbahçe supporters who had tried to beat me up because I support Galatasaray. All these guys know me and instantly attacked them!" Pakize explained proudly.

"I didn't know that futbol clubs allowed girls?" Aseem asked.

"They allow girls who love futbol and who know how to sing and fight," she answered with a wry smile.

The men around them, dressed in red and gold, cheered and shouted and slapped one another on the back in congratulations for chasing off the intruders.

"That will teach those Fenerbahçe donkeys to mess with us!" one of them yelled to the cheers of the others.

The boys walked along with Pakize and the mob of Galatasaray fans and tried to yell with them as they chanted and sang. Someone with paint came and painted the boys' faces red and gold, as they were now honorary members of their team.

"These are the Ultras...the most passionate of all the Galatasaray supporters. They are insisting we go to the game with them. Want to go?" Pakize asked.

"Yeah! These guys are cool!" Aseem replied to the smiles and nods of Fez and Tariq.

Soon, dozens of Turkish men and boys were hugging the boys and welcoming them to the team. They chanted and sang songs and laughed when their new friends tried to sing with them because the boys' Turkish was so bad. Marching through the streets to Union Club Field, otherwise known as *Papazın Cayırı*—the field of the priest—the boys suddenly found themselves in a crowd on one side of the pitch, while the supporters of Fenerbahçe, dressed in yellow and blue, stood opposite them.

Both mobs of supporters sang and chanted and taunted one another until, at last, the teams took to the pitch and the crowd roared for the players.

Each team's supporters cheered and groaned with every pass of the ball. The Galatasaray supporters waved flags, lit dozens of smoke bombs, and fired flares at the Fenerbahçe supporters, who fired flares back at them. They beat drums to keep time with the chants. Surrounded by hundreds of hairy and sweaty Turkish men who laughed, sang, screamed, and groaned, the boys were swallowed up by the passion around them and began screaming, singing, and following the game as passionately as the others. They shouted profanities at the Fenerbahçe supporters and gleefully cheered on the Galatasaray supporters.

After full time, the game ended in a nil-nil draw.

Which wasn't satisfactory to either the Galatasaray or the Fenerbahçe fans.

At the end of the game, both supporter groups charged into one another to the center of the pitch like two armies colliding on the battlefield. The hordes of swarming fans swallowed up the field, which became a melee of red and gold and blue and yellow and swept up the players and referees, too.

"Should we get involved in this?" Aseem asked. Fez and Tariq shook their shoulders.

Just then, a Fenerbahçe supporter struck Pakize and knocked her to the ground.

"Let's go!" Tariq yelled and all three boys joined in the fracas.

Players fought. Referees fought. And, of course, the supporters fought.

The boys picked up Pakize and with the other Galatasaray supporters, found themselves going toe to toe with their opponents.

Smoke bombs were hurled by the dozens and soon the field was covered in a thick smoky haze. Flares flew through the air and drums beat in the background as the crowd hit, kicked, wrestled, spit, and even bit one another.

Finally, after five minutes, the Fenerbahçe supporters were beaten back and began retreating to their neighborhood.

The boys cheered and rejoiced with the Galatasaray players and fans. They chanted and sang until their throats were sore.

Heading back to the safety of the *Osprey*, the boys laughed and reminisced about the game and what fun it had been.

"I never thought futbol would save our lives, but today, it certainly did," Pakize said with an exasperated voice, realizing they had been very fortunate to escape the grip of those gangsters.

"That was great fun! I'd like to go to another futbol match," Aseem remarked to the smiles of both Tariq and Fez.

"Are they always like that?" Aseem asked.

"Pretty much, they often end up in a fight of some kind. Today was actually pretty tame, usually there are knife fights and at least a few people are killed," Pakize casually answered.

"Wow, you take your futbol seriously here," Aseem remarked with the utmost of sincerity.

Abdullah Ozek stood in his warehouse surrounded by twenty of his gangsters. He glared at the henchmen who had been bested by Tariq, Aseem, and Fez.

The men shook in fear in the presence of their leader.

"Twice in the last week I have been insulted. The first time, someone stole the panther. And the second, three young boys made fools of my men. If people see that I can be embarrassed without consequence, then they will openly defy and mock me. Get these boys and make an example of them. I want them found and hung on a lamp post for all to see."

His men didn't make a sound or a move. They simply stared at him.

"Go through every neighborhood and offer three thousand lira for any information on these boys. Someone must have some information on them."

He paced the room, and his eyes were focused and narrow. It had been years since anyone had openly defied him like this. He was accustomed to absolute fear from the inhabitants of Constantinople.

"As for these animals, I want them shipped out as soon as possible. I do not want to lose any more, as the Chinese are giving me the highest prices for them. We will ship them across the Black Sea, through Russia, and on to China. We have some Siberian tigers we will pick up in Bataysk and then make the trek across the mainland to China."

Abdullah Ozek had no doubt that his men understood the seriousness of the instructions. His proven method of dealing with incompetence was to kill anyone who made a mistake. He provided a good life for his men, but it came with certain non-negotiable expectations.

That night Abdullah Ozek lay in his bed. He wasn't a man accustomed to worrying, but recent circumstances had him concerned. The finest silk sheets didn't comfort him. The gold and treasures stacked high on his walls didn't provide him with solace. In his bones, he felt fear. It wasn't the boys or the missing panther; it was the dreams of his dead master that plagued his thoughts.

It couldn't have been an accident that his master had warned him of three boys and then three boys happened to attack his thugs.

But why now?

He had finally started to drift off when the voice of his master came into his head once again.

Find the book. Bring it to Razikov.

Ozek sat up with a start. He expected to find his master sitting next to him, his voice had been so clear.

Instead, he stared at an empty bedroom.

Unable to sleep, he went to his desk, poured himself a double rakı, and wrote down the words that had just been whispered to him.

Find the book. Bring it to Razikov.

What book?

Ozek took another drink of rakı. The name *Razikov* caused his knees to buckle and sent shivers down his spine.

Razikov was a Russian mystic. An excommunicated monk who now ruled Russia's underworld and advised the czar and the royal family. Possibly an immortal demon that conversed with Satan himself and was a master of the black arts. His enemies had tried—and failed—to assassinate him six times. He'd survived an assassin's knife that just missed his heart, a bomb that exploded a second too early, and a poisoning that ended up killing his faithful dog instead.

Peasants maintained that he couldn't be killed.

Ozek had met him just once. Razikov stood over six foot six with a long black beard that gave him a feral look. He was skinny and gaunt with sunken cheeks. It was his eyes that Ozek remembered the most. They were sinister and mesmerizing all at once. Ice blue and hypnotic, Ozek had shuddered in their presence.

Ozek remembered thinking he had to be a madman.

Taking deep breaths, Ozek tried to steady his mind. He was being told something he knew must be important because hearing his master's voice in his head rarely happened. His felt a slight sweat form on his inner wrist and he felt dizzy. His master had been considered a priest of the dark arts and had taught Ozek the ways of the occult. Ozek had always been frightened when his master spoke of forces in the afterlife. At heart, Ozek was a simple thug and such talk of the supernatural terrified and confused him.

But now he was sure his master was giving him orders from beyond the grave. He had to find these boys—and this book—at all costs and deliver them to the mad monk called Razikov.

The next day, the neighborhoods of Constantinople were alive with activity. The henchmen of Abdullah Ozek went to every apartment and shop asking about three boys fitting the description of Fez, Aseem, and Tariq. They offered a reward to anyone with information leading to them.

Finally, they came to a certain bookmaker. Standing before them, he leaned back and smiled.

"I know of these three boys. In fact, I know exactly where they are staying and with whom," he said with a satisfied grin.

The henchmen, all mean and rough looking, pressed him for information.

"When I have the reward, then you will have your information."

The leader made a modest attempt at intimidation, but the bookmaker wouldn't budge. He was accustomed to dealing with Abdullah Ozek, and he knew if he gave the information first then he would never see the reward.

Finally, the coins were produced and placed on his desk. After quickly counting them, the man put the coins in his pocket and leaned forward.

"There is a young thief. A thief who makes a living stealing from Abdullah Ozek. Her name is Pakize and they are with her."

The leader, a stocky man with a broken nose by the name of Goker, listened attentively and then questioned him.

"A girl? Where does this Pakize live?"

"I don't know, but she's in the neighborhood. She sells me things and I give her cash. Ask around and someone will know her. She gives cash to the poor. The lepers probably know of her whereabouts."

Goker studied the bookmaker.

"So, if she is selling you goods, they must be the stolen goods of Abdullah Ozek?" Goker said in a menacing tone.

The bookmaker, suddenly realizing his mistake, tried to cover his tracks.

"Well, not very many things, I don't know where she gets them," he stammered.

It was too late.

"Anyone who steals from Abdullah Ozek will meet his death. You have stolen."

The bookmaker tried to explain but it was of no use.

Goker produced a long, sharp dagger. His two associates held the bookmaker's arms while Goker walked behind the man, placed the blade to his throat, and slid the blade from ear to ear. Blood gushed out and in seconds the bookmaker dropped to the floor—dead. Goker reached in the dead man's pocket and retrieved the coins he'd given as a reward.

"Our next stop is the leper colony. We will find this Pakize, and we will find these boys."

They exited the bookmaker's shop, leaving his body slumped on the wooden floor. A large puddle of blood slowly oozed across the floorboards. The leper colony was only minutes away, and with any luck, they would find the answers they were seeking there.

Pakize's neighborhood park was busy that day. Couples watched their children and cooked legs of lamb on spits over small fire pits. The old men played their chess and bocce while children played games and ran after one another.

Abdullah Ozek's men appeared without warning. A dozen in all, they went about terrorizing the inhabitants, interrogating them about Pakize, demanding to know her whereabouts.

But nobody said anything. They weren't about to tell on Pakize or give away her location. She was one of their own.

In frustration, the thugs smashed the chess tables, ripped up the garden and flowers, and tore down the archway.

Still, nobody said anything about Pakize.

Finally, the henchmen lit torches and threw them down at the base of the weeping willow tree. Mothers wailed—the tree had been there since before any of them were born. The elders pleaded with the men to save the tree. Some of the men tried to fight, but were easily beaten down.

The gangsters just laughed. Soon, the weeping willow tree that had watched over the park for so many years went up in a ball of flames that would be seen from all around Constantinople.

Strong in their defiance of the bullies, not one of the villagers told the gangsters where they could find Pakize—even as their precious park was being destroyed and burned to the ground.

Exasperated, the gangsters gave up.

"Now what should we do?" one of them asked.

"Nothing, perhaps Goker had more success," another answered.

As the thugs departed, the inhabitants frantically tried to save their park, but so much damage had already been done. The garden and flowers were destroyed. The archway, which was over a hundred years old, had been broken and splintered.

And their beloved willow tree had gone up in an inferno.

CHAPTER
— 23 —

REINHOLD AND THE BLACK FOREST

Mia, Margaret, Leopold, and Inez followed the blond-haired boy through the forest. He seemed to know every twig and branch, and it was difficult to keep up with his quick pace. Several times, he ran through a creek, climbed up some trees to get a look from above, jumped down, and doubled back through the trail.

"He has done this before," Mia said between breaths.

Inez studied the boy and decided he was beautiful.

"What's your name?" she asked.

"Reinhold," he replied.

"Reinhold, I like the sound of that. Where are we going?"

"To my grandparents' house. They live just around the bend and over those hills."

"My name is Inez," she said, and felt herself want to giggle, regretting that she was covered head-to-toe with slime.

He turned and smiled at her.

"Nice to meet you, Inez."

After the sun had set, the group came upon a house that sat alone in the woods. The large house was made of rock, with a wooden roof. Smoke rose from the chimney. A stable for horses and pigs could be seen on one side of the house, along with a small barn.

"Hurry, change out of those clothes and I'll get you some fresh ones," he told the group.

Margaret, Mia, Leopold, and Inez stood outside until Reinhold brought them some clean clothes. An old woman, who looked about seventy, came and greeted them.

"So, who are your new friends, Reinhold?" she asked. Her voice was low pitched and sounded as if a rock were stuck in her throat.

Reinhold introduced everyone and then his grandmother introduced herself.

"My name is Ilga and my husband is Christopher," Ilga said.

Her husband was busy chopping firewood, and the sound of his axe splitting wood could be heard in the near distance. Her gray hair was folded under, into a bun, and she had a slight stoop. She looked like a woman who had lived off the land her entire life. Her hands were rough, and her manner suggested a matter-of-factness about life.

"The soldiers are after them. I helped them out of the swamp," Reinhold explained.

"Get them into fresh clothes and I'll prepare some dinner," Ilga replied.

She smiled and went about warming a loaf of bread and some stew on the fire.

The four visitors washed off and soon they all stood in the living room, warming themselves by the fire. Ilga served them hot bowls of stew and fresh bread and butter.

Inez couldn't help but stare at Reinhold and, once, he caught her eye and smiled back.

"It is very kind of you to help us," Mia stated.

Ilga smiled and sprinkled some freshly ground pepper on their stews. The door opened and her husband, Christopher, entered with a bundle of firewood. He almost dropped the pile on the floor when he saw all the visitors.

"Who are these people?" he asked his wife.

"Reinhold's new friends, now put down that wood and get some warm stew in you," his wife scolded him.

Putting down the wood next to the fireplace, he continued to inspect the visitors with a confused look.

"I have to say, I am wondering why the German soldiers would be chasing two young girls from France and an old woman and man," Ilga asked.

"You're being chased by soldiers?" Christopher asked.

"Hush up and get your stew," Ilga admonished him.

Dejected, Christopher fetched himself a large bowl of stew and dipped some fresh bread in the gravy. He was a tall and slight man with short-cropped gray hair. His wool shirt was perfectly clean and tucked neatly into tan trousers held up by a leather belt. His trousers were smartly tucked into shiny leather hiking boots, which had been well polished, with the exception of a bit of mud from his wood-cutting excursion.

"I'm not so old," Mia replied defensively.

The old woman smiled.

"I did not mean to offend. It is just a very strange grouping of people."

Mia and Leopold looked at one another. They hadn't thought of a plausible explanation for why they were there, and how they had all gotten together, and they still weren't sure if they could trust this woman.

"What are your thoughts on the German government?" Mia asked. She wanted to know where this woman stood in the area of politics.

Putting down the stew pot, the woman sat across from them.

"Wars are started by old men and fought by young ones. Even out here in the woods, I hear rumors of war, and no doubt my grandson Reinhold would be one of the first to be drafted into the army. I do not want that to happen."

Reinhold stood and paced apprehensively.

"But I want to fight!" he replied.

"And who would you fight?" his grandmother asked.

"Well, I'm not sure, exactly, but they must have done something terrible."

His grandmother snickered.

"All ready to fight, and you don't even know who or why you are fighting. Such is the foolishness of youth."

This made Reinhold frown and fold his arms.

Mia studied the situation and instantly understood the dynamic and why Ilga had helped them.

"Do the soldiers come through often?" she asked.

"They come on the property to hunt our deer. Other than that, they don't bother us. We are much too far from anywhere."

"Yet you helped us escape?" Mia questioned.

"I didn't help you, but Reinhold certainly did. It sounds like you would have drowned in that swamp—a nasty business that mud pit is."

Mia looked at Reinhold.

"Why did you help us, Reinhold?"

Inez eyed him as well.

"I don't know. I just had a sense that you were good people. If you're running from the troops, I'm sure you have a perfect explanation."

"A sensible answer," Leopold replied.

"And what is that reason?" Ilga asked.

Inez stepped forward.

"They knocked me out and threw me in the back of a truck in France. Margaret followed me by hiding in another truck to try to save me. We were captured and taken to a prison camp, where we met Leopold and Mia. They are helping us return to France."

"Why did the soldiers knock you out?" Reinhold asked.

"Because I discovered they were spies. They are preparing for war," Inez answered, a bit embarrassed.

"Discovered spies? How brave of you!" Reinhold replied and Inez blushed. She couldn't keep from stealing secret glances at Reinhold.

"Preparing for war?" Christopher asked.

"It looks that way," Mia replied.

The group grew silent as Ilga and Christopher contemplated all the news they had been given. Ilga seemed to shrink in stature as she realized a war might be imminent and her grandson might be drafted into service. Or worse, she worried he might be foolhardy enough to enlist.

"This is unfortunate news. What do you need from us?" Ilga asked.

"You've already done enough. We should really be on our way, as the soldiers will be looking for us," Mia answered.

"Nonsense, you'll stay the night and you can depart in the morning. I'm not sure how much the soldiers can do tonight, anyway. It's starting to rain, or perhaps even snow, and it's nearly impossible to track anything, or anyone, in that slop."

Mia glanced outside and, indeed, it had started to drizzle, and it was so cold it seemed as though it would soon turn to snow.

"Very well. Your generosity is very appreciated."

"Reinhold, please prepare some bedding upstairs for our guests in the loft. We have some extra blankets in the dresser."

Reinhold put down his bowl and went to the ladder when Inez interrupted.

"I'd be happy to help you, Reinhold," she said somewhat bashfully.

"Oh, I'd like that, thank you, Inez," he replied a bit flirtatiously.

Inez put down her bowl next to his and joined him as they climbed up the ladder. Margaret sat back in her chair with a puzzled look on her face as she watched Inez disappear with Reinhold upstairs.

"It seems our Reinhold has a little infatuation? Well, that's good, we almost never get any company and I was starting to worry his best marriage prospect would be one of our goats," Christopher said and everyone laughed.

Margaret blushed at the mere thought of a marriage proposal. She was happy for Inez, but a little jealous as well. At fifteen, Margaret still hadn't been kissed and had never had a boyfriend.

Upstairs in the loft, Reinhold went about spreading blankets on the wood floor.

"There's only one bed, so a couple of you will have to sleep on the floor. I'll make it as comfortable as possible."

Inez felt tingles in her body as she stood close to Reinhold and helped him spread out blankets on the floor. At one point their hands touched and they both practically jumped, like their hands were on fire.

"So what do you like to do in France?" Reinhold asked.

"Play sports mostly, or anything in the outdoors," Inez replied and hoped her answer wouldn't be off-putting to him. Boys could be silly about a girl who liked to play sports.

"I love to play sports and be outdoors as well. My favorite thing in the world is skiing. Do they have skiing where you live?"

"A little, but not much. Usually I sled, but I love to go fast. We get a bit of snow on the hills around our school."

"Do you like your school?"

"I love it. The girls are all so nice and the teachers are really smart. I used to get in a lot of trouble at my old school," Inez replied, not sure how much she should say.

"What kind of trouble?"

"Um, well, once I threw a bunch of spiders on my brother and he ran down the stairs and broke his ankle. But I was in all kinds of trouble with my teachers anyway," she replied somewhat awkwardly.

"You poured spiders on him? Ha, that's great. I wish I had a brother or sister to torment. It's just me and my grandparents and they're wonderful, but not much fun."

"Do you get lonely out here?"

"Yes, a bit, that's why I want to join the military and see the world. Then, I want to go to university and become a doctor."

Inez nodded her head and smiled.

"Where did you learn to speak French?" she asked.

"Everyone around here speaks French. We're neighbors with Switzerland and almost everyone there speaks French. I also speak Italian and a bit of English."

"Oh, I only know French and a just a few words in English."

They finished putting down the blankets and some pillows.

"You're very pretty, Inez," Reinhold said and immediately felt embarrassed.

"Um, thanks." Inez replied. The fact was that nobody had ever called her pretty and she didn't know if he was lying or not.

After a few moments, a voice called out from downstairs. It was Ilga.

"Inez and Reinhold, come downstairs—I have some strudel and hot apple cider."

Reinhold and Inez stole one last glance at one another, smiled, and proceeded to join the others downstairs.

Just before dusk, Captain Scopas left his boat. It was getting dark, and he made his way up the streets of Fener before the city came to life for the evening. He kept his collar pulled up over his neck and a wool cap pulled down low over his ears, almost to his eyes.

He'd been delivered an encoded note by courier in the morning asking for a meeting. The note was written in a code he recognized as one used by a Christian underground group, so Scopas knew it to be authentic.

Making his way along the narrow streets, he cut through several alleys to ensure he wasn't being followed.

A high-ranking priest had called him to the meeting in the Greek community. Scopas wasn't told why or with whom he would be meeting. Only that it was very important and he was to come alone and keep the meeting a secret.

After walking for forty-five minutes, he came to a church commonly known as the Church of Saint Mary of the Mongols. It was the site of the last stand of Greek resistance to Ottoman invaders in 1453. The battleground was so bloody, and the Greeks fought with such valor, that the church was named *Kanli Kilise*, which translates to *Church of the Blood*.

Sultan Mehmet II was so impressed by the bravery of the Greek fighters that he allowed the church to remain as a place of worship for Christians. He even provided a written declaration that no future sultan would be allowed to convert it or destroy it.

It would remain then, and for all time, a Greek Orthodox church, and it was one of only a handful of Byzantine churches that hadn't been converted to a mosque by the Ottomans.

The church was small, capable of holding perhaps fifty or sixty parishioners. The architecture was traditional Byzantine with a tetraconch design—meaning there were four apses—each pointing east, west, north, and south. The walls were mostly white, with ornamental yellow stars painted in areas. The carpet was bright red, and the ceiling was a series of arches and stained-glass windows that allowed a good amount of light into the building. A beautiful mural of the Last Supper was painted on the eastern wall. Chandeliers illuminated by candles hung from the high ceiling.

Scopas knocked three times at the gated entrance. The door opened and Scopas was ushered inside by a tall priest with a long gray beard who wore an all-black vestment. A silver medallion with a thick chain hung around his neck, and in his right hand he held a solitary candle nestled in a ceramic holder.

"Come quickly, he's waiting for you. We don't have much time," the priest whispered.

The two went through a courtyard and into the church itself. Rows of wooden benches were arranged in the front of a golden altar. Candles burned on either side of the altar.

In the front row sat a solitary figure. The priest led Scopas to the front of the church and made introductions.

"Captain Scopas, this is Tanju Oktay. He is an officer in the Turkish Army," the priest said.

The man named Tanju Oktay stood and shook hands with Captain Scopas. He was dressed in a military uniform, his posture perfect and rigid, his face handsome, and his eyes curious and alert.

"Pleasure to meet you, Captain Scopas. Thank you for meeting with me," Oktay said.

"It is my pleasure. I have heard about your bravery in Benghazi against the Italians. Holding off a hundred and fifty thousand Italian troops with barely twenty thousand Bedouins and Turks is impressive," Scopas replied.

Tanju Oktay closed his eyes and bowed slightly to acknowledge the compliment.

Scopas and the priest took a seat as Tanju Oktay began the conversation.

"I understand you are enemies with Abdullah Ozek?"

"Yes," Scopas answered.

Oktay studied Scopas before continuing. He fidgeted, as if deciding whether to unload a secret to Captain Scopas. Finally, he sat down, leaned forward and began.

"Captain Scopas, it is no secret that our countries have a long and bitter hatred of one another. I am not here to discuss the war of 1453 or its aftermath. I am here as an enemy of the Turkish aristocracy and monarchy. Turkey needs to change. We must modernize or we risk falling behind the rest of the world. Already the government's bureaucracy and the corruption of the Sultan and his allies are weakening our country. They look only after the interests of the rich and nobody else. We engage in war after war, and this has left the country bankrupt and reeling."

Scopas listened intently and seriously. He studied Oktay and he liked the man. He was forthcoming, and honest, and held a charisma that filled the room.

"You don't like your own monarchy?" Scopas questioned.

"Not at all. In fact, I wish to rid Turkey of the monarchy and convert it to a modern country—a republic with open education, equal rights for women, and democratic ideals," Oktay replied.

Scopas couldn't believe his ears.

"A Turk who wants a democracy, education, women's rights, and modernization?" he questioned.

Oktay let the insult pass over him.

"Captain Scopas, Abdullah Ozek is an extremely powerful figure in Turkey. I don't think you realize how powerful he is. Essentially, he provides the muscle for the government. If Ozek were to fall, it would greatly weaken the power of the Sultan and this government," Oktay explained.

"So, you want me to kill Abdullah Ozek?" Scopas asked.

Oktay hesitated before answering.

"In a word…yes. The Sultan and the current government protect Abdullah Ozek. This Sultan is little more than a puppet right now, and this government has some very sinister ideas…especially when it comes to Christians and Armenians. If I were to go against them, it would be a disaster. However, if he were to be killed by an outsider, especially a Greek outsider, it would draw attention away from myself and my group."

Scopas rubbed his chin and thought about this, then, he smiled broadly.

"And what would I receive in return for killing this gangster?" Scopas asked.

"I would ensure the safety of your group and safe passage out of Constantinople. My organization has members in every area of government. No doubt it would help to have my assistance," Oktay explained.

Scopas breathed deeply and continued to study Oktay. This was serious business, and Scopas knew how to be a serious man.

"What a brave Turk you are. I believe we have an accord," Scopas replied, stood up, and extended his hand.

Oktay stood and shook his hand.

"Thank you, Captain Scopas. I would stay, but as a Muslim and an officer, it is very dangerous to be seen in this neighborhood and this church. I thank you for your assistance—may our respective countries learn to live as friends rather than enemies," Oktay replied.

"That is my hope as well. I wish you the best in your fight," Scopas replied and watched as Oktay made his way to a secret door that opened to a tunnel that extended almost two miles to the Hagia Sophia.

"What an intelligent young man. I think that Oktay has a bright future in government," Scopas said to the priest before exiting the church and making his way back to the *Osprey*.

Tariq hung his feet over the side of the *Osprey* and stared at the water below.

He looked across the horizon, completely lost in his thoughts. He felt the diary around the neck. It gave him solace to touch it, as if Melbourne Jack were still with him.

Standing up, he reached for his right calf and felt a sheath, secured by two leather straps. From it he took out the dagger that Malik had given to him. The blade was ten inches long and the handle was made from solid oak. Malik had shown him how to sharpen it using a rock or brick and instructed him to use grapeseed oil to care for the handle. It had been Melbourne Jack, however, who had taught him how to throw the knife.

Stepping back twelve paces, Tariq widened his stance, putting his weight on his back right leg. Grabbing the knife by the handle, and holding it like a hammer as Jack had instructed him, he brought his forearm up to a ninety-degree angle from his elbow, and then just slightly brought the handle back toward his ear. He launched his weight forward, and the knife flew from his hand, rotated once, and then stuck straight into the beam of wood he'd set up in front of him.

Retrieving the knife, he flipped it in circles, walked back thirteen paces, whirled around, and once again the knife rotated once before sticking straight into the plank.

Fez and Aseem watched Tariq from a distance.

"Fancy moves!" Fez said, walking up to him.

Tariq smiled.

"Jack showed me how to do it. It's hard at first, but after a little practice it gets easier."

Tariq now stood fifteen paces back and released the knife using the same motion. This time it rotated twice on its way to the target

Aseem shook his head in admiration.

Fez was more interested in the book around Tariq's neck than in the knife-throwing display.

"Can I see the diary?" Fez asked.

Tariq took the diary from around his neck and handed it to Fez. Flipping through it very gently, Fez was only able to identify dates and rudimentary sketches of various inventions.

"I wonder what it all means?" he whispered to nobody in particular.

Tariq stopped throwing the knife as Fez continued.

"Whatever it means, that diary meant everything to Melbourne Jack. We will return it, Tariq. It will be a grand adventure!"

Aseem studied the diary along with Fez. He wasn't a natural student like Fez, but the book definitely intrigued him. Finally, after watching Tariq continue to flip his knife at the wood for a few more minutes, he made an announcement.

"Tariq, I will officially never go with you on another bicycle ride. That was crazy!"

Tariq laughed.

"I used to race all around Tangier picking up and delivering packages for Zijuan. I was only allowed to take the bicycle out for deliveries because it was the only one she could afford. I really enjoyed riding it," he replied.

Aseem nodded and smiled.

"I wonder what Zijuan is doing now. I wonder what they are all doing now: Malik, Sanaa, Zijuan…," Tariq said solemnly.

"And Azmiya?" Aseem said with a smirk.

This made Tariq blush.

"Yes, especially Azmiya. I miss Morocco sometimes."

Tariq already felt better in the company of his friends.

"India is such a long way away," he said and, for the first time, let his insecurities about the journey slip out.

"Not for us, it isn't. Think of Sinbad the Sailor or Marco Polo. They traveled the world on their adventures, and this is our adventure," Aseem replied.

Just then, footsteps could be heard coming up the boat ramp.

"I'm so glad you boys are safe! I've looked everywhere for you!"

It was Pakize. She was breathing heavily and sweat dripped slowly from her forehead.

"We've got to hide, Abdullah Ozek knows of your identity and he has his spies looking for you everywhere."

The boys looked at one another and instantly forgot their melancholy. They were in danger.

"Should we wait here for Captain Scopas?" Fez asked.

Pakize shook her head.

"I don't think it will be safe for you. Abdullah Ozek has spies all over these docks. I think it would be best if you came with me," she answered.

"Okay, let's leave word with the crew. We'll hide out and then talk with Captain Scopas about what to do," Tariq agreed, and then returned the dagger to its sheath.

After leaving word with the crew, the four ran off into the dark and the shadows, in hopes that the many spies of Abdullah Ozek had not yet spotted them.

Pakize had a plan for evading Abdullah Ozek and his men.

"When the Romans conquered Constantinople, they built aqueducts to transport water around the city. The aqueducts emptied into hundreds of cisterns located in most neighborhoods. These cisterns served as underground reservoirs to store the districts' water supply. However, I use them to avoid detection, as they are completely unsupervised. After all, I am an exceptional thief," Pakize explained.

"So we've heard," Fez answered sarcastically, and the other boys laughed.

Tariq, Fez, Aseem, and Pakize now crawled on the top of an aqueduct just up from Fener. This particular aqueduct stretched on for almost four miles and ended in a long slide that emptied into the Basilica Cistern. The top was a half circle, about a yard and a half wide and over seventy feet off the ground. It was exposed to the sky, so the four literally crawled on their hands and knees inside the aqueduct so their torsos wouldn't be exposed. A small stream of water was always at their feet and bellies. The moon smiled down as them as they passed over the darkened apartments of Constantinople.

Finally, after two hours, Pakize motioned for them to enter a dark circle that led to the long slide down. One by one the boys entered, and one after another they slid down until they each landed with a splash into a deep pool of water.

It was completely quiet, except for the sound of the gentle movement of water echoing off the walls and ceiling.

The boys waited in the pitch dark for Pakize, who landed with a splash, and then made her way to the side. She hoisted herself to the surface, felt along a wall, until a match was lit, a torch was fired, and the boys could finally see their surroundings. This was one of her hideouts, and she knew it like a mole knows its own tunnels.

She then slowly lowered herself back into the water, careful to keep the torch dry.

They had landed in the Basilica Cistern—a massive underground reservoir that took up two city blocks. It was a huge cavern that acted as water reserve for the city. It was supported by massive pylons in rows and columns. The enormous empty space was both eerie and peaceful. The light flickered to show off two pylons, directly in front of the boys. The columns had been carved into a sculpture of a frightening woman. Her hair looked as if dozens of snakes were striking out from her head, and the expression on her face was horrendous, as if she were warning the boys to stay away.

The boys slowly swam past the sculpture of the woman, whose eyes seemed to follow them.

"This is very scary," Fez quietly said, watching the hideous statue above them.

"It's so silent," Tariq answered, staring at the statue.

"That is Medusa, sculpted in the time of the Romans. Legend has it that one look from her eyes would turn you to stone! Hurry up!" Pakize whispered to them.

The boys studied the statues as they swam by and made their way to the far end of the cistern, where they hopped up on a ledge that led into the doorway. They continued to follow Pakize and her torch along a maze of walkways that led just over the water, through a long and twisting tunnel, up some stone stairs, and finally to a wooden door. After pushing the door open, the boys found themselves in a large cemetery with graves dating back to the thirteenth century. In the center of the graveyard was a huge room with windows poking to the inside. They made their way through the maze of marble graves and exited to a street, which they followed to a large wooden gate in front of a huge mansion.

Pakize knocked three times at the gate, waited, and then knocked twice more.

The gate slowly opened and the four of them went inside before the gate was closed behind them.

The boys found themselves staring face to face with a leper, a man whose face was bloated and pocked with massive scaly warts and whose right eyebrow was so deformed it hung over his eye like a sagging flesh-colored balloon.

Pakize saw the boys' wide-eyed expressions upon seeing the leper, so she took them aside to explain.

"Boys, leprosy is a horrible disease that, at first, causes skin lesions like nasty and oozing cold sores. Eventually, the person's face comes to resemble a burnt marshmallow, and if the disease spreads into the hands and feet, this can cause deformities and permanent disability. It's terribly sad. Leper colonies are full of people affected with leprosy. They have been quarantined and sentenced to a life of exile from the outer world. They don't deserve this, when all they are guilty of is some bad luck. This is why I help them."

The leper held a candle in his hand and urged them to follow him.

"This is Adelet, he will help us," Pakize whispered.

The boys were in shock over Adelet's appearance. They followed behind as Adelet led them up some stairs and around a bend. The wooden stairs creaked under their footsteps and shadows danced playfully on the walls from the light of the candle.

As they approached another wooden door, Adelet produced a key. His hand seemed to shake as he inserted the key into the lock and gently opened the door. As he did so, he gave her a wistful look. Pakize, seeing his expression, was about to ask him what was wrong when he spoke.

"I'm sorry, Pakize. I had no choice," he said tragically.

The door opened and six giant men tackled the four of them. The boys recognized two of the thugs who had chased them. They were powerless, and were quickly subdued by the men, who tied their hands and forced them to sit on the floor.

"Why? All I ever did was help you," Pakize said as tears formed in her eyes and she stared at Adelet.

"I know that, but they said they would slaughter everyone and burn down our homes. I am so sorry, Pakize," Adelet replied with much sorrow in his voice.

One of the henchmen looked at Tariq. He was one of the ones that Tariq had kicked. Without so much as a warning, the huge man reared his hand back and slapped Tariq straight across the face. The slap burned Tariq's skin and instantly turned it a deep shade of red. A second slap burned even more and he felt blood trickle down his lip.

But he didn't feel fear. In fact, he stared at his tormenter with a smirk on his face. He wouldn't give him the satisfaction of seeing him beg.

"Take them to Abdullah Ozek," ordered the leader.

In seconds, the men placed bags over all their heads, blinding them. In no time they were shuffled out of the building, through the gate, and down the city streets. After twenty minutes, they heard a door open and they were led inside. They heard the door slam shut behind them. The room had a sharp, earthy smell. After walking about a hundred feet, another door was opened, their hoods were taken off, and all four were thrown inside a cage.

Once their eyes adjusted to the light, they could see that they were back in the warehouse with all the animals. To their left, a wild hyena paced back and forth. To their right was a full-grown Bengal tiger in a cage that was barely large enough to hold it.

One of the henchmen kicked the tiger's cage and the cat hissed and growled. Laughing, he threw his lit cigarette at the tiger and as the embers burned the cat's fur, it let out a ferocious growl.

Still laughing, the men walked away and out of earshot.

Their cage was so small and low, maybe three feet in height, and only about four feet wide and six feet in length. The four of them were crushed together, two of them facing the other two, and they could just barely stretch out their legs.

"I cannot believe the lepers betrayed me. I thought they were my friends," Pakize whispered.

Fez tried to console her.

"Don't blame them. I'm sure Abdullah Ozek would have killed them if they hadn't given you away."

Pakize didn't take much solace in his words, and her face looked sullen and dejected.

Aseem squirmed a bit and looked around. Everywhere he looked he saw caged animals. The tiger looked scared. The big cat stared into the distance, its body quivering in fear. Aseem felt sorry for it—he knew what it was to be caged and alone in the world.

"It's okay, big guy, we'll get you out of here," he told the tiger and somehow the cat seemed to understand him. Aseem couldn't believe how many cages there were in the warehouse, full of all kinds of different animals. They meowed, barked, and cried, and he was certain that every one of them was very frightened.

"What do you think Tariq? Any way out of here?" he asked.

Tariq smirked and smiled.

"These donkeys, do they think they can keep the likes of us locked up? They didn't even bother to frisk us before they threw us in this cage."

Tariq had that look in his eye: the look of someone who doesn't care about death.

He moved his right hand down to his dagger at his calf, but unfortunately, the guards returned before he could retrieve it. And this time they brought four other guards. The six men placed a sheet over a caged African hyena, slipped a dolly under the cage, and began moving it. The steel wheels squeaked on the wooden floorboards, and it took some effort from the men to move the cage. They were joined by groups of others who were also moving cages down the hallways and out the warehouse door.

"What do you think is happening?" Fez asked.

"I bet they are moving the cages to a ship," Pakize answered.

Throughout the day and night, Abdullah Ozek's henchmen continued to move the cages until the last cage remaining was the one with the four friends inside. An ugly guard with a broken nose took a large blanket and threw it over the cage, covering every square inch.

It was now completely dark inside the cage.

And then the cage began to move. It was brought up on a dolly and then roughly hefted onto some kind of wagon. The four prisoners felt the wagon move beneath them.

In the dark, it was terrifying.

"What do you think they're going to do to us?" Fez asked.

Pakize was quiet for a while before answering in a soft voice.

"Abdullah Ozek generally likes to make examples of people who have betrayed him. Normally, we would just have been hung from the lamp posts for all to see."

This answer caused Fez to go silent, as the thought of being hung from a lamppost as food for the crows almost made him sick.

The cart rumbled along. It was slow moving and the grunts of men could be heard as they pushed the cart around a corner and then another.

At one point it went down a hill and then slowed for a minute before going around a bend.

Tariq didn't say anything the entire journey. He stared forward with a pensive and determined look on his face. He didn't say anything because he was thinking. He was thinking about escaping. He was thinking about killing Abdullah Ozek. He reached down with his hands and brought out the dagger hidden on his calf and handed it to Fez, who began sawing away at Tariq's leather restraints.

Finally, Aseem spoke up.

"What are you thinking about, Tariq?" he asked.

"A window of opportunity," Tariq replied slowly.

Aseem nodded his head.

"We'll have to act fast," he said as Fez finally finished sawing through the straps until Tariq's hands were free. Dagger in hand, Tariq quickly went to work freeing his friends.

"They'll unlock the cage door, probably with one guard, or perhaps two. We'll need to distract those guards and look for an exit," Tariq whispered as he worked.

"They'll handle us roughly, so let's see if we can get them to grab hold of our shirts. Have them loose so we can duck out of them," Aseem replied.

"I can look for the best exit. Usually the guards will be bunched in one area, so I'll look in the opposite direction," Fez said.

"We'll only have a few seconds' head start, probably not quite enough time. We'll need some kind of obstacles to run around or over. Those guys are mostly big and fat, and we'll need to slow them down," Tariq responded as he freed Fez and started on Pakize's restraints.

"An alleyway would be good, or maybe stairs. Our best bet might be to run into a building with narrow corridors and stairs. They'll have to follow us in single file," Aseem said.

"If we get separated, meet back at the boat. If you're captured, don't give up Captain Scopas. Make up a story and stall," Tariq ordered.

Pakize listened to the boys with a sudden interest as her hands were freed.

"You all have done this before?" she asked, rubbing her wrists where the leather straps had been tied.

"You have *no idea*," Fez replied and all three boys smiled.

"You really think we can escape?" Pakize asked.

Fez patted her on the shoulder.

"Trust me, we're professionals."

The cart bumped along for another half an hour. All four were now set to escape once the door was opened.

The cart stopped and the four tightened their bodies and readied for an escape.

Suddenly, the blanket was taken off the cage. Squinting against the sun, they could see that they were now on the deck of a ship. They watched as a man leaped up on top of the cage and fastened a chain to the top.

Directly in front of them was Abdullah Ozek and surrounding him were about twenty of his men. They were a motley crew—most were hairy and ugly, and potbellies hung over the waists of their pants.

A raft of pelicans flew overhead.

"So, here we have our little thieves," Abdullah Ozek said and his crew laughed with delight.

Up close, Abdullah Ozek looked even more fierce. His eyes bore blackness and hatred. Muscles protruded under his shirt.

He glared right at Tariq, who met his stare with not one ounce of fear. Ozek was studying him and Tariq realized he'd noticed something protruding under his shirt.

"What is that?" Ozek asked, and before Tariq could respond, Ozek yanked the diary from his neck.

Ozek took a hard look at the diary and then began flipping through the pages, smiling as he did so.

Find the book.

The memory of his master's voice flooded his mind. The book was encoded, and included many diagrams and illustrations and Ozek was sure this was the book his master had directed him to find.

Tariq went white with horror and then crimson with rage. He wanted to reach through the bars, grab the diary back, and then punch Ozek in the nose. Grabbing the bars with his hands, he spoke directly to Ozek. His voice was steely and his eyes like those of a hungry lion.

"I'm going to get that book back…mark my words, Ozek."

The seriousness in Tariq's voice actually intimidated Ozek for a second. Nobody had dared talk to him in that manner for many years. He glared back at Tariq, and didn't see a boy.

He saw something else. He felt something different. It was as if all of the pain and torment Tariq had ever experienced in his entire life was emerging from him in that moment. The death of so many of his loved ones, and the hardscrabble life of a street boy in Tangier—all the suffering he'd endured seemed to seep through his bones and skin.

Ozek saw not a boy, but a warrior.

"Well, I was just going to kill you quickly. But, I think we need a little entertainment, don't we boys?" Abdullah Ozek yelled and the men laughed sarcastically.

"Secure the cage," Abdullah Ozek ordered.

A small man with greedy eyes placed a thick iron chain around the bars and fastened it with a lock. Once he was sure the lock was tight and secure, he smiled at the four.

"Wouldn't want you to escape, now would we?" he said and laughed.

The cage was then attached to a crane. Abdullah Ozek nodded and the crane lifted the box off the deck and swung it out over the ocean.

Inside the cage, the four were suddenly very panicked. This isn't what they had bargained for. Abdullah Ozek had no intention of opening the cage and giving them an opportunity for escape. They stared at the ocean below them and the thin cable holding them up.

"Let's play a little game called, 'who can hold their breath the longest'!" Abdullah Ozek yelled and the laughter from the crew grew even louder.

Suddenly, the crane's cable started moving and the cage began to plunge downward. Each prisoner held on tight to a bar and prepared for impact.

"Take a deep breath!" Aseem yelled.

The cage hit the ocean's surface hard and instantly started sinking. In a second, they were underwater and moving downward fast. About twenty feet below the surface, the cage suddenly stopped moving. Bubbles were all around them. The boat was just barely visible from that far below. They were surrounded by blue water.

Tariq handed his dagger to Fez, who immediately began trying to pick the lock on the cage. There were now two locks, the one on the cage door and the one on the thick chain that surrounded the cage. Fez was, without a doubt, the best lock picker of all the boys.

Holding the knife steady, Fez understood it was their lifeline. He tried to calm his nerves and keep calm. He couldn't think about drowning. He couldn't think of failing. Closing his eyes, he placed the tip of the knife into the lock and began exploring the pins and tumbler.

Tariq and Aseem immediately went to work on the lock on the chain. Pulling the lock toward them, they didn't have anything to pick it with until Pakize pulled a small piece of wire from her pocket—a necessary and ubiquitous piece of equipment in her profession as a thief—and inserted it into the lock.

For thirty seconds, Fez and Pakize focused on nothing but the locks. Picking a lock is a matter of releasing a series of pins and then the tumbler. When an object of the right shape is inserted in the lock and the right pressure is used, the pins let go. Once the pins and tumbler are released, the shackle will open.

Pakize was growing increasingly frustrated—no matter what she tried, her lock wouldn't open.

Fez felt one pin release and then two. It wasn't a difficult lock to pick, but he also had to concentrate on holding his breath.

Another thirty seconds passed, and Fez could feel his lungs begin to search for air.

The third pin went and then the fourth. Fez felt the tumbler release and the shackle open.

He'd picked the first lock!

A minute and a half and his lungs were now screaming for air. He handed the dagger back to Tariq.

Pakize was frantically trying to pick her lock. A cursory glance and she could see the growing terror on everyone's faces. Fez was starting to look panicked as his lungs grasped for air.

She tried the wire again, but the first pin wouldn't budge. Her hands had begun to tremble with fear and she was starting to get dizzy.

She couldn't do it. She couldn't pick the second lock.

They were going to drown.

Ozek had won.

CHAPTER
— 24 —

TO SLEEP WITH THE FISHES

The barking of the dogs could be heard through the night. It was distant but it was unmistakable.

Inez and Margaret woke to the whispered voice of Mia.

"Come, both of you, we must go, the dogs have found the scent."

Inez and Margaret sat up, got dressed, woke Leopold, and were ready in a matter of moments. Their knapsacks had already been packed for just such an emergency.

Candles were lit and the four tiptoed downstairs and tried not to wake Reinhold and his family. But soon, the light of a lantern illuminated the entire downstairs.

Reinhold and his grandparents stood in front of them, each in their pajamas, hair mussed from sleep, and then began frantically scurrying about.

"They're about a mile away. I imagine you'll have a thirty-minute head start. There's a trail out back. Reinhold, put on a jacket and show them the way," Ilga instructed.

Reinhold threw on some wool trousers, a lambskin coat, and his hiking boots. Taking a lantern with him, he opened the door and the bitter cold from outside rushed into the house.

"It's snowing," he whispered.

Outside, the temperature had fallen ten degrees and tiny snowflakes drifted down from the heavens. It wasn't a full-on snowstorm, just a few flakes here and there.

"Snow is good, it will make it much harder for the dogs to track you," Christopher said.

"But it will be quite easy to track our footprints," Mia exclaimed, a bit testy with Christopher's lack of understanding of their predicament.

"Good bye and good luck. May God watch over you," Ilga said and hustled them all outside.

The biting cold hit their skin and the complete darkness was disorienting. Reinhold moved to a jog and the four others followed behind him. Still sleepy, nobody said a word and the only sound was the snow crunching beneath their boots and the distant sounds of howling dogs.

Soon they entered the forest, and the outline of tall skinny pine trees could just be seen against the dark. They followed the glowing light of Reinhold's lantern as he darted in and out of the trees in an attempt to make a difficult track for the dogs to follow. Soon, the sound of their heavy breathing joined in with the crunching snow. For twenty minutes they ran until they came to a clearing just up a hill.

"Okay then, this is where I leave you. Follow that trail for about two miles and then just keep heading southwest. You'll see a burned out tree and just go to the right. The dogs will have trouble tracking you in the snow, but they'll have an easier time tracking your footsteps in the daylight. Try to make up as much ground as you can tonight and, hopefully, the snow will cover your tracks overnight," Reinhold explained.

Mia nodded her head in thanks and began walking on the trail, followed closely by Leopold and Margaret. Only Inez remained standing in front of Reinhold, sheepishly looking at the ground.

The snow was falling on them, and his cheeks were red from the cold. Steam from their breath disappeared in the mountain air. They stood there for a few seconds, staring at one another.

"Um, thank you for everything," she nervously said.

Reinhold went to her, placed a finger on her chin, and lifted her head up so her eyes could meet his own. Then, he leaned forward and kissed her on the lips.

Inez unconsciously put her right leg in front of her left and it felt as if her entire body was going to go limp. It was her first kiss and Reinhold's lips felt soft and perfect against hers.

"I'll write to you at your school, now go join the others," he told her.

Inez blushed and started to jog after the other three, who had a head start. After about thirty feet, she turned and looked back and Reinhold was standing there watching her leave. She waved her hand goodbye and he waved his hand in return. Then, she started sprinting down the trail with a huge smile on her face, catching the others in no time at all.

"What are you so happy about?" Margaret asked between breaths.

"Nothing," came the reply.

Even in the dark, Margaret could see the huge smile on Inez's lips.

"He kissed you, didn't he?"

Inez broke into an even wider smile and giggled a bit.

"I can't believe it. We're on the run in the middle of Germany and you manage to get your first kiss. I've never even been kissed, Inez!"

Inez couldn't say anything in return. She kept up a silly smile on her face.

"Well, how was it?" Margaret asked.

"It was so romantic and he's such a good kisser. I really liked kissing him in the middle of the forest with snowflakes falling all around us."

"Well, I'm envious of you. You realize you're the first one of any of us to get a first kiss? Sophie is going to be so jealous when she gets word."

Inez beamed with pride. Never in a million years would she have guessed that she would be the first one to get a kiss, and from such a handsome young boy as Reinhold.

"Do you believe me now when I say you're not an ugly duckling?" Margaret scolded her.

Inez continued to smile.

"I guess so," she whispered back.

Major Hostetler drove his men and the dogs relentlessly through the night. Having lost the scent in the mud, he had them walk in circles around the area of the swamp until, after hours, they picked it up again. Lanterns were produced and the company pressed on through the night and the cold.

Hostetler knew that if they waited for daybreak, and it continued to snow, the trail would be lost for sure.

Still, he looked at the dogs and his men and saw their weariness. Running in mud-caked clothes in the cold night was not easy. Bags formed under their eyes from sleep deprivation.

The farmhouse sat nestled in a clearing. There wasn't any kind of light or activity and no smoke came from the chimney.

They followed the dogs, who led them directly to the farmhouse. As he knocked loudly on the door, Hostetler thought it would be a good idea to give the dogs and his men some rest. He continued to knock for a solid minute until, finally, the door opened and Major Hostetler found himself staring into the business end of a shotgun.

"Who are you and what do you want?" Christopher held the shotgun in his hands.

Major Hostetler took a step back.

"I am Major Lars Hostetler of the German Army. We are pursuing wanted fugitives and the trail leads directly to your farmhouse," Hostetler said in a firm voice.

"Don't know anything about any fugitives. Haven't heard anything all day or night. Possible they could have snuck up and then rested in our barn," Christopher yelled at him.

"I'm sure you won't mind then if we search your premises?" Hostetler asked.

Christopher held the gun right at him. He had expected this kind of welcoming, and this kind of answer.

"Of course, anything for the German Army. You and your men must be freezing. Please take your boots off, however, as I don't want my floor to get muddy. Ilga, get these men some nice apple cider and some food."

Hostetler was taken aback by the sudden change in attitude from the old man.

"I'm sorry for the shotgun, Major. As you can imagine, we don't get many guests in these parts and one can never be too careful," he explained, and walked back toward the kitchen. Already, Ilga had lit some lanterns and was warming a pot of cider, a pot of beef stew, and some sourdough bread.

"Search all you want, Major, you won't find anything here," Christopher told them.

Hostetler had his men remove their boots before entering the premises. All of the men were thankful to be getting some shelter from the cold. A wood fire was quickly made and they all sat around it, allowing the flames to heat their frigid bones and dry their damp clothes.

Hostetler took a lantern and proceeded to search the entire house. Searching high and low, he found nothing.

Christopher and Ilga went about preparing the cider and food. They took more time than was necessary and made sure the fire was especially hot and the food fragrant. Ilga mixed some dried chamomile into the cider and stirred it until it dissolved and blended in with the apple scent. Ilga used chamomile as a sleep aid as it was known to be an excellent herbal remedy for insomnia. She also stirred some into the stew with the other herbs.

After twenty minutes, the meal was served and Ilga and Christopher sat around the table with the soldiers. They had made an extra big pot of stew and insisted that the soldiers all have two helpings. They offered them huge hunks of bread and two glasses of the warm cider.

Their generosity was not declined.

"A bit for your dogs as well? They must be cold and tired, running through the night like this," Ilga asked and, before Hostetler could answer, Christopher opened the door and gave a large bowl of stew to each dog. They happily devoured the treat.

Finally, after the food was gone and the cider had been drunk, Hostetler ordered his men to put their boots back on and continue with their search.

"Please check our barn, Major Hostetler. I don't like the idea of any fugitives lurking about," Ilga asked.

"Of course, thank you for feeding my men and for your generous hospitality," Major Hostetler answered. He ordered his men to thoroughly search the barn, but after turning it upside down, they found nothing.

While they had been enjoying their dinner, the snow had begun to come down harder and there was now a light dusting on the ground. It took twenty minutes for the dogs to find a scent outside of the barn that led away into the forest.

"They found the trail," Ilga whispered with worry.

"You put chamomile in their cider?" Christopher asked.

"And the stew," Ilga replied.

"Well, they have more than a ninety-minute head start, and it will be difficult to track them through the night. Trying to run in the dark on a full stomach and a head full of chamomile won't be easy," Christopher said and that made Ilga smile.

After an hour in the forest, Hostetler was frustrated by their lack of progress. The dogs kept losing the scent, and his men were lethargic beyond belief. He even caught one of them napping when they had to stop to allow the dogs to circle and find the trail. Even he was having trouble staying awake.

The hunt was turning out to be more challenging than he had expected.

Pakize felt lightheaded. She wanted so hard to take a gulp of air. She could see the panic on the faces of the others. Just when she was certain they were going to drown, the cage began moving up toward the surface. The minute it reached the surface, all four opened their mouths and took deep gasping breaths. Everyone was drenched, and seawater dripped from their soggy clothes. As the cage was lifted up above the water to the level of the ship, the sunlight blinded their eyes and laughter filled their ears.

The crew was laughing at them.

"Ah, I see you managed to survive. That is excellent work, perhaps some of you are part fish?" Abdullah Ozek mocked them to more laughter from the crew.

The four looked at one another and nobody said a word. Everyone was lightheaded and nauseated from a lack of oxygen.

"Well my friends, it has been interesting, but, now it is time for you all to die. Don't worry, your bodies will go to good use. The tigers haven't been fed today," Ozek yelled to more laughter from the crew.

Tariq saw Ozek nod to a crewman, who released a lever and the cage once again plunged down into the water. Instinctively, everyone took a deep breath as the cage once again plunged below the surface. Only this time, it didn't go underwater just twenty feet, but to thirty feet or more. It was completely dark and they could no longer see the surface or one another very well. Everyone's ears popped.

Pakize immediately produced the wire again and continued trying to pick the second lock. Already lightheaded, she had to force her mind to focus. She thought of her neighborhood and decided right then and there she wasn't going to die. She wasn't going to let a gangster like Abdullah Ozek get the better of her.

In the darkness of the cage, Fez motioned for her to hand him the piece of wire, but she shrugged him off. He looked as if he were starting to panic, his eyes growing wide as his lungs searched for air.

She began to get angry.

Focusing more deeply, she pictured the lock mechanism in her mind. She pictured how it was built, how it was designed, and the alignment of the pins. She thought of her fingers as those of a surgeon—perfectly coordinated, with a light touch. Closing her eyes, she moved the wire just millimeters back and forth.

Her body wanted to lose consciousness, but she forced her mind to focus. She continued to move the wire, and thought of nothing but disengaging the pins.

A shoal of fish swam up to them from outside the cage, perfectly content in their natural habitat. They seemed amused by the humans who looked so out of place in their aquatic world.

The lock opened!

Quickly, Pakize slid the lock and chain off the cage and they pushed the door open. They all swam out, but Tariq could see that Fez wasn't doing so well—his eyes were drifting up inside his head. Tariq looked at Aseem and together they grabbed Fez under the armpits. They were still very deep under the water and they couldn't very well swim straight to the top as Abdullah Ozek and his crew would spot them.

Through the darkness they swam and Tariq could see the life drain from Fez's face. Bubbles rose from his mouth and his body grew limp.

Pakize was swimming up ahead of them and they followed her feet. Tariq's lungs burned and they did everything they could to resist taking a breath, focusing only on saving their friend and getting away from Ozek's men. Now that freedom was so close, they couldn't very well drown.

Tarik saw Pakize's feet begin to rise to the surface. The boys followed her, dragging Fez who was now completely limp in their arms. Up they rose until they finally broke the surface, totally exhausted. They sucked down huge swallows of precious oxygen.

But Fez couldn't; he was unconscious.

They had emerged to find themselves behind some barnacle-infested pilings of an old pier. A boat was tied to the opposite end of the pier. They snuck over to the far end of the boat and flung themselves over the side and onto the deck. Pakize went first, and then had the boys lift the lifeless body of Fez up to her. She gently placed him on the deck of the boat while Aseem and Tariq came aboard.

Fez was unresponsive. Tariq and Aseem looked down at him with wide eyes and a look of terror on their faces. They didn't have time to appreciate their escape or their freedom, all they could think of was their friend who lay dead in front of them.

"Lift his head up and to the side," Pakize instructed. She began pumping up and down on his chest with both her palms, careful so their heads couldn't be seen by Abdullah Ozek and his crew.

"Tariq, breathe into his mouth," she instructed.

Tariq put his lips to Fez's lips, which were ice cold, and blew very deep breaths into his mouth.

"Okay, good, now stop," Pakize ordered and resumed pumping down on his chest.

"Again," she ordered and once again Tariq blew breath into Fez's mouth.

They repeated this twice. Just when they all thought they'd lost him, Fez started choking and spit up what seemed like a gallon of seawater. Lying on the deck, gagging and gasping, he opened his eyes and drowsily stared into the smiling faces of his friends.

They had saved him!

The crew laughed as the cage was lifted out of the water. But this time, the door was wide open and the cage was empty.

All laughing stopped.

Abdullah Ozek was instantly furious and clenched his fists in rage.

"Scour the shores and search the water. I want them found and executed, do you hear me?" he roared.

Without hesitation, his crew searched the waters and shoreline for an hour, but found nothing.

"Perhaps they drowned?" one of them said to Ozek.

He turned and punched the man in the face, breaking his nose and splattering blood everywhere.

"They did not drown, they are mocking me!"

After searching in vain for another hour, the crew gave up and began preparing for departure. Their mood was one of dejection, as it was bad luck to start a sea journey on an unfortunate note. The fact that Abdullah Ozek was now in a murderous mood only made their lives more difficult.

Ozek went to his cabin and began flipping through the diary of Alexander the Great. It contained languages he did not understand and many strange diagrams and pictures. Whatever this book was, it was important. He locked it in his desk.

He then gave orders to go through the Black Sea and directly to Russia.

And then he would personally deliver this book to Razikov.

CHAPTER
— 25 —

A BUCKING AND KICKING
IRON HORSE

Foster tore through the streets of Paris, almost crashing twice. Once when he nearly sideswiped a horse-drawn cart and another when he skidded through a mud puddle and almost dumped the bike on its side. After two wrong turns, he managed to find his way out of Paris and headed north on a dirt road. The bike had quite a bit of power. Once he got to the open road, Foster pulled back the throttle and got it going to almost forty miles per hour. It was exhilarating to speed along the road, dust kicking up behind him, the French countryside as far as the eye could see. He whizzed along, and farmers stopped plowing their fields to wave. He happily waved back. Barely slowing down to go through towns, spectators at cafes either clapped—impressed by his speed—or shook their fists at him in anger as he buzzed through.

He loved the thrill of riding the bike and was eternally grateful for the good fortune of meeting Laurent. He didn't actually believe in good fortune or luck, but he did believe that the Red Hand was somehow guiding him, and he knew he had to make it to Sarajevo in time to stop Wu Chiang from executing whatever devious plan had hatched in his evil little mind. Something inside him warned him that Wu Chiang was capable of unspeakable evil and destruction, and he hadn't a moment to waste.

Foster rode day and night through the countryside on the Indian motorcycle, stopping only for petrol. His entire body was sore from crouching and holding the throttle. His face was caked with dirt and his clothes were dirty and dusty. He ignored the pain and pushed the motorcycle to its limits.

Sarajevo was soon only three or four hours away. Foster was so tired that he had started to see double—he had not slept in over thirty-six hours. He'd been traveling for three straight days and had ridden the length of France, into Italy, and had finally reached the Austria-Hungary Empire. He urged himself on, doing his best to stay alert and lucid. The cold, biting wind easily cut through his clothes. The gloves that Franck gave him provided a good deal of warmth, but still his fingers were almost numb from being on the bike in the elements for so long. It was now dark, and the headlight just barely illuminated the road in front of him. Still, he found it exhilarating to race through the night on the open road. He rarely ran into other traffic, and except for the occasional farmer crossing with some sheep, he had the road to himself. He filled up with petrol when he could, ensuring his tank never reached the reserve level. Looking at his watch, he was surprised to see it was almost one o'clock in the morning.

Finally, he decided that he couldn't ride any longer and had to stop for a rest. He'd been told there was a small town just five miles ahead. He pulled back on the throttle, and the bike accelerated. It was becoming harder and harder for him to stay awake. The countryside became a blur and he almost crashed going around a bend when he nodded off for a moment, sending the bike spinning sideways on the dirt road. He blinked his eyes and shifted his weight to control the slide and straighten the bike out. That little burst of adrenaline helped him stay awake, but only for a few moments. By the time he reached the town, he was almost asleep. Seeing an open corral, he rode the bike right up to it, killed the engine and collapsed in a pile of hay.

"Mister, are you alright?" came the voice. Foster recognized the words in German, as he spoke it fluently.

Foster opened his eyes and found himself staring into the face of an old man with a large nose who wore a black beret. Looking around, it took Foster a few moments to regain his bearings. Realizing where he was, he quickly stood up and reached for his bike.

"What time is it?" he asked the old man.

"Six o'clock. Perhaps you need some coffee and breakfast?"

Foster started the bike. He'd slept for just over five hours. A bit longer than he had wanted, but sufficient as he felt awake and reinvigorated.

"No time, but thank you!" Foster replied. He put his gloves and goggles back on, and backed the bike out of the corral. It started up with a roar and soon he was back on the road again.

The morning was still cold and immediately his face was almost completely numb. Still, it was a beautiful day. The sun was just coming up on the countryside and the light played among the crops and trees. Leaning forward, he pushed the throttle, urging the bike on even faster. He hoped he could make up some of the time after sleeping longer than he'd wished. For forty-five minutes he was at full throttle until he felt a couple of raindrops splash his goggles. Looking up, he saw ominous gray clouds directly overhead.

Just what I need, and with Sarajevo only hours away, he thought to himself.

The rain came down and then began to pelt him harshly—it was now washing down over him in sheets. In minutes, he was drenched and his goggles were so fogged up and caked with muddy streaks that he could barely make out the road in front of him. The dirt road became a minefield of mud puddles, and Foster was forced to slow down in order to navigate the slippery road.

Coming around a bend, the road became much slicker and he felt the bike weave back and forth under him. He lost control, and in a second, he found himself sliding sideways on the road as the bike fell over and both went surging into a ditch.

Picking himself up, Foster felt his ankle throbbing and blood was now gushing from a large gash on his knee. His pants were shredded. He was not only drenched in water, but his back was now completely muddy from the accident.

He limped over, picked up the bike, and backed it out of the ditch. It took him half a dozen tries until it finally started up. But now, it puttered rather than roared, as the engine kicked out dirty water and mud.

Hopping on, Foster continued with his journey, although he was now moving considerably slower than before. He'd gotten lucky with that crash, but it still made a mess of his plans. His ankle and knee felt as if they had been stabbed with knives. He ignored the pain—and the rain and the mud—and continued to his destination.

He had only one thought on his mind. *Stopping Wu Chiang.*

CHAPTER
— 26 —

THE END IS JUST THE BEGINNING

1890—KATHMANDU

On his twenty-eighth birthday, Foster sat across from Lhak-Pa in his kitchen, drinking tea and waiting for his next lesson.

"Foster with Lhak-Pa for eighteen years now. Have learned everything Lhak-Pa has to teach. Have mastered all lessons. Have turned into deadly warrior. Most of all, have proved heart is pure and soul is noble. Now, time to send out into world."

"Into the world?"

"Yes. Want Foster acclimate to old life. Wear suit, present as westerner. Then, Lhak-Pa want Foster start circus."

"A circus?"

"Yes. Certain people, certain objects, very powerful. Foster ever feel powerful feeling from stranger? Imagine entire troupe these people. Foster must seek rarified people. Have join circus. Certain objects attract or oppose good fortune. Foster must find. Keep safe. Circus perfect cover. Avoid suspicion."

Foster rubbed his chin and thought intently about the instructions that were being given to him.

"Mission—keep balance in world. Protect secrets of Red Hand. Dark and powerful forces at work. Responsibility to keep harmony. Good and evil, keep in balance. May need hunt down wicked people. Must spread edict of respect and knowledge. Improve and progress mankind. As taught by Red Hand Scrolls."

Foster listened intently and nodded his head.

"Red Hand Scrolls?"

"Yes. Must guard secrets of Red Hand Scrolls presented to mankind many centuries ago. Like blueprint to advance. Push mankind forward, not regress. Scrolls contain vast knowledge. Secrets of universe. Duty to ensure scrolls never fall into evil hands. No hands of any government."

Lhak-Pa took a drink of his tea and continued.

"Remember red handprints in catacombs? Lhak-Pa not know where come from—simply appear. Lhak-Pa understand prints are markings of the dead, show when on right path. New breakthrough, or new person, print might be on wall next day."

"Like a trail of bread crumbs showing you are on the right track," Foster said.

"Exactly. Not sure how or why. May be symbol of spirit world talking."

"When do I learn about the scrolls?" Foster asked.

"Foster, what think have been learning for last eighteen years? Lhak-Pa only teach about scrolls when sure Foster trustworthy. Small bits and pieces. Think back to lessons—learning jumped leaps and bounds. Foster understand mechanical objects like master inventor. Grasp human body like surgeon. Master of astronomy and physics—breakthroughs came after Lhak-Pa teach Foster lessons of Red Hand."

Lhak-Pa fetched a piece of red chalk and proceeded to draw the outline of a hand on his kitchen wall.

"Each finger on Red Hand different area of knowledge. Areas not separate. All connected. Disrupt one area, others disrupted. Keep room cold, disrupts physical surroundings. In turn, get sick, disrupt physical being. Mind weakens as fights illness. Everything flows together: the physical world, empathy, dreams, thoughts, even the afterlife."

Next to each finger, Lhak-Pa drew an arrow and an explanation:

The Physical World—that of the air, the sea, the land, and the animals.

The Soul—that of the heart and of empathy for fellow man and the world.

The Intellect—that of the mind and of learning.

The Spiritual World—an understanding that there is life after this one and what people do in this life will affect people in the next.

The Body—the mastering and care of human body.

Foster studied the hand and the explanation for each finger.

"Do you know where these scrolls came from?"

"Not certain. Just legend."

"When do I leave to start this circus?"

"One month time. Finish lessons. Lhak-Pa teach how to form circus, what acts, how to travel distant lands. Must learn Legend of Red Hand Scrolls. Foster must not teach secrets of scrolls as taught. Must teach few lessons to select individuals. Complete knowledge of scrolls reserved. Precious few who study with a master."

"And you're a master of the Red Hand?"

"Of course. And now, so are you."

Margaret, Inez, Leopold, and Mia trudged through the mountains in a full-fledged snowstorm. Mia was quite a taskmaster and admonished anyone for slowing down or whining. The snowy air was cold and Margaret couldn't quite get her hands warm as her gloves were thin in the fingers. Nonetheless, the fast pace meant their bodies began to warm up and after a while they were more comfortable in the cold. The snow was coming down in blankets with large flakes that stuck to the ground. Within an hour, six inches of the snow had accumulated on the ground. Walking with any kind of speed became quite difficult. The girls knew better than to complain or risk the wrath of Mia.

After twenty minutes of trudging through the deep snow, Mia had them stop to rest. She went off into the woods and quickly returned with a bundle of long skinny branches. She took out a ball of leather strapping from her pack, cut it into foot-long strands, and began organizing and tying the branches together. After a few minutes, she had constructed a basic pair of snowshoes. Asking Inez to lift her boots, she tied the snowshoes to the bottom.

"Not exactly professional, but the best I could do in short time. It should help with the walking," she said as she went about creating the next pair of snowshoes.

Inez walked around in the snowshoes and it *was* much easier. They protruded about ten inches from both the front and back of her feet and about two inches to the sides. Such long shoes meant she had to lift her knees up very high to take a step.

"Inez, you look like a flamingo!" Margaret joked and even Mia had to smile.

"They help quite a bit!" Inez exclaimed.

After half an hour, Mia had finished constructing all four pairs and they set off into the darkness once again. The fat snowflakes were still coming down in bushels and it was difficult to see more than four or five feet ahead. As they trudged through the darkness, there was nary a sound except for the sound of their own breathing.

"It's beautiful, isn't it?" Margaret said.

"What?" Inez asked.

"The snowfall. Look at how it comes down through the trees and how peaceful it all is."

Inez looked up at the snow falling through the trees and the whiteness all around them.

"Margaret, all I see is stinking snow," Inez replied.

"I thought you were the romantic now. Can't you appreciate the natural beauty around us?" Margaret replied.

Inez took another look around and, she had to admit, it did look pretty.

"Maybe, but I still feel like I'm stuck in a snow globe."

Margaret laughed as they kept walking. Leopold was the slowest and several times they had to take a break to allow him to catch his breath. Mia wasn't as concerned about their pace now, because tracking them in the storm would be very difficult. She wasn't sure if their pursuers had snowshoes; if they did not, their progress would be much slower than their own.

They continued walking in silence for fifteen minutes when, suddenly, in the distance, came a sound that each knew all too well.

The sound of a pack of wolves howling.

Mia listened attentively before providing a bit of commentary.

"They have killed something. That is the sound they make after a kill," she explained.

Inez and Margaret listened to the eeriness of the howling in the darkness. It was a spooky sound and not pleasant in the least.

"How far away are they?" Margaret asked.

"Difficult to tell. Sound carries in the night air. But, if I had to guess, I would say a half a mile."

"Will they attack us?" Inez asked.

"No. Wolves generally avoid humans unless they are starving, and, they would never attack an entire group of humans." Leopold managed a reply.

The snow was coming down even heavier than before and gathering up in deep snowdrifts all around them. They were now blinded by the sheets of white snow enveloping them. The wind blew harshly in their faces and taking just one step was burdensome and difficult. Everyone's breathing became labored and heavy.

Stumbling along in almost complete darkness, they continued to trudge up a trail.

To the relief of everyone, they finally took a break and huddled in a makeshift snow cave. Everyone was cold and tired and nobody said anything. Inez stared straight-ahead and Margaret blew on her hands, trying to get them to warm.

Leopold looked like he'd aged twenty years. He was tired and looked haggard.

Hanging his head in exhaustion, he said, "If I don't make it, if I die, then you must deliver the decoding machine in the case of war."

"What are you talking about?" Margaret asked.

Leopold looked up at Margaret. His breathing was labored and he wheezed with each inhale. His fingers trembled and his face had taken on the look of a defeated man.

"In the event of war, it is absolutely essential you prevent the machine from falling into the wrong hands. It is buried in a cemetery in Munich under a grave marked with the name of Franz Kree. With it you'll find all my notes. The name of the cemetery is the Munich

Waldfriedhof cemetery. Please see that the device, and my notes, are delivered to safe hands."

Margaret and Inez were shocked. Mia stood silently and listened to Leopold, who was now bent over at the waist.

"You're not going to die, Leopold! You can make it…just a little farther," Inez said to him.

"You girls are wonderful, and I trust you. I hope I do live, but I am so weak," he muttered.

They waited for another five minutes, and Leopold seemed to shrink in front of them. Mia offered him some cheese, but he refused, taking only a small drink of water.

"Let's go," Mia finally said, and they exited the cave and trudged back into the howling wind and biting snow. They continued on the trail, each step agonizingly slow, before Mia stopped and yelled through the wind.

"We're going to walk along some treacherous areas. It is better that we tie ourselves together for safety. We'll need to take smaller steps and go slowly. Take off your snowshoes, because the ledge will be narrow."

In minutes, they were attached to one another with the climbing rope after removing the makeshift snowshoes. The incline became more and more steep, and they felt themselves walking up and up into the mountains. It was actually incredible that Mia could find her way through the pass in the near darkness and snow. They walked without much of a break for over an hour. Everyone was focused on taking small steps and feeling the ground in front of them. No one said a word, such was their concentration.

Leopold, continuing to tire, was the first one in line and slowed the group down because they were forced to walk at his pace. He was having difficulty focusing and he felt his steps become more and more erratic.

That's when it happened!

Suddenly and inexplicably.

Leopold felt his right foot slip, and without warning, felt himself falling through the air. He fell for what felt like an eternity, but it was actually only about a second—after falling about five feet, he felt a tug on the rope, slowing his descent. A second later, he was falling again. He heard screaming and shouting from above.

Somehow he had taken a wrong step and plunged off the side of a cliff. Inez, who was tied to the rope next to him, fell along with him and now they were both stuck on the side of a sheer drop.

Margaret screamed as she dug in her feet to keep from following them down. She had started to slide, but Mia grabbed her by the arm and prevented her from going over. Margaret braced her legs as both she and Mia held on tight to the rope, keeping Inez and Leopold from falling to their deaths and taking the whole group with them.

Inez screamed with terror, but Leopold was too much in shock to say much of anything. He was suspended in midair. At one point, his body swung forward and he was able to get a hand onto the side of the cliff.

"Hold on!" Mia ordered as everyone struggled to find their way in the dark.

Mia and Margaret grunted and pulled all their weight backward.

"Pull Margaret, pull!" Mia screamed as both strained to lift Leopold and Inez to safety. Margaret struggled but the weight was just too much. The rope dug painfully into her waist. She could feel it burn against her skin.

For about thirty seconds, they continued their efforts to pull their friends to safety, but the load was just too heavy. Slowly, their feet began to give way and slide toward the edge. Margaret groaned with the exertion and Inez shouted with terror as she felt herself slide inches closer to the abyss.

Leopold, still quiet, reached down, grabbed a knife, and put the edge to the rope that bound him to Inez.

"The weight is too much. I am going to cut loose, thank you all for your help and friendship!" he yelled in the darkness.

Inez, still too frightened to speak, couldn't believe what she had heard.

Leopold dug the knife into the rope, sawed in back and forth, until the rope suddenly gave way and Leopold tumbled through the air to the ground below.

Though shocked by what they had just seen, Mia and Margaret held tight to the rope. The load was lighter now, and they used all of their strength to pull Inez up, inch by inch, until she was able to make her way to the edge and hoist herself up to safety.

Breathing heavily, Inez burst into tears.

"He cut the rope! Leopold cut the rope to save us!" she said between muffled sobs.

Mia and Margaret lay in the snow, exhausted and in shock. It had all happened so fast. Inez continued to sob until Margaret embraced her and held her tightly in her arms. Inez sobbed into her friend's chest as the snow and wind continued to swirl around them.

After a few moments, Mia composed herself. Her demeanor was soft, a change from her usual demanding tone.

"Come girls, we must continue. I am sorry we lost Leopold, it was a brave but necessary choice. If he hadn't cut the rope, we all would have been dragged over the edge."

Slowly, they rose to their feet, secured the ropes, and then continued their journey along the mountain ridge.

Captain Scopas sat at his table, smoking a pipe and drinking ouzo from a tin cup. He studied Tariq, Fez, Aseem, and Pakize as they slurped up *avgolemono*—a Greek egg and lemon soup. They had all changed out of their wet clothes and were now keeping warm in the safety of his cabin. The boys were quiet and calm, and each drank a large bowl of soup—and then another—in an effort to calm their nerves and bring some warmth to their bodies.

The group looked dejected and sad. Abdullah Ozek had gotten the better of them, and they weren't able to save the animals. Tariq, especially, seemed quite depressed. Head down, he stared at his soup and barely said a word.

"Pakize, where will you go now that Abdullah Ozek has you in his sights?" he asked.

Pakize shrugged her shoulders.

"I don't know. It is not safe for me in Constantinople now that he knows of my identity. As long as Abdullah Ozek is alive, I am not safe in this city."

Scopas continued to puff on his pipe.

"Do you know when this ship is leaving? The one with the animals?" Scopas asked.

All four looked at one another before Fez provided an answer.

"No, but it cannot be long. It looked like they had finished loading before trying to drown us. I imagine they will leave tonight."

Fez had recovered nicely from his scare and was back to his normal self. He looked a bit older from the experience. In fact, all the boys looked more grown up. Perhaps it was the stress of the trip, or being far from home, but they all seemed to have matured two years in just days.

Scopas studied the group.

"Why does it mean so much to you to save these animals?" he asked.

Tariq looked up from his soup.

"Because Melbourne Jack said it was our job to protect them. He always said wild animals are sacred. Besides, how would you feel if you were in a small cage, waiting to be killed for nothing more than your pelt? Wouldn't you want someone to save you?"

His words were strong and earnest. Scopas hadn't yet figured out these boys. But the more he thought about it, the more sense it made. He had no respect for anyone who killed an animal for sport. Yes, he hunted animals and fish, but he used every part of the body and absolutely nothing went to waste.

Hunting for trophies was a sport for the weak and the insecure.

"Come," he instructed them after they had finished their meal. They all dutifully stood up and followed Scopas below deck to a large section in the stern of the boat.

Cafu lay comfortably on a blanket inside his cage and didn't growl or hiss. He looked like he was smiling at the group, happy to see them.

"I come down here to spend time with him. I can't explain it, but I love this cat. He even lets me pet him, but I have to be careful. It's as if he knows we are saving him," Scopas explained.

Just looking at the panther lifted Tariq's spirits. He had a regal beauty. The cat returned Tariq's gaze, and seemed to smile, opening his mouth and allowing his tongue to hang over his white teeth.

"Tell me about your brother," Pakize asked.

Scopas rubbed his chin and slumped his shoulders. The planks creaked with the rhythm of the waves and the boat swayed back and forth.

"He was my younger brother. He was quiet and studious and very smart. He was a peaceful chap, and very pious. He believed in right and wrong. One day, he saw Abdullah Ozek beating some peasants for some petty reason and he stood up to him. But he's not a street fighter like me, and he never had a chance. Ozek put a knife in his belly and let my brother bleed to death on the street."

Tears ran down Scopas's face and he wiped them back with the sleeve of his shirt. Fez went and patted him on the shoulder to reassure him.

"I was his bigger brother. I should have been there to protect him," he wailed. The captain's display of emotion was raw and took the boys and Pakize by surprise.

Scopas steadied himself and continued to wipe the tears from his eyes.

"I miss him so much. There is nothing in the world I wouldn't have done for him, and I can't live in peace until I've finished Abdullah Ozek."

Aseem sat on the floor, with his back against a wall, studying Cafu.

"I remember in my village that others would mistreat my family and me because we were poor. They did it to build themselves up. Sometimes I ask myself, why should we get involved with any of this? Animals will continue to be killed and sold for sport. Nothing will change. But then, I realize that is the weak part of myself talking. The lazy part. I want to make a difference in my life, if only a small one. Saving these animals is a very good thing to do, I think. When I am done and the tally of my life is complete, I want there to be far more good deeds than bad. That is the purpose of life, to make a good difference, if only in a small way," Aseem explained.

Tariq had been mostly silent and deep in thought since they had returned. He suddenly perked up as if a firecracker had ignited in his brain. He hadn't brought up losing the diary because part of him was still in shock after almost drowning and saving Fez. He'd been thinking about why Ozek had stolen the book. It was as if he had been looking for it.

"What if we commandeered the ship?" he asked.

"What ship?" Scopas asked

"Ozek's ship. What if we seized it?"

"Do you think he is on it?" Scopas asked.

"Yes, he always accompanies these trips to ensure the goods are delivered safely and the right price is given. I usually wait until he has gone to do most of my stealing," Pakize answered.

Scopas thought for a moment before speaking.

"It would be very dangerous. He will have an armed crew."

"Difficult, but not impossible," Fez responded.

"We would need small boats for a surprise attack. Perhaps a dozen fighters in all? Perhaps more," Scopas continued, to nobody in particular.

"Can we reach the ship?" Fez asked.

Scopas lit his pipe and continued to think. He even started to mutter something to himself in Greek.

"Yes, yes—we can catch them with smaller boats—if the wind is at our back. The Black Sea has good wind this time of year, which will help us. I would imagine they would have a three- or four-hour head start— not an impossible time to make up."

Tariq finally stepped forward. His voice was resolute and stern.

"So what do we need to do to get started?"

Scopas sucked on his pipe, releasing the aroma of the succulent tobacco.

"You sure you're ready for this? Yes, you are brave lads, but you are still very young. These are trained killers."

Tariq never wavered and looked him directly in the eyes.

"Don't worry about us. Get us on that ship and we'll make sure you have your revenge."

Even Captain Scopas was taken back by the maturity and steely resolve in Tariq's voice.

"We'll need an hour to prepare. You can start by sharpening every knife you can find. I'll prepare the boats and arrange for a boarding party," Scopas replied before turning his back and heading to the deck.

The boys and Pakize looked at one another. Each smiled slyly and then began to get busy.

Tariq started by finely sharpening each of his knives, and with each sharpening stroke, he thought of Melbourne Jack and their final moments together. He could feel the anger course through his veins and pound in his heart.

He thought of nothing else but Abdullah Ozek—how he had laughed while the four were caged and nearly drowned and how he'd snatched the diary from around Tariq's neck. He remembered the superior look on Ozek's face when Tariq and his friends almost drowned. The sound of his laugh stayed with Tariq and somehow became mixed up with the feeling of loss from losing Melbourne Jack. The combination of these two feelings was like toxic mixture of gasoline and fire, turning Tariq's psyche into a smoldering mess of anger and vengeance. As he sharpened the knives, his fingers trembled with anticipation.

SHATTERED AND NUMB

Mia, Margaret, and Inez made their way along the mountain ridge. Since the moment Leopold had cut himself free, hardly a word had been exchanged among them. Everyone was frozen with grief and disbelief after witnessing poor Leopold cut himself free to save them. The ridge was treacherous and demanded their complete attention. The wind made hearing one another difficult, and the blackness of the night made it nearly impossible to see more than a few feet ahead. Leopold's fall brought a weight over the entire group, who trudged along with heavy hearts.

At last they cleared the ledge and found themselves in open country. Mia allowed everyone an hour of rest and a little food. However, no one got any sleep, as the horrific event was still too fresh in their minds. Inez, in particular, was taking it harder than anyone else. This was the first time she had experienced such an awful situation, and it had shaken her deeply. Margaret, from her travails in Morocco, was more adept at handling tragedy.

After the hour, Mia had the two girls on their feet and they began trudging through the snow once again. Dawn was approaching, and the emerging light made the walking much easier.

Major Hostetler and his troops followed blindly in the snow. They couldn't find any tracks, but he didn't need any—he knew there was only one route that they could possibly take, and he and his men were following it perfectly.

As dawn broke, Hostetler and his posse made their way across the ridge. They came to the same clearing that had sheltered Mia and the girls, where they easily spotted the sets of tracks in the snow.

Major Hostetler knelt down and studied the footprints. He looked to see how deep they were, and whether there had been any kind of additional snowfall since the steps had been taken.

"We're an hour behind them, maybe less. But, there's something strange about these prints," Hostetler said to nobody in particular.

"What is it, major?" one of his soldiers asked.

"There are only three sets of prints. Two look to be those of the girls, and the other of an adult."

Hostetler stood up and walked with the prints for twenty yards. He was certain there were only three sets of prints.

"What happened?" the same soldier asked.

"I'm not sure, only that there are certainly only three people now. It could be that they broke off and separated, but this is the only route through the range."

Hostetler rubbed his chin, which was now stubbly with whiskers, and tried to think of what could have happened to the fourth person. It was entirely possible that someone had intentionally broken off from the other three, but it seemed implausible, given the isolation of the trail. Where would they go? Perhaps they circled back and decided to take another route?

It just didn't make any sense.

The wind whipped over the Black Sea, and large whitecaps stung the squadron of sailboats over and over as the captains tightened the sails to capitalize on the power of the squall. The boys stayed on the far port side of the deck, as the starboard side was practically submerged in the sea. In the dark, they couldn't see more than thirty or forty feet ahead. At the top of the mast, a lookout had been tethered so they would be able to scan for any sign of the freighter. At the wheel, Captain Scopas did his best to navigate the storm, as salt stung his eyes and his wrists throbbed from hours of steering the boat. He watched over the boys, and more than once questioned whether they were ready for such a mission. In the end, he decided they were tough enough—that protecting and coddling them was not what they needed. So he included them, but still gave orders to other crewmembers to watch out for their safety.

Studying the horizon, Scopas ensured the other three boats followed his lead like a train of baby ducks, each staying close and tight.

On deck, the boys were lying down, except for a slight bend at the waist so they could see over the bow. Each held onto a line and had been given the instructions, "don't let go, because we won't stop to rescue you." With those words of caution, the boys held onto the rope tightly and huddled together to keep warm. Pakize, who was behind them, was getting more and more seasick and finally began to retch over the side. Her face took on a pale green color and cold sweat broke out on her forehead. This was her first time on a boat at sea, and it couldn't have been a more perilous voyage, as the small attack boats were prone to violent motion from the waves.

Fez, feeling bad for Pakize, put his arm around her as a show of friendship. She tried to show her appreciation, but ended up spraying vomit all over his shirt.

"Aaahhh," Fez screamed, but his cries were barely audible over the wind.

"Sorry," Pakize said. She looked as if she might throw up again.

Fez, with vomit covering his shirt, began dry heaving over the side of the boat as the rancid smell entered his nostrils. He wished he could immediately throw off his messed shirt. Thankfully, the seawater washed over it and dissipated the foul smell.

Up at the bow, Tariq stood stone-faced, keeping his eyes fixed on the breaking waves in front of him. The wind blew harshly in his face, stinging his eyes and cheeks. He hadn't said anything during the trip, focused only on preparing for a possible attack.

For three hours they braved the high winds. Pakize's stomach finally calmed down. She felt better, but not altogether perfect. Captain Scopas was about to give up the search when the lookout from above whistled and gave a series of hand signals. The crewman had spotted a freighter about three hundred yards away.

"There, captain—at three o'clock," the crewman shouted, pointing in the direction of the freighter.

The other boats were notified and all set their course for the heading of the freighter. The lead boat picked up speed and for fifteen minutes, knifed through the whitecaps until, at last, the freighter was only a hundred yards ahead. Captain Scopas instructed a crewmember to signal the other boats to break into a two-by-two formation. Captain Scopas's boat and the second one in line would attack from the port side, while the other two would circle around and attack from the starboard side. The two boats broke away and disappeared into the dark. The second boat moved so close to the lead boat that they were practically touching. Scopas knew that moving to the bow of the freighter and then performing a jibe—so their port side would come parallel to the freighter—was too risky in these high winds and breaking seas. A wrong move could easily capsize the boat. The safest approach in these conditions would be simply to come alongside the freighter and hope they could keep the wind at their back.

Using a monocular, Scopas examined the deck of the freighter. The rough seas made it difficult to hold the device steady, but he managed to get a good enough view to determine that there were no crewmembers posted on watch. Which made sense, really—Abdullah Ozek couldn't possibly guess that anyone would attack his ship in these terrible conditions.

Soon enough, the yellow lights from the big ship's portholes could be seen shining through the dark night. They had moved the sailboat very, very close and could now see the massive outline of the freighter. The side of the boat completely blacked out the sky as it bobbed up and down and suddenly Scopas was barking orders at his crewmen and yelling at the boys.

"Take the grappling hooks and prepare to throw them. We won't have many opportunities!"

The boys and Pakize had practiced throwing the hooks for about twenty minutes on shore. The plan was, once the freighter was found, the boys were responsible for throwing up a rope with a grappling hook at the end with the goal of hooking it securely on the edge of the rail. Then, the crew would be able to scale the side of the ship and climb onto the deck. They had managed one practice maneuver with these ropes that contained many knots to grab hold of for traction. It should be easy for the boys and Pakize to scale the side of the boat because they all had a tremendous amount of experience with climbing things.

On each boat, a crewmember would remain behind in case the assault was a failure and the party required a rescue.

It was, undoubtedly, a risky plan, with many moving parts and a high probability of complete collapse.

Captain Scopas approached the freighter as close as he dared in these conditions. Once alongside, he gave the signal and the boys and Pakize immediately sprang into action, each swinging their rope and throwing it to the top of the deck. The rocking motion of the boat and the tight quarters made this extremely challenging—it was nearly impossible to get a firm footing. Of the four, only Pakize's hook found its mark. The other three came crashing down and one almost struck Aseem in the head. They kept trying until Tariq's hook finally managed to find its mark.

"Two will be good enough, let's go!" Scopas ordered.

Captain Scopas was the first to go. He grabbed the rope and scaled the side of the freighter by placing his feet on the side of the ship and walking straight up. He held a dagger between his teeth in case he saw action first thing or was surprised by anyone. On the second rope, two crewmembers began scrambling up the side, followed by Pakize and then additional crew. Tariq was next, followed by Fez and then Aseem and a few more crewmembers. It was different from how they'd practiced, as the winds and rocky seas made for an unsteady ship. Each held the rope tightly and walked as fast as possible up the side. The side was slippery, so they widened their stance to steady themselves and began taking baby steps up the side. Tariq found that bouncing up and down a bit helped, and he hopped the rest of the way to the top. Once on board, he turned to ensure that Fez and Aseem were making their way behind him. Fez was a bit slower, so Tariq grabbed him by the armpits and yanked him over the side. Aseem followed closely behind. Pakize and the other crewmembers had already made it aboard and soon all were kneeling in a line at the side of the ship. Captain Scopas had gone to the starboard side to help the others and soon returned with the rest of the crew.

The landing had been a success! Including the boys and Pakize, there were now sixteen fighters on board. Each took out a knife and held it steady, waiting for orders from Captain Scopas. They were only six feet away from a steel door that should lead belowdecks. Everyone was tense with anticipation and watched the door intently.

Scopas looked at them and then pointed at the door with his right index finger.

It was time for the assault.

Wu Chiang sat in his hotel room in Sarajevo. Decrepit and bare, it was typical of the rooms he rented. He sat at the small wooden desk—the only piece of furniture, save the bed, in the room—and wrote out a series of instructions on two pieces of letterhead. The letters were in code and could only be read by using an extract of lemon juice, ammonia, and a unique compound he'd invented. After being sprinkled with this mixture, within ten minutes the ink would disappear entirely. He couldn't take the chance that someone would happen upon the letter by accident.

The letters said one name and nothing else.

Franz Ferdinand.

Archduke Franz Ferdinand of Austria was scheduled to visit Sarajevo the next day. His visit had received quite a bit of publicity, as it was considered very dangerous for him to visit Sarajevo at this time. Just a month prior, his uncle had barely survived an assassination attempt.

The Austria-Hungary Empire was held together with thread and chewing gum. Since its glory days—now long past—the empire had grown corrupt and bureaucratic. Only the royals and the nobility had enough food in their bellies, while the vast majority of the people were starving, overworked, and uneducated. The people were unhappy and restless. The flames of revolution were mere cinders, but burned hotter and grew larger with each and every passing day.

Wu Chiang took advantage of the people's discontent. Long ago, he'd helped create a group called "The Black Hand"—a group of revolutionaries who wanted to destroy the aristocracy of the Austria-Hungary Empire. These were young men who seethed with hatred at their prospects in life and wanted nothing better than to bring down the establishment.

What's more, Wu Chiang, and others, had spent the last thirty years working their political contacts to influence the signing of a series of treaties among nations. These treaties essentially said that if a country were attacked, then the ally would come to their aid in a time of war.

For instance, Austria-Hungary had a treaty with Germany that decreed if they were attacked, Germany would stand by them against all enemies.

Wu Chiang had orchestrated many of these treaties so that each one depended on the other for success. Just like a row of dominos lined up on a table—topple one, and they all fall.

Franz Ferdinand was the key to everything. If they could assassinate him, then Austria-Hungary would most likely declare war on Serbia. And if Austria-Hungary declared war on Serbia, France would come to Serbia's aid. If France entered the war, then England would be forced to enter the war, because it had a treaty with France. Germany would then enter the war as an ally to Austria. And so on.

And so the dominoes would fall.

Wu Chiang had one goal: to assassinate Franz Ferdinand at all costs.

Organizing the Black Hand had taken a considerable amount of skill, as Wu Chiang never wanted to be actively known, or involved, with the lot. Like a puppet master, he remained unseen, dictating their movements and giving them orders from behind the scenes.

Wu Chiang understood that where there was hunger and poverty, there was opportunity for corruption.

How easy it had been for him to recruit members of the Black Hand and to poison their young minds.

He sealed the envelopes and then hand delivered them to two separate graves in two different graveyards.

That night, a man named Pietri Alespo gathered one of the notes while the other was picked up by a woman named Cassandra Sisspa. Neither Pietri nor Cassandra knew one another, nor were they even aware the other existed. They had both received simple instructions. Collect the note and take it to the leaders of "The Black Hand." They weren't to say where they had found the notes, or from whom they received their orders.

In this manner, Wu Chiang kept himself completely anonymous from the group.

The leaders of the Black Hand met in the basement of a house in a Sarajevo ghetto during the evening. It was determined that six members would attempt to kill Archduke Ferdinand the following morning after his ten o'clock arrival at the train station. They had a map that outlined the route that would most likely be taken by Archduke Ferdinand and his entourage.

That night, the members of the Black Hand drank and smoked and sang nationalist songs. They thought Franz Ferdinand was simply one more aristocrat to kill. They had no idea about the devious plans of Wu Chiang or that the assassination of Franz Ferdinand might set off a world war.

They were merely men who wanted a better future for their country and were being used as pawns in a grand chess game.

Foster arrived at Sarajevo on Sunday, June 28, 1914 at around six o'clock a.m. He was tired and injured from the journey. He rolled onto the tarmac at the Sarajevo train station. His motorcycle was muddy and caked with dirt and his face was brown with mud, save for where the goggles had protected his face. His knee and ankle throbbed.

Barely acknowledging the pain, Foster limped to the concierge desk and was startled to learn that it wouldn't open for another hour. Dejected, he went to the washroom and spent the better part of twenty minutes washing the dirt from his face and hands and even managed to slip into some clean clothes. Then, he found a shoeshine boy who gave his leather boots a nice sheen after rubbing off all the dirt and muck. For the effort, Foster paid him triple his normal rate. After a breakfast of eggs, bacon, and hot coffee, Foster felt much better.

Finally, the concierge desk opened and Foster inquired if they had an envelope with his name on it. The concierge opened a drawer and handed one to Foster. Inside was the address of a hotel and a room number. After asking the concierge for a clean envelope, Foster discreetly placed a fifty-franc note inside, sealed it, and wrote the name "Gerard" on the front. He handed the envelope to the concierge and walked outside to his motorcycle.

The motorcycle hummed to life and soon Foster was navigating the streets of Sarajevo in search of a certain hotel, constantly stopping to ask directions of shopkeepers or even the odd policeman. It took him the better part of an hour before he rolled in front of an old building called "The Million Dollar Hotel."

More like the "Dollar Hotel," Foster thought to himself as he parked the motorcycle down the block. The place was falling apart—the bricks were crumbling, the paint was faded, and even the awning had holes and moldy stains.

The note told him that Wu Chiang was staying on the third floor in room 302. Foster didn't want any kind of mistakes this time. He had to get to Wu Chiang and figure out his plans without running into any obstacles.

As he approached the hotel, he reached into his knapsack for a knife, which he hid up his right sleeve. He felt his heart beating in his chest and made a conscious effort to breathe deeply and exhale slowly. After entering the lobby, he didn't say anything to the old man at the front desk, walking right past him and directly up the wooden stairs, which were dusty, and squeaked under his footsteps. He didn't slow down or try to be quiet as he quickly made his way up the stairs.

Once he reached the third floor, Room 302 was the first room to the right. Taking the knife in his hand, he thought about the best way to proceed. Should he knock and pretend to be a room service attendant? Wu Chiang would probably find that suspicious. He decided just to burst through the door and take his chances. It was an old wooden door, and he hoped the lock would be rusted and would give way easily.

Steadying himself, he counted to three, took a running start, and then brought his foot up and kicked the door.

He was proven correct.

The door burst open in a shower of wooden splinters. In an instant, Foster Crowe was in the bare room.

He found his adversary staring directly at him, still dressed in pajamas and drinking a glass of water.

Wu Chiang dropped the glass of water and it crashed to the floor, sending shards of glass everywhere.

"You!" Wu Chiang said in obvious amazement and surprise.

"What are you up to Wu Chiang? What are your plans?" Foster shouted, knife in hand, warily stepping forward.

Wu Chiang stared at him, still astonished at the persistence of Foster.

Foster took a step forward but Wu Chiang didn't move a muscle.

Captain Scopas slowly opened the heavy steel door to be sure there weren't any watchmen directly below. It was dark and he used his hands and feet to gingerly feel in front of him. His left hand felt for a hold while his right hand held his sword. His toes reached for air and then came to rest on a steel step. The wind slapped against the open door and he forcefully held it open for the next person in line.

"It's a narrow stairwell—tell everyone to be careful," he whispered to the crewmember behind him. The message was passed along and everyone slowly descended into the darkness and followed Captain Scopas.

Once down the stairs, they came to a semi-lit hallway. Turning right, the group moved in single file. Everyone was tense with emotion and anticipation. They had no idea how many of Ozek's men might be on board or where they could be staying. The darkness only added to the excitement. Aseem and Fez were both sweating and breathing a little heavily. Tariq, however, was calm as could be as he eagerly anticipated an encounter with the enemy. He moved stealthily, like a mongoose stalking a cobra, and was hyper-aware of his surroundings.

Moving forward, they came to another steel door, and Scopas heard voices from behind it. He signaled to the group behind him by holding up his right fist, which meant that they were about to meet the enemy.

Taking a deep breath, sword at the ready, Scopas opened the door and rushed in.

Only to be met with a huge surprise.

They had managed to stumble into the galley, and the entire crew was busy eating. There were perhaps twenty-five crewmembers in all, who were all sitting at tables, eating from bowls filled with couscous and fish, and enjoying a bit of rakı.

A few of them men were Ozek's gangsters, but most were crew hired specifically for the voyage. They were not capable fighters and had no allegiance to Ozek.

Scopas immediately went to the first crewmember and thrust his sword through the man's shoulder. The man yelled in pain and stumbled to the ground. There was a chaotic and wild melee as other crewmembers began yelling and charging back at them, surprised by the onslaught. In moments the entire assault party was in the galley and the place was a mess of sword and dagger fighting. Wine was spilled and food was flying.

Tariq rushed in just behind Scopas and used his sword to swipe a man across the chest. The cut was deep, and the man grabbed his wound and fell backward. Tariq, moving swiftly and efficiently, moved onto the next man and his blade pierced through the man's thigh as he attempted to stand up. Screaming in agony, the man grabbed his thigh. Blood squirted everywhere from the sizable puncture in his leg.

Just as Tariq was about to go for a third, out of the corner of his eye, he saw a body flying right at him. Instinctively, he dodged out of the way just as a small and scrappy crewmember lunged at him with a dagger in his right hand. The dagger missed slashing his face by mere inches. However, the man wouldn't give up. He managed to wrap his other arm around Tariq and tackle him to the floor. They crashed hard, rolled around, and finally came to a stop. Tariq could feel the man was stronger than him and he knew he couldn't wrestle with him for very long. He could also tell the man was obsessed with taking him down, so Tariq quickly wrapped both his legs around the man's right shoulder in a kind of stranglehold. Then, he brought up both of his hands and grabbed onto the man's right arm—the one holding the knife.

Strangely, everything seemed to be in slow motion. So much so that the entire scene became clearer, colors were sharper, and Tariq could feel his mind slow down. Tariq was somehow able to anticipate everything before it happened. Malik had trained him for moments just like this. He had taught Tariq to breathe deeply, relax his body, and slow the moment down in his head. They had worked on it for hours. They would wrestle and practice hand-to-hand combat until Tariq felt like things were slowing down and he could begin to see Malik's moves before they happened.

Panic is the enemy. Stay calm and don't allow your emotions to overcome you. Be present, but detached.

Funny how Tariq could hear the words so plainly now, almost as if Malik were right next to him whispering in his ear.

Tariq continued to grapple with the man and in a few moments he felt him tire from struggling to free his right arm. Soon, his wrist weakened. Tariq squeezed his legs a bit tighter around the man's shoulder and the knife fell from the man's hand. They were, however, in a stalemate—Tariq couldn't let go of the man's arm, as that would allow the man to gain further leverage.

That problem didn't last long, because suddenly, a heavy chair came flying through the air and struck the man right on the head. In an instant, he was knocked unconscious.

Looking up, Tariq saw Captain Scopas smiling and waving—he had been the one to throw the chair!

Tariq waved back, stood up, looked for a another crewmember to attack, then took a running start and dove right into him, sending them both flying backward onto the floor.

Fez and Aseem soon found themselves in a scrum with five of the foulest crewmembers imaginable. The men stunk of oily fish and armpit odor and their breath could bring tears to the staunchest of men. Their teeth were yellow and covered in a gray film of plaque and scum.

The two boys tackled a rather large bearded man with rolls of fat dangling from his chin. His breath smelled of rakı and his eyes were glazed over. However, he was strong and was soon overpowering them and pushing them backward. He grabbed both boys in a bear hug, lifted them off the ground, then ran them backward fifteen feet straight into a wall. Both boys felt their backs hit hard and then the man's weight squeezed into them. Up close, his breath was even more rancid than before, and his eyes, still glazed over, were filled with hatred. Aseem had managed to keep his arms outside the man's grasp and were now free. Using both hands, he grabbed under the man's chin, and shoved hard until the man was pushed backward and fell down. It was a move he'd learned from Malik and was very effective in separating from an assailant.

Fez and Aseem quickly wiggled free. Fez kicked the man hard in the left shin and the man shouted in obvious pain. Aseem punched him hard in the esophagus and the man gargled and choked as his breath was cut off.

Seeing a water pitcher on the ground, Fez fetched it and, with a running start, smashed it against the man's head. His eyes rolled back in his head and he fell to the floor.

"Nice work, Fez!" Aseem exclaimed. Then, seeing that Tariq was busy wrestling with another crewmember, he grabbed Fez's arm.

"Come on, Tariq needs our help!"

Mia and the girls trudged along the trail and still barely said a word to one another, exhausted by the journey and still dejected from the loss of their new friend. Suddenly, Mia stopped.

"They're onto us!" Mia yelled and, instantly, all of them forgot about Leopold and began running along the trail. The barking was far off and barely audible. Sound echoed and carried along the mountain corridors, making it seem closer than it was.

For twenty minutes they ran until they ran into a dead end. Well, a kind of dead end.

A huge icefall was in front of them—about one hundred and fifty feet tall and surrounded by canyon walls on every side.

Mia reached into their knapsacks and grabbed all the ice axes and showed the girls how to use them. She fastened a rope around her waist and then tied it to each of the girls. She placed a small ball-peen hammer in the back of her pants and secured it with her leather belt.

After listening to Mia explain how to use an ice axe, the girls fastened crampons to their boots and followed Mia to the waterfall. The crampons crunched in the snow, and the girls could tell they would help with traction on the ice. Mia studied the ice, pacing back and forth, looking for the best possible line for climbing. Satisfied, she dug the axe into the ice with her right hand, and then brought her right foot up and shoved the bottom cleat of the crampon into the ice. Then, she dug the other axe in her left hand into the ice and brought her left foot up. She repeated these steps six times until she was about twenty feet off the ground. Taking out the hammer, she hammered a spike into some exposed rock, placed a metal carabiner into the ring on the spike, and threaded the rope through the ring. Mia was an expert ice climber, and had been using carabiners since their invention.

Mia was secretly a bit scared that the ice would not hold them. It was spring, and normally the ice would have melted and it would be a gushing waterfall. However, the winter had been extremely cold and had lingered on much longer than usual. She only hoped the ice was still strong enough to climb safely.

"Okay, Inez, you go first!" she ordered.

Inez looked up at Mia and gingerly flung the ice axe in her right hand into the ice. The axe bounced off and fell harmlessly to the ground.

"No, you have to hit it hard!" Mia yelled.

Inez picked up the axe, flung it again at the wall, and again it clattered to the ground.

"You must hurry up, girls! We don't have much time!" Mia pleaded.

"Here, let me try," Margaret said, took her own axe, and threw it at the ice.

It, too, fell to the ground.

Both girls looked at their axes and then at the ice wall in front of him.

"The stinking ice is too hard, Mia!" Inez yelled.

"Nonsense, try hitting it at an angle as I instructed, and use your waist and legs for more power."

Inez eyed the axe, took one step backward, and then leaned all her weight into the throw. The axe whizzed threw the air and then stuck right into the ice.

"Yay! Great job, Inez!" Margaret yelled and both girls giggled with glee and hugged one another. Mia rolled her eyes.

"Now, try putting your crampon into the ice with your right foot!"

Inez pulled up her weight and tried to put the spike into the ice. Her movements, however, were too soft and the spike wouldn't stick.

"This won't stick either!" she yelled.

"You have to really kick it in. This ice is hard as rock and it takes a lot of force to get it in there."

"Oh," Inez replied, stuck her tongue out in concentration, reared back her leg, let it fly, and it stuck right in the ice.

"Good job, Inez!" Margaret yelled, thoroughly impressed.

Up above, Mia rolled her eyes once again.

At this rate, the ice will melt and it will be summer before we're to the top, she thought to herself.

After four tries, Inez had stuck her left hand axe in the ice and then her left foot. Trying again, she managed to stick her right-handed axe on the first try and then her right foot.

"Hey, this is fun!" she screamed and Margaret clapped her hands with encouragement.

Another three steps from Inez and then Margaret started. She had difficulty as well on her first couple of tries, but once she got the hang of it, she started to make more and more progress. Soon, both girls were ten feet off the ground and steadily moving.

"Okay, good. Always be sure you keep three points of contact with the ice and follow my line," Mia ordered, and soon all three were moving up the wall of ice in slow, but steady fashion. After half an hour, the girls were thirty feet up on the ice. Once they understood the movements and technique, it got much easier and they were able to increase their speed. The tough part was waiting for Mia to hammer in the spikes to keep the placement of the safety rope going. Both girls found it took all of their concentration to stay on the wall.

"This is so much fun, Margaret. We've got to start doing this back in France," Inez said, grinning as she plunged the right axe into the ice, brought her right leg up, and began moving once again. Margaret was about eight feet below and was trying to match Inez's speed.

They kept moving, and after about an hour they were only fifteen feet from the top. Mia had almost reached the top, but knew the girls were beginning to tire. As she urged them to continue, they suddenly heard voices coming from directly below them.

Looking down, they saw that Major Hostetler and his dogs and soldiers were at the foot of the icefall. The soldiers began yelling at the girls in German and a couple of them brought out their rifles to shoot. But Major Hostetler stopped them.

"We don't shoot women and girls. Besides, we'll be on them in an hour or so. They can't escape us!"

The soldiers put their rifles down.

"Sir, we don't have ice climbing equipment," one of the soldiers explained.

Major Hostetler thought about this for a moment.

"Unfasten your bayonets and give them to me," he ordered.

Within a moment he had four bayonets in hand and tied one to each boot and held the other two in his hands. A small knapsack was on his back with basic provisions. Going over to the icefall, he began climbing it just as the girls had done, only he was climbing without a rope for safety. One wrong move and he would most certainly fall to his death.

Up about twelve feet, he looked back to his soldiers.

"Go back to the clearing just past the ridge and wait for me there. I'll circle back around. If I haven't returned in two days' time, return to the camp."

Looking back at the ice, he began to scale it much faster than the girls had. Each movement was fluid and quick. The soldiers looked on in admiration watching their major climb the icefall with bayonets for crampons and axes and no safety rope.

The girls had now climbed to the top and disappeared from the view of the soldiers. Major Hostetler calculated he would reach the top in about twenty minutes, and that it would take only another half an hour to catch them.

CHAPTER
— 28 —

REVENGE SERVED WITH A STILETTO

Aseem and Fez jumped on the man who was wrestling with Tariq. Aseem wrapped both arms around his neck and Fez held his right wrist with both hands. Caught by surprise, the man fell backward as Aseem pulled on his neck. Tariq, seeing an opportunity, stood up and let loose with a vicious kick right to the man's groin. Instantly, the man doubled over in pain and fell to his knees. Fez, seeing the remains of a smashed chair on the floor, grabbed a piece of wood and smacked the man on the back of his skull, immediately knocking him unconscious.

The mess hall was a sea of bodies as the freighter's crewmembers continued to fight with Captain Scopas and his men. Some swords were drawn and men dueled to the death. Other fights were more like old-fashioned fisticuffs—men traded blow after blow, breaking noses and knocking out teeth.

Aseem saw a mess of netting on the wall and had an idea.

"Let's get that netting!" he commanded and all three boys ran to the wall and pulled off the fishing net. It was heavy, and rather large—about fifteen feet by fifteen feet. They knew it would be strong, as it was con- structed of thick rope.

Spying a group of four crewmembers huddled together, who looked as if they were about to charge on Captain Scopas, all three boys grabbed a side of the net so it was spread out like a spider's web.

"Over the table!" Tariq yelled.

The boys took a running start, quickly turning into an all-out sprint, and then took one leap onto a galley table and launched themselves at the four crewmembers. With Aseem to the right, Fez to the left, and Tariq in the rear, the net was perfectly positioned over the top of the four men, who were ensnared in the net and knocked to the ground.

Scopas, seeing what had happened, came to the aid of the boys and easily disposed of the crewmembers.

"Great job, boys!" he said with a wide grin.

Captain Scopas and his men were now completely in control of the battle. The ship's crewmembers, sensing defeat, were starting to flee out of the room when, suddenly, the door burst open and a gigantic figure filled the doorway.

It was Abdullah Ozek.

A crewman ran by him.

"We're being attacked, master! They have us outnumbered!"

Ozek didn't know what to do. He looked at the scene in front of him and saw that the bulk of his crew were either dead or unconscious. Then, he saw Captain Scopas and half a dozen men screaming and running toward him.

Paralyzed with fear, Ozek did what all bullies do when they stare adversity in the eyes.

He ran.

Launching down the hall, he could hear the screaming of Captain Scopas behind him and his footsteps just ten feet behind him in pursuit.

Running up the stairs, Ozek burst through the door and found himself on the deck of the ship with most of his remaining crew. They had managed to organize themselves into a party of ten, and Ozek joined them.

It was dark outside, yet the light of the moon provided a good deal of illumination on the steel deck of the vessel. It rocked back and forth, swayed by the waves, as Ozek and his men prepared for a counterattack.

A crewman gave Ozek a twelve-inch dagger—his weapon of choice.

Ozek waited with his men outside the hatch door. He held the knife in front of him and when Scopas burst through the door, they charged him.

Captain Scopas, taken by surprise, stepped to his right to allow his men to follow behind him. Ozek was on him immediately, jabbing and swiping the knife at Scopas. Ozek had gotten over the shock of the melee and was now filled with anger and rage as he slashed his knife at the throat of Captain Scopas.

Using his feet to control his body, constantly moving backward and sideways, Scopas avoided the jabs and thrusts. He pulled a stiletto from his jacket pocket to begin his own offensive at the torso of Abdullah Ozek.

Sparks flew like flints as the steel knives slashed through the darkness and reflected off the light of the moon. Like two fireflies dancing in the night, the figures moved back and forth over the ship's deck, thrusting and parrying at one another.

The boys, along with Scopas's remaining crew, were engaged in yet another scrum with Ozek's men. They charged at each other like two rugby teams, and limbs and knives were thrown with impunity at one another.

Tariq, filled with rage, tackled a skinnier crewmember and drove him toward a steel railing on the ship's side. However, Tariq slipped on the wet steel deck and fell hard onto his knees. The pain was immediate and he grimaced in agony. The skinny man, seeing an opportunity, pulled out a knife and was about to stab Tariq when a figure flew through the air and hit the man so hard he was sent flying over the ship's railing and into the cold sea below.

Pakize had swung through the air on a rope and kicked the man overboard! Letting go of the rope, she landed on deck, rolled, and sprung to her feet in one fluid and graceful motion.

Extending her hand to Tariq, she lifted him to his feet with a wide grin on her face.

"Need a little help, Tariq?" she asked with a smile.

Tariq, still grimacing, managed a little smile.

"Nice move, Pakize!" he replied.

Soon, they rejoined the battle as it spread over the entire deck of the ship. Before too long, they had taken complete control of the fight, with the exception of two men.

Captain Scopas and Abdullah Ozek were continuing with their epic battle. Both men had slash marks on their arms and chest and were now dripping with blood, sweat, and seawater. Breathing heavily, they were both too focused on their own fight to realize that the rest of both crews had encircled them, watching intently as their two leaders fought each another to the death.

Ozek decided that Scopas was too skilled with a knife—even for him. He needed to find a way to move the fight in his favor, and that meant engaging Scopas in a wrestling match—where he would clearly have the advantage.

Seeing an opportunity, Ozek bent his legs and bull-rushed himself straight into Scopas, pushing him downward until they were both down on the steel deck.

All the crew could hear was their grunting as both men grappled and struggled for an advantage. Ozek hadn't realized that Captain Scopas was an excellent wrestler in his own right, and Ozek's supposed advantage never materialized.

For three minutes, the match was a mess of tangled limbs and muscles. Ozek managed to flip Scopas on his back. Now that he realized Scopas could wrestle, Ozek was less interested in continuing the struggle. Thinking he could kill Scopas with one blow to the heart, he brought his knife above his head to strike.

It was a foolhardy mistake that proved fatal, as Ozek left his entire torso exposed.

Scopas quickly shoved his steel deep into the man's belly.

Ozek felt the stiletto blade pierce deep inside of him and excruciating pain shoot through his gut. Standing up, he dropped his knife and brought both his hands to the dagger now protruding from his belly. He pulled the dagger out and blood spurted from his guts onto the slippery deck.

Abdullah Ozek's face grew white, and he stared into the eyes of Captain Scopas, who was now standing across from him.

"Why?" he whispered.

"For my brother," Scopas answered dryly and then, with one shove, sent Abdullah Ozek over the side of the ship to the frigid waters below.

Regaining his senses, Scopas realized that the remaining members of both crews had surrounded him. Everyone was eerily silent—they had just watched Captain Scopas avenge his brother by defeating the most notorious gangster in all of Turkey.

"Your orders, captain?" one of his seamen asked.

"Secure the prisoners in a hold below. I'll take command of the freighter."

Scopas turned to walk to the bridge—it was time to steer the ship onto a different course.

The boys and the crewmembers tied up the remainder of Ozek's men in a hold just belowdecks. The men's wrists and ankles were bound, and the access hatch was locked to ensure there would be no escape.

Tariq had another very important thing to do. He went searching and found Ozek's cabin and began rummaging through it. Breaking into a locked desk drawer, he was relieved to find the diary of Alexander the Great, tucked safely in its bag. He brought it to his chest and hugged it. Opening the bag, Tariq flipped through the pages to make sure the diary had not been damaged. He replaced the bag where it belonged: around his neck and under his shirt.

Looking up at the ceiling, he said a prayer of gratitude and gave a nod to Melbourne Jack.

He rejoined the group and they set about checking on the animals. They found the cargo hold and went from cage to cage, making sure that every animal had enough food and water. Many of the animals were malnourished and happily gulped up the fresh water and devoured the food put in front of them.

A mama elephant was tied up to her cage by her front right leg. The shackle, with spikes that tore into her skin, was much too tight and blood dripped down her foot. The shackle was attached to the cage bars by a thick chain and only allowed her to move a few feet in any direction.

Tariq went closer to the elephant and she was looking right at him. He was suddenly overwhelmed by a feeling that the elephant seemed to be pleading with him.

Seeing the shackle and the dried blood, Tariq decided to open up the cage door and climb inside with her. He knew this was risky, as it was a small cage, and a wild elephant could easily kill him. Yet he had no fear.

Instead, the elephant gingerly lifted her foot where the spike was digging into her, turning her head softly toward to Tariq.

Inspecting the shackle, Tariq saw that it was held in place by a bolt with a nut. The nut was tight, but after a few moments, he had managed to loosen it and guide it off the bolt chamber. After the nut was removed, the bolt easily slid out and the shackle was released.

The elephant's leg was now free and fully exposed, and Tariq could see the extent of the damage. Punctures where the spikes had dug in formed a circle of wounds around her leg. Blood and pus oozed out of each sore.

Tariq fetched a sponge and went about cleaning the wounds, dousing the punctures with clean water and a bit of soap.

Once finished, he stood up and looked at the mama elephant.

Tears were streaming down her face.

"I won't let anything happen to you," he whispered, and suddenly felt a wave of relief come over his entire body. It was as if Melbourne Jack were in the room with him, smiling next to him, as Tariq gently stroked the elephant's belly. He closed his eyes and took a deep breath.

The next moment, he felt something caress his face. Opening his eyes, he realized that the mama elephant had wrapped her trunk around his neck, as if embracing her own child.

Tariq hugged her trunk, and it felt so warm and gentle. It was her way of showing joy and gratitude at being released and cared for.

During this moment of quiet, Tariq took out the diary of Alexander the Great from the bag around his neck. He flipped through it and tried to understand some of the diagrams and the language. Whatever was in that book was massively important—so important that Abdullah Ozek had stolen it.

Tariq still had a duty to perform. He still had to return this diary to Melbourne Jack's circus.

In these moments with the elephant, looking over the diary, he almost felt himself age and grow wiser. He was no longer a boy, and probably hadn't been for some time. He was turning into a man, and would now be presented with all the pressures and responsibilities that come with manhood.

He would not shirk his duties. He would not bow under the weight of expectation.

CHAPTER
— 29 —

THE CLOCK STRIKES MIDNIGHT

Foster Crowe looked right at Wu Chiang. Just as Foster was about to charge, Wu Chiang spoke.

"Who are you?" Wu Chiang asked.

"Someone who is sworn to stop you," Foster replied.

Wu Chiang smiled slightly and, amazingly, bowed to Foster. Confused, Foster paused for a moment when he heard a loud crunching sound. Wu Chiang had bitten down on something hard. In seconds, a white and foamy liquid started to pour out from Wu Chiang's lips.

Cyanide!

With the same slight and devious smile, Wu Chiang didn't wait for Foster to attack him. Moving quickly to his left, he took three steps and then threw himself out of the hotel window. Crashing through the glass, Wu Chiang's body hurled through the air in a cloud of glass shards and splinters. In a moment, his body traveled to the ground and landed with a thud.

Foster went to the window and looked down.

The body of Wu Chiang lay motionless and dead on the ground below. A shallow stream of blood trickled from his lips and formed a puddle in front of his face.

Foster wasn't sad to see him die. He was an evil man and if he hadn't committed suicide, Foster probably would have killed him anyway.

Nevertheless, he was now at an impasse. Wu Chiang had killed himself for a reason, and that reason was to prevent Foster from learning of his plans.

Foster did a quick inspection of the room and found nothing. Wu Chiang hadn't even unpacked. As he searched the room for clues, he heard a commotion outside as a crowd had begun to gather around the body. Not wanting to draw attention to himself, Foster left the hotel room and vacated the hotel via a backstairs exit.

What could Wu Chiang want in Sarajevo?

Walking out of the hotel and down a city street, he tried to think, but nothing came to him. Wu Chiang obviously had agents in Sarajevo and had given them instructions. But how could he find these agents? He didn't have any leads to go on.

He was at a complete loss. The man was dead and had given him nothing.

Archduke Franz Ferdinand stepped off the train with his wife, Sophie, and a contingent of security. They were whisked through the train station to a fleet of waiting automobiles. The motorcade sped through the streets of Sarajevo on the way to the governor's house.

Suddenly, a man burst forward and hurled a grenade at the car transporting Franz Ferdinand and his wife. The grenade bounced under the car and then detonated, missing the archduke's automobile completely, but exploding under the car traveling behind them.

The archduke's driver, seeing what had happened behind them, honked his horn to urge the cars in front of him to speed up.

Somehow the rest of the motorcade managed to speed through the streets and make it unscathed to the governor's house.

The man who had thrown the bomb was a member of the Black Hand. His name was Nedeljko Čabrinović. It was supposed to have been a much bigger and more coordinated attack, but at the last moment, some of the other Black Hand members backed out when they learned the archduke would be traveling with his wife. Killing a woman was not what they had signed up for.

The assassination attempt was a failure.

The girls were in an all-out sprint since climbing up the icefall. Mia urged them onward and wouldn't let them slow down, even for an instant. They had nowhere to hide, and Mia had run out of strategies for evading their pursuers. They would simply have to outrun them or be captured.

Finally, after running at top speed for an hour, Margaret stopped, bent over, and dry heaved into the snow. She was breathing so hard she couldn't catch her breath and was nearly at the point of hyperventilating.

"We have to stop, Mia. Margaret is cooked and so am I," Inez explained, bent over and gasping for breath.

Mia nodded her head. She was sweating profusely and, truthfully, was exhausted herself.

"We rest for ten minutes and no more," she replied, took out some food and water, laid out a towel for the girls, and placed the meal on the towel. The girls hurriedly ate and drank and were so grateful for a break.

As the girls munched on sausage, a voice greeted them from behind.

"Quite a bunch of rabbits you all are, and quite impressive for an old woman and two young girls."

They looked up and saw the imposing figure of Major Hostetler standing in front of them. He was dressed in a German military uniform, and while a bit dirty, he otherwise looked the part of an officer.

The girls froze as he stepped toward them. He didn't seem very antagonistic—actually, he seemed slightly impressed and even friendly.

"A nice trick your friends at the farm pulled, getting my troops sleepy, and the icefall was brilliant. Unfortunately for you, I've been scaling icefalls since I was a boy."

Inez and Margaret looked at one another. Inez gulped and gazed wide-eyed at Margaret, who was obviously scared.

Major Hostetler looked at Mia when he spoke his next sentence.

"Where is Leopold?" he asked.

Mia stared back at him. She knew she had been captured, and there was nothing left to do.

"He fell off the ridge," she answered.

Hostetler didn't seem overly surprised.

"I figured that someone had fallen off the ridge when there were suddenly only three sets of footprints."

Hostetler studied the girls. They were so young. What they didn't know was he had a daughter of his own about their age. In fact, with her blond hair and slender face, Margaret looked very much like his own daughter.

"You're taking them all the way to France?" he asked.

Mia nodded her head.

He sighed deeply and studied their footprints. He wanted to be sure they weren't hiding Leopold. After surveying the area for a minute, he was satisfied. He only saw three sets of footprints and no more.

Scratching his head, he took out a cigarette, lit it, and blew smoke into the crisp German air.

He thought for a bit, took another drag on his cigarette and studied the girls.

"Courageous girls you have there. May I speak to you for a second?" he said to Mia.

Mia slowly walked over to Hostetler and they talked alone for a few moments. The girls couldn't hear what was being said until, finally, Mia came back and joined them.

"Make sure you deliver these girls safely to France," he said, extinguished his cigarette, and began walking away from them.

Margaret questioned him as he left.

"Wait—why are you letting us go? You pursued us for so long...," she asked.

Hostetler turned to look at her.

"I'm afraid for what is going to happen in the world. I'm afraid for Germany. You need to get back home to your families."

The girls watched Hostetler disappear around the bend. They laughed and gasped with delight. They wouldn't be going back to the concentration camp!

"What did you say to him?" Margaret asked Mia as she didn't speak German.

Mia packed up the food, put on her knapsack, started to walk down the path.

"I think…I think he is a good man. When he saw Leopold wasn't with us, he decided to let us go."

Inez quickly caught up to Mia.

"But he knew we helped Leopold, and you helped us all escape," she pressed, completely baffled by Hostetler's sudden change of heart.

"As I said, I think he is a good man," Mia answered firmly, and soon they were hiking through the woods and making good time.

Archduke Franz Ferdinand and his wife decided to visit the victims of the car bombing at the local hospital. After a quick discussion with the governor, they were ushered to their car by a team of security guards, who got into another car to lead their motorcade. After they had been on the road for a few minutes, the car in front stopped, realizing they were headed back to the hotel and not to the hospital as intended by the Archduke. The drivers reversed course and backed down the street. As they turned around a lone figure recognized them from across the street, just off the Latin Bridge.

Gavrilo Princip, a member of the Black Hand, sat drinking a cup of tea at Schiller's Delicatessen and mulling over the missed assassination attempt earlier this morning. All the frustrations borne from his life of poverty were stirring in his head when he saw the archduke's caravan back up and turn around right in front of him. He instantly recognized the archduke and his wife in the back of one of the cars.

How the fates had provided him with this opportunity.

Without a second thought, he got up from his chair and removed a pistol from his coat pocket. It was a Browning Model 1910 and not an especially powerful gun, so he knew he would have to get very close in order to assassinate the archduke.

His mind went blank as the car stalled in front of him. In slow motion, he saw the archduke and his wife just feet in front of him. The archduke turned and saw Princip walking toward him with a determined expression on his face.

Princip walked within a foot of the car, raised his pistol, and began firing into the rear seat that contained the archduke and his wife.

The first bullet ripped through the archduke's neck and the second went straight into his wife's abdomen.

The archduke, in spite of the bullet wound in his neck, cried out to his wife, "Sophie dear, don't die, stay alive for the sake of our children!"

Some security members and pedestrians immediately tackled Gavrilo Princip. He was thrown to the ground and subdued.

The driver of Franz Ferdinand's car kicked it into gear and sped toward the hospital. It was too late.

Both Archduke Franz Ferdinand and his wife died en route.

Wu Chiang had succeeded, even in death.

Word of the assassination spread through Sarajevo like a huge gust of wind. It was the only topic of conversation in every household, saloon, and restaurant.

Foster Crowe sat at a bar and nursed a cognac. He looked like he'd aged ten years in a matter of hours. Swollen bags had formed under his eyes and his skin was a pale white.

The assassination of Archduke Franz Ferdinand was obviously the work of Wu Chiang.

He ordered a whiskey and tried to think about what he could have done differently. He had stopped Wu Chiang, but not the assassination.

He didn't have any clues except that he'd learned from the evening edition of the local paper that the man who had been arrested, Gavrilo Princip, was a member of the Black Hand. It couldn't have been a coincidence, could it? The Red Hand Scrolls and now the Black Hand?

It all seemed too impossible to be a coincidence.

He tried to think of his next move, but he just couldn't fathom what to do next. All he had to go on was that an underground organization called the Black Hand had killed the archduke.

And just hours before, Wu Chiang's body lay lifeless on a Sarajevo sidewalk.

Foster knew what this meant. He'd studied Wu Chiang's plans and understood what he was trying to do. Wu Chiang's ultimate goal was to start a world war, and the killing of Archduke Franz Ferdinand was just the spark to ignite unrest among nations. He'd tried to have Germany declare war on Serbia through the bombing and near-poisoning of the ambassador. When that didn't work, he shifted his tactics, assassinating an Austrian archduke in order to get Austria to declare war on Serbia.

A few tables over sat a group of laborers, with large muscles and day's growth of hair on their faces. They were getting more and more drunk. After a while, they began to sing nationalistic songs. After a few more drinks, they began to shout and threaten anyone within earshot.

"I'm glad that Franz Ferdinand is dead! We are not Austria's lap dog," said one.

"I hope Austria wants to go to war, I'll be the first to sign up and fight those turnips!" said another.

Foster sighed again, took a sip of his whiskey, and dejectedly stared at the bar in front of him. This was exactly what Wu Chiang was planning…to get the people riled up so they would actually want to go to war.

He didn't know where to go or what to do. He wished he were back with the circus and his people. His thoughts drifted to Melbourne Jack and he wondered if he'd found the diary of Alexander the Great. Lately, however, he'd been worried that something had happened to Jack. Something terrible, possibly even death. It was just a feeling he couldn't shake.

He ordered another whiskey.

The freighter cut through the sea with Captain Scopas at the helm. His crew manned the ship's stations and it was safely under their control. Fez, Aseem, and Tariq stood next to Captain Scopas on the bridge as he guided the wheel with the steady movement of his hands. It was very difficult to see out the front window due to the darkness and the rain. A cup of warm tea sat at his side.

"So boys, we have a ship and a freighter full of animals. Any idea of what our next plans should be?" he asked.

The boys looked at one another in agreement and then produced the Red Hand map, unfolded it, and spread it out on a counter next to Scopas.

"What is this?" he asked, as he gave the map a closer inspection.

"It was given to us. I think it's the route we're supposed to take," Tariq answered.

Scopas studied the map closely while keeping the wheel steady, a skill he'd developed managing his own ship.

He then took a sip of his tea and seemed to be in deep thought.

"This route takes us through Russia and down through Afghanistan. I have to say, there are quicker routes, and much safer ones," he remarked.

"We know, but somehow this map is telling where to go, and we think we have a duty to follow it," Fez explained.

A crewmember came up and interrupted the discussion.

"Captain, we might have a problem," he said in Greek and then spoke at length with Captain Scopas before exiting the bridge.

"Boys, we have another problem," he explained.

"What is it?" Aseem asked.

"These animals are meant for delivery to Razikov," he said and there seemed to be fear in his voice.

"Who is Razikov?" Tariq asked.

Scopas sighed and took another drink of tea before continuing.

"He is a Russian. An ex-monk who now is a master of the dark arts. It is said he is a demon and cannot be killed. I know for a fact that even the roughest Russian criminals are terrified of him. If these animals are meant for him, it will be very dangerous for us in Russia."

"Do you think he's really a demon?" Tariq asked.

Scopas glanced at Tariq.

"I don't know…I know only that he creates fear across the country-side. We should steer clear of him at all costs."

The boys stood silent, looking at the map, and then looking at one another.

"What should we do?" Fez asked.

"Boys, I know of a place in Africa. It's a unique place run by missionaries who have sworn to protect wild animals. Instead of delivering them to Razikov, we could easily drop the animals with the missionaries who would then release them safely into the wild. I could then sell the freighter on the black market in Port Sudan. This plan would be good for you, and good for me. I would then escort you boys to India through the Arabian Sea. It is a much safer route and most importantly, we avoid Razikov."

The boys were silent.

"It does make sense," Fez replied softly.

Tariq suddenly felt a weight return to his shoulders. The route made sense. They would be protected by Captain Scopas and his clan and would travel a much safer, and faster, route to India.

But something nagged at him. It was like a muffled voice in the back of his mind. He stared at the map and it almost spoke to him. His eyes traveled to the red hand print that seemed to pop out at him.

"We'll have to think about it," he whispered.

That night, Tariq, Fez, and Aseem sat at a wooden table, the map spread out in front of them. Each of them studied it in silence, trying to understand the meaning of the symbols and lines, and what the path represented. Tariq even opened the diary of Alexander the Great and placed it next to the map because Fez suggested it might provide some answers to the map's mysteries.

"The lines are longitude and latitude, I know that from studying the charts that Scopas showed me," Fez explained.

"What are those symbols?" Tariq asked.

"They are warnings that the depth of the water is low—useful to keep us from running aground."

The collection of lines and symbols zigzagged across the map. Tariq studied the path, and to him it looked like such a long way. There was the

Black Sea to navigate, then a long, hot march through deserts, and treks over treacherous mountain passes. All of this over such a long distance.

"It says our journey will end in Delhi—that's strange," he whispered.

"Why?" Aseem asked.

"Melbourne Jack told me to go to Bangalore. They are both cities in India, but Bangalore is far south while Delhi is up north."

Leaning back, Tariq looked at his two friends.

"Going with Scopas would be much easier. We would be safe with him and his clan, and we would be at sea. This route looks so long and treacherous. I'm not even sure if this map was meant for us...maybe it's just a coincidence?"

He sighed and continued to stare.

"If we follow the map, we would need to sail the entire distance of the Black Sea. We don't even know how to sail," he said dejectedly.

"I can sail, Tariq. I've learned everything there is to know about a boat. I can even read charts," Fez answered.

"Then what about all these mountain passes and crossing over deserts? We don't have money or supplies. How are we supposed to walk all that way? I've heard that Afghanistan is full of bandits and vicious warlords. How will we pass safely through all these valleys?" Tariq responded.

"Well, Marco Polo traveled that far, and he wasn't that much older than we are. If he could do it, why can't we?" Fez again answered.

Tariq sighed heavily again.

"Why do you want to take this route, Fez? We've barely escaped with our lives twice now. It would be much easier to go with Scopas," Tariq finally asked him.

"Because I think we were meant to find this map and follow it. Everything happens for a reason, Tariq," Aseem answered before Fez.

Tariq shook his head.

"If I follow this map, I can't ask you to join me. The distance is so long, and what if something happens to either of you? Then I would feel responsible. I don't know what this map is, or what we're doing. It seems crazy to me."

Tariq looked deeply into the map, all the while shaking his head as he pondered.

The boat creaked with the rhythm of the sea and the candlelight flickered softly as a gentle breeze fluttered in through an open porthole. The boys were silent.

The map seemed to stare at them, but no answers were provided and no voices told them what to do. Only the sounds of the old boat and the sea could be heard in the small room. Tariq closed his eyes.

He didn't have an answer.

CHAPTER
— *30* —

STEPPING INTO THE BREACH

In a week's time, Mia and the girls crossed over the German border into France. They walked along dirt roads surrounded by wild maple and birch trees, their leaves in full color, creating a wall of gold, orange, and red. They camped often, and Mia even taught them a bit about fishing and trapping and eating wild plants and herbs. They were invited into local homes for dinner and sometimes even enjoyed a warm bed and bath. Mia, in spite of the long distance, seemed to be quite comfortable away from home and enjoying her time with the girls.

One morning, after they had finished packing and were headed onto the road, Margaret asked Mia a question.

"Mia, do you think we should send a telegram to our school? I'm sure they are deathly worried about us."

Mia remained silent for a bit.

"Perhaps it would be wise. But, we've already covered so much of the journey that there is not much of anything they could do but wait. If something were to happen to us on the remainder of the journey, it would be horrible for your families to think you were safe, only to find out they couldn't protect you. I'm sorry, I'm very pragmatic. For me, we will be safe only when I deliver you to your school."

"I think I understand. Right now, they don't know we're safe, but if we told them, and something happened, they might feel awful for not coming for us," Margaret answered.

"Exactly."

"And, I want to see everyone's faces when we come waltzing into school. Don't you, Margaret? Don't ruin it with a stupid telegram," Inez answered cheerfully.

"I suppose it's settled. It still feels strange to not let my family know I'm safe. I'm sure they are worried something awful," Margaret explained, still a bit puzzled by the answer.

They continued to walk and Inez was especially quiet. Finally, Margaret couldn't stand it.

"Inez, whatever are you thinking about? You've had that silly grin on your face all day."

Inez blushed and finally answered.

"Today is Reinhold's birthday. We said we would think of each other on our birthdays," she explained with a sheepish grin and blushed even more.

Mia and Margaret both burst out laughing.

"I knew it was all about Reinhold," Margaret gushed and tickled Inez as she protested and giggled.

As they walked further into the French countryside, they began to notice more and more French soldiers. At first, it was just a few patrols in the towns and the girls didn't think anything of it. However, as they went deeper and deeper into the rural areas, they noticed more and more soldiers digging trenches and going through maneuvers. They didn't stop to ask the soldiers about their exercises, as they looked quite serious and determined.

For six more days they traveled, helped by hitching rides with various horse carriages and even on the bed of a couple of trucks, which were scarce. At last, as they headed around one last bluff, their school came into view.

Only, it wasn't at all what they were expecting.

There were hundreds of French army troops everywhere and dozens of tents had been set up all over the grounds. The soldiers were running through drills in their uniforms of blue shirts with silver buttons and red pants with black boots.

Dirty, sweaty, and exhausted, Margaret had wanted nothing more than a warm meal and bath. Now, she was more concerned with the surroundings in front of her.

Going to the main schoolhouse, they were stopped by a young man in a uniform.

"Who are you?" he asked.

"We are students at this school," Margaret replied.

The soldier looked at the dirty and grimy girls with a look of disbelief.

"Well, we kind of got lost," Inez answered.

"Come with me," he said and walked straight to the school headquarters.

Opening the door, they were not greeted by Sister Anne as would be typical. Instead, they saw that a gruff and older-looking officer had set up the room as his own. Giant maps were hung on each wall as he read some documents on his desk.

"Sir, these girls say they are students of the school," the young soldier told him.

The officer, about fifty with a gray moustache, looked up from his papers.

"All the students were evacuated a week ago," he answered.

"Well, we kind of got kidnapped and sent to Germany," Inez answered.

The man's mouth opened and he instantly stood up.

"Are you Margaret and Inez?" he asked.

"Yes, sir," Margaret answered.

He got up from his desk and approached the two girls. He gave them each a warm hug.

"My dear children. You were the reason the school was evacuated. We thought you were both dead!"

"Where is everyone?" Margaret asked.

"Once you disappeared, there was an inquiry and German agents were discovered at the farmhouse nearby. It was decided the school was too dangerous and the students and staff were evacuated," he answered.

"But why are the soldiers here?" Margaret asked.

"My dear child, we are preparing for war. Surely, you must have heard?"

"Well, we saw a lot of soldiers, but we don't really know what is going on."

"After Archduke Ferdinand was assassinated, Serbia declared war on Austria. Because of their treaty with Austria, Germany was obliged to declare war on Serbia. Then, Russia declared war on Germany and Austria. And France is an ally of Russia."

Margaret and Inez stared at him blankly.

"Which means that France is going to declare war on Germany and Austria any day now."

Inez almost burst into tears.

"What are you talking about? We were just in Germany. In fact, this is our friend and she's German and she saved us!" she cried.

The man stared suspiciously at Mia.

"I understand your confusion, and it's obvious you've been through an awful ordeal. I must get back to work, but before I do, there are some people who would like to meet with you."

The man proceeded to escort the girls out of the headquarters and up to their old dorm room. Opening the door, Margaret was suddenly face-to-face with her mother. Louise Owen let out a scream and hugged Margaret as tightly as she could.

"Where have you *been*?" she asked as she held her daughter tightly.

"You won't believe it," Margaret whispered.

Coming up the hill, a voice yelled out.

"Inez!"

Inez looked out the window and her brother, Michel, was running toward the building. Inez ran out to greet him and Michel practically tackled Inez, lifted her off her feet and swung her around in circles.

"I can't believe you're alive!" he cried.

Inez had never been hugged by her brother, or at least, not any time that she could remember. He had never shown her any kind of emotion or told her that he cared about her. Now, here he was, hugging her, screaming, sweeping her off her feet and whirling her around in circles.

"Michel, you're going to make me sick!" Inez laughed and finally Michel let her to the ground.

"Mother is here, she's down washing clothes, let's go!" he said and grabbed Inez by the arm and pulled her down the hill.

Inez's mother was carrying a load of laundry when, upon seeing Inez, she immediately dropped the load, let out a scream, and ran into the arms of her daughter. She stood there for thirty seconds, holding her tightly against her chest, stroking her hair, not saying a word.

Finally, Inez had to break the silence.

"I'm sorry I worried you, I know we should have sent a telegram or something," she said, feeling terrible at the thought of making her mother worry like this.

"All that matters is that you're safe now," her mother replied, still not wanting to let Inez go from her embrace.

Finally, Inez's mother let her go and looked at her daughter's face. Inez's cheeks were caked with dirt from the journey and she looked a bit haggard.

"Where have you been?" she asked.

"I was kidnapped and sent to Germany. Margaret followed the kidnappers and freed me. Then, we met this German woman Mia who led us home. There was a nice man, Leopold, but, well, he died on the way," Inez replied and her voice was full of dread as she mentioned Leopold.

Her mother smiled and hugged her again.

"Well, I only care that you're safe. Come, we have so much to tell you, and I want to hear of all your adventures. Oh Inez, if your father could see you now."

The group congregated in front of the dorm room and there was more crying and hugging as the mothers couldn't let go of their girls for long before wrapping them up in their arms again. Margaret's younger brother, David, finally appeared after an uneventful afternoon of fishing. He wasn't as outgoing as the others with his emotions, but was still obviously glad to see his sister and began following her around like a little puppy.

As they were catching up, a squadron of six airplanes flew over the school, perhaps only two hundred feet from the ground. Margaret looked up as the planes flew overhead. A man in a black leather helmet and goggles captained the lead plane. Even from the ground, his white scarf could be seen flying in the wind. Upon seeing Margaret, he waved his hand furiously and even wobbled the plane's wings back and forth.

Margaret instantly knew who it was.

Her father!

"C'mon, let's go greet him!" her mother said. Margaret shrieked with joy at the thought of seeing her father once again.

Margaret, David, and Louise Owen ran up a hill to a pasture behind the school that had been turned into a makeshift landing strip. The planes had landed and Charles Owen was shaking the hands of the other pilots when he spotted his daughter. Without missing a beat, he sprinted across the field and hugged her as she jumped into his outstretched arms. He was wearing a brown leather jacket, and his face was dirty and oily. His eyes looked like a raccoon's from where the goggles had covered his eyes. His blond hair stuck to his sweaty brow, and three days' growth of whiskers darkened his square jaw.

"Where have you been?" he asked.

"I have so much to tell you!" she answered.

Father and daughter hugged for several minutes and tears soon streamed down Charles's face. Margaret, in her father's embrace, realized how much she had missed him. It was as if her entire body relaxed in the safety of his embrace—she felt like a caterpillar warmed in its cocoon.

"Well, I guess I'm second banana in this family when it comes to adventures," he finally said and managed a laugh. It had seemed like only yesterday that his daughter had found him locked in a French cage, having been condemned to death as a pirate. Their bond had grown so close that he now viewed her as more his equal than his daughter.

"I see you're flying again," she said, looking at the planes.

"Training these French pilots is like training a poodle to cook an omelet. They don't listen, they do whatever they want—it's a miracle none of them have died," he replied, obviously a bit frustrated with the French independent spirit.

Margaret beamed as she looked at her father. He had always been her hero, and to see him flying again, barking out orders, as noble as ever in his pilot's clothing—she couldn't help but be proud.

"Well, enough of that. I want to get washed up and hear about where the devil you've been for almost two months. Your mother and I were worried to death."

Margaret frowned and looked at the ground. She knew she should have sent word at the first possible moment, but Leopold's death had been so much to bear. She'd needed time to be quiet and grieve. She had hoped that in the end, her family would understand.

After dinner, Margaret joined her father and mother for a small glass of port. On special occasions, they allowed her to have a small glass of the sweet wine, and this made Margaret feel so grown up.

"So why are you training these French pilots?" Margaret finally asked her father.

"Oh Margaret, there's so much that has happened since you've been away," he replied, took a small sip of wine, and cleared his throat before continuing.

"I'm afraid there's going to be a war my dear, and not a small war…a massive war the likes of which the world has never seen. I'm here to help the French prepare for war against Austria and Germany."

"So that explains all the soldiers?" Margaret replied.

"Yes, unfortunately France is ill-prepared for a war of any kind. There's so much confusion and so many preparations to make. And at the moment, the right hand doesn't know what the left is doing."

Margaret grew silent as she thought about what her father had just told her.

"And you're sure about this? I mean, you're certain there will be a war?" she asked.

"I'm afraid so. Some of the more diplomatic politicians are holding out for an accord, but I don't see it as a possibility. England will be drawn into the war because we are allies with France. London is already making preparations."

"And what happened to my schoolmates? Where have they gone?"

"To a school in Switzerland. Sister Anne thought it would be safe. Saint Catherine's is now being used as a makeshift command center. We expect there to be a lot of action around these parts."

Louise Owen could see Margaret was upset by this news. She put her arm around her daughter's shoulder, brought her in close and kissed her forehead.

"As long as you're safe, darling," she said and rocked her daughter back and forth in her arm.

"But I was just in Germany. It's a beautiful country and a German woman saved us. I don't understand this at all," Margaret said and there was obvious pain in her voice.

"Don't ever confuse governments with people, my dear," her mother replied.

Charles Owen gazed at his wife and daughter and he wondered how much time he might have with both of them. He knew all too well what was coming. The Germans would attack France and he would immediately be called into duty. He knew the war would be vicious and, most likely, a long one. He didn't hold out any hope for a treaty or peaceful solution.

Sipping his wine, he just wanted to be with his family for whatever time they had together now.

He understood his world—and his family's—would soon be turned upside down.

Just then, four English soldiers appeared with Mia in handcuffs. Her hands were bound behind her back.

"What are you doing?" Margaret shrieked.

The soldiers looked at Margaret and, finally, a young lieutenant stepped forward.

"I'm sorry, but I'm afraid I have some bad news," he told Margaret while looking sheepishly at Charles.

"What is it? This woman helped my daughter escape from Germany and you are treating her like a prisoner? There better be a good explanation for this," Charles barked at the young lieutenant.

"I'm afraid, sir, that we believe this woman is a spy," he answered.

"What? That's impossible!" Margaret yelled.

Charles stared at the lieutenant. He was a good man, and a fine soldier.

"What makes you think this?" he asked.

The young man produced a rudimentary map from his pocket.

"We found this in her satchel as she was attempting to leave. It's a map of all of our positions including supply lines, trenches, troop levels, and there's more," he answered, handing the map to Charles.

Studying the map, Charles could scarcely believe his eyes.

"What is the meaning of this?" he asked Mia.

She looked at the floor. Charles went away and talked with the lieutenant. After a few moments, he returned and looked at Margaret, who stood there, stupefied, with her mouth hanging open, staring at Mia in disbelief.

"I'm afraid it's true, darling," he told Margaret.

"Mia!" Margaret shrieked.

Slowly, Mia looked at her. There was a different look in her eyes. It was defiant and shameful all at the same time.

"I am sorry," she whispered.

"What do you mean you're sorry? All this time…you were just a spy?" Margaret screamed at her.

Mia continued to look at Margaret with a blank look, and it was obvious, at that moment, that everything the young lieutenant had just said was true.

Margaret felt a sudden rage course through her body. Without further thought, she reared back and hit Mia hard across the face with the palm of her hand. Tears streamed down Margaret's cheeks.

"What about Leopold? Was that an accident?" she screamed.

"It had to be done," Mia answered, her left cheek now flushed red from Margaret's blow.

For the first time, Margaret saw a glint of evil in her eye.

"You murdered him! You made it so he would slip off the cliff! You were in cahoots with Hostetler the entire time! Now he knows where the decoder machine is located!" Margaret yelled.

Her father and the soldiers stepped between the two. Mia was now staring stoically and defiantly at Margaret.

"Let her go, darling. Let her go," Charles whispered, trying to gently calm Margaret and ease her away. He could see the hurt and anger in his daughter's eyes. He led Margaret to the back of the room, where she burst into tears and hugged him.

"I trusted her, spent weeks with her. I thought she was our friend," she said and sobbed into his chest.

Mia was led away by the soldiers. Margaret continued to cry for two minutes, her breath heaving into his chest, until she finally pulled away from him.

"Why would she do that?" she asked.

"War is hell, Margaret. She's probably been giving away positions all the way, which is why she didn't want you to send us a telegram. We're not sure how she communicated with the German high command," he answered.

"So she just used us to get into France?" Margaret asked.

"You were the perfect cover. A couple of schoolgirls traveling with an old woman. It was a very good plan," Charles explained.

"What does this mean?" Margaret asked.

"It means that the Germans have a good idea of our positions and they are poised for an attack. Having Leopold fall off the cliff was the perfect cover. She was able to glean information from him that he wouldn't dare tell the German officers and then kill him without anyone asking any questions."

Margaret stared at her father.

"I have to help. I have to help in any way I can. I have to make up for what I've done," she said.

"You haven't done anything, Margaret...you were trying to help a friend," he said. He tried to console her but she was despondent.

"I don't care. I want to do anything and everything to help the war effort. I have to make up for this somehow," she said and Charles could see the hurt and determination in her face.

"Okay, my darling. Okay. We'll get you set up to train as a nurse. That will be the best area for you," he said.

"I don't want to be a nurse. I want to fight. I want to hurt these Germans the way they hurt Inez and me and Leopold. I want you to teach me to fly and fight," she answered, with steely resolve in her voice.

Charles stepped away and stared at her.

"Margaret, they don't allow girls to fly fighter planes…," he answered.

"I don't care. I want you to teach me. They need you, right? You're the best pilot in the RAF, right? They'll do whatever you say, and if you say I can learn to fly, then they will have to let me. I want you to teach me to fly."

Charles could see he had no chance of winning this argument.

"Okay, Margaret. Okay. I'll do everything I can. I'll teach you how to fly."

Margaret stared at her father, tears still streaming from her eyes, the salty taste wetting her lips.

"Good. Let's get started right now."

Zijuan sat cross-legged, her back flush against the trunk of a birch tree. The spot was secluded, in the countryside out of Tangier, and overlooked a pasture and a small valley.

She had discovered the spot years ago and came to it when she felt the need to be alone and away from the daily duties of running the orphanage.

Ever since Malik had been named the new caid, things had been eventful. He had made peace with the Sultan, and the French, and already began repairing the countryside. They were building schools and hospitals and had begun the work of healing the many wounds created under the rule of the evil Caid Ali Tamzali. With Sanaa at his side, they made a powerful couple. For once, the future in the countryside looked bright.

Yet, Zijuan was never at peace. Nightmares plagued her each and every night. Usually, they involved Tariq.

Closing her eyes, she breathed in and out until her breath relaxed and her mind drifted to a deeper and calmer place. After a few moments, images flooded her mind. Images of Tariq, Fez, and Aseem. They were on a boat of some kind and headed to a distant port.

Breathing deeper, more images came to her. She realized the boys had passed the first test. They had taken a large step forward, but there were many more to come.

The image of a Caucasian man then came to her in an instant. It was a steady image and not a flash. He was older, with a long, scraggly beard and a skinny, malnourished face. His face embedded itself in her mind—as if he were staring straight into her. The man's ice-blue eyes were hypnotic.

Evil oozed from every pore of the man's skin.

That's when Zijuan realized this wasn't a dream. This man had somehow found her. It was as if he were peering into her thoughts and her mind. He *was* staring at her.

Just as quickly, the image of Fez, Aseem, and Tariq flashed in her head. They were headed straight for this man. He was watching and waiting for them.

Zijuan abruptly ended the meditation and stood up, shaking her hands and walking in the grass. She felt completely intruded upon, as if this man knew every thought in her head.

Then, a voice came into Zijuan's head. It was a female voice, young and ethereal with a pleading tone, as if it was trying to warn Zijuan of something awful and evil. The voice said one word in the form of a whisper.

"*Razikov.*"

The small sailboat skimmed along the surface of the Black Sea. A light wind kept her steady at four knots as she bobbed up and down in the gentle waves.

Tariq sat at the stern with a calm hand on the tiller. He watched the main sail, taut with a belly full of wind, and kept an eye on the tell-tail, which provided the direction of the wind. The moon smiled overhead.

At his port side, Aseem sat and watched the horizon. Water, as far as the eye could see. Fez sat at the starboard side, dutifully tracking a compass in his lap and watching the stars above. He was using celestial navigation, allowing the stars to guide them, and keeping close tabs on their course.

They were headed to the port of Rostov-na-Donu in Russia.

The boys sat in silence, listening to the rhythmic sounds of water splashing against the wood hull. All were nervous being alone on the water again, after their near-death experience in the Mediterranean, and none were eager to venture on their own into the depths of the Black Sea.

In the hold below, stretched out over a small table, was the Red Hand map. In a decision of faith, the three had agreed that they would follow the course given on the map—even though they would be alone and their journey would be undoubtedly difficult and dangerous.

Together they made the difficult decision to leave Scopas and his clan.

It took a long evening of negotiating, with many shouts and much emotion, but finally Scopas allowed them to leave with a small boat from his fleet. He agreed to deliver the animals to Africa and return Pakize to her home in Constantinople. With Abdullah Ozek dead, he had no doubt her life would improve tremendously.

Just prior to their departure, Scopas, with tears in his eyes, gave the boys a letter with a name and address of a contact in Rostov-na-Donu. He told them this man would help the boys on their journey, and promised to send a telegram to Zijuan, confirming the boys' safety and alerting her to their future plans.

Tariq felt the diary of Alexander the Great on his chest and he thought of Melbourne Jack. Looking up at the sky, he said a silent prayer.

We will need your help, Jack. We will need you to guide us.

He looked at his two friends and experienced a mixture of both gratitude and regret. He was so thankful they were with him, as he knew he could not complete the task on his own. Yet, he felt responsible for them and terribly worried harm might come to them. He was excited and anxious at the same time. They would need to travel thousands of miles, across some of the most desolate and treacherous terrain known to man, to reach their final destination of India.

Mindful of the arduous trek ahead, each boy felt a twinge of danger and the unknown in their blood and bones. It was quite a thing to be free with no agenda or timeline to worry about. They were no longer boys. Although young in age, their minds and bodies were those of men.

Suddenly, a squadron of bottlenose dolphins emerged and began swimming at the bow of the boat.

"Look!" Fez exclaimed and pointed his right index finger toward the dolphins.

All three boys smiled as they watched the dolphins' heads bob up and under the water in the direct line of a moonbeam shining down on the water's surface.

As if the dolphins were leading the boys on their journey ahead.

The boat drifted through the night. The boys took turns sleeping and steering. The weather cooperated and the sailing was smooth.

In the distance, dark storm clouds formed on the horizon. They were ominous and gray, as if a monster lay in wait to swallow the boys whole and spit out the skeleton of their small boat. Thunder echoed in the distance and lightning tore from the sky.

And then it began to rain.

Adventures continue in:

Ghosts of the Hindu Kush

"Watch your thoughts: They become your words.

Watch your words: They become your actions.

Watch your actions: They become your habits.

Watch your habits: They become your character.

Watch your character: It becomes your destiny."

—Upanishads

ABOUT THE AUTHOR

The idea to write the *Red Hand Adventures* first came to Joe O'Neill while he was on safari in Sri Lanka. As he was driving along in an old jeep, under a full moon casting silhouettes of wild elephants against the jungle wall, the image of a rebel orphan in old Morocco popped into his head. While he wishes he could take full credit for coming up with the idea, it was, in reality, a story that was already out there, waiting to be told.

Joe O'Neill is the CEO and founder of Waquis Global, which has given him the opportunity for world travel and the experience of many different cultures.

JOIN THE RED HAND!

The Red Hand isn't just about reading books,

but also having a sense of adventure,

being curious about the world—where we've been,

and how we've gotten here.

It's about giving back to those less fortunate and

having a sense of justice in our everyday lives.

As a member of The Red Hand, you'll be privy to new books

and other cool stuff before their release to the general public.

To join The Red Hand, please go to

www.RedHandAdventures.com